PRIMAL
WHISPERS

PRIMAL WHISPERS

A NOVEL

Kim Rowley

ELKRUN
PRESS
COLORADO

2010 ELK RUN PRESS, LLC TRADE PAPERBACK EDITION

www.ElkRunPress.com

Library of Congress Control Number 2010929739

Library of Congress Subject Headings

1. Relationships—Fiction. 2. Hollywood—Fiction.
3. San Francisco—Fiction. 4. Women motion picture producers and directors—Fiction. 5. Adoption—Fiction.
6. Man-woman relationships—Fiction. 7. Colorado—Fiction.
8. Friendship—Fiction.

ISBN 978-0-9845331-0-7

Printed in the United States of America

First Edition

For Those I Love the Most . . .
Steve, Blythe, Kelsey, Gil, Mom and Dad

ACKNOWLEDGEMENTS

Many people helped me accomplish my dream of writing this novel. I'm most grateful to my husband, Steve, without whose support this book never would have happened. Thank you Carolyn Campbell, poet, artist, teacher and friend, who taught me how to channel the words and gave me the courage to write fiction. Laura Abbott—I couldn't have gone forth without your tireless encouragement and insightful suggestions. Thank you niece Kelsey for staying up late the night before leaving for college in order to be the first to read my novel and offer giant words of enthusiasm. My sister, Blythe, showed her love for me by graciously reading and critiquing several rewrites. A special thanks to my mother—a voracious reader who encouraged me through all stages of my writing. And finally, thank you to these special friends who helped me along this journey: Kathy Shinn (designer extraordinaire), Janice Drickey, Lin Gentry, Sally Bergstedt, Jeff Marschner, Donna Park, Marc Abbott and my intrepid critique group—Kathy, Debbie, Lu, Judy, Dan and Barb.

PROLOGUE
Summer, 1967

Tall and slender with an engaging smile, Kate rarely walked into a room. She swept into gatherings with a grace and energy that evoked people's attention. On this day, she slumped in a chair in her parents' backyard, her eyes red from tears.

"You're pregnant?" Kate's mother rose from the patio table, her stature eclipsing the California sun from her daughter's tanned body. Still water in the nearby swimming pool mirrored the ice of the older woman's wrath. "We've spent a fortune on your education. Is this how you repay your father and me? You're going to ruin your life. How could you do this to me?

In Kate's twenty-two years of living, it had always been about her mother. She wondered why she thought this situation might be different. "Do you think I wanted to spend my first year in graduate school pregnant?"

"Who is the father? Or do you know?"

Kate clenched her teeth and straightened her posture to brace against her mother's attack. "Of course, I know. But he won't want this baby any more than I do."

"Good. Then no one will contest you having an abortion."

Kate's mouth dropped open. "Abortion?" Her hands fell across her stomach. "Just like that? No discussion? Is an abortion even legal?" She fought back tears. "How can you be so callous?"

"I'm being pragmatic, dear. These things can be arranged."

Cold as granite, her mother's glare told Kate all she needed to know.

Her predicament was a black mark her mother would never forgive or forget. There would be no comforting arms to embrace Kate, no hankie for falling tears. Kate wouldn't be able to talk to her mother of the affinity she felt for a young man she had only known just a few days. She feared her mother would only call her a slut anyway. Her affair hadn't been like that.

Kate sat in silence as the older woman's voice droned into the milky fog of Kate's fumbled attempt to enlist her mother's aid.

"Doc Swanson probably won't want to do the abortion, but I'm sure he'll be able to recommend someone. I'll make an appointment for you to see him right away."

Kate might have laughed at her mother's imperious bearing had the thrust of her scorn not felt like a jagged knife. As a child, her mother's "evil eye" had delivered the warnings necessary to rein in Kate's behavior, to keep her from crying or acting out. Today, there was nothing that could erase her pregnancy or undo the hurt she had inflicted upon her mother. Kate dropped her head to avoid the disappointment in the older woman's eyes.

Upon hearing her mother's footsteps disappear into the house, Kate allowed the tears to escape onto her lap.

Seconds later, her mother addressed her from an open doorway with a voice ripe with condescension. "Kate, dear…"

Kate jerked her head up but kept her gaze on the swimming pool, its glistening water rippling upon the arrival of a silent breeze.

"Please make sure Doc agrees not to tell a soul about your unfortunate situation."

Kate wiped her wet cheeks with the back of her hand and squeezed her eyes shut to manage her emotions. "I'm sure he'll be discrete."

The heat of summer beat down on Kate. Yet, whispers of fear, longing and regret gripped her senses and chilled her body. She reached for the beach towel draped over her mother's empty chair and wrapped it around herself.

Kate's thoughts shifted to her father. How would he react to her news? Her body seized in shame when she imagined the fallen expression on his face. She shook her head with uncertainty. Perhaps Doc Swanson would be her lifeline to what lay ahead. He was not only their family doctor, but also a close and trusted friend. By hastily shoving her off to Doc, Kate's mother might have provided her with the means to weather this ordeal without the added emotional strings of a parent's involvement.

Rebelling against the self-pity washing over her, Kate suddenly pulled herself out of the chair and threw off the towel. "What am I doing?" she whispered. Familiar rhythms pounded through her body. She had been raised to stand up to adversity and take control of things, not succumb. She would show her parents how successful she could be in life, even with this setback. She knew immediately what needed to be done.

CHAPTER ONE
Spring, 1989

A shrill ring jolted Kate from a sound sleep. Heart racing, she fumbled through the darkness hoping to answer the bedside phone before it could wake her husband, Parker. Instead, she knocked it to the hardwood floor, barely missing the rug that might have deadened its final, resounding crash.

Parker's voice reached through the confusion of broken slumber. "What? Who is it? What's the matter?"

Kate gathered her jarred nerves and spoke as calmly as she could. "I've got it."

She hung over the side of the bed, found the phone and pulled it toward her until she had the receiver in hand. "Hello," she whispered into the mouthpiece.

"Kate?" asked the voice on the phone.

"Yes."

"Kate Cochran?"

"Yes." Kate's voice grew stronger. "Who is this?"

"It's Becky."

"Who?"

"Becky Madison," the voice enunciated more clearly.

"Huh? Becky?" Kate's mind stumbled out of drowsiness. Why was her childhood friend calling at this unsettling hour after more than twenty years of silence? "My, God, it's been years. What's wrong?" she asked.

"Where is she?" Becky demanded.

"Where is who?" A rush of uneasiness washed over Kate. Not only was Becky's voice huskier than she remembered, but her words were slurred as if she had been drinking.

"My daughter. Where's my daughter?" Her voice grew with intensity.

"What daughter? What's this all about?" asked Kate. "I didn't even know you had a daughter." Her hand tightened around the receiver. She could hear Becky gasping for breath, as if the woman was struggling not to cry.

"You know what I'm talkin' about. Where else would she go? No one knows more 'bout me than you do."

Kate pulled herself into an upright position and replaced the phone's base on the bedside table. She didn't know how to react. "I used to know you. That was before you ended our friendship. Remember? No letters, no phone calls. No explanation. Nothing but silence since our senior year in college." Kate grimaced at the harshness of her tone.

"But I thought…"

"You thought what?" Kate's body swelled with rising irritation.

"Why else would she be in Denver?"

Kate took a deep breath for sustenance. "I'm at a loss. I don't know your daughter."

The subject of a daughter, anyone's daughter struck a raw nerve in Kate. The emotional upheaval of her recent miscarriage had already unleashed memories and regrets about the child she had given up years earlier Her breathing quickened. Don't go there, she warned herself. Gathering her wits, Kate knew that Becky could only be calling about her own daughter, not the child Kate looked for in the eyes of every young person she passed on the street.

"Where are you calling from?" asked Kate in an attempt to ground both of their heightened emotions.

"I'm here, in Denver."

Parker nudged Kate to get her attention.

"Hold on, Becky." Kate turned and spoke to her husband. "It's Becky Madison, an old friend."

He rolled out of bed with an exasperated sigh. "I'll be watching television."

Kate reached for him. "I'm sorry. Stay here and go back to sleep. I'll move into the other room."

"No. It's okay. I'm already wide awake." He patted Kate on her shoulder and disappeared through the bedroom door into the darkened hallway.

Kate grabbed her robe and moved to the fireplace across the room. Glowing embers emitted enough heat to offset the chilling sight of snow falling outside her window. Their golden retriever, Rusty, lay at her feet, still curled in sleep. Returning to Becky, she asked, "Is your daughter okay? Did she run away? What's happened?"

"I think she's okay," said Becky in a calmer voice. "I just don't know where she is at this moment."

"I'm a little baffled. Why are you calling me about this?"

"I know, I know. This is probably quite a shock to be hearin' from me."

"Shock is a good word. Even your brother has been close-mouthed about you to all of our old friends, at your request, I understand."

"Well, perhaps we, ah, we can talk about that. I'm only here for a short time, but it'd be nice to see you."

Kate was uncertain how to respond. Becky's quixotic jump from panicked mother to long lost friend was unsettling. "What about your daughter?"

"My fear got the better of me. I need to be patient. Somethin' I'm not good at. I know she'll call me."

Becky's flippant dismissal of her situation did not sway Kate's concerns. "This isn't a good time for me, Becky. I don't want to get involved in anyone's family problems."

"We could just talk—for old times' sake. I'm sorry I flew off the handle. I was out of line."

Not wanting to appear heartless, Kate left Becky an opening. "Why don't you call me in the morning if you still want to talk."

After hanging up, Kate joined Parker in the library.

"What was that all about?" he asked, putting his arm around Kate as she snuggled next to him on the sofa. "Who's Becky?"

"She used to be my best friend when we were kids. She's in Denver and suddenly wants to see me again." She shrugged her shoulders. "There's something going on with her daughter."

Parker took hold of Kate's hand. "Is this wise? You don't need the weight of other people's problems right now. Especially when it relates to their children."

"Darling, I need to move forward with my life. Just because a doctor says I can never give you a child is no reason to avoid people who can and do have children. It's been weeks since my miscarriage. I've mourned long enough."

"Don't minimize the impact this has had on you. The fact that you gave up your chance at motherhood years ago has compounded your grief."

"There is no need to remind me."

"I apologize, Kate."

Kate brushed a shock of Parker's hair back from his forehead and laid her head on his shoulder. "Why did I give up that baby? I assumed I'd have more children. Now, I can't."

"Oh, Kate." He sighed. "You did what was right for you at the time. You're a different person now. You know you can't look back." He pulled her closer to him. "I love our life together, just as it is."

Rusty walked into the room and laid on the floor just within Kate's reach. "Hello, you," she said to their four-legged companion, scratching the top of his head. She looked back at Parker. "Why did I get so wrapped up in my career? Why didn't you and I meet before it was too late?" Kate stayed in the comfort of Parker's arms while he stroked her back and she petted Rusty.

"You really need to let go of this."

"I'll get there. You may not have noticed, but I'm not waking up in tears anymore." Kate looked at Parker with a hint of her broad smile and blinked with dry eyes to reinforce her improvement.

"I noticed. But, I'm still concerned about you."

"I know. But you don't need to worry anymore. I really will get over this." She relaxed into his comforting embrace.

Moments later, Parker asked, "What are you going to do about Becky?"

Kate frowned. "I doubt she'll call again."

Parker gently removed his arm from around Kate and rose from the sofa. He leaned over and kissed his wife on her forehead. "It's very late. Can I convince you to come back to bed?"

She nodded. "In a moment."

She whispered, "I love you," as he left the room with Rusty trailing after him.

How lucky I am to have found this man, she thought. His broad, athletic shoulders and powerful hands reminded Kate of her own father, who had always been her protector and a man who could fix anything from a broken bicycle to her self-confidence.

After staring blindly at the flickering TV screen for several minutes, Kate flipped off the set, routinely straightened the pillows, put a vase back in its place and looked around the room, admiring the warm, scholarly effect she had created. Where once she had supervised set designers, managed intricate shooting schedules and multi-million dollar budgets as a Hollywood television producer, she now honed those skills on home remodeling projects.

After their marriage, Kate and Parker had relocated from Beverly Hills to Pine Mountain, Colorado, an intimate mountain community nestled high above the glow of Denver's lights. The view of the Continental Divide's towering peaks looming beyond their great room's expansive windows had cinched their life-changing decision to leave their stress-filled lives behind. Just outside the windows resided Kate's latest acquisition—a life-size bronze statue of an eight-hundred-pound elk. Kate had laughed the first time she eyed the majestic look-a-like standing in their rock garden. She wondered whom she was fooling. The elk was as real as the image she projected of a contented woman.

Kate knew her pastoral life wasn't enough anymore. It was time for new dreams.

The fast-moving snowstorm had lifted by the time Parker left for an early business meeting in Denver the next morning. A geologist with a law degree, Parker consulted for a U.S. oil company. He worked out of his home office unless a project necessitated a personal appearance.

Shortly before noon, Kate was rummaging through her pantry for a snack when she heard the doorbell. Still in her warm-ups after a hike with Rusty, her hair damp with sweat, she headed to the entry hall and pulled open the massive front door.

Standing before her was a robust, middle-aged woman who looked vaguely familiar. A moment passed before the stranger refreshed Kate's memory with an elfish smile.

Kate's eyes widened. "Becky."

"Hi Kate." Becky bit at her lip. "Sorry to surprise y'all like this."

It was the same whiskey voice Kate had heard on the phone, but now the words weren't slurred. Kate also detected the southern accent Becky had affected during a family trip to Georgia one summer. "Y'all" had apparently become a mainstay in Becky's persona.

"I figured y'all wouldn't see me if I called first. Not after that terrible phone call last night."

Kate grimaced. "Truthfully? You're probably right. But since you're here, come on in." Kate took Becky's coat and hung it on the hall tree.

The two women had laughed, cried and experienced jealousy as children growing up together. Before people jogged, their mothers had walked together almost everyday while pushing their sleeping daughters through the neighborhood in baby buggies. The young girls had survived a night in the woods when they became separated from their Girl Scout troop on a wilderness hike. Their friendship had risen above the difficulties of teenage cliques and cheerleader competitions. But they were no longer children.

Kate felt a flutter of nerves race through her stomach. She was leery of her visitor's intensions. She zipped up her running jacket and pulled it down over her narrow hips. "I was about to fix myself something to eat. Care to join me?"

"Maybe something to drink." Becky followed Kate into the kitchen.

Kate poured a glass of iced tea for Becky, to which Becky added a scoop of sugar from a canister she found in a cupboard. They had once treated each other's familial homes as their own. Today appeared to be no exception.

"You have a beautiful home," Becky said as she looked around the room. "Everything in its place, just like your old bedroom when we were kids. Remember how you always lined up all your stuffed animals in a certain order? I'll bet your spices are alphabetized." Becky opened a few cabinets until she found them and let out a hearty laugh. "Oh, my God, they are."

Kate rolled her eyes. She was embarrassed at the discovery. "What can I say, it was a long, cold winter this year. I needed something to do."

"Since when do you need an excuse to be organized?"

Kate ran her finely manicured fingers through her silky, chestnut brown hair. "I don't, I guess. That's the way I was raised."

"It's hard to believe we were once friends. Look at me." She spread out her arms with the gusto of an opera singer. "Overweight and in need of an emery board, and you with pressed pleats in your workout pants." She gestured toward Kate.

Kate looked at Becky, whose youthful figure now filled a sweater that was designed to be baggie. The sweet voice had deepened to a husky tone, probably born from too many cigarettes. "Do you still smoke?" she asked.

Becky shook her head. "Not as much since I swore off alcohol."

"What do you mean?" Kate didn't remember Becky having a drinking problem. Then again, Becky's slurred speech during her phone call the night before had sounded to Kate as if Becky may have been drinking.

"Let's just say I'm a nicer person when I don't drink. And since smoking seems to go with drinking, I've cut back on the smoke-bombs as well."

By now, Kate had prepared a tray of food artistically garnished with bunches of grapes and fresh parsley.

Becky eyed the food. "That looks wonderful. Perhaps I will have something to eat. Is it warm enough to be outside?" She walked over and opened the French doors. The bleak, gray morning had transformed into a blue-sky day, pure as a baby's smile. Melting snow trickled down drain spouts while clumps of slushy snow reluctantly slipped from surrounding pine trees. "Look at this gorgeous day. What happened to the snow storm?"

"Springtime in the Rockies!" Kate walked outside with the tray of food. "If you don't like the weather, just wait another five minutes, and it will change." She set the tray on a weathered, teak table and flipped down cushions on matching chairs.

Becky leaned on the balcony railing inhaling the fresh air. The distant barking of a neighbor's dog floated above the ruckus of three blue jays squabbling over sunflower seeds in Kate's bird feeder. A woodpecker knocked on a pine tree in search of bugs while swallows swooped through the air carrying nesting materials in their beaks. Kate spotted elk tracks in a surviving patch of snow and pointed them out to Becky.

"It's a veritable 'Call of the Wild' around here," said Becky. "I thought my home in Seattle was a beautiful place, but this tops everything. You're very lucky."

Kate smiled. "So, you live in Seattle?"

"Yes. I have a small house in a wooded part of town, but it lacks this view. My bay window overlooks a creek infested with poison oak. But rest assured, I always keep the window closed between me and the poison oak!"

Kate chuckled. "We did have an ugly run-in with poison oak once. Didn't we?"

"How could I forget? My body dripped pus and itched for weeks."

Both women laughed at their misadventure.

Kate settled into one of the chairs at the table and motioned Becky to join her.

"With whom do you share this grand view?" asked Becky.

"That would be my husband, Parker. How about you? Are you married?"

"Once…a long time ago. How about children, Kate?"

"No, just a spoiled golden retriever."

"Really? I envisioned you with several children."

A seed of grief caught in Kate's throat. She turned away to regain her composure and noticed with some relief that the pain seemed duller. Kate looked back at Becky. "One of those things that wasn't meant to be. I spent years wrapped up in my career. No time for babies."

"Oh. My brother told me about your Hollywood career, but not much about your personal life. Les isn't one for gossip. Typical of a man, I guess."

Kate thought of all the times she had asked Becky's brother, Les, about his sister. He'd always left her in the dark with no information. She shifted in her chair. "So, it was okay for you to know about me, but not the other way around? Was it Les who told you where to find me?"

"Yes." Becky snugged her sweater tighter around her body as if to protect herself from Kate's scrutiny. "I guess this might be the time for an update." She sipped her tea.

Kate nodded, leaned back in her chair and waited for the woman her childhood friend had become to fill the void hanging between them. Neither woman touched the food Kate had set before them.

"About the time you were probably plotting your glamorous career in Hollywood, I was changing diapers and struggling to make the rent. I got pregnant in college. It happened the same time my mother was dying of cancer."

Kate closed her eyes, saddened by the reminder of Becky's loss. "Yes, I knew about your mother. I tried to reach you when I heard about her death."

"I know you did. But it was all too much for me. After my mother died, I distanced myself from almost everyone around me."

"But why? That's when you might have needed us the most."

Becky pursed her lips and glanced down before answering. "Kate, I don't know what to say. My life changed. I thought..." Becky hesitated. "We were so young. It was a very complicated and difficult time. I did what I did to survive."

"You should have told me. We had more in common during that time than you might imagine."

"I don't know how you can say that. Having a child is the most powerful thing a woman can experience. Nothing can affect you more, except losing a child."

Becky's words pierced Kate like an ice pick. She wanted to tell Becky of her own losses, but instead, lingered in the shadow of Becky's building emotions.

"I'm so sorry for my behavior last night. That's why I wanted to see you today, so I could apologize in person. I owe you that much. I had a lot of nerve attacking you. I hate to use alcohol as an excuse after telling you I don't drink anymore, but having a Coke in the hotel bar last night wasn't enough to calm my nerves."

"I appreciate your apology." Kate's growing compassion brought back feelings of their old friendship. "Will you tell me more about your daughter?"

Becky shifted in her chair. "I'm so lucky to have her. It's just that she wants to know certain things that..." Becky stopped and stared into the distance as if seeking guidance before looking back at Kate. "What am I doing? I can't expect you to understand, or ask for your help."

"Why so evasive?"

Becky pushed her hair behind her ears. "I was upset as all get out last night. I had no idea where she was. I was grasping at straws."

"Did you find her?"

"Yes. The mix-up is really Les's fault."

Kate looked quizzically at Becky and waited for an explanation.

"He promised to call me with the address of where my daughter is staying as soon as I arrived in Denver. When I didn't hear from him, I started calling around. Then I called y'all, the only person I know in Colorado."

Kate was baffled. "If you know where she is, why aren't you with your daughter now?"

"She's a curious young thing on a treasure hunt, and I won't help her with the clues. Y'all know young kids today. They're always looking to fulfill fantasies and ideals that have no relation to reality. After Les finally called me with a phone number this morning, I tried to contact her, but she refused to talk to me."

"I'm sorry."

Becky shrugged. "The difficulties and heartache of being a mother, I guess. I've got to give her some time to cool down. This may seem odd, but I wouldn't be surprised if she tries to contact you."

"Me?" Kate threw a hand to her chest. "What's she looking for? If it's information about you, then she has come to the wrong place. I don't know anything about you anymore."

"She doesn't know that. Over the years, Les and I may have mentioned your name in passing. My daughter never forgets anything. That's why I thought she was with y'all. Kate, you and I once shared everything—clothes, toys, dreams. But I can't share my daughter. She's too precious. Everything I've done in my life has been for her."

Kate threw up her hands. "What are you talking about? Don't worry. Your daughter is all yours."

"You're right. I'm being silly."

Encroaching clouds cooled the sun-drenched afternoon. Becky glanced at her watch. "I've got a plane to catch. I'm sorry about all this. I didn't mean to dump my problems on you." She rose from her chair. "I'm truly sorry for my behavior."

Surprised by Becky's sudden departure, Kate walked Becky to the front door.

"I'd like to keep in touch, if you're willing to forgive me for the past twenty years of silence." Becky slipped a piece of paper into Kate's hand.

Kate glanced at the paper and shrugged her shoulders. "Let's see how it goes."

The two embraced, a gesture made awkward by the years that had distanced them.

Moments after Becky left, Parker arrived home to find Kate staring out a window in the living room. He walked up behind her and wrapped his arms around her waist. "Who was pulling out of our driveway?"

"Becky." Kate leaned into his embrace, chuckling in disbelief. "She showed up unannounced."

"Probably wanted to see for herself that her daughter isn't here."

"Oh, Parker. You're shameful."

"Still, pretty brazen behavior after last night's episode, don't you think?"

"Peculiar. Unsettling. Somehow I might be involved in a mother-daughter conflict, and I have no idea why."

"What?" Parker let go of Kate. "Does that mean you plan to see each other again?"

Kate turned to face him. "Maybe. At least, now, I have her address." She opened her fist to show Parker the piece of paper Becky had given her. "It's so odd. I'm more confused than I was last night. I'm sure she came here with the intention of getting my help, but changed her mind." Kate sighed. "There was a time Becky and I shared our deepest secrets with each other."

"Do I detect a note of sentimentality in your voice?"

"A little."

"Do women still tell-all to their friends? By this time in our lives, I imagine that most of us have lived too much of life to remain an open book. Don't you think some details of our pasts are best kept in the past?"

"Maybe so." Kate knew she lacked the courage to tell him the only secret she had ever kept from him.

Becky pressed persistently on the doorbell until Les opened the front door of his San Francisco home. The robust man in horn-rimmed reading glasses loomed over Becky with an accusatory expression that vanished when Becky moved from his shadow into the light flooding through the open doorway.

"Becky, my God! What are you doing here?" Les picked up his sister's satchel and guided her from the damp fog into his living room. "How long has it been since you were last in California? Twenty years?"

"I guess. Does it really matter?" she muttered. Becky felt downtrodden and exhausted.

"Did you find Lily?"

"Yes, but she wouldn't see me."

"What do you mean? After flying all the way to Denver for the specific purpose of seeing your daughter, she refused to meet with you? That doesn't sound like Lily. The two of you have always been so close."

"She wouldn't even talk to me on the telephone." The bitter words of a stranger still rang in Becky's ears: *"Perhaps it's best if you give Lily a little time."*

Becky closed her eyes briefly and released a deep sigh. "I'm sorry. I don't know why I'm bothering you with this. Maybe you could just hold me for a bit."

"Of course." Les enveloped his sister in a bear-sized embrace.

Unfortunately, his comforting gesture wasn't enough to calm Becky's raw nerves. Released from his arms, she slumped into the nearest chair and dropped her head into her hands. Les's wife, Margaret, entered the room, but Les motioned her to leave them alone for awhile. He rested his hand on Becky's back and waited until she was ready to talk. Margaret returned briefly with two cups of tea, then left them alone.

Les sat on the ottoman near Becky's chair and spoke quietly and soothingly. "Becky, what's happened? I told you everything I know on the phone last week"

"Tell me again."

Les took a deep breath. "Lily was here, but only for one night. She was very preoccupied. She borrowed my car one afternoon, but didn't tell me where she was going. And I didn't ask. I figured it was none of my business."

Becky glared at her brother. "Your niece shows up unexpectedly, and you don't ask why? Weren't you the least bit curious?"

"Yes, but I'm her uncle, not her keeper. And she's twenty-one, now. Lily and I have enjoyed a great relationship through our years of letter-writing. I figured if she had something she wanted me to know about, she would have told me."

"That's it?"

"Pretty much. When I dropped Lily at the airport, she said she didn't want to talk to you, but asked me to let you know she was all right. Why wouldn't she talk to you, herself?"

"I don't know." Becky blew her nose and wiped some tears with a tissue. "I'm scared. First, she shows up on your doorstep. Then, she flies off to Colorado and refuses to speak to me. I thought if I could retrace her steps, I would find out what she's up to."

"So, tell me what you know."

"Well, I imagine it must have started in Chicago. She went there as part of her special studies program. She called me about midway through her conference and said everything was going great. A few days later, I got a phone call from her college roommate, Doreen. She was worried because Lily never returned to school after the conference. Doreen told me she thought Lily was going to California. I didn't know what to do. I was frantic. That same day, you called to tell me Lily was with you."

"What do you think happened in Chicago? You must have some clue," prodded Les.

Becky shook her head. "I was hoping she told you something. Perhaps you left something out when you called me last week. Did Lily ask you any questions?"

"You mean, about you?"

"Yes."

"She gave that up years ago, once she understood I wouldn't tell her who her benefactor is." Les pondered for a moment, then continued. "Is that what this is about? I thought she had forgiven you for keeping her trust fund a secret all those years."

"I thought she had, too."

"Do you think she may have discovered who gave her all that money?"

"Not unless you told her." Becky glared accusingly at Les.

"I promised you, I'd never tell her. I've kept my promise, Becky."

"Okay. I'm sorry." Becky sipped her tea, then continued with restrained persistence. She wanted to learn more without raising her brother's curiosity. "So why did she rush to San Francisco, then, suddenly, dash off to Colorado? And where is she headed next?"

"I know she contacted Doreen. Apparently, both girls finished their semester study programs early. Doreen was headed to her parent's home in Denver, and I guess Lily wanted to join her."

"There must be something more," Becky insisted.

"Wait a minute," said Les. "Do Donald's parents still live in Chicago? Do you think she went to visit them? Is that it?"

A chill rattled Becky's spine. She felt her cheeks flush. She had never dared to imagine that possibility. Her brief marriage to Donald ended when a tragic auto accident took his life. Lily was only three weeks old at the time. After his death, his parents had severed all connections with Becky.

She struggled to gain her composure. "What?" she asked.

"I said," continued Les, "Donald's parents live in Chicago. Perhaps Lily learned the truth about her trust fund from them, something I hoped you would have told her years ago."

"They never approved of my marrying their son. Remember?"

"That's something I'll never understand. Why wouldn't they want to know their granddaughter?"

Becky grasped the arms of her chair to hold herself in check. "You'll have to ask them."

"What haven't you told me, Becky?"

"Les, please." Becky's thoughts whirled. What if Lily's suppressed curiosity about Donald's parents finally had led her to confront them? If what Becky feared was true, there was good reason for Lily's mercurial behavior. Patience and time must suffice as Becky's temporary allies. In the meantime, she would cling to one hope. If Lily did go to Colorado because of something she learned in Chicago, then Becky was certain Lily must be on the wrong track. The only connection Becky had to Colorado was Kate Cochran.

"You were in Colorado for less than thirty-six hours. Why didn't you stay longer? Perhaps Lily would have changed her mind about seeing you."

"I don't think so. She's too stubborn. So, I made do with a visit to Kate Cochran."

"Kate? You called her? I can't believe it." Les shook his head. "It's wonderful that you reconnected with her. But why now?"

"I was distraught and frightened. I thought Lily might be with her. I woke Kate up in the middle of the night and accused her of hiding Lily from me. I behaved horribly."

"You didn't!"

"I did. She's still beautiful, with that same self-assurance I envied in high school." Becky paused, reflecting back on her time with Kate. "Seeing her brings up a question. Is it a coincidence Kate lives in the state where my daughter seems to have exiled herself from me? You and Kate have remained friends over the years. Have you ever mentioned Kate to Lily?"

"Not that I can remember."

"Perhaps I should stay in contact with Kate, just in case."

"What did you tell Kate about Lily being in Colorado?" asked Les.

"Barely anything." Becky laughed pathetically at herself and dropped her head. "Not even Lily's name or that I changed my name from Madison to McGuire. What would Kate be able to do?"

"Maybe it's time you tell Lily what she wants to know."

"I don't think I can."

"Then be prepared for the consequences when Lily finds out on her own. She's a tenacious young woman, Becky. A trait you should appreciate. Eventually, she'll uncover what you're hiding from her."

"Are you certain Kate doesn't know anything?"

Les threw up his hands. "Maybe she does."

CHAPTER TWO

The morning after Becky's visit, Kate awoke riddled with thoughts of Becky's mysterious visit and the worry Becky exhibited about her daughter. Knowing that exercise was the best antidote to shake herself free of nagging troubles, Kate slipped out the back door and trudged up the mountainside with Rusty in the lead, his tail wagging with excitement. At first, Kate's pace was slow. But gradually she quickened her steps. And as she did so, clarity began to pump through her veins. The harder she breathed, the more fog cleared from her conscience.

Allowing her mind to wander, she reflected on the road her life had taken since she last saw Becky. The lust for her career and the time she had spent in a dead-end relationship had unwittingly transported her to the far side of her childbearing years by the time she met and married Parker. While other women in their forties were able to give birth, Kate had not been able to carry a child to term. She and Parker had wanted a family, yet they had chosen to let nature, rather than the whim of an adoption agency, decide their destiny as parents.

Kate's jogging smoothed into a run. Her swiftness lured Rusty from his side jaunts back onto the trail where he could keep pace with her. Soon, her heightened energy glided to a lightness in her step. As if awakening from a deep sleep, she stretched out her arms and opened her fists. A sense of calm washed over her with the sudden realization she no longer felt constrained by the emotional anchor of her miscarriage. Having seen the agony of Becky's estrangement from her daughter, she felt relief in accepting the fact her legacy would not include children. Moments of grief may still overcome her, but today was the first time she had felt a sense of freedom from that burden.

She credited Becky's visit for triggering this shift in her path back to normalcy.

After returning from her workout, Kate showered and dressed, then joined Parker, who was reading *The Wall Street Journal* at the kitchen table.

"Wow, don't you look professional," he said, putting down his newspaper. "Ready for your first big day?"

"It's not a real job. I only volunteered to help Susan when she's desperate for help. Overall, I think it's going to be fun."

"Based on what you've told me about Susan Alston, she may be calling on you a lot."

Kate laughed. "Yes, no one knows that better than I do. But I set very clear ground rules. No stuffing envelopes, no phone solicitation, no filing...even for a candidate I believe in. I did that when I was an idealistic college student."

"That's my girl." Parker laughed. "Even so, I wonder how long it will be before your days as a volunteer begin to multiply, grow into longer hours, then slip into weekends."

"Don't worry. I'm not ready to sacrifice my peaceful lifestyle for a full-time plunge into the political battles that lie ahead of Dottie Emerson's run for the Senate. That's Susan's job as the campaign manager."

"Just as long as you're enjoying yourself. That's the main thing. I think it's a good idea for you to spread your wings again."

She walked over and kissed Parker. "Thanks for being so supportive. Now, I'd better call Susan and apologize for not showing up yesterday. Based on her phone message this morning, I don't think she realized I called her office yesterday to say that I wouldn't be there."

"Huh. That's odd. A youngish-sounding woman called here late yesterday asking for you when you were taking your bath. I assumed she was from Susan's office. She seemed content when I told her you would be at campaign headquarters today, so I didn't bother to tell you about the call."

Kate acknowledged his remarks with a light shrug and proceeded to dial Susan's office. She barely had a chance to say hello before Susan hit her with a barrage of questions.

"Where were you yesterday? That is so unlike you to be a no-show. How soon can you get here? I'm pulling together a news conference for Dottie this afternoon. I can really use your help to contact the media."

"I'm on my way." Kate's response was cool and calm. She was used to Susan's brusque manner and knew not to take it personally. But she wondered how Susan managed to maintain the loyal enthusiasm of the younger campaign volunteers if her friend was as rude to them as she could be with her.

Kate and Susan had first met when they both worked for a private public relations firm in Hollywood. Eventually, Susan moved to Washington D.C. and evolved into a savvy, East Coast political operative. She had been recruited to supercharge Dottie Emerson's senatorial campaign in Colorado. Kate had also moved on with her career—to excel on the production side of the television business.

Although the two women admired each other's successes, a competitive rivalry had existed between them that had precluded a close friendship. Once Kate married and was no longer gainfully employed, their rivalry had diminished.

Though Susan had never said as much to her, Kate presumed her old rival felt isolated in the hinterlands of the Rocky Mountain time zone. Thus, the woman had recruited her former colleague for support. This opportunity suited Kate for her own reasons. She needed to emerge from the protective embrace of her mountain home. There was nothing left to remodel and the screenplay she had written since moving to Colorado seemed destined for the Hollywood rejection pile. She hoped a timely foray into the mind-boggling mishaps of politics would buoy her to new horizons. Returning to her roots as a press agent seemed to present the best starting point.

During her half-hour drive down the mountain to campaign headquarters, Kate thought about her earlier visit there and the high-octane volunteers who had stimulated her interest in working on the campaign. They were wildly enthusiastic, dedicated to Emerson's ideals and willing to work all hours of the day or night. Some had come from out of state to work on the campaign. They were mostly college students or recent graduates looking for an entry into national politics.

Kate knew she might be old enough to be the mother of some of the volunteers and envied the youthful passion exhibited by their eager participation. It was the same overwhelming drive and ambition that had once propelled her to the top of her profession. By joining their efforts, she hoped to reignite that spark in herself. There were too many years left in her life to rest on her laurels. Her nerves bristled with anticipation as she headed off the freeway into the snarl of Denver traffic.

Kate walked into headquarters shortly after ten o'clock. She wound her way through a sea of desks spread across the worn wooden floor of the second-story loft in a dingy building that had once housed the finest furrier in town. Years of neglect had left cracked windows and blistered paint peeling from the walls. However, the ample square footage, city-center location and donated rent made it a perfect campaign headquarters.

The volunteers were abuzz with indignation over the attack by Emerson's opponent on the legality of her campaign contributions. Plans for a full-scale counterattack, in the form of a press conference, were under way. Susan was in a closed-door meeting. For the time being, Kate was happy not to be caught up in the political slings and arrows of the opposing candidates.

Per Susan's directions, Kate headed over to a bulletin board on which was pinned a list of twenty reporters Susan wanted Kate to invite to the press conference. Along with it was a copy of a release that would go out after the event.

A smile crossed Kate's face. Hmmm. No script to follow, she thought. It amused her that after all these years, Susan was finally willing to admit Kate had enough gray cells to glean the necessary information.

Kate sat at an empty desk nearby and began to work her way through the list. Ed Horton had been with the *City Journal* for over thirty years. His reputation as a hard-hitting journalist was probably one of the reasons the paper had the largest circulation in the state. He was abrasive, impatient and noncommittal. Kate mimicked his style and grumbled the information to him, sounding as if she didn't care if he came to the press conference or not. She already knew he would show up because there would be free food, and his editor played golf with Dottie's husband every Saturday morning.

The television stations responded with the same comeback: they might come if a crew was available. Kate knew they would be there because Dottie would be addressing a juicy controversy that had been brewing around her campaign. The television stations could use it to hype viewership for their news broadcasts.

Some of the names on her list were stringers for small local papers in rural parts of the state. Kate understood that less than marginal budgets sometimes forced these smaller papers to hire reporter wanna-be's who qualified by having taken one correspondence course in journalism. For this caliber of reporter, she suggested detailed ideas to help them pitch the story to their overworked editors. If she talked directly to an editor, she would introduce herself, then throw out the headline. Giving enough specifics to practically write the story usually guaranteed ink from these one-man operations in which the editors did eighty percent of the writing themselves. They did not have time to attend the press conference but needed to fill a certain number of pages for their advertisers.

Phone calls completed and press releases faxed to those papers whose people couldn't attend the press conference, Kate didn't want to wait any longer for Susan to emerge from her closed-door meeting. Earlier, Susan had asked her to stand by because there would be much to do when the meeting broke up. But that was two hours ago. On the next occasion Susan came out of her office, she had just waved off Kate. That was all Kate needed to justify her early departure.

She was packing her things to leave when she noticed two young women walking toward her. They whispered something to each other, then one of them, a zaftig young woman with lush dark hair and intense green eyes, walked up to Kate.

"Hi, I'm Doreen Finch. And you are?"

"I'm Kate Cochran. Nice to meet you."

Doreen motioned to her companion to move in closer to be introduced, but the young coed held her ground. "That's my college roommate, Lily McGuire," said Doreen, gesturing toward her friend.

The friend offered a demure smile and raised one hand in a slight wave. Her redder-than-auburn hair was pulled back into a ponytail with delicate wisps of curls spilling out from her temples. She defied her gentle femininity with a preppie hound's-tooth jacket she wore over a crisp white shirt, jeans and sockless loafers.

Doreen proceeded to lead the conversation as Lily continued to hang back. "Lily's visiting me for awhile, so we thought we'd come down here to find out about volunteering. Boy, this place seems to really be jumping…like something really major is happening." Doreen was wide-eyed with enthusiasm, while Lily seemed somewhat preoccupied. "I understand that we need to talk to Susan Alston. Is she around?"

"Susan is behind closed doors, and if her day continues as it started, it appears she'll be there for some time," offered Kate.

"Well, I wonder what we should do. No one seems to have time to help us."

Lily finally stepped in closer and belied her timid demeanor with a spirited voice. "What are all the volunteers wound up about?"

At the sound of her voice, Kate tipped her head slightly and focused on Lily before handing each of the girls a copy of Susan's press release. "Perhaps this will help explain what's going on today."

"Thanks," replied Lily and Doreen in unison, glancing over the release.

Kate slipped on her jacket and gathered up her briefcase and purse. "Well, I'm off to grab a quick bite to eat before heading home. Nice to meet you both."

Lily looked up from reading and quickly interjected, "Could I come? I mean, hmmm, how about we all three go to lunch while Susan's in her meeting?" As if to explain her sudden interest in joining Kate for lunch, she added, "I'm starved."

Kate shrugged at the unexpected invitation. "Sure. Why not?"

Doreen scrunched her face into a hesitant expression. "I don't want to risk missing Susan when she gets out of the meeting."

"Oh. Well, perhaps we can all have lunch another day," said Kate.

"Sure, another time would be nice," agreed Doreen. "Nice to have met you. Thanks for helping us." Doreen sat at the desk Kate had vacated to continue her vigil for Susan.

"Doreen, I'd really like something to eat," Lily murmured with a sense of urgency in her voice. Turning to Kate, she said, "I'd like to have lunch with you today, if that's all right."

Kate smiled at Lily's persistence. "That would be fine."

Doreen prodded her roommate again. "Lily, what about Susan Alston?"

"Perhaps I can meet her later this afternoon."

Doreen rolled her eyes and waved goodbye. "Whatever."

Lily followed Kate down the dimly lit staircase that led them into the blinding sunlight.

"Boy, it's nice to be outside," said Lily as the two started down the sidewalk. "I'm surprised Doreen passed on lunch. At first I couldn't convince her to come down here, and now she's the vigilant one. I think Doreen's mother might have gone overboard with her be-an-involved-citizen pep talk."

Kate was amused. "I assumed you were both political groupies anxious to press your idealistic views into action."

"Sort of, I guess. But I'm a bit surprised at Doreen's enthusiasm." There was a note of amazement in Lily's voice. "She's one of my best friends at school, primarily because she isn't into all this political double-talk like some of our friends. Don't get me wrong, I'm all for democracy, equal opportunity and women's rights. I'm just not an activist."

Lily threw up her hands for emphasis. "I just can't get over Doreen. I thought we'd stop by for a little while to check out things, see if it's any different from other campaign headquarters. But, it's pretty much the same." She shrugged. "The workers all have a phone glued to their ear while they sap some poor soul out of a few bucks, or they're stuffing envelopes with propaganda. Now, if we could have been in that meeting with Susan, we could've learned the real dirt, not just the watered-down agenda they pass along to the anxious volunteers."

"Whoa. You're certainly cynical for someone so young. How come?" Kate steered her companion through a maze of orange cones in a construction zone and down another block.

Lily raised her voice to be heard over the rattle of a jackhammer. "Not cynicism. I'm a realist. They probably didn't report all of their campaign contributions accurately, contrary to what the press release states."

"Perhaps not. But what are our choices? We often have to support the least objectionable candidate. Hopefully, our candidate lies and deceives a little less than the others. It's often the career staffers who are the real experts at strategy and cover-ups. That's why the politicians need them. They also need as many young, idealistic volunteers as possible to continue the process. Hence the closed-door meetings. If the less-experienced volunteers knew the truth, many of them would probably quit."

"Ignorance is bliss."

"A cliché, but true."

"So what brings you to this campaign, Kate?" Lily asked with a softer tone in her voice.

"I'm just another volunteer. I'm helping Susan Alston with media relations."

"Why do you do it if you believe they are a bunch of liars? What's in it for you?"

"Good questions. More importantly, what would you like to eat for lunch?" The two women had reached the end of the block where they were now waiting for the signal to change before crossing the congested street.

"I'm sort of a vegetarian, when it's convenient. Is there something suitable around here?"

Kate pondered for a moment. "Not that I can think of. If we had more time we could drive over to Marty's Veggies and Grits. It's sort of a southern-style vegetarian restaurant."

"I've got time if you do."

"Won't Doreen be waiting for you?"

"Oh yeah. Is there a hamburger stand close by?"

Kate laughed at Lily's schizophrenic turn from vegetarianism. "On the next corner."

They walked in silence to the Hamburger Kitchen. Lily had left her purse at headquarters so Kate stood in line to buy the cheeseburgers, fries and chocolate shakes. Lily wiped off an empty table with a handful of napkins and threw packets of ketchup and mayonnaise on the cleaned space.

"Here we go," said Kate, setting down a food-covered tray. "Two fat-filled beef burgers, deep-fat French fries with plenty of salt, and two cholesterol-filled chocolate shakes, no calories spared!" Both women laughed.

"Here's to your health," said Lily, raising her condiment-slathered burger in a mock toast.

As the two hungry women ate, Kate looked more closely at her young companion. Lily had inquisitive, sparkling blue eyes and a creamy complexion glowing with youthful luminescence. Her face was devoid of makeup, and she wore gold loop earrings and a child-sized gold dolphin ring hanging around her neck on a thin gold chain. The ring reminded Kate of a similar one she had received from Martin Kelly, the man she had once loved and from whom she had parted years earlier. The unexpected memory of that relationship surged through her heart with a quickness of light that jarred her for a moment.

"I like your ring," said Kate, motioning toward Lily's necklace. "I used to have one just like it, only in silver. Mine was from Greece."

"Mine was a gift when I was very young."

"Is it from Greece, too?"

"I don't know."

Lily shrugged lightly in denial of the symbolic weight her ring actually carried and let her mind wander. Since her trip to Chicago a week earlier, she had replayed over and over in her head the circumstances that had induced her to recover the ring from obscurity.

The year before high school graduation, when many of Lily's friends had already applied to college, her mother, Becky, kept asking why Lily had not applied. The older woman encouraged her to do so, "just for fun."

Her mother's insistence felt to Lily like a cruel joke. She had always dreamed of attending an East Coast college…some place more sophisticated and intellectually engaging than the predictable West Coast universities to which her friends aspired. Yet when it came time to apply for college, Lily hadn't bothered. She understood her higher education would be limited to living at home and attending a nearby junior college, something she considered a mere extension of her high school experience. She didn't blame her mother. Lily understood all too well the economic realities of being raised by a single mother.

Her mother never let Lily forget the sacrifices she had made. How she had worked full time to keep a roof over their heads while completing her PhD. How she had limited the growth of her own career so she could expose Lily to as much of life as Becky could afford.

But when Lily entered high school, Becky had pushed aside motherhood, the life she claimed to cherish, and turned her attention to her aspirations of a career and making a name for herself. Lily knew money might become a part of their lives, but not in time for her college education. At least, this is what Becky allowed her daughter to believe.

Bolstered by her dreams, Lily eventually took on her mother's challenge and applied to several colleges. Every school accepted her. It wasn't until Becky stopped Lily's attempt to apply for financial aid that Lily learned about a gift that would change her life.

Becky always enjoyed giving her daughter little surprises. Until then, they had been limited to token souvenirs like sugar cubes from a restaurant, storybooks from the grocery story or tee shirts from a museum. The gift-giving events were always moments of lightheartedness between mother and daughter. But on the night Becky sat Lily down to give her this one special present, her tone was somber and ominous. Haltingly, Becky revealed that money for Lily's four-year college education was waiting for her in the bank.

"How can this be?" Seventeen-year-old Lily was bewildered, her heart pounding from the shock. "Why didn't you tell me before? Why did you let me believe I wouldn't be able to go to a four-year college?"

"That was terribly wrong of me. I never should have let you think that." Avoiding eye contact with Lily, Becky took a deep breath and launched into her explanation. "On your second birthday, a lawyer notified me of a trust fund being set up in your name. It was a very small amount, so I didn't give it too much thought. When I did learn how large the trust had become, I decided it was best you didn't know about it just yet." Becky turned her gaze on Lily. "Money doesn't make you strong, Lily. Life makes you strong. I wanted you to have your dreams and to give you the tools to make them happen by yourself. Like I have."

Lily tried to absorb what her mother was telling her. Some stranger, a mysterious acquaintance of her mother's, had established a trust fund for her future. Lily could afford to attend any college in the country, all expenses paid with plenty left over. This revelation left Lily astonished and giddy about her good fortune, yet, suspicious of her mother's duplicity in keeping this a secret.

"Why would someone give me all this money? Who gave it to me?" she asked her mother.

"The trust was set up out of guilt, not love or a sense of responsibility. The benefactor's only purpose was to drive a wedge between us. Look how this has upset you already." Her mother took gentle hold of Lily's shoulders and looked into her face. "I love you, that's why I haven't told you about the trust until now. I'm the only one who has ever taken care of you. Don't you see that? I always hoped that somehow I would find a way to provide for your college education without a stranger's help."

Lily wasn't sure what to believe. She thought about all the times she and her mother had spent together exploring museums, attending the theater, playing in the park, bicycling through the San Juan Islands, attending Seattle Ballet performances…wonderful, adventurous times. Yet in the past couple of years, since her mother dedicated all of her free time to work, Lily had felt abandoned. Now, the revelation of this secret trust fund had uncorked Lily's curiosity about all the unanswered questions of her childhood. Thoughts of betrayal swept through her. What did she really know about anyone in her mother's past, including her own relatives?

"Mama, why has it always been just you and me? Except for Grandpa Madison and Uncle Les, why have you kept me from my other relatives? I know they aren't dead. Don't they want to know me? I've asked you a million times about them, but you never talk about them or anyone from your past."

"Lily, this is not about my past. It's about your future."

"But it looks to me like someone from your past is providing me with my future."

Lily knew from Becky's piercing glare that her mother would not be answering many more questions. Yet, that didn't keep Lily from wondering what else her mother was keeping from her. Where there was one secret, there were always more. Maybe her father hadn't really died when she was a baby. Was he the benefactor? Or his parents in Chicago?

"Who gave me this money? Please tell me," pleaded Lily.

"I can't."

"You can't, or you won't?"

"I can't." Becky spoke in a calming voice. "Distribution of the trust is contingent upon the benefactor remaining anonymous."

"You sound like a lawyer." Lily couldn't resist asking another question. "Was it my father?"

Becky sighed. "Donald died too young to afford a trust of this size. Your benefactor tried to keep in touch during the first two years of your life but eventually lost any contact. He has a life of his own to pursue."

"He? The unnamable is a he?"

Lily allowed her mother to gently take hold of her hand. "My darling daughter, I understand your curiosity, but I hope you will put it aside and` celebrate your good fortune." Her words were met with Lily's challenging stare. Becky hesitated before conceding one final piece of information. "I can tell you only this…and it's about the gold dolphin ring you used to wear. Do you remember it"

"I think so. Why?"

"Your benefactor left it for you on your second birthday."

Lily waited, but her mother offered nothing more. "That's it?" Lily asked in frustration. "You're not going to tell me anything else?"

Becky answered her daughter with silence.

Unable to comprehend the bestowal of this life-changing gift, Lily retreated from her mother before her confusion took on another manifestation she would regret. She knew her building anger might be an unfair reaction toward her mother, yet she could not get past her mother's unwillingness to tell her who was behind the money. She needed time to absorb the significance of her newfound fortune. To rejoice in the excitement money might bring to her life, the independence it would offer, the world it would present to her. To be lifted from her narrow boundaries so suddenly was mind-boggling. But at what price? Her search for excitement quickly melted into a sobering fear of how much her life was about to change.

Back in the sanctity of her room, Lily rummaged through her toy box of beloved objects representing forgotten memories—a worn, stuffed panda, a faceless cozy bear, dog-eared golden books, a plastic tractor, deflated kick ball, broken crayons and Barbie doll clothes. All of these things had colored her childhood of dreams.

At last, she found the dolphin ring in a small jewel box. She slipped it on a long chain and hung it around her neck, a symbol of her new financial freedom and a reminder of the confusion she felt about her mother's secrecy.

As she glanced into her bedroom mirror, Lily whispered a promise to her reflection: "Someday, I will find my benefactor."

When it came time to withdraw some of the trust money for college, Lily's only splurge was to replace the dime store chain with a fourteen-karat gold necklace to match her ring. The opportunity to fulfill her promise hadn't occurred until now, almost four years later, at the conclusion of her junior year at college. On a whim, she had taken advantage of a trip to Chicago to visit the Thompsons, her dead father's parents. Meeting them had opened a door to her mother's past and widened Lily's search to encompass more than just the identity of her benefactor. It also reopened the dormant wound of distrust and confusion she had once harbored for her mother.

Clattering sounds in the restaurant brought Lily back to the present. She was still clutching the dolphin ring that hung on her necklace and wondered how long she had been gazing out the window. She considered telling Kate about the ring's origin, but was afraid to reveal too much so soon. For now, she was keen on maintaining control of her emotions.

"Are you okay?" asked Kate. "You seem to have drifted off."

Lily relaxed her furrowed brow. "Sorry. Yes, I'm fine."

Pulling Lily back into conversation, Kate asked where she was from.

"My mother is from California. I was born in California, but I never lived there. I grew up in Washington State." She hoped Kate didn't notice the strain in her voice.

"Where in California did your mother live?"

"I'm not really sure," Lily responded, nibbling on a French fry. "Somewhere in northern California. She never talks about her childhood. Apparently she left right after high school and only went back a couple of times."

"I'm from the Bay Area. What about her family? Do they still live in California?"

"I stay in touch with my uncle. I correspond with him occasionally, but I don't see him very often. My mother's parents are both dead, and I've only met my other grandparents once." Lily shifted around in her chair before continuing. "The way my mother tells it, she married my dad after she got pregnant. But he died in an auto accident a few weeks after I was born. So, I guess his parents sort of blame her and me for his death, or something." Lily shrugged. "My mother's pretty independent. She never married again."

As if to stop herself from talking, Lily filled her mouth with a whopping bite of her hamburger. Swallowing her food, she continued. "Geez. I've sure been going on. I don't usually tell strangers about all this stuff."

"Lily, I'm flattered you're comfortable enough to tell me those things. Please don't feel self-conscious."

Lily wiped a drip of ketchup from her chin, then dropped her head, but not in time to hide her flushed face. "So Kate, how often do you volunteer for the campaign?"

"Today's my first official day. I'll probably come down two or three times a week. We live in the mountains. Normally, I might not get downtown more than once a month."

"What do you do up there? No offense, but I think I'd be bored silly living so far away from the action."

"I would have been at your age, too. I've had my time in the spotlight. I'm enjoying my retreat to the mountains to hike, read and write."

"You're a writer?"

"I've written a novel and a screenplay based on the novel, but nothing has come of them, at least not yet. A producer friend in Hollywood is trying to help me."

"You have connections in Hollywood?"

"I used to work in the television industry in L.A." Kate sipped her shake, as if to allow time for Lily to ask all the inevitable questions that people usually asked about Hollywood, but Lily didn't pursue the topic. Kate smiled at her young friend. "What about you? What is your major in college?"

"Poli Sci and English with a minor in Theater."

"A double major. I'm impressed. What an interesting combination. But I thought you didn't like politics."

"I do, some of the time. I haven't decided what I want to do with my life yet, so I've dabbled in enough classes to give myself two majors."

"Good for you. If you go into politics, you'll need some acting ability. And an English literature background might help you create some wonderful fiction for political campaigns or the theater."

Lily laughed. "I never tied it together like that." She glanced at her watch. "Speaking of politics, it's probably time we head back. Doreen's going to be stressing that I took so long for lunch."

At that, the two women walked the short distance to headquarters in silence. Standing outside the building, Kate spoke. "You never told me what brought you to Colorado. How long do you plan to stay?"

A warm smiled crept over Lily's face. "That all depends."

"Depends on what?"

Lily thought for a moment. "Too soon to tell."

"Sounds like an adventure in the making," prompted Kate.

"So far, meeting you has been the highlight."

"Wow. Then I hope things will pick up for you."

"I didn't mean that negatively. Please don't be offended, but it's been a long time since I've connected with someone your age. My mother and I are on the outs, so to speak, but I miss the relationship we used to have. Somehow, I felt that connection with you today. I hope we can see each other again while I'm in Colorado."

"I'd like that too, Lily. Thanks for joining me for lunch. I really enjoyed it." Kate pulled out a piece of paper and scribbled on it. "Here's my phone number and address in case we miss seeing each other at headquarters again."

Kate and Lily gave each other a warm embrace. "Say goodbye to Doreen for me," said Kate. "And tell Susan I asked you to help her with the press conference." With a knowing smile she added, "It beats stuffing envelopes."

"Thanks, Kate. Do you think you'll be at headquarters later this week?"

"Yes, I suppose so. Perhaps we'll see each other then."

As Kate turned and walked away, Lily called after her. "Thanks for lunch. I owe you one."

Kate smiled and waved back.

Lily watched Kate leave, then looked at the note in her pocket. The address Kate had given her matched the one she already had. She tossed the paper Kate had given her into a nearby trash can.

CHAPTER THREE

Over the next two weeks, Kate mentored Lily through the machinations of managing the volatile relations between Emerson's campaign and the local press. There was a curious energy and ease in their new friendship. They often went to lunch together. Sometimes Doreen joined them, but usually it was just Kate and Lily indulging themselves in unusual epicurean adventures they found within walking distance of campaign headquarters. After one particularly long lunch, Kate decided to head home; Lily returned to headquarters.

"Where have you been?" asked Doreen, clearly miffed at Lily's lengthy absence. "You missed the staff meeting."

"I'm sorry, Doreen. I had no idea we were gone that long, honestly."

"Susan invited us to an important reception for Emerson, but now it's too late for us to go."

"You should have gone without me."

"Right. And left you behind. Just how would you have gotten home?"

"I'm not helpless, Doreen. I would have figured something out. Listen, there must still be plenty of time to make the reception. Can't we try?"

"No."

"Why not?"

"I don't know where it's being held. It's at a private home somewhere near the country club. I was so bummed at having to wait for you, I didn't think to get the address. Now, practically everyone has left."

Lily rolled her eyes. "Doreen, what's going on with you? It's not like you to give up so easily."

"Nothing is going on. I'm fine," Doreen snapped back.

"Look, let's check around. There must be someone left who knows something about this party." Lily scanned the expansive block of empty desks until she spotted Jake, a high school intern who was notorious for knowing everything around headquarters.

After learning all she needed to know from Jake, Lily returned to Doreen. "Wow, if Jake is right, it sounds like the who's who of corporate investors and political big wigs will be at the party. This might be a little over the top for us, but when did that stop us," said Lily. "First we'd better go to your house and spruce up a bit. That is, if you still want to go."

"Okay, yeah, sure. If you want to."

"What do you mean, if I want to? Didn't you just pounce on me for ruining our chances of going?"

Doreen gave her a sheepish look.

"All right then. Grab your purse and let's get out of here."

Thirty-three thousand feet over the Rocky Mountains on his flight from San Francisco to Denver, Martin Kelly reached into his briefcase for the private investigator's report he had received days earlier. He already knew what it said, but he looked at it again for reassurance. The report clearly stated that the object of his search, Lily McGuire, was in Denver. It went on to report that Lily was spending time volunteering for Dottie Emerson's Senatorial campaign headquarters. The investigator was very thorough in his report and had included the names of the volunteers who also frequented there. One name on the list had startled Martin. Under his directive, the investigator later confirmed that the name on his list was the same Kate Cochran Martin had known years earlier. Further, Lily and Kate were working together at headquarters.

Already scheduled to give a speech at a banker's conference in

Denver, Martin saw the trip as a logical opportunity to set up a meeting with Kate. He was certain she would help him arrange the ideal meeting between himself and Lily. He dismissed the notion that Kate might not want to help him and ignored the emotions he feared might arise in a reunion with Kate, the only woman he had ever loved. For the moment, his single-minded determination centered on meeting Lily. He had acquiesced to Becky's wishes to stay out of Lily's life long enough. Now that Lily was twenty-one, he no longer felt obliged to hide his identity from her.

After departing from the plane in Denver, Martin proceeded to a limousine where the private investigator awaited him with directions to a cocktail reception for Dottie Emerson.

"Are you sure Kate Cochran will be at this reception?" Martin asked the investigator as the limo pulled away from the curb.

By the time Kate arrived home after her lunch with Lily, Susan had left three messages on her answering machine to call her immediately. The first two were in Susan's normal condescending tone. By the third message, she was almost frantic. Kate was in no hurry to return her calls. She was changing her clothes when the phone rang. With no thought of who might be calling, Kate instinctively answered the phone.

"Kate. Finally. How come you haven't returned my calls?"

"This must be Susan," said Kate.

Susan ignored Kate's sarcasm. "Kate, I need your help."

"Look Susan, if you needed me so badly, why didn't you say something when I was at headquarters earlier today? I thought you had everything under control."

"*Au contraire.* This party… I did tell you about the cocktail reception for Dottie, didn't I?"

"No."

"Well, that's beside the point. I know you. You wouldn't have come if I had told you about it. But now you must come. Senator Patricia

Fitzpatrick is flying in from Washington this very minute, a day early. I have someone picking her up at the airport, but would you meet the Senator at her hotel and bring her here, to the party? This event has ballooned into a very delicate affair. Our most important contributors are due within the hour. There are just too many egos to soothe and schmooze for me to handle it without your help."

"Why not have the same person who's picking her up at the airport bring her to the party?"

"Yes, yes. That would make logistical sense. But I need a professional here, and I need you to meet her. You are so experienced with these high-profile types. And since you've already arranged her press schedule for the next few days, it would be logical for you to accompany her. She's a tough campaigner and eager to help Dottie, but she needs hand-holding. I don't want to slight her by having some pimply-faced volunteer be her escort. Patricia Fitzpatrick is a powerhouse in the Senate who deserves all the T.L.C. we can give her." Susan fell silent.

Kate knew the Senator was dynamic, inspiring, intelligent and intimidating—all the characteristics that usually drew Kate into challenging situations. But she resented Susan's manipulation and the fact it was working on her. She tried to suspend the ticking seconds while she decided what to do. She didn't want to drive back downtown, but what else did she have to do tonight? Parker was out of town. She might as well fill her evening with some activity.

Her adrenaline began to pump as she wondered whether or not she could maintain an intelligent conversation with Senator Fitzpatrick. The next words out of Kate's mouth gave Susan her answer. "At what hotel will she be staying? Can you give me some details about the party?"

An hour later, Kate walked through the door of Fitzpatrick's hotel suite and was met by Doreen. Lily was sitting across the room. An extravagant gift basket of tropical fruit and nuts swathed in colorful cellophane and a flamboyant ribbon dominated a nearby table. Kate recognized Susan's touch of hospitality even though she knew the card would have Dottie Emerson's name on it.

"You two again," whispered a surprised Kate. "So you are Susan's newest recruits, stepping into the breach to save her butt." It was a rude comment Kate regretted the moment she said it.

"I'm not sure what you mean," said a wide-eyed Doreen. "We walked into the party and Susan gave us the greatest welcome. She managed to introduce us to a couple of people and then asked us to do her a big favor. I mean, can you believe she asked us to pick up Senator Fitzpatrick? Was that cool, or what?"

Kate noticed that even the more cynical Lily seemed excited to be here. So she didn't tell the girls their dynamic new charge was actually less important than all those potential donors they had left at the party. Otherwise, Susan would have been here instead of the three of them. The beauty of it was, Senator Patricia Fitzpatrick would probably be far more interesting than most of those CEOs in gray suits, even with all their money and influence.

"So, why are you here, Kate?" asked a curious Lily.

"The short version is, Susan asked me. Where's the Senator?"

"Freshening up." Doreen pointed across the room to the closed bedroom door. "Isn't this place something else? What a view!" It was a sprawling corner suite with a spectacular panorama of downtown and distant snowcapped mountains.

"So what do you think of the Senator?" asked Kate, ignoring Doreen's glee.

Before either girl could answer, Fitzpatrick entered the room talking as rapidly as a machine gun spits bullets. She appeared outraged by a local news story about Dottie she had just seen on the television in her bedroom. She turned on the big-screen set in the living room area, but baseball scores filled the screens on all the local channels she flicked through. She clicked the television off and mumbled something about the idiocy of anyone who worried about baseball scores this early in the season. Upon seeing Kate, she walked across the room and introduced herself. A light pink suit hugged the Senator's petite figure, suggesting a softness that was quickly offset by the strength of her handshake.

"Are you the one who set up my press schedule while I'm in town?"

Fitzpatrick asked Kate.

"Yes. I'm Kate Cochran," were the only words Kate uttered before the Senator continued.

"Okay. Good. Maybe you can tell me why it's so important I spend time with these people instead of working with Dottie on her campaign strategy."

"Perhaps I can while we're driving to the party. Dottie would like you to meet some important contributors, there. We should get going so you don't miss anyone."

"Good. I'm ready." She returned to the bedroom, reemerging with her purse in hand. "Is there someone in particular I should spend more time with at the party?"

Luckily, Kate had been briefed about the more influential contributors, but before she could share this information, the Senator hurried everyone from the suite. Fitzpatrick led them down the hall, barely missing an elderly couple sauntering toward the elevator. The two moved aside to allow the group of women to rush by them.

"Where's the car? Perhaps the girls should run ahead so we don't have to wait too long for the valet to bring it up."

Kate had anticipated this. "It's okay. We can take my car. I asked the valet to keep it out front for us."

Doreen looked at Kate with a sigh of relief and mouthed a silent "thank you" to her.

Kate's years in Hollywood had numbed her impressionability to all but a few mega-stars. What she hadn't encountered for some time was Fitzpatrick's exuberant intensity and power oozing from every pore. No wonder she had captivated an entire nation with her political speeches over the years. Patricia Fitzpatrick emitted a sense of commanding control, though she knew little of what was to take place in the next couple of hours.

Kate believed power was an intoxicating drug to unsophisticated souls who came in contact with it. Billionaires, captains of industry and heads of state were most often imbued with it. Even some luminaries of the entertainment world exhibited certain nuances of power.

However, most people would not brush close enough to these rare icons to experience the stealth-like clarity of their strength.

Some of those powerful tycoons were gathering now to assess whether Dottie Emerson not only had the guts and drive, but the intelligence and charisma to carry off a winning campaign. A degree of malleability was a quality some of Dottie's guests might also find desirable. Kate winced at her vision of Dottie being examined like a specimen under a microscope.

The Senator let Kate precede her through the front door of the stately Tudor home that was the site of the party. She had ignored Lily and Doreen since Kate had arrived at the hotel. The women greeted some volunteers in the foyer and followed the conversational buzz and tinkling of ice cubes toward a living room packed with men and a sprinkling of women. Standing on the steps overlooking the living room, Kate quickly scanned the room for Susan, but couldn't see her. However, she did spot Max Weingard, Chairman of Petroleum America, and walked over to him with the Senator in tow. Doreen and Lily headed off on their own.

Kate had met Max several years earlier at a party she had organized in his honor for a Los Angeles Philharmonic Guild fund-raiser. Max was in his mid-fifties, about six feet tall, athletic, yet showed some softening around his waist. Dressed in a Brooks Brothers suit and conservative tie, he mirrored the look of many attendees surrounding him.

Upon seeing Max, Kate couldn't help but reflect on her past personal relationship with him...and others associated with him. Max's company was owned by a European conglomerate, EXLT, one of the largest corporations in the world. It was mere coincidence Kate had become friends with Max during the time she was having a long-distance affair with the dashing Chairman of EXLT, Lars Karlstrom, a Swede she had met while vacationing on the Amalfi Coast. Kate had always been discreet about their relationship and never told

Max she knew his boss.

Lars held such immeasurable international influence and stature as Chairman of EXLT, that protocol required him to meet with heads of state of whatever country he visited on business. At first, Kate had felt unworthy of being in the company of such a prominent businessman, but Lars's obvious delight in spending time with her had boosted Kate's self-confidence. His playful chiding had taught her how to laugh at herself and her mistakes. He also validated the Swedish reputation for uninhibited sex, starting with their first episode of lovemaking on a rocky cliff above a crowded beach. If it hadn't been for the scenic rapture of the sapphire blue Mediterranean engaging the sunbathers' attention, their private tryst might have been spotted by those below.

Now, years later, Kate still relied on the strength and influence of Lars to help her level the mental playing field at times like this, when she was in a room filled with high-powered executives who might otherwise intimidate her. No matter how wealthy, influential or intelligent she might perceive someone to be, she now saw herself as an equal.

"Max, Kate Cochran," she reminded him. The two shook hands.

"Kate, yes of course. My favorite Perle Mesta of the West Coast. You're looking as glamorous as ever. What are you doing in this neck of the woods?"

"So nice of you to remember me after all these years. I'm living here now." Kate put one arm around the Senator's back to bring her into the conversation. "Max, I'd like you to meet Senator Patricia Fitzpatrick. Senator, this is Max Weingard, Chairman of Petroleum America."

Once Max and the Senator were fully engaged in conversation, Kate excused herself and moved on to find Susan. It was time for Dottie and her paid staffers to take over. She suspected Susan would appreciate having the next crack at introducing the Senator to a few of the strong and powerful she liked to claim as her own personal friends. Kate chuckled at the thought of Susan's surprise when she discovered that her old colleague actually knew someone at this soiree.

Kate spotted Susan across the room in animated conversation with three men. Susan was clearly enjoying the attention, so when Kate caught Susan's eye with the intention of interrupting her, Susan shifted her glance back to the threesome as if to say, "not now." Kate ignored the obvious signal. She wanted to relinquish her package to Susan and go home.

"Excuse me, Susan," interrupted Kate with a determined voice.

Susan wasn't going to miss a beat. "Oh, Kate, how are you? So nice to see you," she said in a dismissive tone.

The man with his back to Kate turned toward her. Kate couldn't believe her eyes. Her heart skipped a beat before it began to palpitate wildly. Her throat tightened. Feeling her palms turn clammy, she took a slow, deep breath to keep from hyperventilating. All of this happened in an instant, but it seemed like an uncomfortably long time to Kate. She silently reprimanded herself for her schoolgirl reaction. Where was the poised woman she took pride in portraying? Perhaps her mind was playing tricks on her. For years, she had spotted Martin Kelly's familiar profile in a crowd, only to discover a look-alike. After awhile, she understood it would always be someone else's profile reminding her of him. But this time, it was Martin's blue eyes meeting her stare.

He tilted his head and studied her with the quizzical expression so familiar to her. It was a look of a thousand questions. A look that asked, *where have you been, how are you, what are you thinking, what am I thinking, how are we supposed to react to this situation?*

Kate knew she should say something before someone detected the electricity flowing between them. But she was frozen in place.

"Kate?" prompted Susan, "Are you looking for me?"

Kate did not move her gaze. She ignored Susan's question. "Martin," she said to him as he moved over to her.

"Kate."

Kate was vaguely aware that Susan and the two other men in the group had excused themselves and moved away to join others in the crowd.

"Can I give you a hug?" asked Martin.

"That would be appropriate for two old friends," she replied, trying to present a calm demeanor. She thought her love for Parker had eclipsed any lingering passion she once felt toward Martin. Yet, her heart was beating rapidly. She hoped Martin wouldn't sense her nervousness. Her mind flashed back to the memory of their first brief fling in college. Perhaps that's when his Svengali-like grip first took hold of her heart. But she was certain that nothing more would have transpired between them if not for a chance meeting a few years later. It was that encounter and his encouragement that prompted Kate to conveniently cling to Martin's tenuous love while allowing him to sweep in and out of her adult life.

He held her close and whispered into her ear, "You look fabulous. I mean you really look great!"

Kate gently moved out of their embrace. "Thank you. It's really good to see you, too."

Martin took a step back and ran his gaze unabashedly from her head to her toes and back up again. How many times before had he done this to her? She always wondered whether he tried to charm every woman he knew with this gesture, or if he reserved it for her. In any case, it made her uncomfortable, as if she was supposed to perform some circus trick to make his long look worthwhile. He smiled and shook his head, "Boy, you look good."

"Martin, don't embarrass me." Kate was anxious to move the conversation to a less personal topic. She couldn't believe she was reacting to him in the same helpless way she always had. He had thrown her off balance with his infatuation before she married Parker, and he was doing it again. Shouldn't his power over her have waned by now? He was the only man, besides Parker, she had ever loved, but they had never been close or at ease with each other the way she and Parker were.

Indeed, when Parker had entered her life, Kate had been able to open her heart to him and allow her passion for Martin to recede into her past. Ironically, it was Lars Karlstrom's reconciliation with his estranged wife that had helped Kate open herself to Parker. By watching Lars and his wife reconcile, she had lost her own fear of marriage and had begun to believe that she deserved more from a relationship than the flash of her random encounters with Martin.

"What are you doing in Colorado?" she asked him.

"I'm giving the keynote address at the Colorado Bankers annual meeting tomorrow." Martin continued while holding her in his gaze. "I came in early for some private meetings. One of my hosts brought me here on our way to dinner. Said it might be entertaining."

"And?"

"And I find this party has taken my breath away."

Kate couldn't help but smile. "Perhaps I can resuscitate you over lunch tomorrow." Kate cringed at her flirtatious response.

"I will remain breathless until then. Call me in the morning and tell me where to meet you."

"Where are you staying?" Kate asked.

"At the Brown Palace."

"What if I just meet you in the hotel lobby at noon? I'll make reservations for some place nearby."

"Sounds like a plan."

"I've got to go." Kate took a step away from him to break the spell. "See you tomorrow." She melted into the crowd like a butterfly flitting across an open meadow to safety. She hadn't even given him a chance to pursue any further conversation.

Perfect, she thought. She had left him curious, wanting and smiling. She was a little off balance and hoped she had left him that way, too…for a change. Although she silently berated herself for inviting him to lunch, she knew the gesture had been her way of appearing relaxed when all sense of decorum was breaking loose within her.

Kate didn't get far before she smacked into someone. "Oh Lily! I'm so sorry. I didn't even see you."

"I noticed that. You were a thousand miles away." They both laughed.

"Yes. I guess I was. I've got to run. Do you and Doreen need a ride or anything?"

"No, thanks." Gesturing to a young man standing beside her, Lily said, "Malcolm has offered to give me a lift when I'm ready to leave. Doreen just left with someone who's going to take her back to the hotel to pick up her car. Will I see you at headquarters tomorrow?"

"Actually, no. I have other plans."

Lily lowered her voice and moved in closer to Kate. "That man you were just talking to hasn't taken his eyes off you. Anything you'd like to share?" she teased.

Kate felt the hint of an involuntary smile cross her face. "Nope. Hope to see you soon." She gave Lily a peck on the cheek and forced herself to saunter casually out of the room.

CHAPTER FOUR

The next morning, Kate searched through her closet for the appropriate outfit to wear for lunch with Martin.

"What do you think of this one, Rusty?" Kate pulled a pink dress from her closet and showed it to the dog who lay at her feet. Rusty wagged his tail at the sound of his name.

"No. A bit too revealing, I think." She put the dress back and flipped through the row of clothing. "Ah, here we go." From the back of her closet Kate reached for a conservative black pantsuit and a silk blouse. It was simple, understated and not the least bit suggestive.

The dog yawned and laid his head on the floor.

"Too drab, Rusty? I'll add a few modest accessories for a look of casual elegance. I don't want my old friend to think married life has made me boring and dowdy."

She hoped seeing Martin today would put a realistic perspective on the role he played in her life. "But I'm not being honest, am I?" She patted Rusty on the head. "There's something much bigger between Martin and me than I care to face." Kate noticed the dog's ears beginning to twitch and smiled. "Maybe I'd better not tell you anything more."

Kate caught Martin's eye as he was coming down the stairs from the hotel's mezzanine banquet rooms surrounded by a knot of businessmen. He looked sophisticated in his light gray suit, carrying his thin black briefcase—something designed especially for carrying his speeches, she was sure. She could easily imagine him presiding over a huge gathering of bankers, impressing them with statistics only they could appreciate.

He shook hands with the men around him, then walked across the elegant lobby to join her. She felt her pulse quicken the closer he came. Damn, she thought.

He greeted her with a friendly kiss on the check.

"How was your speech?" she asked.

"It was fine. They had a lot of good questions, so I guess they were listening. That's about all I can hope for. How about we find a place where we can have some privacy?"

Kate let the word privacy mean more than perhaps Martin had intended. She was forced to clear her throat before speaking. "I've made reservations at a restaurant just a few blocks from here. It's a gorgeous day. I thought you might enjoy a little walk."

"Absolutely."

She noticed a thin smile cross his lips, making her feel a bit foolish. She was certain he had noticed her nervous reaction to his privacy remark.

Once outside, Martin made some perfunctory comments about how clean the downtown area was and then they walked in silence. Occasionally, he commented on the architecture, or Kate pointed out a landmark. She felt his hand brush the back of hers when they waited for a streetlight to change. Kate wasn't sure whether it was an accident or intentional.

After another block, they fell into a flow of relaxing small talk. It felt normal and very comfortable for her to be with him again. Their life together had always been full of separations and reunions. There seemed to be little difference in the rhythm of this get-together.

Martin raised his arm to drape it around Kate's shoulders. There were times she had longed for his touch and almost let him put his arm around her now. Instead, she casually moved a half-step away to thwart his overture. Perhaps his inclination to touch her was all in her imagination, but it left her with a shameful desire.

The Glenmore Grille was one of Kate's favorite lunchtime retreats. It was a stylish, understated restaurant with dark mahogany paneling, white linen tablecloths and tuxedo-clad waiters, some of whom had worked there for thirty years. Haunted by newspaper reporters and an occasional anchorman from one of the television stations, it also bore the closest resemblance to a movie studio commissary she had found, with its ambiance of camaraderie and the pressure of impending deadlines pulsing through the patrons.

At the end of the bar, she spotted a local columnist who waved when he saw her. Martin must have observed the exchange, but he said nothing. The maitre d' seated them at one of a long line of tables-for-two. Martin looked around the room and gave Kate a look of approval. She knew it was similar to restaurants he frequented in the financial district of San Francisco.

The clatter and buzz of the room faded into the distance as they looked across the small table at each other.

"It's been a long time," he said, reaching across the table to take hold of her hands resting on the table. She was curious to feel the bare touch of his hand on her skin, so left her hands in place.

"It has."

Silence fell between them as they melted into the sight of one another. The bravery only years can provide, allowed Kate to feel a level of comfort she had never experienced with him before.

She gently pulled away her hands and spoke in a soft, nostalgic tone. "It's really nice to see you."

"It's good to see you. I've missed you."

"I've missed you, too," she confessed.

"Well, you can't have missed me too much. I understand you have a wonderful man in your life."

"Yes, I do. I'm very lucky. He's a very good person and loves me very much. If I had known it would be this easy, I would have gotten married years ago."

"Why didn't you? You have so much to offer." Then, enunciating every syllable as if to dramatize the meaning of each word, he said,

"You have always been a dynamic…intelligent…beautiful…woman with a great sense of humor."

She laughed at his flattering remarks out of modesty and because of their irony. If she was so wonderful, why hadn't he married her when he had the chance? "I think you had a lot to do with my waiting in the wings for so many years."

"Me? That's crazy," he said. "I always thought you were too involved in your career to be bothered with me. Let alone a relationship with me!"

"No, it was *your* career that was so important. I was always ready to spend more time with you, but somehow it never happened."

This was clearly a conversation they should have had years ago. Kate knew she should let it go, but she couldn't. She quickly continued, using lightness in her voice to camouflage the note of bitterness welling from deep within her. "But it all turned out for the good. I had a fabulous life immersed in the trimmings of Hollywood. I suppose my ambitions might have added to the barrier between us, but it was more out of self-defense. I didn't want to appear needy. That would have sent you running for sure. I knew, and accepted, what your priorities were."

"I had no idea."

"Oh, I think you did," she said. "Didn't I propose to you once?" A warm blush spread across her cheeks.

Martin answered Kate with an uncomfortable look of puzzlement. "You couldn't have. I never would have turned you down."

"But you did. Too bad for you."

Kate would never forget the embarrassment she had felt from the brevity of his careless dismissal of her proposal. *I don't think so.* He had responded as if she had asked him out to dinner. Then he had sent her off in a cab so he wouldn't be late for a meeting.

"And what about you?" she continued. "Do you have a significant other in your life?"

Martin smiled. "I'm not sure if I would call it significant, yet. She's a wonderful lady, but we're not living together or anything. She reminds me a little of you. She's outspoken, fun and keeps me guessing."

"I hope her opinions penetrate your thick skull better than mine did."

Martin laughed. "You'd be surprised how much I listened to you over the years. Your opinions on politics and business definitely influenced my life."

"I wouldn't have imagined. I'm flattered."

"I guess there's a lot we never talked about."

Kate found solace in his admission. "I would agree. Why do you suppose that was?"

Without missing a beat, he accepted the challenge of her question. "Oh, I think we were both so involved with our careers there wasn't much energy left over. You were always fighting with one studio or another for more money or better facilities for your projects. I loved hearing your stories." Martin leaned back in his chair like a proud father while Kate listened, her elbows on the table and her chin relaxing on her clasped hands. She thought his vision far out-glamorized her work as a line-producer, but she let his words of admiration wash over her like a cooling breeze refreshes the desert.

"You really endured a lot in your battles with all those men, and you, one of the few female producers at the time. I've always admired your determination. My own struggles seemed tame compared to the high drama of your celebrity world. I used to read about the people you worked with in the newspapers. My world of investment bankers and real estate developers isn't known for its flamboyance. A rather dull group, absorbed by the price of money. No tattoos, or scandalous sex lives worth reading about."

"Oh, you certainly had your moments," she countered with a laugh. "Remember the time you introduced me to President Reagan at that fund-raiser for the San Francisco Opera? Very impressive. And then there was that presidential oversight committee you served on, International Banking and Commercial Real Estate Development in the U.S., or something to that effect. I've never been in the Oval Office like you have."

"Wow! What a memory. I'm not sure I'd be able to remember the name of that committee."

"Your appearance at the cocktail party last night tells me you're still very well connected."

Martin shrugged. "It goes with the territory. How have you adjusted to your new lifestyle? Don't you miss working in Hollywood?"

"I used to. It took me a couple of years to adapt to the more languid pace of a mountain woman, but now I don't think I could ever go back to Hollywood, at least not a steady diet of it."

" What are you doing now?"

There was that often-asked question again. Martin never would have left his career dangling in midair like she had. He had suffered his identity crisis early on when he'd been cut by the Buffalo Bills football team. In one summer, he tumbled from the summit of achieving his childhood dream of becoming an NFL draft choice into the murky waters of obscurity. He had been used and discarded, and vowed it would never happen to him again. He had grabbed onto a new career and never slowed down, not even when he reached the top of his profession.

"Parker and I play a lot of golf. I've become an addict. Do you still play?"

"I play enough so I'm not embarrassed when I have to entertain clients. I travel too much to play as well as I used to. Gone are the days of my three handicap."

"You look like you're in great shape."

"Nice of you to notice. Fortunately, many hotels have a gym."

A hovering waiter captured their attention long enough to take their orders. Each of them chose the vegetarian salad and a glass of Chablis.

Martin steered the conversation back to Kate. "It's still hard for me to imagine that you walked away from all of your success. What are you doing to keep your creative juices flowing?"

"I do a lot of writing."

"You were always good at that. I still have your letters to prove it."

Kate's eyes widened in astonishment. Her heart warmed. "You're kidding. You don't really?"

"Would I lie about something as sentimental as that?" He rubbed his chin and looked around the room, apparently embarrassed by his admission, then recuperated by asking another question. "What kind of writing are you doing?"

Kate wanted to ask about the letters, but she allowed his question to guide her thoughts. "Fiction. I write fiction. I've written a novel and a screenplay based on the book."

"That's just great! Did you have it published?"

"I tried, but no luck. Do you remember me ever speaking of David Backus?" Martin's expression told her he wasn't sure. "He's one of the few producers I still keep in touch with in L.A. He's trying to put together a movie deal for us. Last I heard, it was still on a list of scripts-in-development at one of the television networks."

"And I suppose it's all very confidential," added Martin.

Kate laughed at his insightful remark. "You'd think they were developing nuclear weapons the way they guard their acquisitions. David calls me occasionally to say we're very close to getting the go-ahead. Frankly, all of his illusive hope drives me crazy."

"At least your script is collecting dust in Hollywood and not lost under a layer of pine pollen in Colorado."

"Very funny." It felt good to talk to Martin about her writing.

Martin shared little about his commercial real estate company except to say business was good. After lunch was served, Martin and Kate updated each other on mutual friends and complained about the moral demise of the country. The conversation swung back and forth easily between them. It wasn't one-sided, with Kate doing most of the listening, as in the past. Kate wondered why they had never been able to have such a free-flowing dialog before now. Perhaps things would have been different if they had. The protective veil that had always hung between them was suddenly gone.

Curious about the woman in his life, Kate prodded Martin for more details.

"She's not you, but I think she's very special. We've talked about getting married."

"I would call that a significant step for you." Kate's heart sank at hearing about his serious relationship with another woman. "Congratulations," she said, attempting to rise above her irrational jealousy.

"How about you, Kate? Any thoughts about children?" he asked.

"We're very happy with just the two of us. At this point in our lives, I guess that's the way you must feel as well." Kate gritted her teeth. She hated the thought of Martin having children if she couldn't. Somehow, it didn't seem fair, since he was the prime reason she had not married until she was beyond her ability to have a child.

The waiter whisked away their plates and offered them coffee, which only Kate accepted. Martin used the brief interruption to change the direction of their conversation.

"Kate, it wasn't a coincidence I ran into you yesterday." His voice had become very serious, almost ominous. "I went to that reception yesterday with the hope of finding you there."

Kate was startled. She pulled herself up in her chair and looked at him in bewilderment.

Martin hesitated a moment before he went on. He was clearly nervous, as if the weight of what he was about to reveal might harm her. "I've got something very important to tell you. It will most likely be a shock." He paused again before proceeding. "I don't know how else to put this except just to say it."

Kate locked her gaze intently on Martin to let him know she was ready to hear whatever he had to say.

"Kate, I have a daughter. I've had a daughter for almost as long as we've known each other."

Kate was silent. She pressed her lips together in an attempt to freeze her emotions.

"I don't know why I never told you this before."

"Let me just take a breath here," said Kate as she rested the weight of her forehead against her hand. She felt like she had been punched in the gut. She fought to contain the tears welling inside of her, then allowed a few words to escape. "I don't know what to say."

Martin slowly continued, his eyes reflecting the anguish she felt in her heart. "My daughter doesn't know about me, but I've always known about her. I had a girlfriend my senior year in college. We...she got pregnant just before we broke up at the end of the term.

"Would that have been the same summer you and I first met and dated for all of two weeks?" Kate's tone was curt.

Martin shrugged. "Yeah, about that time, I guess. Kate, I know what you're thinking. But I had already split with her before we met."

Kate clenched her fist. "Oh, you have no idea what I'm thinking."

Martin looked quizzically at Kate, then continued. "I really cared a great deal for her, but I wasn't in love with her. I did offer to marry her." He chuckled nervously. "To her credit, she wanted no part of a loveless marriage. I only saw my daughter once when she was too young to remember me. I sent letters and tried to stay in touch, but the only reply I received was from a lawyer, telling me to cease and desist. I was angry and hurt." Martin closed his eyes and shook his head. "Perhaps I shouldn't admit this, but at that point in my life, I didn't need a child to worry about. My girlfriend's insistence on keeping me out of the picture made it easy to bail on my responsibilities."

Kate squirmed in her chair. "Why are you telling me all of this now?"

"Please, just hear me out."

Her curiosity let him continue with the story he clearly needed to tell.

"Two years later, I started a trust fund for my daughter. Over the years, it built to quite a considerable sum—more than enough to put her through college and keep her going after that. I contacted her mother's lawyer to inform her about the trust fund. Apparently, my ex-girlfriend wasn't pleased. She contacted me and said she didn't need any help, that I should keep my money. I reminded her this was my child, too, and whether she liked it or not, I had every legal right to set up a trust fund for whomever I chose. She even tried to tell me the child wasn't mine."

"And you didn't believe her. Why not?" Kate asked.

"Without going into details, I knew she was lying. Anyway, that was the last time I ever heard from her. Instead of being happy her daughter's college would be paid for, she cut off all contact."

"But how do you know anything about your daughter if her mother is so secretive?" asked Kate.

"Lawyers sometimes talk about their clients in ways they probably shouldn't. In my case, her lawyer has kept me informed, but has respected his client's desire to conceal their whereabouts until now."

"Why now?" asked Kate.

"Lily and her mother had a serious falling out."

Kate's body tightened. She leaned slightly forward upon hearing a familiar name.

"Lily? That's her name?"

"Yes."

Suddenly, Kate felt very foolish. It was painfully apparent her lunch with Martin had little to do with any love she thought they might have shared. "Where do I fit into all this? How did you know where to find me last night?"

"I hired a private investigator to learn more about Lily's activities."

Kate shook her head in resignation.

"Kate, this is a tough world. No one's daughter should be left to find her way without someone who cares. But, I don't know how to approach her on my own. I'm afraid her mother might have prejudiced any hope I have to befriend her."

"What a funny coincidence. "I don't suppose your Lily is the same Lily McGuire I've been working with at Emerson's campaign headquarters." Her lungs collapsed with a deep sigh.

Martin grimaced as if to apologize. "Lily McGuire is my daughter."

Kate put her hand over her mouth and moved her head side-to-side in disbelief.

"This is perfect, don't you see? I planned to visit Denver when I learned that Lily was here, and then I found out that you know each other. It's kismet! What better person to help me than you? What do you think of her?"

"I'm stunned! I'm...I'm shocked! I mean... How can you ask that question so casually? And what do you mean, I can help you? I don't know what to say or think about any of this right now. Why should I believe that my meeting Lily was an accident?"

"What else could it have been? Kate, you know more about my daughter than I do, and you just met her. This is very awkward, I know. But for the moment, would you suspend your feelings and judgment of me?"

Kate removed the napkin from her lap and reached under the table for her purse. "What I'd like to do right now is get out of this restaurant. I'm having a hard time breathing." With that she rose from the table and left.

Kate was almost half a block away from the restaurant when she felt him by her side. Her pace increased to keep time with her heartbeat. He matched her strides and said nothing. Ten blocks later they were in City Plaza. The midday sun beat down on concrete pathways curving through flower beds of early-blooming tulips and scattered daffodils. She led him to the center of the plaza where all the walkways converged on a circular area lined with stone benches. They were alone, except for a few lunchtime stragglers soaking up springtime warmth from the afternoon sun. Suddenly, Kate stopped dead in her tracks and turned to face him head-on.

"Do you have any idea what's running through my head right now?" Martin stood silently in front of her.

The words poured out of Kate like the launching of a rocket that couldn't be stopped. "You were the love of my life for most of my adult life. I wanted to marry you and have your children. I accepted your swinging-door relationship because it was better than not seeing you at all.

"You called me when it was convenient, or when you needed a date for a special event. But we never just hung out like normal people who enjoy spending time together, not even during those first couple of years when we lived in the same town. Yes, I went along with it all those years. I was an equal player. It was convenient for me, too.

"On those rare nights when you were in town for twenty-four hours and had time to see me after a business dinner, we would talk until you began to fall asleep mid-sentence. We would go to bed and make love. Then you would roll over and sleep, not out of disinterest. I knew that. You were usually suffering from jet lag or exhaustion from the impossible schedule you kept.

"Did you know I never slept during those nights you stayed over? I knew those were the only hours I would spend with you for several weeks or even months. I didn't want to waste one minute of our time together by sleeping. Pretty pathetic, don't you think? In the mornings, you barely took time for a polite cup of coffee before you left."

Martin grimaced.

"I'm embarrassed by my own behavior," she continued, throwing her hands up into the air. "Where was my self-esteem? I always made excuses for you. I truly believed you would have spent more time with me if it hadn't been for your all-consuming career. Of course, I thought your career and I were the only mistresses in your life. But that wasn't true, was it? Over time, I began to face facts and deal with the evidence I had always ignored. And now your revelation of a daughter."

He started to say something, but Kate charged over his words. "Finally, one day I woke up and realized I deserved more from a man than you were capable of giving. Good for me!" Kate turned her back to Martin and walked a few steps away to gather her thoughts. She realized she had his attention, and he appeared willing to listen to her for however long she needed to speak. Martin had slipped his hands into his pockets, but dropped them back to his sides when she returned.

"Unfortunately," Kate went on, "I unknowingly surrendered the likelihood of having children while I was waiting for you. That was my fault and something I've had to deal with. This might sound old-fashioned coming from me. It's the dogma I was raised on before the feminist movement led us in a new direction. But here it is. In my gut, I believe motherhood is the most basic truth of a woman's earthly purpose, which therefore makes me inadequate and nonessential as a real woman. I don't care how *Cosmopolitan* Magazine glamorizes the successful careers of single, childless women. To me, it's all meaningless. I feel sorry for the young women today who go to bed reading the latest folklore from Helen Gurley Brown, because I know they will still wake up lonely.

"I've tried to reconcile my childless status. Somehow, the belief that you would never have any children either, helped to soften my own pain. My reasoning may seem strange, but I don't know how else to explain it. In essence, I chose my career and the hopes of a relationship with you over the experience of raising children. But now you have a child and I don't. Lily is the daughter we should have had together. How the hell would you expect me to feel?"

Kate's anger finally reached its end. She turned her back on Martin to wipe her tears with an old tissue from her pocket. She had kept these emotions inside for years, but the knowledge of his having a daughter had pushed her over the edge. She exhaled deeply and felt surprising relief. She turned back and looked at him with a raised eyebrow, gripping his shoulders with each of her hands while she patiently and quietly addressed him. "And now, you have casually walked back into my life to ask a favor."

Kate noticed that Martin had not taken his eyes off of her during the entire outburst. Even in her rage, Kate saw her agony mirrored in his face.

Martin spoke softly. "What can I say? I'm sorry. I had no intention of causing you so much pain. Then or now."

"I know. I've been holding this in for a long time. But since today is a day of confessions, it's only fair you know what I've kept pent up inside of me. I'm not going to apologize for my eruption. I actually feel pretty good now that I've unloaded."

He chuckled, "Good. I guess I deserved some of it."

"Some of it? Don't dilute my tirade. You deserved all of it," she corrected him.

"I'm not proud of the way I treated you, but I was only doing the best I could at the time. I didn't know how to love you then. Letting you get away has been a big loss in my life. I don't want to make the same mistake with my daughter. I can't walk away from her without a fight. Based on what you just told me, you of all people must understand that. She is at a point in her life in which I might be able to give her more than just my money, but I need your help."

"Martin, I have no idea how I can help."

"You said you've spent some time with her."

"Yes, I have, and I like her very much. Our personalities seemed to click somehow."

"Tell me what you think of her. Do you think she's happy?"

"I'm not comfortable with this."

This time, Martin put his hands on her shoulders. "Please, Kate."

"I don't know, Martin." She shrugged her shoulders, but he kept his hands in place while she thought. "She seems a bit confused about her life and what she wants to do right now. But isn't that normal at her age?"

"I don't know. You and I always knew what we wanted to do."

"Yes, but I'm not sure everyone is as passionate about their careers as we were."

"Kate, please! Spend more time with her."

"Martin, I don't know how to hover. I've never been a mother."

"Exactly. You'll treat her like an adult instead of being overly protective like her mother has been."

"I can't do this. You're asking me to spy on Lily."

"Kate, I'm worried. Something happened to her just before she came to Colorado, only I don't know what."

"How do you know this?

"I told you before. I've always kept track of her."

"Then why do you need me?"

"I trust your judgment. You're more like me than anyone I know, only better."

"Better?"

"You're a woman. You have more compassion and insight."

"Don't feed me that line. Why won't you try talking to Lily

yourself?"

"Why should she talk to me, the father who deserted her?"

"Don't be childish. You didn't desert her. You were prevented from seeing her."

"Kate, there is a young girl out there who might need help." He placed his hands on his hips and looked down at his feet for a moment. He looked back at Kate and continued. "Of course I want her to know who I am, but she might need help before I have the luxury of trying to bond with her. What if she goes into some kind of a depression, or something? You told me, yourself, the two of you felt connected in some way. We've got to watch out for her."

"We? Shouldn't you be having this conversation with her mother?"

"Unfortunately, that's not possible. Would you at least think about it?"

"This is crazy. Why should I do this?" His persistence was beating her down. "If Lily and I spend time together, it has to happen naturally, not at your insistence. We've talked about her coming up to Pine Mountain, but now I can't be the instigator. Being friends with Lily doesn't seem honest anymore."

"It is if you really like each other, as you say you do."

Kate walked Martin back to his hotel, the brisk afternoon breeze chilling Kate. They said their goodbyes in the shadowed courtyard outside the hotel entrance, giving each other a perfunctory hug, appropriate for old friends.

Kate turned and walked away from him with her heart racing. She went about twenty feet, turned around and walked back to him. His eyes were riveted on her. She took one of his hands in hers and gazed back into his eyes. "I love you, Martin Kelly, and I always will." She let him pull her into his arms.

"I love you, too," he whispered into her ear.

In all of their years together, they had never spoken those words to one another. They held each other close until he relaxed their embrace to kiss her gently on her lips before letting her go. Tears of what might have been ran down her flushed cheeks as she turned and walked away.

CHAPTER FIVE

Kate cried for most of the return drive to her mountain home. She cried for the emotional paralysis that had kept her and Martin apart, that had prevented her from truly loving any man before Parker. She cried for too many years of empty nights dissolving into lonely dawns, for the children she had once longed to bear with Martin and then with Parker.

She felt guilty and confused by the tears for Martin. She loved her husband, sometimes to the point of actually aching inside. Parker was the one constant in her life. His unconditional love had shown her the way to love herself. Apparently Martin had learned how to love as well. But neither she nor Martin had learned this valuable lesson in time to love each other.

Suddenly aware of familiar surroundings, she steered the red Jeep Cherokee up her curving driveway and was surprised to see Parker's car sitting in the open garage. She hadn't expected him home for another two days. She parked her vehicle next to his, pulled her limp body out of the car and walked back out to the mailbox, deciding that the activity of retrieving the mail would give her eyes more time to dry before Parker saw her. She mindlessly flipped through the mail, barely registering the card from Becky Madison. She would read the card when her mind cleared. Completely wrung out, Kate thought only about submerging in a hot bath to loosen Martin's unexpected grip on her emotions.

There was a note from Parker on the blackboard in the mud room. *Rusty has taken me on a fast hike up the mountain. We left at 3.* She guessed she had about thirty minutes before he returned. Relieved, she found her way into the bathroom and started the water to which she added a healthy dose of foaming bath gel. Back in the bedroom, she absent-mindedly scrolled through incoming phone numbers on the answering machine while removing her clothes, lazily dropping them into a heap on the floor around her bare feet.

David Backus's number was in the list of callers. He had called three times in the last two days, but she hadn't had time to return his calls, or even listen to his messages.

David was the only executive producer with whom she had a true friendship outside of the entertainment business. When her search to find a literary agent had come up empty, David had become her angel. With a handshake, they agreed to let him have a crack at getting her novel published. He even paid her for the right to option the book for a movie and insisted she write the screenplay. The money wasn't much, but it made her feel like she was still part of the game.

In the year that followed, she fed from David's flamboyant hyperbole about her screenplay's inspiring brilliance and guaranteed success. But over time, like over-used swear words that lose their punch, so had David's rhetoric lost its impact on Kate's belief in her project. Today, she was not in the mood for his ongoing hype or updates on his other projects in development.

Kate heard the back door slam. Parker's footsteps burst into the house, sounding like those of a kid who had just won his first baseball game. The sound of Rusty's toenails clicking across the wooden floor let her know he was scrambling close behind.

"Kate, Kate!" Parker yelled enthusiastically. "Where are you?"

"I'm here, in the den." Comfortably slumped in an overstuffed chair, Kate was sipping a glass of wine as she relaxed after her bath. The unopened note from Becky was sitting on the side table near her.

Rusty bounded into the room, tail wagging, tongue hanging out from his vigorous romp. He lopped up water from his bowl and plopped down beside her chair as Parker appeared carrying a chilled bottle of champagne and two glasses. Drenched in sweat, he leaned over and gave her a salty hello kiss. Kate's clouded mood couldn't match his exuberance.

Parker stepped back from her with a look of concern. "Hey, what's wrong? Are you okay?"

"Yes, just a little tired."

Apparently satisfied with her explanation, Parker revved up to his initial enthusiasm. He put the wine flutes on the coffee table and filled them with champagne while Kate looked on. "I talked to David Backus today. He said he's left a zillion messages, but you haven't returned his calls."

"So, how are things with David?" she asked halfheartedly.

"He's great. Just great! I was going to leave you a note to tell you what's going on, but I wanted to see the look on your face when you heard the news."

"What?" she asked, finally beginning to feel his excitement.

"Your screenplay. They're going to make a TV movie out of it!"

"Oh, Parker. David's been saying that forever. He's been shadow-boxing with the network for almost a year on this project, and I don't see that he's made any headway."

"No, no. They really are. That's why David is so desperate to reach you. He was going to fly out here to tell us the news in person if he hadn't reached one of us on the phone."

Kate laughed at the exaggeration and eagerly leaned forward in the chair. "What else did he say? Did he give you any details?"

"He didn't have time. He was calling from JFK and was rushing to catch his flight. He just said to tell you it was a 'go' and they want to start pre-production in the next few weeks."

"You're kidding!" she screeched. "You're kidding! I can't believe it. Are you sure?"

Parker could only shake his head and laugh as Kate leapt out of the chair and began to jump up and down.

"I thought he was calling with the same old promises. I've been too busy to chat with him. I was planning to phone him later this week."

"Well, you'd better call him tomorrow morning, but not until after ten, West Coast time. He said he'd be working out with his trainer until then."

"That figures. First, he's desperate to talk to me. Now, he wants to torture me by making me wait for details. Nothing doing. I'll never sleep. I'm going to phone him now!"

"Kate, his plane is still in the air."

"Well, then I'll give him another hour."

She swept up her champagne flute and clinked glasses with Parker in celebration.

Kate finally reached David at two in the morning. By then, sleep had completely eluded her. He scolded her for not returning his messages and threatened to remove her from the project unless she promised always to reply promptly. Silliness, laughter and excitement propelled their conversation.

"This is too good to be true," Kate insisted. "I won't believe it until I see the signed contract." But Kate knew David would not make a joke out of something this important to her. "David, I'm going nuts. I never thought I'd react this way. I'm near tears, but too excited to cry."

"Darling, you deserve to act however you feel. You're a professional screenwriter now. I knew you couldn't just walk away from Hollywood without a backward glance."

"Ahh. But it took the isolation of living in Colorado for me to write a screenplay. What happens next? How involved do I get to be? Needless to say, I want to be in on everything. Do we have a cast? Is your company producing it? When do we start?"

David, the businessman, kicked into gear. Kate marveled at his seamless ability to slip out of tee-shirt mode and into the efficient business demeanor symbolized by a button-down collar. The fun-loving jokester all but disappeared when money was on the line. He methodically began to answer all of Kate's questions. "My production company is the sole proprietor of the project. That's why the deal has taken so long to pull together. I had a lot of negotiating to do. I didn't want to co-produce the film with the network's movie division. We wouldn't make as much money, to say nothing of losing more control of the project than is already inherent with a network movie deal. I thought you understood all of this."

"Sorry, David. I remember now."

"Since Bill Blackman returned to the network as president of the movie division, our project has turned to gold."

"You mean your status of favored son has been reinstated?"

"You got it. Bill has promised me as much creative license on the project as possible. We are sitting pretty. Now, the first thing I need from you is a rewrite."

"Oh, David! Not another one," she groaned, feigning exasperation.

"Not to worry. Just some fine-tuning and a change in the setting. We're going to shoot it on location in Napa and San Francisco."

"That's fabulous!"

"What makes it especially appealing is shooting in Northern California further distances us from the network's scrutiny. And, Blackman promised me he wouldn't send one of the fresh-faced program execs they hire right out of college to babysit us. I would lay odds Blackman will be the only network suit to walk on the set. He's always welcome. He's creative and knows how to cut to the chase.

"Kate, I'd like to meet with you next week in San Francisco for a few days before you start your rewrite. We can talk about actors, directors, locations. It'll be fun. I'll call you tomorrow to work out the details. And don't forget. I expect you to take all of my calls from now on." He laughed.

"Yes sir!" she answered with military briskness. Then her voice softened. "And David, thank you so much. I can't believe we're really getting to do this. You're magnificent!"

"Yes, I know. Now let me get some sleep. I'm exhausted."

"Good night."

"Good night, my foxy screenwriter."

CHAPTER SIX

Kate danced and cartwheeled her way around the house for the next two days. Every time the phone rang, she charged to answer it, thinking it might be David. In fact, he only called once to set up their meeting in San Francisco. He told her he wouldn't be calling for another few days, but that didn't dampen her enthusiasm for racing to the phone.

Each day, she took Rusty on long hikes through wildflowers that seemed to bloom more brilliantly than she had ever noticed before. Blankets of bright yellow false lupines spread across grassy knolls, stealing attention from the delicate white sand lilies that were spring's earlier triumph over winter. Envisioning the Napa Valley setting of her screenplay, her mind's eye painted the mountain ridges surrounding the house in lush, tender green to match the rolling hills of California's wine country, whose vineyards would be aglow with mustard this time of year.

Kate relegated thoughts of Martin and his daughter to the back of her mind. She had decided not to tell Parker anything about Martin, except that she had met an old friend for lunch. But in all of her excitement, she had never told him even that much.

Kate and Parker were on their deck, soaking up spring's preview of summer warmth, when the phone rang. The sound dislodged Kate from one of her rare moments of inactivity since learning about her movie deal. Parker smiled as Kate sprinted for the phone with childlike zeal. He had teasingly dubbed her borderline hyperkinetic, and needled her about his eagerness to turn her over to David for a few days.

"Hi!" she blurted into the receiver. She was sure it would be David.

"Kate?" a youngish voice asked in reply. "This is Lily."

Kate drew a momentary blank.

When Kate didn't respond immediately, Lily added, "Lily McGuire, from campaign headquarters."

Kate's mind snapped into focus. Her whole life had changed in the past forty-eight hours. It was as if a ghost from her distant past had returned to haunt her. Kate's heart pounded as the emotions from lunch with Martin flooded back. A flush of heat washed over her. She instinctively touched her face to confirm the sensation.

"Lily. Of course. How are you?" She cringed at her blunder and hoped she had not made Lily feel uncomfortable.

"I'm fine, thank you. I, hmmm, we've missed you at headquarters."

"I guess I should have called, but I've been a little preoccupied," explained Kate.

"Is everything okay?"

"Oh, yes. Everything is fine."

"Well, I was just wondering." Lily hesitated a moment before continuing. "Doreen is going out of town to visit her grandparents, and I was hoping to take you up on your offer to come and visit for a few days. That is, if the offer is still open."

Kate's mind raced. Spending time with Lily, now, would be like spending time with Martin. Kate's instinctual desire to hide Lily's connection to Martin was a betrayal of Parker's trust in her. Her thoughts scrambled for an excuse to quash Lily's visit without hurting her feelings. "Lily, I'd love to have you come up, but my husband just got back in town, so I'd like to check with him first. Can I call you back in about an hour? I'll tell you what, why don't you plan on coming up for lunch this afternoon, at the very least." Trying to outguess herself, Kate thought there would be no harm in lunch.

"I'd like that. I wouldn't be asking, except that we did talk about my coming for a visit sometime. But if this is a bad time, I don't want to impose."

"Don't be silly. Plan on lunch, and let me call you back on the other."

Kate gave Lily directions to her house, which unbeknownst to Kate, Lily would be able to record in her datebook alongside the entry where she already had Kate's address in bold letters. At the top of the page was another name and address Lily had circled with an arrow pointing down to Kate's name.

Torn between her desire to see Lily and not wanting to accept responsibility for bringing Martin's daughter into their home, Kate relinquished the decision-making to Parker. She felt sure he would agree to lunch but draw the line at having a college student he didn't know invade their privacy for a longer visit. Kate was flabbergasted when Parker encouraged her to invite Lily to stay for a few days.

"Why not?" he asked. "You said you really get along with her, and she obviously is drawn to you. She'll give you something to think about besides the movie."

Kate sighed and looked away from Parker when she spoke. "I love thinking about my movie. And, we only have a few days together before I leave town. Besides, she may have some quirky habits I don't know about that could drive us nuts."

"I doubt that. At twenty-one, she couldn't be too quirky."

In the early months of her budding romance with Parker, Kate knew he had considered Martin a rival for her love. She tried not to think what her husband's reaction might be today, if he knew who Lily's father was.

After calling Lily back to tell her she should plan on staying for a few days, Kate returned the cordless phone to the table in the den, where she noticed Becky's unopened card. She ripped it open and scanned the note. Becky's words were brief. She thanked Kate for lunch and wanted to keep in touch. Kate pocketed the missive with the intention of answering it later.

Lily arrived at noon with everything she'd brought to Colorado—three bulging duffle bags and a set of golf clubs. She had hitched a ride with two of Doreen's friends. Kate invited them for lunch, too, but they politely declined and left.

"I hope you don't mind if I just park my stuff in some corner. I couldn't decide what to bring, so I brought everything."

Kate laughed. "I can see that." She gave Lily a welcoming hug. Now that she saw the girl again, Kate understood why she had felt so comfortable with Lily from the first moment they had met. She had Martin's sparkling blue eyes, his light coloring, a nose lightly sprinkled with freckles, even his quirky, enigmatic smile and his impatient energy. But her sprite-like figure was in stark contrast to her father's robust, athletic stature. She looked more like an underfed ballet dancer than someone who lugged around a hefty-sized golf bag, almost bigger than its owner.

"So, how long have you played golf?" Kate asked.

"All my life," Lily responded with a smile.

"Parker and I love golf. Maybe we'll have time to play while you're here." Kate surmised from Lily's expensive set of clubs that the girl might be a fairly good golfer.

"I'd like that."

Kate helped Lily move her things into the guest bedroom before proceeding to the kitchen, where Parker was searching the refrigerator for a beer.

"Lily, I'd like you to meet my husband, Parker."

"Hi," she said, reaching out to shake his hand.

"Hi, Lily. Welcome to Colorado and our home. Kate tells me you're a very special young woman." His greeting was warm and sincere.

"That's very kind of her," responded Lily, nervously shifting her weight from one foot to the other.

Lily seemed slightly intimidated by Parker. Perhaps it was his distinguished good looks and comfortable air of sophistication, thought Kate. The light sweater he was wearing over a pair of walking shorts enhanced the outline of his tall, trim body. His silver hair was lush and thick. Kate had wanted to run her fingers through it the first time she'd met him, for no other reason than to make sure it was real. She wondered if other women had the same curiosity.

"Can I get you something to drink?" he asked. "A Coke, Seven-Up, orange juice?"

When Lily didn't respond right away, Parker followed up his offer by adding beer to the list.

Lily smiled. "No. I'd better stick with a Coke, but thanks for the offer."

"Where are you from?" he asked her.

Before Lily had a chance to reply, Kate jumped in. "Parker, Lily's a golfer." In steering what she believed were two avid golfers onto the same teeing ground, Kate hoped to deflect the conversation away from Lily's personal life. She was instantly rewarded when Parker and Lily jumped on the topic. Golfers are all the same, thought Kate. Even twenty-somethings.

"When did you start to play?" asked Parker.

"When I was about six months old." Lily laughed at Parker's dumbfounded expression, then went on to explain. "My grandfather gave me a red, plastic golf club to drag around. Mostly, I just chewed on it. I didn't really get hooked until I was about three. He had a miniature set of clubs made especially for me so I could hit balls with him on the driving range. I used to spend hours mimicking his golf swing."

Parker could only shake his head.

Once the trio had finished their drinks, Kate tried to direct Lily and Parker onto the sunny deck, but they ignored her. They were anchored in conversation. "How about tuna sandwiches for lunch?" she asked them.

Her only response was a nod of agreement from Parker, who didn't miss a beat in his conversation with Lily. "This is great," he said. "We should definitely play golf while you're here."

Relieved Parker and Lily had hit it off so easily, Kate listened to them talk as she prepared their lunch. They were both lighthearted and enthusiastic about their golfing war stories. Apparently, Lily had a temper on the course, as did Parker. They confessed to being "recovering club throwers" and compared notes as to how far each of them had flung a golf club across the course.

"Have you played much tournament golf?" Parker asked.

"A little. Just for fun. When I was younger, I liked hustling money from unsuspecting people I used to play with. Because I was a girl, and small for my age, no one thought I'd be able to beat them. After my grandfather taught me how to press a bet, I made enough pocket money that I never had to get a regular summer job."

Parker howled with laughter.

Kate handed each of them a plate with a sandwich and chips. "Come on," she prodded them. "Let's eat outside. It's too nice a day to miss."

Rusty was sleeping on the deck and jumped up to greet their guest. Lily instinctively raised her plate out of his reach. The dog's entire body wiggle-waggled against Lily's legs, hampering her forward movement.

"What a beautiful view," Lily said in awe, catching hold of the railing to prevent Rusty from knocking her off balance. "I can see why you abandoned the city."

Apparently seeing her discomfort with Rusty, Parker called the dog over to him. "Sorry about that. He's a big galoot, but perfectly harmless, I promise you. The worst he'll do is leave your sweater covered in dog hairs."

"I haven't been around too many dogs," explained Lily.

Moments after she was comfortably situated at the table, Rusty wormed his way around the table legs and put his paw in Lily's lap. She reluctantly patted his head. As much as Kate hated to exclude her dog from any activities, she coaxed Rusty away from the table and led him by his collar to the far end of the deck.

"Boy, that sun is hot," observed Kate, rejoining the conversation in the shade of the umbrella table

"What do you plan to do when you graduate?" Parker asked Lily.

"I haven't decided yet. That's why I'm not going back this fall."

"What do you mean?" asked Kate in a sudden burst of maternal interest. "That's news to me."

Lily fell back in her chair with a startled look on her face.

Kate tempered her words. "I'm sorry, Lily. That is your own business. I assumed you'd be returning to school in the fall. I'm just a little surprised, that's all."

Lily dropped her head and fingered the dolphin ring hanging from its chain around her neck, just like she had in the restaurant the day she and Kate had first met. She looked up with a smile on her face. "Kate, you sounded almost like my mother for a moment." Then she laughed. "Fortunately, you're nothing like her. Which reminds me, when are you going to take me on one of your hikes you've talked so much about? This little city girl could use an injection of Mother Nature's finery."

Kate was impressed by Lily's adroit handling of an uncomfortable moment. She also sensed a need in Lily to be alone with her. "I know just the hike."

Later that night, when Kate was left alone to clean up the dinner dishes, her anxiety over the duplicitous nature of her relationship with Lily finally imploded when she accidently dropped a dinner plate on the floor, smashing it to pieces.

"Shit! What am I doing?" She pushed the hair back from her face as she bent down to pick up the broken pottery. Her concern was not for the broken dish, but for the secrets she was keeping from Parker and Lily. Yet, she knew any chance for openness lay deadlocked by her confused emotions for Martin.

CHAPTER SEVEN

The next morning, Parker usurped Kate's plans for a hike. He arranged a tee time for Lily, Kate and him to play golf, even though the course was in a slow state of recovery from a colder-than-usual winter. Small patches of stale snow lingered in the deeper shadows, and dead splotches of winterkill left an irregular pattern of large brown polka dots in the greening fairways. Hoof marks from a herd of elk that used the golf course as their winter playground had left deep scars on the greens and fairways.

Undaunted, the threesome headed off to the first tee.

"I haven't hit a golf ball in almost six months," warned Lily. "I'm not sure where this ball might end up." After a few warm-up swings, Lily addressed her ball and launched it two hundred and twenty yards down the middle of the fairway.

Parker smiled. "Not a problem."

"Boy, the ball sure goes a lot farther at this altitude." Lily sounded amazed.

"Yours certainly does." Kate chuckled in agreement while keeping the blemished irony of the day to herself. Where she had once played golf with Martin, the cycle of life had placed her on another golf course with his daughter.

Going into the back nine holes, Parker and Lily were tied at three over par. Kate was nowhere near their level of ability. She simply kept her ball in play while watching Lily's fine round. Parker, on the other hand, seemed more focused on his game than usual. Kate figured he didn't want to be beaten by a spry, one-hundred-fifteen-pound girl.

After eighteen holes, Parker had barely eked out an eight-over-par round to Lily's six-over. When they had finished putting out, Parker gave Lily a congratulatory hug. "I don't know when I've enjoyed a round of golf more. That was great. Your game is such a pleasure to watch."

Parker's demonstrative enthusiasm over Lily's game stirred a twinge of jealousy in Kate. "You make it sound like my game isn't worth much," she said to Parker. In fact, Parker's overall enjoyment in their houseguest had taken Kate by surprise.

That night at dinner, Parker proudly brought up the subject of Kate's movie.

"What's it about?" asked Lily.

"It's based on the novel I haven't been able to get published. It's called *Love Among the Vineyards*. A city girl, totally ensconced in her career as a stockbroker, inherits a winery she must restore before assuming legal ownership of the property. Naturally, the girl has no interest in the project, but her fiancé becomes obsessed with viticulture, to the point of neglecting her. And the story unfolds with more conflicts. It's a lighthearted, romantic comedy. Or, at least, that's what I hope it is." Kate took a deep breath. "So, instead of a novel, I've ended up with a screenplay and several fun-packed weeks of shooting a movie on location in California."

"David and Kate are going to put on a show like Mickey Rooney and Judy Garland in *Summer Stock*," joked Parker. "David Backus is the executive producer—"

Lily interrupted him. "I love Judy Garland! Old movies are my favorite." Turning to Kate, she asked, "What will you do on the film if the screenplay is already written? Will you still work on the Emerson campaign?"

"I already told Susan she'll have to do without me for a while. I'll be busy with some rewrites," Kate replied. "My first changes begin this week. I'm meeting with David on Wednesday in San Francisco to scout locations and go over some other things."

"Sounds exciting," said Lily.

"Actually, David's just looking for an excuse to have Kate to himself for a few days. They don't think I know about their little romance," quipped Parker with a conspiratorial smile and wink directed at Lily.

Kate punched Parker in the arm. "Enough, you two. Parker, you're going to give Lily the wrong idea. It's usually actresses who have affairs with producers, not the screenwriters."

"Where is that axiom written?"

Kate ignored Parker and continued, "Once things get under way, I'll just be around if they need me."

"What if an actor demands a scene change because he thinks his dialogue is demeaning to his character or something?" teased Parker.

"You've seen too many movies." Kate laughed at her husband's jibes. Then she turned to Lily. "The shooting schedule for a television movie is too tight and rigorous for the luxury of major rewrites. We might shoot as many as eight pages a day, whereas, a theatrical feature can take days to shoot only one page. Once filming begins, a standard two-hour TV movie is shot in only four or five weeks."

"I thought it took months," said Lily.

"Features do, but not TV movies…unless it's an epic miniseries like Alex Haley's *Roots* or Herman Wouk's *Winds of War*. But the networks rarely invest in those anymore."

"Do you get to be on the set and meet the actors?" asked Lily.

"That's the price of admission." Kate smiled. Lily was showing more interest in her movie than Kate had expected based on their initial conversation over hamburgers two weeks earlier.

"If I came out to California, would you be able to get me on the set for a visit?" Lily asked.

"Sure. That would be easy. In fact, you could hang out for a few days if you want to."

"Oh, I'd love that!"

"Kate, since Lily doesn't know what she wants to do with her life yet, maybe you could get her a job on the movie as a gofer or something," prompted Parker.

Kate looked at him quizzically. How could he be so presumptuous? He was really placing her on the spot. Although, it hadn't escaped Kate's thinking that Lily's presence in San Francisco would present the ideal opportunity for Martin to meet Lily.

"Oh my gosh. That would be so cool," gushed Lily.

Kate wanted to put a lid on this idea quickly, at least until she had a moment to sort out the implications. But she wanted to be diplomatic. "It would be fun. But I really don't know what I can do."

"Kate, don't be so modest. Of course you have influence. Just ask David," said Parker.

Kate didn't appreciate Parker's pushing her into a corner about this. She looked at him with a crinkled grimace Lily couldn't see, and kicked him under the table with her bare foot. "I'll see what I can do."

She turned toward Lily. "Is this something you really might want to do? What about your work at campaign headquarters?"

"Working on the campaign has been fun, but I can do that anytime. This is a neat opportunity I'd be crazy to pass up. I'd positively love working on your film. I always thought it would be fascinating to be part of the movie business. You know, hang out with all of those creative people. What do I have to know to be a gofer?"

"You just have to know someone who can get you the job," said Kate.

"Don't be so cynical, Kate. Tell her what a gofer's job is," Parker insisted.

"Well, hmmm, a gofer does just about anything someone needs doing, as long as it doesn't infringe on a guild or union worker's job description. Get coffee, run errands, deliver scripts. Gofer, as in go-for. If you're working with Paul Newman, a gofer makes popcorn every afternoon. Being a gofer also gives you access to everyone who works on the movie. You get to hang out, ask questions and learn a lot. It can be boring, and if you don't like doing other people's schlep work, it can be demeaning."

Hearing her slant toward the negative, Parker imparted a warning glance.

Kate shifted in her chair and said to him, "I just think it's good to know all sides of a job." Turning back to Lily, she continued. "I will admit, if I were your age and was interested in breaking into the movie business, I'd jump at the opportunity. I'd offer to work for free. In fact, if you get the job, you practically will be working for free. But for paltry wages, they'll call you a production assistant instead of a gofer."

Rusty scratched his paw along the glass door, signaling his need to go out. Lily, who had warmed up to Rusty during her stay, volunteered to take him, leaving Kate and Parker to clear the dirty dinner dishes.

Once alone, Kate grilled Parker. "How come you're so anxious to help Lily get a job working with me?"

"What are you talking about?"

"Don't be coy."

"No, really. I don't know why you're so upset. I thought Lily was your friend and you would want to help her."

"I hardly know her. We only met a couple of weeks ago. Yes, I feel some kind of connection to her. But what do we know about her, really?"

Kate blanched at the dishonesty of her comment. She knew more about Lily than Lily knew about herself. Lily was Martin's daughter, and he was the provider of a generous trust fund he had anonymously established for her. She had his sense of humor, his natural athleticism, his intelligence, his intensity. Lily tipped her head sideways when she was confused, just like Martin. Even some of her hand gestures were similar to his. Those things really astounded Kate, since the two of them had never met.

"Well, I like her a lot," said Parker. "Especially her golf game."

"Yes, I noticed," she said, somewhat perturbed.

Parker shrugged his shoulders to dismiss her remark. He spoke to her with gentle concern. "Why are you uptight? Look Kate, as it turns out, Lily does want to be a gofer. It wouldn't hurt to at least ask David about it, would it?"

"I guess not. But where will she stay?"

"Don't get bogged down in details. Just ask David first. Then if he says yes, let him work out the logistics. Okay?"

"Lily, are you ready?" Kate yelled down the hall to the guest room. "Rusty is chomping at the bit for his morning hike."

"Here I am." Lily joined Kate outside, where she fell in step as Rusty pranced handsomely ahead, tail wagging. "I kind of pushed you into a hike this morning. Are you sure you're okay with this?"

"Of course," said Kate. "Rusty needs to get out, and I promised you a hike. I thought we'd head to a beautiful spot we call the enchanted glen."

"Sounds perfect. Lead on."

Their route followed a sunny trail that worked its way around the base of the mountain until Kate veered off the path. She led the way up a rocky slope shaded by ancient pines…some growing miraculously out of solid stone outcroppings. The body heat the women generated by their skyward ascent kept them comfortable in the cooler temperature of the forested terrain.

At times, the going became so steep, the pair needed their hands to help climb up granite rock faces that Rusty cleverly circumvented. Near the top, the landscape folded into a gentle meadow.

"This looks like a pretty place to stop," observed Lily.

Kate answered with motion of her hand for Lily to follow and trudged onward over rolling mounds of fresh dirt, unearthed by tunneling voles. The hikers carefully maneuvered around hundreds of fallen aspens strewn like pick-up-sticks across the broad meadow. On the far side, the meadow sloped downward, melding into a glade of healthy aspens shading them once again from the warming sun.

Continuing up another ridge, they said very little. Kate hoped Lily wouldn't be suspicious of her motive for bringing her to such a remote area. Earlier that morning, Kate had shoved aside her worries about Martin long enough to wonder about the oddity of a college student wanting to spend time with her and Parker. She hoped the isolation of time and place, where no one knew their whereabouts, would provide a safe haven for them to talk openly.

Finally, they came upon a mountain stream overflowing with spring run-off. Rusty dashed into it, splashing water in a frolicking frenzy. They both laughed at the dog's playful antics. "Just a little farther," Kate assured Lily, not leaving her any choice but to follow.

They plodded upstream until their bushwhacking carried them around one more bend where they could hear the crashing sound of a mountain waterfall. A few more steps and the cascading water came into view.

"This is it," pronounced Kate with the aplomb of a wagon train scout.

"It's beautiful. How did you ever find this place?"

"Parker and I just happened upon it one afternoon. It's one of our favorite spots, although it's a bit of an excursion getting here. I hope you didn't mind the uphill grind."

"Not at all. I really needed a workout. I actually feel quite invigorated."

"Good. So do I."

They perched on boulders. Rusty began sniffing the territory.

"Do you want an apple, Lily?"

"Not right now, thanks."

They sat in silence, savoring the tranquility of the woods surrounding them and the calming reassurance of the tumbling water. After a few minutes, Rusty settled on a cool mat of grass near Kate's feet. Lily slipped off her backpack, which seemed to unleash her thoughts.

"I had a miscarriage a year ago." Lily blurted out her confession as freely as an uninhibited child might walk up to a stranger and say hello.

The abrupt leap into this traumatic topic jarred Kate. She hadn't expected Lily to share something so personal with her, at least not so soon. Kate wondered if Martin's concern about his daughter's emotional stability was justified after all. But, the timing of the miscarriage did not fit the more recent event she thought Martin was concerned about. She made no comment and let Lily continue.

"Fortunately, Doreen found me passed out on the bathroom floor of our dorm room."

"I'm so sorry, Lily. That's a horrible thing to go through. I assume you saw a doctor afterward?"

"Yes. Doreen made sure of that. I'm fine now." Lily smiled in response to Kate's concern-filled words.

"I know this must be a painful topic. But, from the little time I've spent with you, I'd say you've endured your miscarriage and continued on with your life without missing a beat." She added in a softer tone, "Was it difficult for you? I don't mean to pry, but since you brought it up, I imagine there's some unfinished business surrounding it."

"Maybe a little." Lily adjusted her position on the granite boulder and riveted her eyes on Kate. The polarizing effect of Lily's focus secured Kate's attention as Lily continued. "I shut it out of my thoughts for months. Even denied it ever happened. But I learned something about myself very recently, which has made me think more about the significance of my miscarriage and the life I want to create for myself. I never thought I'd be stupid enough to have sex without any protection, let alone get pregnant. But I did. And the consequences could have been life-changing."

Kate nodded her head in agreement and continued to listen.

"I prefer to be in control of my life and make decisions based on positive choices, not because I need to fix a mistake."

"We all make mistakes in our lives."

Lily took a deep breath. "Yes, I understand that. And this was one mistake I'll never make again. I know I'm not ready to have a child. The miscarriage actually made things easier for me. I didn't have to choose between an abortion, or giving up the baby for adoption." Lily kept her eyes on Kate. "Perhaps, that's why I don't seem to have any emotional scars from this particular bump in the road. The miscarriage got me off the hook. But, the experience did make me wonder about what happens to other young women who go through unwanted pregnancies."

A chilling flow of uneasiness pulsed through Kate's body. She didn't want to risk an emotional meltdown by sharing the pain of her own unfortunate pregnancies right now. Kate maintained her composure before asking her next question with cautious curiosity. "And did you come to any conclusions?"

Lily offered a warm smile. "Let's just say, my discovery put me on a path I didn't know existed."

"Care to expound on that one?"

Lily broke their connection by looking away as she spoke. "I think I want to learn more before I'm ready to talk about it."

Kate wondered if Lily's discovery might be the mysterious event Martin was worried about. Her curiosity to learn more about Lily's mother prompted the next question. "Does your mother know about the miscarriage?"

Lily's expression hardened. She tipped her head to one side and shrugged her shoulders in a "who cares" gesture. "We don't have that kind of relationship anymore." She spoke with a distinct edge to her voice.

Kate sensed Lily's unease and gently tried to soothe her. "That's too bad, Lily. Maybe in time, you'll regain that closeness."

Her comments seemed to stir Lily's agitation. "My mother is a very controlling woman. Fortunately, the pull of the world saved me from her apron strings. Besides, I'm not sure I will ever be able to forgive her lies about my father, whoever he may be."

What lies? wondered Kate. She didn't have a chance to ask before Lily continued. "My mother was dead set on my earning an MBA in college. Do you know how boring business classes are? After my freshman year, I decided to pursue my own dreams…not my mother's."

"And what are those dreams?"

"That's the problem. I can't narrow it down to one thing. Golf would be right up there. But I don't have the single-mindedness to be a professional golfer. Same problem with ballet, even though I was a fairly decent dancer."

Kate nodded. "I thought you had a dancer's carriage the first time we met. I was thrown when you hauled a set of golf clubs into our home instead of a tutu."

"Yeah, that surprises a lot of people." The lightness in Lily's demeanor was returning.

"What else have you pursued?"

"Acting. That's been the most fun. But I hear actors are treated like beef in Hollywood. Is that true?"

"The expression is 'meat,' not 'beef,'" corrected Kate with a slight laugh. "It's especially true for unknown actors, but certainly can apply to established actors. They're treated as a basic commodity. Something to be rejected or accepted on the subjective whim of a quirky producer or casting director who has a fondness for brunettes the week you bleach your hair blonde. Or maybe an actor wears red shoes to an audition and the director hates red. Or the actor has a darling pug nose, but they want a Bob Hope schnoz. It almost doesn't matter how much talent an actor may have.

"It's an incredibly cruel profession, but maybe you could be one of the lucky ones. You could get one acting job that could lead to the next one, and before you know it, you're the next Veronica Lake."

"Who?"

"Never mind. She was quite the thing in the forties, a few generations before your time…and mine, for that matter. Anyway, you don't want to look back on your life in twenty years with regrets. If you seriously want to be an actress, then go to Hollywood. Succeed or fail on your own. At least you'll have tried." Kate threw her hands into the air for emphasis. "And that's my twenty-five cents' worth of advice."

"Good advice. I guess I can apply that to anything."

Rusty leapt to all fours, flying after a squirrel who darted across some rocks. The squirrel quickly ended the chase by streaking up the nearest ponderosa pine. Safely perched on a branch fifteen feet overhead, it looked down, taunting the dog. Rusty stood at the base of the tree barking with a steady upward gaze.

"Rusty, that's enough," commanded Kate. Rusty let out a few more barks before lying at the base of the tree to keep the squirrel from escaping.

"Tell me more about your acting, Lily."

"I'm not sure acting is what I'm most interested in. I also enjoyed launching the college productions I was in. I loved stage design and lighting. Costuming. I'm not good at drawing, but I had lots of ideas that were used in our productions."

Kate reached into her red knapsack and pulled out two Granny Smith apples. "How about an apple now?"

"Yes, thanks." Lily took the fruit from Kate and instinctively rubbed it against her sweatshirt to give it a shine. Then she took a juicy bite. "Ohhhh, this is tart!"

"I guess I should have warned you. So, tell me more."

"I'm running at the mouth this morning. Are you sure you want to hear more?"

"Please."

"Okay. My other passion is politics. That's why I wanted to go to school back east, so I would be near Washington, D.C. I was offered an internship by Congressman Gorenson, but lost that when I participated in a protest demonstration he opposed.

"I've never been subtle about expressing my opinions. I think that's my problem with men. I scare them off with my honesty. I'm afraid I can't stand playing games."

"I never could, either." Kate shook her head. "As people get older, they lose the need to play games. Or, at least some people seem to play fewer games. I think your options with men will improve the older you get. I just hope you don't take as long to find the right man as I did."

"How old were you when you and Parker got married?"

"Too old to have everything I dreamed of when I was your age."

"You mean children?"

"Uh-huh."

"Well, I definitely want children, but not right now. I don't even want to get married for a few years."

"When do you want to get married?"

"Oh, I don't know. Maybe when I'm twenty-eight or so. By then I will have done most everything I want to do on my own, I think."

Kate was amused by Lily's certainty in scheduling her future. "I thought I would have done everything by the time I was twenty-three." Kate laughed. "It took me another fourteen years before I was ready for marriage. I hope you don't wait that long, Lily. Marriage is a wonderful institution."

"Institution? That sounds like jail."

"Bad word choice. I ran away from marriage most of my life because I thought it would rob me of my independence and my dreams. What I've experienced is just the opposite. Lars Karlstron, a married man I once knew, told me something that virtually saved me from myself. He said that the everyday mundane you expect with marriage is the life-saving sanctuary everyone needs from the upheaval of the outside world.

"His words switched on a light bulb in my head. My marriage is a safe, nurturing environment where I don't have to justify my existence. Loving someone is actually very liberating. It opens up your soul to all the good things in life. Some people might call it a spiritual experience.

"I may never experience the powerful love or precious moments a mother has with her child, but with Parker, I've experienced another kind of unconditional love and tenderness."

Kate looked over at Lily, whose eyes were filled with tears. "Oh, Lily. How insensitive of me. You just bared your soul about your miscarriage and the problems with your mother, and here I am going on about the beauty of children and my own misfortune. It must sound like I'm berating you for being relieved you lost your baby. That's not the way I meant it at all. Please forgive me."

"Oh, don't be sorry. What you had to say was beautiful."

"I got a little carried away. You certainly don't need a sentimental sermon from me."

Kate pulled up bits of fresh grass curling around her hiking boots for a distraction, then turned back to Lily, who was watching her. "Hopefully, you found my point in all that rambling. A career is great, but it can't fill the empty moments in our lives. Pursue your dreams of a successful career, material possessions, prestige, notoriety, or whatever gives you joy, but make sure your desires don't crowd out the love that can make all those things seem trivial."

Rusty left his sentry position under the bantering squirrel and sniffed the territory for new prey. He returned to Kate and Lily, proudly presenting a four-foot-long pine branch he had dragged back across the creek."

"Rusty's trying to get our attention, but let's get back to you, Lily."

"I think I've talked too much already."

Kate reached over and tried to reassure Lily by gently patting her on the shoulder. "Perhaps we'd better head back then. I've got some phone calls to make, and I need to pack for my trip to California."

"Thanks for the lovely morning and thanks for listening. I really needed to talk."

"I'm glad you were able to share so much with me." Kate turned to stuff things back into her knapsack while continuing to talk. "Sometimes it helps to put things on the table before you make any decisions. I'll see what I can do about the production assistant's job. Maybe it will get you a little closer to finding what it is you're after."

"I'm already closer than you could ever imagine," mumbled Lily.

"I'm sorry. What did you say?"

"It's nothing."

"Well that's settled." Kate plopped on the sofa in Parker's office. She still had a smile on her face from her phone conversation. Since returning from their hike, Lily had been stretched out on the deck with a good book, and Kate had launched into making arrangements for her trip to San Francisco the next day.

"What's settled?" asked Parker, looking up from his desk, where he had been working all morning.

"I just got off the phone with Annabella."

"So, how's the Italian beauty?"

"She sounded great. We didn't have time to talk much. But the important thing is, she invited me to stay with her."

"You knew she would."

"I guess." Kate smiled. "She is my closest friend."

"I, for one, am delighted. Now, I know you have a chaperone. There will be no traveling businessmen hitting on you at the Fairmont Hotel. They'll all be after Annabella!"

"Thanks a lot," she snipped at his snide remark. "I'm glad I'll be staying with her, too. I haven't seen her in a couple of years. We have a lot of catching up to do."

"I'll bet you have."

"Parker, we need to talk about Lily. What are we going to do with her?"

"What do you mean?"

"I'm leaving tomorrow, and I'm not sure it's a good idea to let her stay here alone with you."

"Why?" he asked.

Kate opened her eyes wide, hoping he would see in her expression a suggestion of impropriety.

"There's nothing wrong with Lily being here with me for a few more days. Look, we can't just tell her to leave. Didn't you say that she was pretty much on her own?"

"Yes. But she does have money."

"What do you mean she has money?"

Kate had not meant for that to slip out. She had learned about Lily's trust fund from Martin, not from Lily. Kate fumbled for her words. "Oh, ummm, you know how college kids are. They always find a way to get by."

"Look, Kate. She won't be in my way. I've got a ton of work that should have been done by now, but I was having too much fun with you and Lily to get to it. So, I'm pretty much going to be stuck in this office until I get caught up. Why don't we let her stay through the weekend? By that time, you might know about the gofer job for her. I'll set up Lily with your buddies, Nancy and Wendy, for a round or two of golf. I have to go to Houston next Monday for two days and—hey, wait

a minute. She could take care of Rusty for us. Then all appearances
would be more proper. Is that what you're worried about, that people
might talk?"

"Sort of."

"What people, and who cares? Kate, I can't believe you would make
this an issue. Lily is young enough to be our daughter. The fact she isn't
related doesn't mean anything."

"I certainly know that. I'm just nervous."

"Nervous about Lily or about your movie? Don't be anxious. Things
are going to go great in San Francisco. If David gives you a hard time,
just call me, and I'll help in any way I can."

Parker had hit on the truth about Lily. Kate was nervous about the
girl and everything surrounding her. She parted her lips to tell Parker
about Lily and Martin, but the idea caught in her throat. Instead, she
found relief in Parker's assumption that her nervousness was related to
her movie.

Later that day, the couple talked to Lily about Parker's plan.

"I'd love to take care of Rusty," said Lily. "That will give me time to
organize myself before I go to California."

Kate looked at Parker, then back at Lily. "But Lily, I won't know
about getting you a job on the movie for awhile yet."

"After our talk today, I've decided to go to California, no matter
what happens."

Kate didn't know what to make of Lily's pronouncement. Tangled
thoughts of Martin and Lily had clouded Kate's mind since her trek
back down the mountain that afternoon. She shuddered from the chaos
of emotions smoldering in her mind.

That night, Kate tossed and turned until she fell into a fitful sleep
and dreamed of struggling barefoot through a thicket of prickly brush,
eventually finding relief in a blackened forest. There, she wandered
toward an opening illuminated by a multitude of flickering candles
floating over the glow of red hot lava oozing toward her. Magically
elevated above the bubbling caldron, her body floated into a tented
room of gossamer silk drapes billowing through the whisper of a

gentle sea breeze.

Martin lay in the middle of the vaulted chamber on a pillowed bed of roses, beckoning her to him. Kate tried to slip from his view, but a powerful entity pulled her through misty skies, and slowly, slowly released her of all garments as she drifted closer to him. Separated by a breath of air, she allowed his hands to trace the outline of her nakedness until she settled softly beside him. Overcome by her desires, she urgently pressed her body against his and luxuriated under his fondling touches until her body erupted in pleasure.

Kate's eyes burst open in a jolt of guilt and panic. She searched through the darkness to find her bearings. Looking to her right, she saw Parker sleeping beside her.

Her mind reeled. Could a dream make her an adulteress?

She curled into a fetal position with the covers pulled around her, but could not fall back to sleep. She blamed Lily for her unsettling dream. The only solution was to banish Martin's daughter from her home…and her life. Yet, Lily had reached out to Kate like a child seeking the nurturing and guidance of a mother. It touched on the markings of a mother-daughter relationship Kate thought she would never have. Neither had she counted on Parker's paternal-like affection for Lily, or the possibility that Lily might look upon Parker as the father she had never known.

But Lily was Martin's daughter. Not hers and Parker's.

Kate was being pulled into the heart of Lily's life, and she was afraid of what it might do to her own. Martin must have known it would be like this. He had set her up. Kate was boiling with fear and anger. She knew she had no choice but to meet with Martin during her trip to California.

CHAPTER EIGHT

The next afternoon, Kate's taxi pulled into the narrow driveway belonging to the building in which Annabella's Telegraph Hill flat was located. It was a warm spring day in San Francisco. A giant flowerpot, nestled in a corner by Annabella's front door, exploded with pink geraniums, their tendrils entwined around the balustrade at the top of her porch. A Victorian-styled birdhouse hung between two pillars. Annabella had always been the nature lover, thought Kate.

Annabella had kept the flat after the divorce from her husband, Dennis Holliberry. He was a charming man, oozing with sex appeal, madly in love with Annabella, but hopelessly unfaithful. Thanks to his generosity in the divorce settlement, Annabella would never have to work again.

From her vantage point within the cab, Kate saw two doors on the porch, one for each of the two flats. They were painted robin's egg blue. Annabella's was embellished with a colorful, hand-painted floral design. Kate noticed a note on the door.

She asked the driver to wait while she ran up the steps to check it out. It read:

Welcome, Katherine. My neighbor in 1B—you remember me talking about Mrs. Stokes—has the key to let you in.

Kate was relieved. She didn't want to haul her stuff around while she killed time waiting for Annabella to return.

She paid the taxi driver and looked back at the building in time to see an older woman peering out a window while trying to hide behind a set of sheer curtains. Presuming the woman to be Mrs. Stokes, Kate smiled and waved at her. The woman quickly withdrew from view. Kate recalled what Annabella had told her about the neighbor. The woman rarely left her home and spent most of her time watching over the neighborhood, especially the comings and goings in Annabella's flat. "She's better than a security system and much cheaper," Annabella had claimed.

Kate also remembered hearing how Mrs. Stokes tried to fatten up Annabella with homemade casseroles and cookies. The casseroles were usually burned on the bottom, and the health food cookies were like cardboard—sugarless and over-baked. Always the kind-hearted neighbor, Annabella would secretly dispose of the food and thank Mrs. Stokes profusely when returning the clean platters. Unfortunately, Annabella's display of appreciation had resulted in the older woman continuing to prepare food for her.

Mrs. Stokes opened the door to 1-B before Kate had a chance to ring the doorbell. "Katherine?"

"Yes," replied Kate, standing very straight when she heard the name uttered in an authoritarian fashion reminiscent of the way her mother spoke to her.

"What's Annabella's middle name?" asked Mrs. Stokes.

How typical of Annabella to require a secret code to gain access to her apartment, thought an amused Kate. "Maria," she replied crisply, matching the older woman's brusqueness. Kate was also relieved that for once, her memory hadn't failed her. It had been years since she had learned Annabella's middle name.

With that, Mrs. Stokes handed over the key and abruptly shut her door. Kate could hear a deadbolt locking and the rattle of a security chain settling into place.

Annabella's lock glided open with a gentle turn of the key. Kate picked up her luggage and nudged the door open with her shoulder. A steep stairway just inside, led to the second-floor flat, perched over the city like a bird's nest in a tree. Kate dropped her bags at the top of the stairs and walked down the narrow hall to the airy, sunlit living room with its dazzling panorama of San Francisco's financial district. The

Transamerica pyramid building rose like a white phoenix amid the clutter of buildings.

After releasing the view's hold on her, Kate walked back through the rest of the flat, glancing at photographs of Annabella with friends, family, and her surrogate children—two departed schnauzers. Both dogs had died the year before Annabella moved to San Francisco. Otherwise, she might never have left her Santa Monica cottage with its secluded backyard, a haven for her cherished dogs.

On the round oak table in the kitchen was a note scrawled in thick black magic marker:

Hi Kiddo! Had a slight change in my schedule. Should be home by 6. Please make yourself at home. Chardonnay and munchies in fridge.

Kate opened the refrigerator door and found another note that read:

If you prefer red, you'll find a bottle of cab in the back closet. Hang your stuff in the guest bedroom.

In her designated room, Kate found yet another note, this one mounted on the closed bathroom door.

Guest bathroom being remodeled. We'll share the master bath. Hope you don't mind. Help yourself to the bath oils for a luxurious soak.

Kate kicked off her shoes and unpacked. She decided not to change clothes until she found out about their dinner plans. She knew David was flying in tonight, so didn't expect to hear from him until much later.

She called Parker to let him know she'd arrived safely, but there was no answer. He was probably outside with Rusty. Renewed focus on her movie and being in San Francisco allowed her to push aside thoughts about Lily for the time being.

Kate poured a glass of chardonnay and took it into the living room, where she eased comfortably into one of Annabella's overstuffed armchairs. Even though she was tucked safely away in the flat, she could still feel the energy of the city pulsing around her. She watched the sailboats maneuver the bay's forbidding tides on their return to safe harbors while the evening commuter traffic crept slowly across the Bay Bridge. Lights were coming on in the office buildings rooted below.

"Katherine." Annabella's voice boomed from the bottom of the staircase. "Come help me!"

Kate jumped with a start. She hadn't heard the door open. She pushed herself out of the plush hold of the chair. "Bella!" Kate looked down the staircase at her friend, who was juggling giant billows of bulging plastic bags.

"I'm so nuts, but I couldn't resist," explained Annabella.

Kate joined Annabella to help with her bundles. "What's all this?" Kate helped Annabella with her balancing act by grabbing a few of the bags.

"Macy's! That's all I can say. It's my downfall. You can have Neiman's or all those trendy boutiques. I love Macy's. These were all on sale. Wait 'til you see what I got. I don't know if you noticed, but I'm in the middle of remodeling the guest bath. Don't even consider remodeling until you've consulted with me. But that's another story. Anyway, I saw all of this stuff and couldn't resist such a great deal. They will look fabulous in the guest room. I'm into soft, fluffy and comfy. These should make the room irresistible."

The two women hauled the bags of softness into the guest room. From one of them, Annabella yanked out a puffy off-white comforter and tossed it across the bed, covering the few clothes Kate had laid out. Each woman pulled a stash of pillows from the other bags and tossed them on the comforter—brocade, satin, cotton…beige, white, wheat and barely yellow. Some elegant, some simple, some tassels, some lace.

"Do you love them?" she asked, dropping onto the pile of pillows, knocking some of them to the floor.

Kate picked them up and threw them back on top of Annabella.

"Katherine. It's so good to see you. You've cut your hair!"

Kate ran her fingers through her hair. "It's great to see you, too! You're just as crazy as ever."

"And you, you're a screenwriter now. I can't believe it. Yes I can. I always said you had talent. Didn't I? Now you've shown everyone. I'm so excited for you."

Kate plopped on the end of the bed and the gabfest began, launched by decorating tips, propelled by a stream of gossipy information and juicy updates on mutual friends.

"He's getting married again," stated Annabella matter-of-factly.

"Who's getting married?"

"Dennis." The name of her ex-husband came out with sadness in her voice.

"Oh, Bella. How do you feel about it?"

"It hurts. But I have no claim on him."

"I'm so sorry. Who is she?"

Annabella clutched one of the new pillows close to her, as if to soften the pain. "A twenty-seven-year-old loan officer. They met during his latest acquisition."

"Which was?"

"Three restaurants in Santa Barbara. He introduced me to her a couple of months ago. She's quite attractive and apparently very astute in banking matters."

"Well, what else would you expect? He's always been able to attract money and beautiful women."

"I assume you're including me in the beautiful woman category." Annabella nodded. "The money thing he did on his own. My money expertise peaks at balancing my checkbook. As for her age, he's picked a young one because he wants to have children."

"Children!" Kate shrieked. "What's his sudden attraction to being a parent? Isn't he almost fifty?"

Annabella laughed. "You and I might be too old, but men never seem to be. She really wants children, and he's decided he would make a pretty fun dad." Annabella stopped and threw a hand over her mouth. "Oh, Kate. That was so thoughtless of me. I wasn't thinking."

"It's okay. I'm getting better about things."

"Did the doctor say for sure you couldn't have any children after the miscarriage?"

"Not unless I want to die."

"Hush. Don't say things like that."

"Well, it's the truth. Something I'm learning to deal with. I've been moping around long enough. I'm trying to move on."

"Sure you're okay?"

"I'm sure. Let's talk about happy things."

"Okay. Here's something pretty wild. Dennis wants me to be his 'best man' in the wedding!"

"What?" You're not going to do it, are you? He's impossible!" gasped Kate.

"Well, I am his best friend. But I did remind him I'm also his ex-wife, and I couldn't imagine that Missy—that's my name for her—would feel comfortable with his ex-wife in the wedding. Besides, it would be rather painful for me."

"Does he know that?"

"Yes. I gave him an earful one night to remind him of the heartache he had already caused me and that I had no intention of setting myself up for more. The saddest part is, once he gets married, I won't be able to see him anymore."

"Why?"

"I just don't think it would be a good idea. We have too much history together."

"But if you're just friends…?"

"But we're not just friends. You, of all people, should understand that. Speaking of which, I ran into Martin Kelly a few weeks ago. Do you plan to see him while you're in town?"

A chill ran through Kate. She wondered if Martin had said anything about seeing her in Colorado. Before Kate could respond, the phone rang and Annabella jumped up to answer it.

"Hello. David! Hi. How are you?" Annabella turned back to Kate and mouthed, "It's David Backus."

Kate smiled. "I guessed that."

Annabella switched on the speaker phone so they could all hear.

"Is my screenwriter there?" asked David.

"I'm right here," said Kate.

"Here's the deal. How about we all get together for dinner tonight…the two of you, me, and Holliberry?"

"You, me and Kate sound fine," said Annabella. "But the mister of Holliberry and Holliberry is out of the picture. I guess you didn't hear about the divorce."

"Oh, Kate did tell me, but I forgot. I was sorry to hear about that. He was a great guy."

"Still is. He's just not my great husband anymore. Where are you staying?"

"At the Fairmont. How about we all meet at Pescale's at eight o'clock?"

Kate and Annabella looked at each other and nodded in agreement.

"Okay with us," said Kate.

"I'm looking forward to this. We haven't partied together in years. See you soon." David hung up.

And frolic they did, starting with martinis and wine over dinner, then a blissful romp through the city with additional bar-stops for Irish coffee and too many shooters of Jameson Irish Whiskey. The trio did not head home until almost one-thirty.

What a contrast from my quiet nights in Pine Mountain, thought Kate. She had not been on a drinking expedition with her friends since she married Parker. Darling Parker. She wondered how he and Lily were getting along without her.

Kate was wide awake by six-thirty the next morning, even though she didn't have to meet David until nine at his hotel. Her body begged for more sleep, but her mind was whirling with ideas of locations for her movie. She hauled herself out of bed, threw on some sweats and shuffled into the kitchen to splash water on her face. Then she eased open Annabella's bedroom door, hoping it wouldn't creak so she could get into the bathroom without waking up her friend. Annabella was breathing heavily. Kate realized there was little chance of waking her for another couple of hours.

Once outside, Kate surveyed her surroundings and decided to plod her way farther up the hill to Coit Tower. Perching high above the city would invoke good karma for the success of her new adventure as a screenwriter. She did not slow her brisk pace when the hilly terrain presented staircases instead of sidewalks. She jogged along one deserted street that finally dead-ended at the historic Julius' Castle restaurant. Winding around the restaurant, she found another stairway that climbed to the base of the tower through a dark covering of gnarly pepper trees and Italian stone pines, leafy shrubs, thorny pyracantha and blooming hydrangeas. She briefly flashed on the possible danger of being in this wooded area alone. She might have to tangle with a mugger or a desperately hungry and crazy homeless person. The sound of chirping birds quickly distracted her.

She ran up the eighty-one steps, hardly noticing any exertion. A mugger would have to be in good shape to catch me, she thought. Standing atop the last step, she inhaled the freshness of the day and walked out of the cool shadows into early morning sun streaking through the elegance of the surrounding cypress trees. The aroma of peeling eucalyptus trees permeated the air. From below, she heard horns honking, engines starting up, a garbage truck crunching glass and debris, even sea lions barking from the piers.

This is my world, she thought. Kate Cochran was in San Francisco on business. She sauntered around the tower's base, savoring every view of the city before heading back to the flat via the Greenwich Street Stairs—three hundred and eighty-eight wooden steps winding through gardens of orange and yellow blooming nasturtiums, showy foxgloves, and dancing fuchsias.

Kate arrived for breakfast at the Fairmont exactly on time and was surprised to find David already ensconced in one of the booths. She walked up and peered over his shoulder to see the notes he was writing on her script. He didn't bother to look at her. "Where have you been? You're usually early."

"And you're usually late." She kissed him on the cheek and slipped into the other side of the booth. A waiter quickly moved in to pour her a cup of coffee and refill David's. "How does your head feel after last night?"

"Actually, I feel remarkably alert. I didn't go to bed until I sobered up enough for the room to stop spinning. That's my secret. Then I'm never hung over the next morning."

"So what time was it when the room stopped spinning?"

"About five-thirty. That's one of the drawbacks. Sometimes I miss out on a night's sleep. But I used the time to go over your script. I've made some notes."

"Those should be fascinating."

"Actually, I was just looking them over, and I think I was right on the mark. Perhaps I should always mix martinis, wine, whiskey and script notes." He winked at her.

"I'll be the judge of that," she teased in a stern tone.

During breakfast, David went through his notes with her. Always cognizant of budget restrictions, he wanted to combine some scenes to save on the expense of too many different locations. Combining two of the characters into one would also help above-the-line costs. For her part, Kate took ravenous notes during their two-hour session.

"Is that all?" she asked, when they appeared to be done.

"For now." He smiled.

Actually, Kate wasn't as irritated as she might have been normally with so many changes. David's insights and understanding of her characters impressed her. She had heard he was very masterful in working with writers. Now, she could appreciate his talent firsthand. His enthusiasm and faith in her abilities made Kate anxious to please him by making the script changes work.

"Has Bella read the script?" he asked.

"I doubt it. I brought her one, but I don't think she's had time. Why?"

"I'd love to have her ideas on casting. She's always been able to come up with the most inspired suggestions that go against the norm. Do you think she'd be up for that?"

"Are you kidding? Miss Trivial Pursuit Champ who never forgets an actor's name no matter how obscure it may be? She might not be a casting director anymore, but she's still a compulsive movie-goer and loves to show off her knowledge."

"Okay. I get your point." He signaled the waiter to bring the check. "Let's go up to my suite. I need to make some calls before Ken Ferrer picks us up. You can call Bella. Ask if she can meet us around six tonight in my suite."

"Who's Ken Ferrer?"

"He's about the best location manager I've ever worked with. I used him on *Wayward Watson* five years ago. He can get us into places no one else has even thought possible. He's gruff around the edges, but worth the abuse. You'll learn to love him when you see the locations he finds for us, and after he saves our ass with some of the local unions."

"I'll take your word for that. But our locations shouldn't be that hard to find."

"Katie, Katie, Katie. Don't you want your film to have a sensational, one-of-a-kind look to match your scintillating script? Yes, you do. And Ken is the man who'll get it for us."

"How about our Napa locations? What about the rundown winery?"

"Ken's our man. But those locations are on tomorrow's agenda."

"Whatever you say. I guess I'm just a bit anxious about everything right now."

"That's good. You should be. But remember, you're not the producer. Leave the anal, left-brain details to me, for now."

"You're right. It's just that I'm so used to being a part of the production team that my mind still whirls with logistics, schedules, crew needs…"

"Kate, that's the beauty of having you as the writer. Anyone else would have fought me tooth and nail about the script changes I suggested this morning. But the producer in you understood the need for my suggestions. I respect your abilities as a producer and am open for all the ideas you may have in that regard. But remember, your chief concern is the script."

"Why not?"

"Why not, what?" he asked.

"Let me help you as a producer. You said yourself I'm good at it. Writers often serve as producers. There won't be much for me to do as the writer once filming starts. Frankly, you can use my help. It will allow you more time to stay on top of your other projects."

David raised an eyebrow. "Interesting idea."

Annabella burst into David's suite at the stroke of six to find Kate and David in disheveled heaps on opposite sofas. Kate reclined with a washcloth over her forehead, suffering from a headache and nausea after six hours of rocking up and down San Francisco's hills in the back seat of Ken Ferrer's shock-worn, spring-free, fifteen-year-old Range Rover. David was slumped on the couch with his feet on the coffee table and a phone to his ear. Annabella's arrival cued David to finish his heated conversation by slamming the phone back on its receiver, causing Kate to wince.

"What a sorry sight," said Annabella with a note of disappointment. "By the looks of you two, I'd say the casting brainstorming isn't going to happen."

David answered by pulling himself to an erect sitting position. "Here you are," he exclaimed with a renewed sense of enthusiasm. "The shot of adrenaline we both need."

"Hi, Bella," said Kate in a weak voice, not moving from her position. "You wouldn't believe the places we've been today. We must have been in fifty restaurants and two hundred apartments. David's location manager is a very thorough man."

"She exaggerates. But it was a productive afternoon," said David.

"What locations did you scout today?" asked Annabella.

"We needed to find a couple of restaurants, a cozy neighborhood park, and the apartments for the characters of Cassie and Bob," answered Kate while propping pillows behind her head so she could sit partially upright. "Ken is truly visionary. I saw places I never dreamed existed in San Francisco. Even in all my years of watching reruns of *The Streets of San Francisco.*"

"The only thing I ogled on that television series was Michael Douglas." Annabella pretended to fan a heated libido. "Who cared about the scenery?"

"Ken did a great job," said David. "Next week he'll lock in the street exteriors and the stockbroker's office, so we don't need to worry about those."

David's trust and confidence in Ken was astounding to Kate. But from her own experience as a producer, she recognized that while David had the reputation for being a control freak, he also knew how to surround himself with exceptionally capable people, then let them do their jobs.

"So Bella, I hope you've read the script," said David.

"Of course." She turned to Kate. "Katherine, I am so impressed. I love your story!"

"I appreciate your enthusiasm. But I don't know if it's that good."

"Don't be so modest. Just say thank you," instructed Annabella. "You never were any good at taking compliments, let alone believing them."

Kate acquiesced to her friend. "Thank you."

"*Love Among the Vineyards* is a very good script," added David. "So let's get started on casting Kate's characters."

David outlined the qualities he wanted in the two lead characters, Cassie and Bob. He named some actors and actresses he thought would fit the roles. Kate had a couple of names to add to his list. Then they put them in order of their preferences. Annabella didn't contribute to this discussion. Her turn came when they got to the list of supporting actors and minor characters.

David hauled out the two *Player's Directories* he had brought with him, one for males and one for females. The volumes were as thick as phone books, with pictures of almost every viable actor and actress in the business. Annabella would need them to show David and Kate about whom she was talking.

Kate listened in awe as David and Annabella threw names back and forth over the Chinese food that had finally arrived. David had insisted on ordering from some obscure joint that existed in the subterranean recesses of Chinatown. None of it smelled good to Kate. After a tiny bite of the squirmy, green stuff in one container, she decided to stick with the rice. David and Annabella gorged themselves on everything as if the food was filling them with ideas.

They talked about skinny, pug-nosed waitresses versus those who were pear-shaped, pointy-nosed waitresses; mustachioed, well-fed, apron-draped, Italian-accented vintners versus youthful, sophisticated Armani-suit-clad ones. Sometimes their ideas sent them all into fits of laughter. By the time they had run out of food, they had assembled a list of at least four to six possibilities for each of the characters in the script, including the names of local actors Annabella knew. But until they nailed down the two main characters, nothing definitive could be decided about the supporting players.

Back at Annabella's flat, Kate soaked in soothing bath oils until she felt the quickness of her mind begin to relax. She lathered her glowing pink skin with lotion and slipped into her nightgown and one of Annabella's terrycloth robes. Annabella had a steaming pot of tea brewing and some Godiva chocolate truffles waiting when Kate emerged from the bath.

"Pretty exciting day?"

"Stimulating would describe most of the day. Exhausting is the word I would use now." A large yawn overtook Kate as she settled onto the sofa. "I'm a little concerned, though. I never heard from Parker. I tried to reach him a couple of times today, but there was no answer. The message machine didn't pickup either."

"Oh. I completely forgot. Parker called just before I left to meet with you. He had wondered why the phone hadn't rung all day, only to discover that the lines were down again. He was calling from the grocery store."

"Did he say anything else? When will the phone lines be repaired?"

"By tomorrow sometime. He said to tell you he loves you and hopes everything is going okay. He also said Lily says hi and don't forget to ask about the gofer job."

Kate grimaced slightly at the mention of Lily's name.

Annabella raised an eyebrow. "Who's Lily?"

"Oh, Bella, that's a long story I'm not sure I have the energy to get into right now. I'll tell you about Lily, but not tonight."

"Now you've raised my curiosity. How do you expect me to sleep with that dangling over my brain?"

"It's no big deal. I promise you. She's a friend's daughter who wants a job on the movie. I told her I'd see what I can do." Kate knew that if Annabella had any idea Martin Kelly was Lily's father, there would be no hope of sleep until she revealed all. She was anxious to share her concerns about Lily and Martin with Annabella, but later.

CHAPTER NINE

Ken Ferrer and David picked up Kate at seven the next morning for a full day of scouting in Napa Valley. At least half of Kate's screenplay took place at a rundown winery. In the booming wine industry, finding that look would prove daunting. As Ken's Range Rover bumped over the city's streets toward the Golden Gate Bridge, Kate was glad she had taken a Dramamine to ward off a recurrence of yesterday's carsickness.

Ken showed them eight different vineyards between Napa and Calistoga, and four others in the neighboring Sonoma Valley. Unfortunately, there wasn't a single property offering all the elements they needed.

Weary from the hours of driving and fearful her Dramamine pill was wearing off, Kate asked, "Aren't you guys getting tired?"

Ken glanced at Kate without saying anything. David continued scouring the map Ken had given him.

Kate's stomach growled. "Did you hear that?" she asked them.

"Hear what?" asked David. "Is there something wrong with the car?"

Kate sighed. She allowed another minute to pass before speaking out again. "It's two o'clock. If you guys expect me to go a mile farther, you must feed me. I'm getting very crabby."

"We noticed," said David. "Ken, I think we're all a bit discouraged. Where's a good place to eat?"

"Just up the road."

Ken bypassed two restaurants that looked perfectly acceptable to Kate. He continued driving for a few more miles until he turned down a long gravel driveway lined with century oaks whose stately branches canopied over the roadway. It led them to a sunny expanse of vineyards rolling up a hill. A large adobe building perched on the top of a knoll afforded visitors a gracious view of the valley below. Ken pulled his Range Rover into an opening between a new Mercedes and a dusty pickup truck.

"Interesting mix of clientele," observed David.

"Best food in the valley," said Ken.

"What a perfect spot." Kate stepped from the car and scanned the area with her hands resting on her hips. "This would be ideal for the after version of our winery."

"Not a chance," said Ken.

David gave Kate a "whatever-he-says" shrug of his shoulders and followed Ken into the reception area. Kate trailed behind. A host led them onto a broad, flagstone patio and seated them at a table shaded by overhanging latticework entwined with grapevines. The few remaining patrons were quietly lingering over their wine while enjoying the view and the warm afternoon sun that slipped through the vines.

Kate and David relaxed over a glass of wine and a salad of vegetables grown in the restaurant's garden while Ken preferred coke and a gourmet hamburger. Feeling the food ease her nerves, Kate soaked up the atmosphere of their civilized escape from Ken's bump-mobile, as she now referred to his Range Rover. She couldn't understand his attachment to such an overrated bundle of bolts.

Their conversation settled on what each thought would work for Cassie's winery. After awhile, it was just Kate and David who threw possibilities back and forth while Ken sat in silence.

Finally, he interrupted them. "None of it's any good!" His forcefulness caused Kate and David to freeze in place—Kate with a fork of food in her hand, David in mid-sentence. "We could make some of it work, but it's still not what I had in mind."

Ken's arrogance astounded Kate. What did Ken have in mind? Wasn't he supposed to take them to locations so they, the producer and writer, could make the decisions? Kate said nothing.

"What did you have in mind?" asked David.

"I know the place I'd like, but even I can't get us permission to use it. The property is owned by a consortium of entrepreneurs who are also prima donnas. I've used every connection I have, but they won't allow any filming." Ken couldn't hide his contempt for the elite club of capitalists who had thwarted his efforts to nail down the perfect location.

So why even bring it up, thought Kate. "Where is it?" she asked. "Maybe it won't be right even if they would allow us to film there."

"Oh, it's the right place," he insisted.

David must have felt the thickening tension between Kate and Ken because he jumped in with his own suggestion. "When we're finished with lunch, let's go take a look."

"We'll have to hike in. They've got locked gates leading into the property," warned Ken.

"Okay with me. I'm up for a hike, just as long as we don't encounter any armed guards or vicious dogs," said David. "I gather we don't have permission even to look at the property."

Ken nodded to confirm David's suspicion.

Kate was skeptical, but she was up for an adventure. Anything to get her out of the bump-mobile.

The Range Rover heaved back and forth as Ken navigated the narrow road twisting into the mountains separating the Napa and Sonoma Valleys. He slowed at several small side roads until he found the one he was looking for. It was marked by a row of rusty, tumble-down mailboxes, the only indication that anything existed on the all-but-abandoned road. A single lane snaked its way through a dense growth of scraggly valley oaks and overgrown bushes. Venomous tendrils of poison oak reached toward the passing car. Eventually, the pitted pavement disintegrated into a dirt road. After three miles of ruts and potholes, Ken stopped the car on the side of the road.

"This is where we begin our hike."

David and Kate shared a look of disbelief. They were in a narrow, damp valley surrounded by steep terrain. The only way to go, besides the road, was straight up the muddy bank. They both understood Ken enough not to question his decision. If this was the spot from which Ken expected them to hike, then this is where they would begin.

"This better be good," Kate whispered to David.

"I'm sure it will be."

Kate glanced around her. It was too early in the season to easily detect poison oak by its reddish coloring, but she knew it was out there. She looked down at her clothes. Her shorts covered most of her thighs, but her calves were exposed. She pulled up her socks as close to her knees as she could.

Ken zigzagged his way up the hillside to lessen the difficulty of their climb. The higher they hiked, the less foliage they encountered. After about fifteen minutes, they were traipsing through a pasture spotted with gracious broad oak trees. California's summer gold was already taking hold of the green grass that swept them toward the crest of the ridge.

Ken was leading them over a wide outcropping of craggy rocks when he suddenly stopped, causing Kate, who had been following close behind, to smack into him.

"Sorry," she said with a start.

Kate and David looked around to see why Ken had stopped.

"Oh, my God!" said Kate. The vision she had created in her own mind while writing the screenplay lay before her.

David said nothing. He didn't have to.

Spread over the gentle rolling hills that formed the intimate valley below were acres and acres of overgrown vineyards, ripe with blooming mustard plants and thistles. On the valley floor was a stone barn lost beneath a rusted metal roof and an overgrowth of creeping vines. Nestled up the far slope in a grove of centennial oak trees lurked the boarded-up remains of a once stately, two-story Victorian farm house with a wrap-around porch.

Kate knew David's trained eye was scanning the area the same way she was. There were no telephone wires or unsightly power lines a camera lens would have to avoid. An open space near the stone building provided an ideal area in which to park equipment trucks and trailers for the cast.

"David, we've got to have this place," whispered Kate.

"I know."

On their drive back to San Francisco, David quizzed Ken for more details on the ownership of the property called White Oaks. Ken explained the consortium had been in litigation over the property's ownership for five years. He had heard rumors the lawsuits had finally been settled, but no one would confirm this. Ken admitted he had hoped to find other locations that would have worked instead of White Oaks, but after today's outing, he was determined to land White Oaks.

"David, you know how I always get you what you want," said Ken.

"You always have. But maybe this one is beyond our grasp?"

"It might be too far out of my league," admitted Ken reluctantly. He surprised Kate with his admission of possible defeat. Ken was arrogant, conceited, sometimes rude and tough. But rarely, if ever, defeated. If Ken couldn't make it happen, then Kate assumed no one could.

"I didn't say we couldn't get permission to use the property," Ken continued. "I just said it might be out of my reach." Addressing David, he said, "Perhaps you have the connections to make it happen."

"I'm listening," said David.

"Let me call you tonight with more information. I need to make a few calls first," said Ken.

"There's something I probably should pass along to both of you," said David.

Kate and Ken both looked at David with concern as he continued.

"I don't mean to put any pressure on anyone, but if we don't get this property, there might not be a production. The network has very high expectations and giving them the look they envision might be the difference between a final thumbs up or down on this project. There's also another little issue about my reputation. If I can't deliver on this movie, there might not be others in my future."

"What?" said Kate, astonished. "I thought we already had a go."

"It's just one of those final details we need to take care of."

"It sounds like a big detail to me," she insisted. "I don't want to lose this project because the stupid owners of White Oaks won't talk to us. We've got to figure out something."

Ken dropped off Kate and David at the Fairmont Hotel a couple hours later.

"I'd like to know more about this consortium," Kate said, as she and David headed for the entrance to the hotel. "Sounds very suspicious. Do you think there was a death involved? Are they hiding something? Maybe my next book could be a mystery about it."

"Let's just stick to your current screenplay for now," David said with a wry grin. "Come on. Let's get a drink." He ushered her through the revolving glass door into the hotel. They found an open table in a bar just off a lobby filled with well-dressed businessmen and women, and settled into overstuffed chairs.

"David, you never told me who's directing. And, why isn't he or she scouting locations with you instead of me?"

"Still asking questions." David laughed. "Although I can't believe you haven't asked this one long before now. Jonas Waring is my first choice. Do you know him?"

"Doesn't ring a bell, but I've been out of the loop for a long time now."

"He's young, ambitious, daring, creative and not too expensive. He's also the current darling boy of the network. That's the part that worries me."

"You are so cynical," said Kate.

"Yes. But I have cause. In Jonas's case, however, I happen to agree with the network. I think he'll be a great director some day. He was a production assistant on *Wayward Watson* just five years ago. Now he's directing. See what I mean about ambitious? Anyway, we're finalizing the deal with his agent. Jonas thinks he owes me one for letting him work on *Wayward*. He doesn't. But let him think that, and we'll have ourselves a very special director." David seemed pleased with his own cunning. "I asked him to come up here, but he's finishing another project and won't be free for another week. Then he's all ours."

David flagged down a passing waiter who took their order—wine for him and water for Kate, who was now slumped in her seat. She was still woozy from Ken's erratic habit of accelerating and decelerating while cruising down the freeway.

Reluctantly, Kate decided to broach the topic of hiring Lily as a production assistant. She hoped it would require no detailed explanation. "David, speaking of production assistants, if you don't have one lined up yet, I have a friend whose daughter is anxious to break into the business. She's very bright and has a background in the theater."

"I don't see why not," he replied.

That was simple, thought Kate, relieved by David's easy compliance.

"Kate, you look exhausted."

"I am. And a little carsick too, I think."

"Why don't you head back to Bella's, and I'll call you in a couple of hours after I've heard from Ken."

"What about our drinks?" she reminded him.

"What about them? You ordered water. You can probably find that at Annabella's."

Kate nodded, relieved to follow David's suggestion. Annabella had a date, so Kate would have the apartment to herself for a few hours.

David didn't call until ten o'clock. "Bad news, Kate. Ken came up empty."

"What are we going to do? Do you know someone who might help us?"

"I've exhausted all my resources, too. This isn't good."

The inevitable was staring Kate in the face. She'd hoped the burden wouldn't fall into her lap, but now it had. She didn't want to go home to Pine Mountain defeated before they had shot one frame of film.

Kate swallowed hard to remove the lump in her throat. "I might know someone who can help us."

"What? Why didn't you say so earlier?"

"I'm not positive, but it's worth a try. He's negotiated land deals in the Napa and Sonoma Valleys for years. He has connections we can only dream about. If anyone will know about this consortium, he will."

She took a deep breath to suppress her rising anxiety.

"How badly do you want White Oaks?"

"What do you mean? You saw it. The look is better than anything we could have hoped to find. I thought we were in agreement."

"Yes." She sighed.

"Why the doubts? What aren't you telling me?"

Kate took a deep breath. By saying his name out loud, she knew she would have no alternative but to deal with Martin.

"Kate, who is it?" he prodded.

"Martin Kelly."

"Well, well!"

Kate winced at David's reaction, but wasn't surprised by it. She had cried to her friend about Martin too many times over the years for him not to understand the love-hate relationship she probably still had with the man.

"I had no idea he was that successful," David added.

"Very successful. He's involved with development deals all over the state."

"When was the last time you saw Martin...six, seven years ago? He used you for years, Kate. Perhaps, it's payback time."

"I hate asking him for anything."

"Hmmmm. Remember all those business conflicts he had, which were actually dates with other women, or those meetings of little import he chose to attend at the expense of breaking another date with you? It's time you use him for a change."

"David!" Her stinging tone resonated through the phone line. "Let's not get into all of that. You might as well know. I saw Martin two weeks ago. I ran into him at a political fund-raiser in Colorado."

"No kidding. That must have been a shocker for you. I assume it was unexpected."

"Seeing him made my knees buckle. I can't explain my reaction, but I was shocked at the electricity that still flowed between us. I wish I could say I felt nothing."

"Oh, my dear Kate. After all this time? What about Parker?"

"That's what I keep asking myself. I feel so foolish. It's a teenager's reaction I had to Martin. It doesn't mean I don't love Parker."

"How about if I talk to Martin?"

"Thanks for the offer, but I know him too well. Once Martin realizes I'm involved in the project, he'll insist on talking to me. I might as well deal with him from the start."

"Kate, I know you can handle him. Just keep your emotions out of this."

"Easy for you to say."

David had never met Martin. The only insight he had was from Kate's perspective, so she couldn't blame David for his feelings of animosity toward the man. Kate also knew she couldn't tell David his new production assistant was Martin's daughter. He wouldn't stand for it.

"Just remember, Martin had his chance with you. Don't let him creep back into your life. You've moved on, Kate. You know what he's about, now. That gives you the upper hand."

Intellectually, Kate knew he was right. "Don't worry. If Martin is our key to White Oaks, I will get his help without entangling myself in his mystique. This is a business deal." She was trying to convince herself as much as David.

"I assume Martin is still based in San Francisco?"

"Yes."

"If you can, why don't you stay over long enough to meet with him."

Kate bowed her head and squeezed her eyes shut. "I can do that."

CHAPTER TEN

Martin's assistant answered the phone in the officious manner of an overly protective secretary. "Mr. Kelly is unable to take any calls at this time."

"Just let him know who's on the line," insisted Kate.

Ten seconds later Martin picked up his phone. "To what do I owe this pleasure?"

"I'm hoping you might be able to help me with something."

"I'm happy to help in any way I can, but I'm in the middle of a meeting. Where can I reach you?"

Kate sighed. "I'm in San Francisco. I'm staying with Annabella."

"Then let's talk over dinner tonight."

Damn, thought Kate. A phone call would have been too easy. She reluctantly accepted his offer. "How about Jack's, six-thirty?"

"No atmosphere. The Carnelian Room at seven."

She loved the Carnelian Room, but not with Martin. The restaurant's sweeping view of San Francisco's twinkling lights would offer too many romantic memories of their past. He was insistent, and she didn't want to argue, so she agreed and hung up the phone with a grimace.

Digging deep into Annabella's closet, Kate found a dull blue business suit and white tailored shirt. She held it up to herself as Annabella came into the bedroom.

"What do you want with that ugly suit? It's way too big for you."

"No, this is perfect." Kate moved out of Annabella's reach.

Kate had spent most of the morning telling Annabella about meeting Martin in Denver, including the emotional tilt-a-whirl on which it had placed her. Instead of calming her nerves, renewed focus on

Martin seemed to inflame Kate's anxieties.

"I can't believe you agreed to have dinner with him. Couldn't you have dealt with him over the phone?"

"It has to be this way."

"I don't get it. What hold does he have on you? After all this time, would you please explain that to me?"

Kate pulled more and more clothes out of the closet. "We go back a long way."

Annabella rolled her eyes. "There's something more to this thing you have with Martin. I can tell by the mess of clothes you've heaped on my bed that you aren't thinking straight. I think I'd better come with you."

"I knew that was coming. I don't need a chaperone." She looked sheepishly at Annabella. "It's not all Martin's fault." Kate took the blue suit off the hanger and laid it on the stack of clothes, then slipped out of her robe to try it on. "Seeing him again will give me a new perspective on what our relationship is now."

"You mean you want to keep him as a friend?" Annabella's face wrinkled with distaste. "I have this Medusa vision in my head, only it's a tangled web of libidinous desire taunting you with thoughts of Martin."

Kate laughed. "You do have a flare for the dramatic." The laughter seemed to relieve some of her tension.

"What will Parker think about your plan?"

"I'm not sure he'd be thrilled if he knew I was still friends with an old lover…a rival, to be more precise. Good God, I'm mixed up. Why can't I put this issue to bed?"

"To bed?" Annabella raised an eyebrow.

"Bad choice of words." As if a sideshow had distracted her, Kate looked into the full-length mirror and saw herself dwarfed in Annabella's blue suit. "This does look ridiculous on me. Maybe I'll just wear the black dress I brought with me. It's conservative. I'll just use a scarf to conceal any hint of cleavage."

A little later, Kate switched her focus to David's script changes, but thoughts of her imminent meeting with Martin diluted her creative juices. How would she greet him? A kiss on the cheek? A handshake? What about Lily? Would he still want her help? And what about White Oaks?

She finally gave up work on the script and lost herself in a rerun of *The Golden Girls*. The comedy classic with Bea Arthur and Betty White made her laugh harder than the first time she had watched this same episode years earlier. She was closer in age to the characters now. Scary thought.

How could she still be so mixed up with longings for Martin? What made her think he was still interested in her? But the chemistry had been there two weeks ago. There was no denying that.

Kate abandoned the modesty her scarf would have provided and left it on the bed when she departed for her dinner meeting.

Martin was waiting for Kate at a window table in the restaurant, fifty-two floors above the city. The room was only partially filled with diners at that early hour. The final gasp of daylight hanging over the city was an innocent prelude to the romantic luxury darkness would bring.

Feeling a bit like a teenager on vacation without the scrutiny of parental supervision, Kate walked over to Martin's table, her heart thumping in anticipation of being somewhere her parents would not approve.

Martin stood to greet her, took both her hands in his, and kissed her on the cheek. Her eyes closed when she felt the touch of his lips. The maitre d' helped Kate with her chair, then moved away.

"Thank you for seeing me." She pushed back her shoulders in an attempt to maintain her composure. She almost laughed out loud at her attempt to appear regal when what she envisioned was falling naked into his embrace.

The sommelier swept in to serve them wine, then placed the bottle in a stand beside their table.

Martin picked up his glass as if to make a toast. "I hope you don't mind. I took the liberty of ordering wine."

Kate raised her glass to meet his and smiled. "Nice."

Martin kept his eyes on Kate as he sipped.

She drank in his tenderness and let the silence linger. She felt giddy. He's doing it to me again, she thought. She used to search his gaze for the words he would never say. The rhythm of his movements and voice had once filled Kate with a lyrical vision of their life together.

What were the words she had wanted him to say so many years ago? *I love you. I want to spend the rest of my life with you. You're the most important part of my life.* What would the lyrics be now? She had been too frightened to ask in the past.

"Are you going to tell me what you're thinking?" she asked.

He smiled. "I was thinking how beautiful you are. Now, more than ever. You have a sense of peacefulness that is new to me."

These weren't the words she was thinking of, but they were good.

"I've been very confused since our lunch in Denver," he continued.

Instinctively, Kate knew he meant the flush of energy still flowing between them. His admission pumped her with pleasure.

"Me, too."

"Where did we go wrong? We came very close to getting married once."

His statement threw Kate back into her chair, almost causing her hand to knock over her wine glass. "Did I miss something? I don't seem to recall you ever discussing marriage. Could we have been that out of touch with one another?"

Martin tipped his head and leaned into Kate. "I thought it was assumed. Certainly, we knew there was a time it might happen."

A prickling sensation washed through her body, almost signaling a cry for tears. She swallowed hard and looked down a moment. She could only smile at his vague recollection. "That was a long time ago. God knows, we certainly had our chance."

"I can't help but wonder if we made a mistake."

Kate opened her mouth to speak, but stopped. The shock of his admission jolted her senses. "I think I'm with the right man, now. I love my husband very much." Kate spoke from her heart, but that didn't deaden the feelings she still felt for the man sitting opposite her.

She took a sip of wine to calm her nerves and reconsider her intentions. Her emotions sputtered into a flush of embarrassment. "I think I've given you the wrong impression tonight. I'm not here for us. I can't be."

"Of course not. I never should have presumed."

Silence underlined their sudden discomfort. Kate looked away until she heard him speak.

"Are you here about Lily? Have you been able to spend any time with her since we last talked?"

"Well, no. It isn't about Lily. But yes, I have seen her." She was grateful to talk about anything that would change the subject. "In fact, she's staying at my house in Colorado right now."

"That's fantastic. I knew you would help me, Kate."

"It's not what you think. Actually, I had decided not to get into the middle of your problems. I didn't call Lily. She called me." Kate went on to describe how Lily had arrived for lunch and charmed Parker into letting her stay for several days. "She's a wonderful young woman, Martin. Very bright and insightful, a little scary, actually. Mature and levelheaded for her age. I think she can be a bit too serious at times. But she's also got a great sense of humor."

"Sounds like you know her pretty well for someone who wasn't going to get involved."

"Yes, well, as I told you before, we get along."

"Maybe for the same reasons you and I have always felt a bond between us," he said.

"Like father, like daughter, eh?"

"Exactly."

A waiter returned to pour them more wine and offered them menus. After years of eating at the Carnelian Room together, the pair knew exactly what they wanted without the need of menus. Kate asked for her favorite dish of roasted asparagus and salmon and Martin ordered prime rib.

"I think I have some good news for you," said Kate.

"Don't keep me in suspense."

"Lily's coming to California to work on my movie."

"What movie? You mean the screenplay you wrote? How did this come about?"

"Right after we met in Denver, a network picked up my screenplay for a movie-of-the-week, or whatever they're calling TV movies now."

"Congratulations. I knew we'd see your name in lights one of these days." He looked at her with a smile of admiration.

"Thanks. I'm pretty excited. Anyway, we're shooting the film in San Francisco and, hopefully, somewhere in the wine country. Lily expressed interest in working on the film and the producer agreed to hire her as a gofer."

He gave her a quizzical look. "A gofer?"

"The director's job was taken." Kate smiled. "She'll be a production assistant. It's entry level, but a wonderful opportunity to break into the business."

"Kate, I'm stunned. Does this mean Lily will be in San Francisco for awhile?"

"At least as long as we're in production."

"When? When will she be coming?"

"I don't know for sure. We haven't locked in the start date, but it could be within a few weeks. "

"What about her college?"

"It's her semester break."

"Of course." Martin looked out the window and stroked his chin.

Kate used the pause in the conversation to butter a piece of sour dough bread and take in her surroundings. The room had quietly filled with starchy mannered patrons who positioned folded hands into their laps while straight-backed waiters politely nodded and took their orders. Everyone looked pretentious to Kate. A glint of home fluttered into her consciousness. What a contrast to her jean-clad friends sipping beer while huddled near an outdoor fireplace on a cool night.

She lightly touched Martin's elbow to recapture his attention. "What are your intentions regarding Lily?"

Martin turned back to Kate. "I want to know my daughter. If my life continues on its current course, she will most likely be the only child I'll ever have."

"So what are you going to do, just walk up to her and say, 'Hello, I'm your father'?" Kate looked intently at Martin.

"Of course not. Don't be so unmerciful. That's why I need your help."

"Oh God, Martin. I don't want to be involved. I've got my movie to think about. It's more than I can handle right now."

"I promise you. It'll be fine."

"How can you make that promise? You have no control over everyone's emotions."

"Trust me. When the time comes, we'll be careful. You're one of the most sensitive people I know. You won't let me make a mess of this."

"I appreciate your faith in me, but don't try to build me up. Lily may need a father, and as much as I'd like to help her…" Kate's voice trailed off. She looked up at the ceiling, then back at Martin, who appeared to be hanging on her every word. Realizing the inevitable, she fell back into her chair and reluctantly cracked a smile. "We have to take this slowly."

Martin folded his arms across his chest. "That works for me. Thank you, Kate."

During dinner, Martin probed Kate for details about Lily. She reluctantly obliged by extolling the virtues of his daughter's magnificent golf game, how they had hiked in the mountains around her home, and about Lily's exploits in theater and politics.

Finally, when their coffee was served, Martin asked, "What is it you needed to talk to me about?"

When Kate told him about White Oaks he gave her a one-word answer. "Yes."

"Yes? What do you mean, yes?"

"I'm very well acquainted with the new owners and their plans for White Oaks. We've done a lot of deals together. Knowing them, they can't be bothered to help you. But with me to run interference, there won't be a problem. Your timing couldn't be better. Your filming will be completed long before they start work on the property."

"You'd do that for us?"

"For you, Kate."

"Don't you need to check with somebody?"

"Merely a formality. I'm guessing you'll want to block out two or three weeks for set up and filming. How soon do you want to start?"

She looked at him in amazement. "You're sure about this? White Oaks is a major key to the success of our project."

"I understand." Martin laughed. "When you agreed to meet with me in person, I knew it had to be something important. Otherwise, you'd have pushed for a simple phone call." He shook his head. "Don't you know by now? I would have helped you, no matter what. But I'm glad you joined me for dinner."

Kate sighed.

He reached across the table for her hands, but she pulled them down to her lap, pretending she needed her napkin.

Kate was able to catch a late flight back to Denver that night. She wouldn't get home until almost two in the morning, but she needed to be with Parker.

Killing time before her plane, she browsed a postcard rack of San Francisco's famous landmarks—Chinatown, Ghirardelli Square, Golden Gate Park, San Francisco Zoo. All stirred fond memories of her childhood. She wondered if her favorite animal, Puddles, the hippopotamus, could still be alive. She and Becky had always run to see Puddles before any other animals in the zoo.

Her thoughts shifted to her childhood friend and she recognized she still had feelings for Becky no matter what may have happened over the years. Feeling guilty she had never answered Becky's note from days earlier, Kate jotted down a few words and dropped the postcard in a mailbox.

CHAPTER ELEVEN

A postcard of San Francisco's Japanese Tea Garden rested atop the clutter on Dr. Rebecca McGuire's desk. Reference books, client files and notebooks crowded her work area in teetering stacks. They surrounded the coffee-stained blotter, which was covered with scrawled reminder notes and phone numbers—some circled, some starred, some scratched out.

The tearful mother of ten-year-old, bed-wetter Charlie Hobbs sat on the sofa across the small, dimly lit room. Becky sat silently in her oak chair, occasionally fingering Kate's postcard, patiently waiting for the mother to gather herself so Becky could end the session. When Mrs. Hobbs finally calmed, Becky confirmed her next therapy appointment for Charlie and walked Mrs. Hobbs to the door.

Alone in her office, Becky glanced at a note from her brother, Les:

As promised, here's an update on Lily. She's coming to San Francisco to work on Kate Cochran's film. How did she meet Kate? Coincidence?

A knot tightened in the pit of Becky's stomach. Next, she reread Kate's postcard:

Visited our favorite city to scout locations for a screenplay I wrote and thought of you. We're shooting the film in Northern California this summer. Drop by the set if you're in the area.

Becky was happy with herself for thinking to leave a note for the postman to deliver mail addressed to Becky Madison. Since Kate didn't know she had changed her name to McGuire, Becky might not have gotten the card that presented an invitation she would accept.

Dr. McGuire used her short break between patients to jot out a return note, asking Kate to keep her posted on her filming schedule. She was careful to match Kate's tone. She was intent on knowing what was going on in San Francisco without drawing attention to her own agenda.

Becky had been scheduled to leave for a conference in Europe in a few weeks, but after hearing from Kate and Les, she decided to cancel the trip so she would be able to go to California instead. She thought about calling Kate, but didn't want to appear too eager. It was important for her not to meddle prematurely. Her mind clicked on different scenarios until she noticed the red light flashing on her desk signaling the arrival of her next client.

Becky's reply to Kate, suggesting she might come to San Francisco if she could star in the movie, amused Kate. It sounded like something the old Becky would have joked about, unlike the dour visitor to whom Kate had opened her door weeks earlier. Their childhood fantasies had included the dream of becoming famous movie stars.

I could get her into the movie as an extra, thought Kate. Why not? So far, David was open to accommodating her minor requests.

She sent off a reply offering Becky a job as an extra. *The pay won't even cover your expenses, but it might be fun. I'll let you know when we lock in the shooting schedule.*

Working on a movie was not a real job to Kate. She looked forward to it the way she had anticipated recess as a child. It was a playground where everyone's energy was happily spent; where cast and crew, writer and director contributed their individual resources to create the newest cultural phenomenon, hopefully a ratings-grabber as well. They would gather every day in a giant sandbox to form hills, sculpt roads and build towns populated by interesting characters whose every move would be carefully plotted by an overseeing director. As the writer, most of Kate's work would be completed before filming began. She could use her free time to become reacquainted with Becky.

Since returning from San Francisco, Kate had isolated herself from her normal routine at home to complete the script changes she and David had discussed. There was no time for a morning run, no time to fix meals, make a bed or hang out with Parker and Lily. David's barrage of daily phone calls challenged her writing skills, twisted her nerves and gave her headaches. Then, on the third day of this compulsive merry-go-round, Kate noticed her shoulder muscles had relaxed, she wasn't wringing her hands anymore, her typos had become fewer and fewer. She had slipped into a Zen-like work mode she hadn't experienced since marrying Parker. As a side benefit, her work had provided a buffer from the guilt she felt about not telling Parker about Martin.

The phone rang at ten o'clock one night, just as Kate completed her final rewrite on the closing scene.

"Kate, Jonas Waring here. Hope I haven't caught you at a bad time." His voice was energetic.

"Jonas, the director," she reminded herself out loud. "How nice to hear from you. Welcome aboard. How are things going so far?"

"So far so good. We start casting next week. The reason I'm calling is, I have a few changes I want you to make."

"Really." Her body stiffened. "I was just finishing some modifications in the last act."

"Well, hold off activating your printer. Let me tell you what I have in mind."

Kate listened in deafening silence as Jonas described his changes. They completely contradicted her concept of the two main characters David and the network had applauded. This was more than a minor annoyance. It was unbelievable gall in the face of her hard work. She tried to maintain a calm voice, but inside she was livid. "Interesting ideas, Jonas. Have you talked these through with David, yet?" She spoke through clenched teeth.

"I didn't feel that was necessary."

"Okay. Let me see what I can do." Seething with anger, she eagerly ended their discussion and immediately called David at home.

"What's going on? Do I have to rewrite this script every time a new member of our cast or crew signs on to this project?"

"Slow down. Back up a minute. What are you talking about?"

She related her conversation with Jonas, then flew off at David again. "You and I have been working for days on this final draft, and now he wants to change the character's motivations completely. It's ridiculous!"

"Kate, simmer down. I agree with you. He never talked to me about this, so I don't know what he's after. Let me handle this. Give it a rest tonight. I'll call you tomorrow morning."

Kate hung up the phone and launched herself into the den, where Parker relaxed watching a televised baseball game. "What a cocky, arrogant kid this director is." She stomped, arms flailing. "I'm so angry I could spit. I've been working like crazy on this script and just like that"—she snapped her fingers—"he wants to change everything!"

"Kate, don't let yourself get all worked up," Parker said calmly with one eye on Kate and the other on the three-and-two pitch about to be delivered.

"I've never even met this kid and already I despise him."

The batter swung and missed to end the inning. Parker flicked off the television and turned his full attention on Kate. "What happened?"

Kate started to retell her story with venom in her voice until Parker interrupted her. "It won't solve anything to get so worked up."

She let out a deep sigh. "I know. I'm probably overreacting. I'm tired." Her body slumped as if to prove her point. "I've been working every day for a solid week to try and get this damn script right, and now this punk director wants me to start all over again. I'm not sure I'm cut out for this." Kate looked forlornly at Parker.

"Of course you are. Come over here, darling." He reached out to comfort her.

She slipped into his arms and curled her body close to his on the sofa. She adored it when he called her darling. It was so continental, so calming and civilized. His tone was so loving.

She spoke softly into his chest where her head was resting. "I think I'm starting to get nervous. The reality of real actors saying my dialogue with a jaded, cynical film crew of fifty people watching from behind the cameras is starting to hit home."

"What are you afraid of? The network wouldn't be making your movie if they didn't think it was good."

"Yes, they would. They make lots of bad movies." She sighed.

"I don't think yours is one of their normal rape and mayhem movies. *Love Among the Vineyards* is intelligent…it has heart… And it's very funny in places."

"I have visions of the crew snickering about corny dialogue behind my back. How humiliating."

"Kate, you're letting your fears get out of hand."

She momentarily pulled away to look into his face. "What if they laugh in the serious parts?"

"That's not going to happen." He caressed her back when she settled into him again.

"It could," she whimpered.

Parker let Kate ramble through her fears while he continued to stroke her back. After she stopped, he lifted her chin and kissed her tenderly on the lips. "I love you."

"I love you, too. Thanks for listening."

This is always what it came down to. Their truth was the love they shared for each other. Everything else was superfluous, especially at times like this, when they were in the protective custody of each other's arms.

"Kiss me again."

He cradled her head with both of his hands and pressed his lips against hers. She melted into him with a passionate filled with longing. Parker pulled Kate closer so she could feel the excitement of his arousal.

"Kate, I was just thinking," he whispered, caressing the inside of her thigh. "Maybe it's better if you don't go to California. I think you should stay here with me."

"Okay, Parker. Whatever you say," she murmured between kisses, her desire building.

Parker eased Kate away from him, pulled her up from the sofa and led her toward their bedroom. "Good, I'm glad that's settled."

"What's settled? What did you say? You've been distracting me in the most wonderful ways."

"You agreed not to go to California, darling." Parker nuzzled up to her when they reached the darkened bedroom and started to unbutton her blouse.

Determined not to break the romantic spell, Kate said in a breathless whisper, "No I didn't. Of course I'm going to California."

Kate touched her lips against his, but he withdrew from her. "I really don't want you to go."

"What? You're serious. Don't be silly, sweetheart." Kate tried to pull him back into her, but he resisted.

"I'm worried about what will happen to us if you go back to your old life."

"What old life?" A sting of fear twisted her thinking. "Nothing is going to happen to us. What's this all about?" Did he know about Martin? How could he? Just because she equated Martin to her old life, didn't mean Parker did. Kate flipped on a lamp by their bed. "It's only one project. But it's a very important one for me. I thought you understood that."

"Yes, but why do you have to be in California for the entire shooting schedule? We never really discussed what this commitment was going to entail."

"I didn't realize I needed your permission to work. We've always been supportive of each other."

"Kate, you've already changed."

Kate's mouth dropped open in disbelief. She plunked onto the edge of the bed and looked up at him, exasperated. "What are you talking about?"

Parker sat beside her. "We've barely spoken since you got home from San Francisco. In fact, you've been preoccupied since the day you learned your screenplay was going into production."

Kate knew he was right. Parker had always been able to sense the slightest turmoil in her disposition. But he was wrong about what had distracted her at first. It had started the day she'd had lunch with Martin, when she had learned about his daughter. It had had nothing to do with the screen play at that point.

Her chest tightened with guilt. "I've been distracted. I admit it. But you can't expect to be the center of attention all the time."

"Oh, that's unfair."

"Well, aren't I right? Parker, I'm going to California. And that's it." Kate cringed at her harsh words, but made no attempt to soften their blow. Right or wrong, it felt strangely satisfying to blurt out uncensored thoughts.

Parker shot back at her. "Anything you say, darling. Is that what you want to hear? No need to include me in decisions that affect both of us."

"There's nothing to discuss."

"I thought there might be, but apparently, I'm wrong in caring about what you do." Parker stood and walked from the room.

A moment later, she heard a door close down the hall. She did not go after him, but sat in the darkness of her empty victory until her shoulders slumped with regret.

Kate awakened in predawn light and saw that Parker had never come to bed. She curled around his empty pillow and fell back to sleep.

She didn't wake until almost eight o'clock. She never slept this late. If the sunlight didn't wake her and Parker by six, then Rusty's urgent need to go outside always did. She heard Parker in the shower and pulled herself out of bed so she could join him for a cup of coffee.

Kate found a note from Lily on the kitchen counter. She had taken Rusty for a hike. It had become her morning ritual to hike to a meadow where she gracefully glided her body through the various movements of T'ai Chi.

Thankfully, she had been out last night when Kate and Parker had argued. Since Lily would be working on the film, they had all agreed it made sense for her to stay with Parker and Kate until she was needed in California. In the meantime, Lily kept herself busy by continuing her volunteer work at Emerson's campaign headquarters.

Parker walked into the kitchen, dressed for work, briefcase in hand.

"Leaving already?" she asked him, pouring water into the coffee maker.

"No time for breakfast. I have a nine-thirty meeting this morning. Of all days to oversleep." He put his briefcase on the table and walked past Kate toward the refrigerator.

"Why didn't you come to bed last night?" She knew why, but didn't know how else to test the depth of his lingering anger.

"It was late. I didn't want to disturb you."

Kate flipped on the coffee machine and turned toward Parker. "I'm sorry about last night. I was wrong about what I said."

"Yes you were."

"But, Parker, I've got to go to California."

"I know. But I don't have to like it. Perhaps I'm being unreasonable and selfish, but that's the way it is."

Kate hugged Parker from behind as he searched the refrigerator for something to take with him.

He turned out of Kate's embrace. "I'll call you this afternoon." He brushed her check with a perfunctory kiss, stuffed a cold muffin into his briefcase, and left.

"I love you, Parker," she whispered into the empty room.

Rusty's sudden appearance at the kitchen door didn't allow Kate's clouded thoughts a chance to build. The golden retriever wagged his tail in eager anticipation and pressed his wet nose against the perpetually-smudged glass door. Lily bounded up the outdoor stairs moments later and let them both in the house. The dog rushed over to Kate and pressed his head into her legs.

"Hello, my precious," said Kate, reaching down to scratch Rusty behind the ears.

Lily slipped out of her vest and threw it over her shoulder. "Good morning. What a gorgeous day."

"Morning."

"I hope I didn't wake you guys when I came in last night. Actually, it was more like two a.m."

"I didn't hear a thing." Kate left Rusty to check on the coffee. "Just out of curiosity, where were you until two? There's not much going on up here at that hour."

"You're telling me!" said Lily. "After the movie, I ran into some people I met hiking, Greg and Lisa. I think I told you about them. Anyway, they invited me over to their house to play pool. Very fun." Lily filled a glass with water and chugged it down. "I worked up a good sweat. I'd better jump in the shower." As an after thought, Lily turned back to Kate, "Did I tell you I stink at pool?"

"It's nice to know you don't excel at everything!"

Lily was standing by the phone when it rang. "Do you want me to get it?"

Kate nodded.

"Hello. No, this is Lily... Sure. She's right here." Lily handed the phone to Kate and left to take her shower.

Kate answered with an upbeat hello.

"Aren't you cheery so early in the morning." The voice on the phone bristled.

Kate's smile drifted away. "Oh, hi, Mother." Coolness replaced the lightness of her conversation with Lily. "How are you?" she asked with a sense of duty.

"Not that it matters, but I'm fine, now. Are you going to tell me who Lily is?"

Kate responded with quiet restraint. "She's a new friend."

"She sounds very young, Kate. You aren't thinking of adopting, are you? Ever since your miscarriage, I've worried about that. You just never know what you might be getting. If God wanted you to have a child..."

"Mother, you can stop right there. You're way off base."

"Well then, that's a relief. What I called about is your father. I'm worried about him."

"What's wrong with Daddy?"

"He's acting like an old man. He just shuffles around the house. I tell him to pick up his feet, and he still shuffles."

"Well, Mother, he is an old man."

"But he never used to shuffle."

"And he was never seventy-nine before. Daddy is just slowing down. It's normal." Kate reminded herself that her mother was becoming more vulnerable to the trials of aging.

The older woman's list of complaints continued for another ten minutes. Over time, Kate had learned her mother needed a listening post to purge frustrations. This was one of those times, so Kate held the phone to her ear until her mother finished talking. She thanked Kate for listening and was about to hang up when Kate asked, "Would you like to know what's new with me?"

"Oh, yes, dear." She spoke in a robotic tone. "What's happened?"

Kate shrugged off her mother's apparent disinterest. "One of the television networks is going to make my screenplay into a movie!"

"A TV movie? Aren't those movies all about violence? Your play isn't one of those, is it?"

Kate sighed. Why couldn't the woman be happy for her instead of finding fault? "No, Mother. They're producing the screenplay I showed you last Christmas. It's a kind of love story about a girl who inherits a winery."

"Oh, yes. Well, that's very nice, dear. I'm glad one of us is having something nice happen in her life. Your father and I don't do anything any more."

"Well, I just thought you'd like to know."

"Yes, I'm happy for you."

Kate heard the words but could detect no sincerity in them.

"We'll be shooting on location in San Francisco and Sonoma Valley. You could visit the set."

"Could I?"

"Yes, of course. It would be fun. Maybe Daddy would come, too."

"Maybe, yes. He might want to do that. We'll see."

By the end of their conversation, Kate's mother seemed to perk up with the idea she could be a part of Kate's experience, too. Kate hung up the phone and poured a cup of coffee, but before she could take a sip, the phone rang again

Kate knew it would be her mother calling back. "Hi, Mother."

"I was just thinking. I don't suppose you would come and stay with us while you shoot your movie? Since you're going to be so close."

"Mother, that's a great idea, but I don't think it will be very practical. I have to be on the set by six-thirty every morning and by the time we look at dailies, I won't be finished until about nine or ten at night. Palo Alto is just too long a drive."

"I see. Perhaps you're right."

Kate realized that her mother would go into a jealous rage if the older woman knew she was staying with Annabella, so Kate suggested a preemptive peace offering. "I could visit you and Daddy before production starts."

"Oh. That might work, as long as I have nothing on my calendar. Goodbye, dear."

"Bye, Mother."

At that moment, Kate flashed on the various people she had invited to the movie set. Lily would be working as a gofer. No doubt Martin would be there in hopes of spending time with his daughter. Annabella would be a constant visitor. Becky, someone she barely recognized anymore, might be an extra. And, now her parents. She put a hand to her forehead. Maybe I *should* stay home with Parker, she thought.

CHAPTER TWELVE

It was now mid-June. The tulips in Kate's garden had reached their vibrant peak, at least those that hadn't been eaten by the foraging elk traipsing down the rugged slopes in search of goodies. The daffodils had already begun to dry up. The wildflower seeds that would grow to replace the fading tulips were sprouting green leaves, still too tender to be identified.

Misty rain drifted from distant clouds onto Kate's deck where she sat partially protected under the eaves of her house. An open book rested in her lap while she wandered through her thoughts. She was undisturbed by the whispers of wet nothingness that managed to leave droplets of rain on her legs before evaporating under the sun's subdued warmth.

The network had accepted Kate's revised script with only minor changes that David insisted he was planning to ignore. Casting was complete. In two weeks, the staff and crew would be moving into offices in San Francisco to begin shooting. Tomorrow, Jonas would be starting rehearsals with the six major cast members before they descended on San Francisco. These rehearsals were a luxury not often available to a director for a television movie. It wasn't in their budget or the actors' contracts. But Jonas had insisted on the need for them. He didn't make them mandatory, but not one actor declined his request. They were eager to exercise their acting muscles and agreed to oblige his whim.

For Kate to say she was nervous wouldn't be accurate. Excited? A little. Anxiety-ridden? Without question. Copies of her script were now in the hands of everyone involved in the production: critical actors and designers, cynical technicians, gaffers and grips. She felt as exposed as if she were walking naked through town. Now, everyone would know what kind of a writer she was, good or bad. She remembered having the same feeling when she submitted her first press release after becoming a publicist. Only then, she thought she'd be fired. As it turned out, it wasn't the best press release ever written, but it hadn't been the worst, either.

No matter how much David and Parker encouraged her to let go of her fears and listen to the network prophets who had praised her script, she couldn't. She remembered her own behavior from years past, when she had been the one to roll her eyes and share a few snide remarks with a crewmember about corny dialogue or bad acting. Now, she might be the target of that same ridicule.

Earlier that day, David's secretary had called Kate in a panic. "I need to know the name of the production assistant you want David to hire."

"Why?" asked Kate.

"Jonas wants someone to take notes for him during his rehearsals, and I can't find anyone on such short notice. David suggested I call you."

"Her name is Lily McGuire, and I'm sure she's available."

Kate hung up the phone after sorting out the details, then went to Lily's room to give her the news.

"They want me now?"

"On the next flight."

"Wow. Should I do it?"

"Absolutely. It'll be fun. And you'll have a neat title—Assistant To The Director. At least for the week of rehearsals."

Lily stood taller and waggled her shoulders. "That sounds a lot more important than the subhuman title of gofer."

After a flurry of packing, booking the first available flight to Los Angeles, and faxing the necessary paperwork to get her on the official payroll, Lily was on her way to the airport two hours later. Kate gave her enough cash for emergencies and taxi fare to David's house, where

Kate had arranged for her to stay.

The morning of the first rehearsal, Lily steered David's silver Audi through a maze of narrow, potholed streets, past dilapidated, clapboard bungalows with dried-up weed beds where lawns had once flourished. Since the actors wouldn't be on the official payroll for these rehearsals, David wanted to stay under the radar of any union watchdogs. So, he rented a rehearsal hall at a long-forgotten studio in an obscure neighborhood in Hollywood that slipped over the hill into the shabby outskirts of downtown Los Angeles. It wasn't convenient for anyone, but it was cheap and out of the mainstream.

Lily passed a vacant lot nestled between two houses, a rarity in any neighborhood. The area inspired visions of a silent film she had seen in a film history class. In it, the Keystone Kops raced through similar streets—when the picket fences were still standing—as a camera truck followed in close pursuit, a knickers-clad director yelling instructions through a megaphone.

As Lily neared an intersection, she returned her thoughts to the present and rechecked David's directions to avoid getting lost in this snug, hilly area.

Hidden in a twelve-foot wall of ivy-covered stone was a narrow, green door with the number 102. The zero dangled on a single nail below the rest of the numbers. Twenty yards from the door, the stone wall gave way to a ten-foot square, rusty, wire mesh gate with two rows of barbed wire strung along the top. Directly to the right was a wooden guard stand, painted the same green as the door. It was barely four feet wide with a flat roof extending about a foot over the opening for shade. It didn't have a door. Inside was a crusty, old studio guard, slumped uncomfortably on a three-legged stool, which might have been used for milking cows in an old western movie. He looked up from his newspaper when Lily turned the nose of David's car into the short expanse of driveway leading to the wire gate. Without looking, he reached down beside him for his yellow legal pad, which displayed a short list of names.

"Morning. You here for them rehearsals?" he asked.

"Good morning," replied Lily. "Yes, I am. This place is certainly not easy to find."

"Not nowadays."

Beyond the rusty gate, Lily could see two sound stages and a number of smaller buildings. They looked abandoned.

"What is this place?" Lily's vision of Hollywood was based on what she'd seen in movies: sprawling studio complexes bustling with technicians and costumed actors hustling in and out of huge sound stages, equipment trucks and elaborate sets moving through the alleys formed by towering rows of buildings. There should be high energy everywhere she looked. But she didn't even see a cat lurking in the shadows here.

"This is old-time Hollywood, sweetie. Ever hear of Mack Sennett?"

"No."

"Should know your movie history," he scolded her. "He's one of the giants who made this business what it is today. He worked at this studio. Made several silent films here."

Lily shrugged her shoulders. "I guess." She was somewhat bewildered by the gruff old man. The significance of this rundown studio's place in the scope of Hollywood lore was lost on Lily. She had come to L.A. hoping to find a clue about the origin of her dolphin ring and anything else related to it. But surveying the bleak surroundings where she would be isolated for the next week, she doubted the wisdom of her decision. How had David ever found this place?

The man unlatched the lock and pushed the sweeping fence across the driveway. "Better park over by the beige building. Building number three, just off to your right." He pointed out the direction to her. "Your rehearsal's in the main room at the east end of the building. Can't miss it, Miss McGuire."

"How did you know my name?"

"Simple deduction. You're the only one on my list who ain't here yet."

"How long has everyone been here?"

" 'Bout forty-five minutes."

Lily looked at him and shook her head. Just great, she thought. My first day and already I'm late. She pulled into a dusty spot between two other cars and checked her watch. It said nine-forty-five. So did the clock in David's car. She wasn't due until ten. Her stomach flip-flopped as she realized she may have been confused about the starting time.

She flew out of the car and started toward the main building. Then came to a screeching halt when she realized she'd hadn't locked the car door. David had implored her to treat his classic, 1980 Audi with care. She returned and locked the car door, then took a deep breath to settle her nerves.

Around her, weeds thrived in cracked asphalt leading to the creaky, wooden steps of the building. She walked in and turned left down a long hallway flanked by an unfriendly lineup of locked doors. The transoms above each door supplied the only available light.

Lily reached the end of the hallway where she could barely make out the lettering on a set of double doors reading, "Rehearsal Hall A." She hesitated at the doors, trying to hear what was going on inside the hall. Nothing. She put her ear up against the crack separating the two doors. This time, she thought she detected the sound of deep breathing. What was going on inside? Did she dare enter? She waited another minute, then carefully pushed open one of the doors a crack so she could peek into the space without being noticed. Unfortunately, the seldom-used door hinges let out an agonizing squeak.

Not wishing to appear like a peeping Tom, Lily opened the door and entered, all the while forcing herself to adopt the posture of a confident young woman and not appear to be the apprehensive outsider, which is how she felt.

Before her, seven bodies lay on the floor, each one stretched out, face down, with palms pressing against the hardwood floor at about shoulder level. Everyone was still. Finally, the group began to move in unison, pushing their upper bodies away from the floor into arched positions, then flat again. Then, with arms reaching to the floor, they pushed their buttocks back to rest on their feet. Taking deep breaths, everyone continued through a sequence of postures, eventually bringing themselves to a standing position. Once on their feet, a few of them looked toward the door where Lily stood, but no one acknowledged her.

One of the participants broke the silence. He spoke to no one in particular. "Okay, that felt good. But don't expect me to salute the sun like that ever again!" He looked to be about thirty, definitely uncoordinated and slightly overweight. Lily guessed he might be playing the role of Morgan, the male lead's best friend in *Love Among the Vineyards*.

"Tommy, it's good for you," insisted an athletically taut, petite blonde. Since she was the prettier of the two girls, Lily assumed she had the starring role.

"Denise, enough, I said." Tommy pushed a hand through the air as if thwarting Denise's attempt to lure him into more exercise. "Humor your sweaty little self at someone else's expense. Raising my arms to light a cigar is the most exercise I care to indulge in."

The group chattered and laughed as they sauntered to various clumps of satchels spread around the room to swill stowed bottles of water or dig for a towel to pat away their sweat. Finally, a tall man glided across the room toward Lily with a grace surprising for someone of his lanky stature. He looked too young for the day-old shadow that grew on his face.

His penetrating eyes locked onto Lily's gaze as he stopped in front of her. "Are you my assistant?"

"If you're the director, I am."

"Jonas Waring." He reached out and gave her a perfunctory handshake. Before Lily had a chance to introduce herself, he continued. "Glad you were able to make it here on time."

Lily thought he was being sarcastic. "I thought the rehearsal started at ten."

"It does. I was merely expressing my gratitude that you could get here from Colorado on such short notice."

"Sorry, I just…"

"Is this your first movie job?"

"Yes."

"No need to be nervous. We're all a team here. That's what will make it great fun. You must be pretty well connected for them to fly you in from Colorado to take notes for me."

Lily wrinkled her brow. There was an edgy clip in her reply. "I, umm, I'm not sure what you mean."

"There you go again, getting defensive."

"No, I'm not."

"Look, ah… What did you say your name is?"

Lily shifted from one foot to another. "Lily McGuire."

"Lily, I just like to know where I stand with everyone. By knowing who got you this job…

Lily interrupted before he could finish. "I see. You want to know whether you have to be nice to me or not." Lily was surprised by her own insolence and wondered why she was reacting this way toward Jonas. Perhaps it was because the director didn't seem too much older than she was.

"Ouch!" Jonas shook his hand as if he'd burned it on a hot stove.

"Let's not worry about whom we each know. I'm here to take your notes. If you don't like the job I'm doing, then you can fire me."

Jonas smiled. "Deal." He put out his hand to solidify their agreement.

Lily shook his hand, but did not return his smile. What a jerk, she thought.

Jonas walked away and called the actors to gather at a table where scripts sat in front of each chair. He didn't specifically invite Lily to join them or bother to introduce her to the group. Nevertheless, she pulled up a chair at the far end of the long table and listened to them read through the script.

After the initial read-through, they took a short break before Jonas began running the actors through the first scene to work on their motivation. He handed Lily a clipboard with a note pad and asked her to stand near him, which wasn't easy because he spent much of his time nervously pacing back and forth while listening to the actors. Occasionally, Jonas walked up behind Lily and whispered an observation or stage direction to her, which she wrote down. When the actors finished the scene, Jonas took the clipboard from Lily and referred to her notes in his discussions with the actors.

On the second go-round, Jonas appeared to settle down. He mostly stood behind Lily's right shoulder with one hand to his chin and the other arm clasped across his body as he concentrated on the actors and whispered his notes to her.

During their next break, Lily briefly introduced herself to the actors. Their replies were distracted as they remained trained on Jonas's every move and direction.

At one o'clock, Jonas called for a lunch break. He asked his leading actors, Denise and the boyish Simon, to join him so the pair could go over his notes in more detail. The remaining four actors—bookish, soft-spoken Beth; Taylor, a roguish English actor with dapper good looks; John, the oldest of the group, very fit for his late fifties; and Tommy—walked off together, leaving Lily behind. She felt awkward, out of place. She presumed these people viewed her as nothing more than a Dictaphone. She looked around the room to see if anyone had witnessed her embarrassment at being excluded.

Left to her own devices, Lily went outdoors to explore. She found an unlocked side door to one of the sound stages and cautiously walked inside. It smelled musty, but was too dark for Lily to see the expansive area she could feel around her. Back outside, she walked to the far end of the lot, where she found a lone tree offering shade as respite from the afternoon sun. She tested the legs of a rickety wooden chair positioned under it, before plopping onto the seat. Throwing back her head, she let out a deep sigh. She wasn't sure she liked the movie business. So far, it had made her feel like a second-class citizen.

An hour later, Lily was the first to return to the rehearsal hall. Moments later, the first group arrived, giggling and laughing. Finally Jonas, Beth and Simon showed up, thirty minutes late. Without apologies to anyone, Jonas resumed the pattern of his morning rehearsals until five o'clock. At that point, he thanked everyone and called for a ten o'clock start for the next day.

By the time Lily made her way through the clogged veins of Los Angeles' evening traffic back to David's house, it had taken her two hours to maneuver the route she had traveled in thirty minutes that morning. She promised herself to pump David about an alternate route home.

He was out for the night, so Lily had his place to herself. The cool blue of David's swimming pool beckoned her for a refreshing swim she hoped would calm her nerves. Alone in the privacy of David's secluded backyard and without a swim suit, she stepped out of her clothes at the pool's edge and dove naked into the tranquil water sparkling under the last rays of the setting sun. She returned to the surface for a breath of air, then launched into brisk laps, swimming freestyle as fast as she could. She didn't slow her pace until she felt the anger and frustration drain completely out of her body.

She continued swimming, this time with an easy breaststroke, her head out of the water, finding additional comfort in the lush gardens surrounding the pool. The choppy water settled around her, further calming her nerves. Contentment filled her as she wallowed in the luxury of her surroundings. A melodious rhythm waltzed through her body as she performed smooth, balletic somersaults and surface dives with the ease of a porpoise.

When her thoughts tumbled back to *Love Among the Vineyards*, she remembered her promise to call Kate with a bulletin on the rehearsals. It was almost nine o'clock in Colorado. She figured Kate would be pacing by now. Lily slipped out of the pool and wrapped up in one of the fluffy beach towels stacked on a chaise lounge. Her empty stomach churned and groaned. She compiled a dish of cheese and crackers, poured a coke, then plunked down at the counter by the telephone and dialed Kate's number.

"Lily, how are you? How did everything go today?"

"Fine." Her voice sounded tired and disinterested to her ears as she munched on a cracker.

"Only fine? Didn't you have fun? Is anything wrong?"

"Really, everything went very well." Lily didn't want Kate to know what an unpleasant time she had actually experienced. She was afraid of sounding ungrateful. She told Kate about the rundown studio where they were rehearsing and about how she walked in on the actors doing yoga.

"How was Jonas?"

"Very intense."

Kate laughed. "I suspected as much. How about the actors? Did they like the script?"

"I don't know. They didn't talk about it, at least not when I was around."

"Okay, then. You're probably exhausted. Thanks so much for calling. Are you sure you're all right? You sound a little down. I thought you'd be a little more exhilarated after your first day."

"I'm just tired. You know how things are when everything is new. I'll call you later in the week to let you know how it's going. Night, Kate."

"Goodnight, Lily."

"Was that Lily calling?" Parker walked into the kitchen as Kate hung up the phone.

"Yes."

"Oh. I was hoping to talk to her. How's it going for her?"

"I'm not sure. She sounded pretty tired."

"You know…" Parker hesitated a moment before continuing. "Richard Haulk in our L.A. office wants to meet with me in the next few days. Maybe I'll fly out tomorrow morning. I could meet with Richard and then check up on Lily."

"Check up on Lily? She just got there, Parker."

"I think it would be nice to offer her a little moral support. She's not used to the hard knocks of breaking into a new job." Parker grabbed some cookies from the cupboard and joined Kate at the kitchen table.

"How about a cookie?""Sure." Kate took a bite. "Aren't you being a little overly protective?"

He gave her a sheepish look. "Maybe."

"You seem to have grown awfully attached to Lily."

He shrugged. "She's fun."

"Parker, what does that mean? Should I be worried?"

"Hardly."

"Then why am I suspicious?"

"Oh, Kate." He sighed. You're being silly."

"You think I'm being ridiculous? You're the one who seems to have a crush on Lily."

"Good grief, Kate! Where did you come up with that idea?" He got up from the table and returned the jar of cookies to the pantry.

Kate wondered if the guilt she felt about her own behavior of late had caused her to mistrust Parker's intentions to help Lily. Still, his sudden business trip bothered her. "What's going on, Parker?"

"Nothing," he insisted.

"Then why are you rushing off to L.A.?" She turned around in her chair to confront him straight on and keep him from leaving the room.

"Kate, aren't you the one who said we didn't have to ask permission to live our lives? I have a business meeting in L.A. Dinner with Lily would make it a far more pleasurable trip."

"Are you doing this to get even with me for the other night?"

"If I had any immoral thoughts, which I don't, I wouldn't be telling you about my plans to see Lily."

"It may not be your intention, now. But after a few drinks in the presence of a nubile beauty like Lily, you might be tempted."

Parker appeared bewildered. He shook his head. "Your writer's mind is full of fantasy tonight, Kate. I think we should end this conversation before either one of us says something we might regret."

"Why?"

"Kate, let's not do this. Do you know what's really going on here?"

"I'm sure you're going to tell me."

Parker rejoined Kate at the table. "I'm not sure what it's

called…pre-separation anxiety syndrome, or something like that. If you and I are fighting, then it will be easier for you to go to California for a month to escape the unpleasantness at home. It often happens to military families just before a serviceman must leave on extended duty. Disagreements erupt over picky, unimportant things, real or imagined. But Kate, I want you to miss me. So, I'm not going to argue with you. We usually don't fight. Remember?"

Kate reached across the table to hold Parker's hand. "I'm sorry." She hoped Parker was telling the truth, and she was anxious over nothing.

Lily's lunch break the next day was a repeat of the first day. The actors and Jonas took off in the same two groups, leaving her behind. Never mind, she thought. Parker had called early that morning and had arranged to have dinner with her. She would be seeing him in just a few hours.

Parker was waiting for Lily at the bar when she arrived at the restaurant that night.

"Wow," she commented. "You look so distinguished. I've never seen you in a business suit."

He smiled. "Distinguished? That makes me sound old."

"How about handsome, then?"

"Yes, I like that better. Thank you for the compliment." He got up from his stool and gave her a hug. "They have a table ready for us. Are you hungry?"

"Starving."

Once settled at their table, Parker took a menu offered by the host and looked back at Lily, "How did things go today?"

"Did Kate send you down here to spy for her?" Lily laughed.

Parker laughed, too, and held up his hand. "I'm sworn to secrecy. But Kate did say you sounded a little down after your first day on the job."

"First days must always be the hardest."

"Sometimes, I guess. Anything in particular happen?"

"I'm not sure you want to hear about my silly problems."

"That's why I'm here. Don't forget, I live with someone who used to work in the industry. I know it can be rough."

A waiter came over to take their drink order. "Lily, would you care for anything?" Parker asked.

"Nothing, thanks. I'm driving David's prized Audi, so need to be on the straight and narrow."

"Do you mind if I have a martini while you sip on a soda?"

"Have a double. Then I won't feel so guilty about taking up your time with my problems."

"You could never be a waste of my time. Fire away."

Lily smiled at him. "Well, to start with, hardly anyone even acknowledges my existence when I'm in the same room. Then, everyone takes off for lunch and never thinks to invite me along. If that's the way people are treated in this business, then I'm not sure I want to be a part of it."

"I can understand that. But I'm sure your bright smile and charming personality must have gotten through to them after two days?"

"Are you trying to make me feel better?"

"Yes. Is it working?"

"Maybe a little." She felt heat radiating from her cheeks and knew that her face had turned red, but she pressed on with her story. "Two of the actors managed to say goodnight when I left. Jonas, the director, was still too preoccupied to do more than offer a slight smile."

"I'll bet you didn't smile back."

She leaned into the table, toward him. "How did you know that?"

"Just a hunch. Did you say goodnight to the other actors or did you wait for them to say it first?"

"Well, I… I guess I waited for them to say something first. But they wouldn't even make eye contact."

"Lily, can I pass on a few things I've learned from Kate about the sorry state of being an actor?"

"Please do."

"For starters, they're some of the most insecure people you'll ever meet. Their lives are filled with rejection. It's the nature of their profession. So, they're not going to set themselves up for any more disappointments than they're forced to. Their paranoia of rejection often makes them appear to be self-centered and aloof, which, of course, is what many of them become."

Lily remembered her own conversation with Kate about actors. "So, what am I supposed to do about it?"

"Two things. Ignore them and find someone else to have lunch with...which, I suspect, is not acceptable to you. Or, you can become the social director. They'll never recognize you're as uncomfortable or insecure as they are, so don't be."

Lily fidgeted with the dolphin ring hanging from her necklace while listening to Parker. By being here, giving her advice, Parker was proving to be the father she had never known. It felt good.

"They'll never offer you the acceptance you're looking for," he continued. "Instead, you must reach into their little bubbles and pull them into a cushy safety net with you. Ignore what appears to be their avoidance of you. It's not personal. They're just snubbing you before you reject them. It's too early to know if they like you or not."

"Maybe I could ask them to join me for lunch or something," enthused Lily.

"That's the idea."

"But I don't know any restaurants."

"That's easily remedied. I'll give you the names of some fun places."

"Okay, but they always seem to have a plan before I arrive in the morning. They all do yoga together before the rehearsals."

"Then you do the yoga, too."

"But I think the yoga's just for the actors and Jonas."

"Nonsense." Parker gestured with a hand for emphasis and almost knocked their drinks from the tray the waiter was carrying to their table. He smiled at the waiter and placed both of his hands in his lap to show the man it was safe to serve their drinks. After he'd left, Parker raised his martini and offered a toast. Lily raised her soda to clink his glass. "Here's to the success of your new job, Lily."

"Thank you."

"Now, back to our strategy." His smile seemed conspiratorial. "What time do they start their yoga?"

"I'm not sure…"

"What time?"

"About nine-fifteen, I think." Lily looked away from Parker's gaze, unsure she wanted to hear his plan, but curiosity drew her back.

"Tomorrow morning, you be there at nine-fifteen and join them. Do you get the idea? You're excluding yourself from things that don't require an invitation. Become an equal participant, Lily. They're only better than you in your own mind. Their arrogance is only a front, like that Jonas fellow. He's probably scared to death someone will find out he's just faking his way through right now. No doubt, he may have a lot of potential, but it's his attitude of competence that's his best ally. If he's smart, keeps an open mind and listens to some of the veterans around him, he'll probably become as good as he already pretends to be."

Lily's eyes opened wider as she tried to take this all in. "You're so smart."

"Not really. I've just been around a few years longer than you have. Lily, you're an astute young woman. You'll catch on quickly. Now, how about we order some dinner?"

"Good idea. I need a little time to digest some of the things you told me."

"Not to worry. You'll do fine."

Before they parted after dinner, Parker wrote down the names of some restaurants. She accepted his suggestions with an uncertain smile. "Don't back out on me, Lily. What have you got to lose? You're adventurous, or you wouldn't have taken this job in the first place."

"I'll try. Thanks so much for your help. I'm really glad you had to come to L.A."

Parker smiled. "Me, too. I wish I could stay longer, but I want to get home to Kate."

"Shuttle diplomacy, eh, Parker?"

He laughed. "Something like that."

Lily kissed him on the cheek. "Thanks for being concerned about me. Give my love to Kate. And tell her I'll call with an update on how things are going."

"I will. Good luck to you."

Lily didn't phone Kate again until the night before the final rehearsal. Her breathless exuberance was a far cry from the lackluster tone of her initial call to Kate earlier in the week.

"Wednesday we had lunch at an absolute dive in downtown L.A., but it's the most 'in' spot you can imagine. Parker was so wonderful to think of it for me. We waited in a line stretching halfway around the block. They seat everyone at picnic tables you share with total strangers, only they aren't all strangers. Vanessa Redgrave was sitting at the table across from us! She's starring in a play at the Dorothy Chandler Pavilion. John, he's one of the actors, pointed out a couple of TV producers he's worked with. And get this, the menus were decoupaged onto the picnic tables as place mats. It's called Tiny's Grill. We're going back for lunch tomorrow, and Jonas is even going to come with us."

Kate knew the local dive where cops, drug dealers, entrepreneurs, writers and actors mingled for Sunday morning breakfasts. Parker had taken her to Tiny's on their first breakfast date. They considered it their special place. Parker's willingness to share it with Lily felt like a wet rag in the face to Kate.

"They've been teaching me yoga," continued Lily. "So, on Saturday morning, four of the actors are going to meet at the beach so I can teach them T'ai Chi."

"Sounds like you've made some friends already. How are the rehearsals going?" asked Kate.

"Pretty well, as far as I can tell. Jonas has really made a lot of changes that seem to be helping."

"What kind of changes?" Kate could hear her alarm in her voice.

"In the actors' performances. You know, in how an actor says a line, emphasizing a verb, or adding a pause, or gestures, body movement. That kind of thing."

"He's not changing any lines, is he?"

"Only in a couple of instances, but don't worry, Kate. It's been very minor, involving only one or two words. I promise."

"Has David been by?"

"No. I haven't seen much of him at all, not even at his house. One of the actors told me Jonas has forbidden any visitors."

"David is hardly a visitor."

"I don't know what the deal is, but everything seems to be fine. Of course, I'm a bit lacking in the experience department."

"I trust your instincts, Lily. Anyway, these rehearsals were Jonas's baby, and they'll probably improve the performances. So I guess I shouldn't worry." Maybe Jonas wasn't such a bad guy, thought Kate. She would reserve judgment until she met him face to face.

CHAPTER THIRTEEN

Friday night, after the final rehearsal, Jonas took everyone to dinner…including Lily. They met at Billy's Bistro in Santa Monica for drinks and then moved on to The Crab House in Venice Beach for a feast of cracked crab, luscious green goddess salad and fresh sourdough bread flown in from San Francisco. Denise and Beth nibbled on the crab and sipped from glasses of white wine while Lily and the guys gorged themselves like hungry sailors. Lily didn't care when the melted butter dripped down her chin. She was having too much fun.

Lily had never been around such an entertaining group. They regaled her with stories of Paul Newman teaching John how to butter a bowl of popcorn using a knife, Jonas's run in with a high voltage country star whose bodyguard was a former president of the Hell's Angels motorcycle gang—and Tommy's childhood dancing debut with the legendary Ray Bolger. Their high energy repartee was like being on *The Tonight Show*.

Even though their stories and personal experiences were peppered with the names of famous people Lily had only heard of, Lily couldn't call what she heard name-dropping. These celebrities were either her co-workers' friends, or people they had worked with over the years. Lily almost pinched herself to make sure she wasn't dreaming.

Around ten o'clock, the group had dwindled to three: Jonas, Lily and John. When John left, Lily felt a little awkward being alone with Jonas. But she had been having such a great time, she didn't want her evening to end.

Jonas moved to the center of the long table so he was sitting directly opposite her. "So, Lily. It looks like you've claimed a prominent spot amongst our little family."

"Yes, I guess I have," she replied with some pleasure at her accomplishment. "I wasn't so sure after my first day, though."

"You were a bit uptight."

A few glasses of wine had relaxed Lily's inhibitions. "And you didn't help much."

"No, I probably didn't."

"I thought it was the director's job to make everyone feel comfortable."

"Where did you come up with that notion?" Lily could hear amusement in his voice.

"Isn't that what the best directors do to get good performances out of their actors?"

"Some do, I guess. But we're not social directors. Different techniques work with different people."

"And what about the other people you work with? Don't you care if the only other person in the room with you, beside the actors, is uncomfortable?"

"You are talking about yourself, of course. I had the impression from our first meeting that you are used to taking care of yourself."

"So you chose to ignore me?"

Jonas smiled and stared into her eyes. "I wouldn't say that. I have a tendency to submerge myself in a scene to the extent that if a fire broke out, I probably wouldn't notice it. In the process, I guess my social graces fall below the standards of Emily Post."

"Perhaps I'm being overly sensitive." Lily relaxed in her chair.

"No, you're probably right. I'm sorry if I made you feel uncomfortable, Lily. But you seem to have recovered from my neglect."

"I had a little help."

"From your mentor?"

Lily laughed. "Are you still wondering how I got this job?"

"Always curious," he said with a smile.

"Well, I'm not going to tell you. Not that it matters. But since I know you're so desperate to know, I'm just as determined you don't know."

"You like shrouding yourself in mystery, eh?"

"Yes. That's the only way I know how to keep you a little off balance."

"I'm intrigued, Lily McGuire. How about we go for a walk along the beach? I'm ready for some fresh air."

"Is it safe to walk the beach in Venice?"

"Not here, but I know a place up the coast. Are you game? It's a gorgeous night, and a walk will help us both unwind." As if he could read her mind, he added, "No hankie-pankie."

Lily laughed, not sure she could believe him. A walk on the beach sounded wonderful, but was it worth the risk of putting herself in a compromising situation? "I don't know…"

"Come on."

Her heart raced. "Well, okay. That does sound inviting."

"Good, then let's go."

Jonas drove up the coast toward Malibu, to a stretch of the Pacific shoreline guarded from the highway by a lineup of beach houses perched shoulder to shoulder on stilts. He slowed and cautiously waited for a break in the oncoming traffic before turning into an open carport, their only haven between the highway and the front door of the attached beach house.

"I hope you know the people who live here." Lily concluded that if he didn't, he certainly possessed a lot of chutzpah parking his car in a stranger's garage.

"I know the person very well. I'm renting this beach house from a friend."

Jonas walked around the parked car to open Lily's door, then continued on to unlock the front door of the house. Lily hesitated a moment, still worried about Jonas's intentions. Assuring herself she could handle the situation, she stepped out of the car and followed him inside. The boom of crashing waves overtook the roar of the highway when she shut the door. Before her stretched a long, narrow room, ending at a wall of floor-to-ceiling, sliding glass doors.

Jonas slipped open the doors to let in the salty ocean air and turned back to her. "The best way to access the beach is right through here. Care for some wine, first?"

Lily eyed Jonas. "No, thanks."

"I didn't think so." Jonas seemed to sense her unease and led Lily onto the balcony. "Follow me."

With a feeling of mixed relief, Lily trailed behind him to the bottom of the stairs, where she slipped out of her shoes. Her feet sank into the cool sand, the tiny granules pooling around each toe as the lure of pounding surf pulled her away from the lighted house and into the darkness. She picked up a stubby stick of driftwood and tossed it toward the ocean. Jonas kicked off his shoes and caught up with her.

"For a girl from the mountains, you sure seem comfortable on a beach."

She smiled at this. "I'm not from Colorado. I was only visiting for awhile."

"Ah, the mystery continues."

"No mystery. I grew up in Washington State. We have an ocean there, too. Not as warm as your Southern California beaches, though. I've missed the ocean. It has such a calming effect."

"For me, too. That's why I decided to rent out here."

"I'm surprised. You strike me as an A-type personality, someone who always needs to be in the middle of the action."

"True. Thus, my apartment in Beverly Hills. But I recently discovered I need to be alone sometimes. This business can burn out people in a short time. I intend to be a long-time survivor, and in order to do that, I need a retreat where I can escape the pressures of deadlines and long hours. This is a great place to unwind, do some creative thinking, meditate or even read a book."

"How nice you can afford such a luxury."

"No argument there."

Walking in silence along the water's edge, Jonas took Lily's hand.

Her first reaction was to pull away, but the unexpected comfort of his reassuring touch helped Lily release the leftover strain of her trying week. The need to rebuff any further advances washed away with the tide and a calmness that overcame both of them. It was the perfect walk on the beach after all.

It took them an hour to walk to the end of the beach and back, after which, Jonas drove Lily to her car in Santa Monica. Whatever his intentions might have been earlier in the evening, Jonas had endeared himself to Lily.

She looked up at the tall figure standing next to her. "Thanks for a great dinner and the nice walk, Jonas."

"You're welcome."

"Taylor, Denise, Beth, Tommy and I are meeting for T'ai Chi and breakfast tomorrow morning. Care to join us?" She tried to sound as casual as possible.

"I might, but don't count on me. Where?"

"Lifeguard stand ten, just north of the Santa Monica pier. Ten o'clock."

Lily had almost completed teaching some basic T'ai Chi movements to the group by the time Jonas arrived. When she spotted him walking down the beach toward them, a nervous dose of adrenaline and excitement shot through her body. She waved at him and then, as if to seem more interested in her exercise routine than his arrival, refocused on the T'ai Chi postures and didn't look his way again until the group had run through their final form.

"Eh, Jonas! How's it going, man?" Tommy greeted Jonas with a handshake.

"Hey, Tommy. I thought you were finished with exercising after our yoga class this week."

"Oh yeah, right. I thought I'd give this a try since I was planning to put in a little beach time today anyhow." A bare-chested Tommy flaunted the tan of a year-round beachcomber.

Taylor, Denise and Beth gave Jonas an obligatory kiss on the cheek and a hug, in turn. Unused to this demonstrative show of affection between relatively new acquaintances, Lily stood off to the side as an observer.

Jonas turned toward her. "Morning, Lily."

"Hi," she replied with a shy wave of her hand.

"Sorry I missed your T'ai Chi."

"That's okay."

"Can I talk to you for a sec?" he asked her. He turned back to everyone else, saying, "Excuse us for a minute. I've got to take care of a little business with my assistant." Putting his arm around Lily's shoulders as if he had something confidential to tell her, Jonas led her away from the group.

Lily turned back to the group and shrugged her shoulders under a wide-eyed expression to show them she was just as surprised as they were about his actions.

"What's up?" she asked him.

He walked her farther down the beach before he replied. "I had a really nice time last night."

"Me, too. That was terrific of you to take us all to dinner."

"It's our walk on the beach I'm talking about."

"Oh." She suddenly felt giddy.

"Listen, Lily," he said, ushering a sense of intimacy into his voice. "I had planned to join you this morning for T'ai Chi and breakfast, but something has come up. I got a call this morning from David Backus, our producer."

"I know who David is."

"I wasn't sure. Anyway, he needs me to fly up to San Francisco today to check out a couple of locations we need to lock in for the film."

"What's that got to do with me?"

"I just wanted you to know why I couldn't meet you this morning. I'm on my way to the airport right now."

"Thanks for letting me know. It wasn't necessary though. This was just a casual thing. You never said you were planning to come for sure."

Lily was thrown off guard. Jonas had gone out of his way to find her at the beach. And she was surprised at how happy she was to see him. She didn't want to discourage the possibility of a personal relationship with Jonas, but she wasn't sure she wanted to encourage anything, either.

Lily returned to David's house early that afternoon to find him home and available to talk for the first time since her arrival. Though she had become sidetracked by her new job, this was the opportunity she had been waiting for. Lily and David relaxed under the shade of an umbrella table by the pool.

"Jonas tells me you were a tremendous help during rehearsals," said David. "I was wondering if you'd be willing to stick around long enough to work in our L.A. production office until we move our operations up to San Francisco."

"I'd love to. Is it okay if I stay with you until then?"

"You bet."

Summoning up her courage, she felt for her talisman—the dolphin ring hanging around her neck—and plunged into the topic that had brought her to Los Angeles in the first place. "Tell me about Kate Cochran. How did you two meet?"

David laughed. "I thought that question might eventually come up. It's a little embarrassing, but I'll tell you anyhow."

Lily encouraged him with a smile.

"We met years ago. I was fresh out of college. CBS hired me as a program executive—someone to tell Norman Lear what was wrong with his scripts."

"Wow."

"What a joke, is more like it! I hadn't worked three days in the business, and I was expected to critique *All in the Family*. I think the show was in its last season. The production company was cordial when I showed up for the rehearsals. They said hello and offered me a cup of coffee. From then on, they went about their business as if I were a dust ball blowing around in the corners."

"Is that standard treatment in this town, to ignore new people who are working with you?"

"What do you mean? Has that happened to you this week?"

"Jonas treated me as a second-class citizen for most of the time."

"I didn't realize that. You should have told me."

"And have you admonish the director on my behalf? I don't think so. That would have made matters worse. I think I eventually smoothed out things on my own."

"Good for you, Lily. Kate said you were pretty self-reliant, with definite ideas of your own. I wasn't so fortunate in my first job." David tipped his chair and balanced on the two back legs. "Eventually, some of Lear's writers befriended me enough to, at least, share some jokes. But they made fun of the script notes I offered. It was pretty humiliating.

"Kate was working for Lear's company at the time and threw me a lifeline when she saw me drowning. She suggested I downplay my role with the network and take advantage of my assignment to learn the business from Lear's crusty writers. Some of them had written for Milton Berle, Bob Hope and Lucille Ball during the golden age of television's early classics."

"How come Kate was so wise? She must have been pretty young then, too."

"She was. I guess she was just better at seeing the obvious."

"Did you and Kate ever date?"

"Hardly. We're just great friends." David gave her a funny look suggesting she should have guessed that.

Hoping the sight of her talisman might prompt some kind of reaction from David, Lily slipped the dolphin ring back and forth on its gold chain.

"What is that around your neck?" He leaned in for a closer look.

She held it in place for him to see.

"A dolphin ring. Very nice." He settled back into his chair. "Kate used to wear one like that. They weren't very common years ago."

David's observation confirmed her belief that the origin of her dolphin ring might be a clue in her search.

"Do you know where Kate got hers?"

"No. Probably from an old boyfriend."

"Really? Who?"

"Oh, I'm not going to tell tales on my old friend." He smiled. "How long have you known Kate?"

"Actually, we barely know each other. I met her about a month ago. I don't know. I guess we just clicked. I feel like I've known her my entire life. I can talk to her about almost anything. And Parker, too. He's very special. He and I are both avid golfers."

"He's pretty much a fanatic."

"They were kind enough to let me stay with them for a couple of days and next thing I know, here I am. Speaking of which, I have a favor to ask."

"What's that?"

"Would you mind terribly if we didn't tell anyone how I got this job, or that I've been staying with you?"

"What difference does it make?"

"It seems to be very important to Mr. Director, Jonas."

"So?"

"We got off to a rather shaky start, partly because of his need to know if I had any important connections to anyone associated with this production, or presumably anywhere else in this industry."

"Ah, yes. Jonas likes to know where the bodies are buried. His lack of subtlety can be annoying."

"Is that what you call it?" She laughed. "What's his story anyway? He's pretty young to be a director, isn't he?"

"Not really. Directors seem to be a lot younger today than they used to be. And Jonas has a natural gift I don't mind nurturing. Did you know I gave him his first job five years ago as a production assistant?"

"He was a gofer? How old is he, anyway?"

"What would you guess?"

"Twenty-eight maybe, but sometimes he acts like eighteen."

"You're not too far off in either direction. He's twenty-six, and he's already directed two television movies and a small independent feature."

Lily's eyes opened wide in disbelief. "Are you telling me that in five years, I could be a director too?"

"That's a loaded question, Lily. What is it you want to be?"

"That's a loaded question, too. Maybe I'll know more at the end of this production."

"Fair enough."

"So, do we have an agreement? Will you promise not to tell Jonas that Kate got me the job?"

"I don't see what difference it makes, but I promise."

Lily hoped David had not detected her infatuation for Jonas. She didn't want to appear unprofessional or immature in his eyes. Besides, the newly ignited spark between her and Jonas might fizzle into nothing more than an uncomfortable clash of two strong-willed personalities.

CHAPTER FOURTEEN

"Parker," Kate called from the bedroom. "You'd better bring me both of those giant suitcases."

One week before production was to begin in San Francisco, Kate's nerves percolated with excitement. She could pack six weeks of clothing in one carry-on bag for a trip to Europe. However, the parameters of driving to California for six weeks of filming allowed her the freedom of abundance. She could take enough clothing to accommodate San Francisco's bone-chilling fog in July and a cotton wardrobe for the Napa Valley's stifling summer heat. When Parker reminded her that most of the crew would be in jeans and tee shirts, she pointed to a stack of carefully folded jeans. There was little he could do but shake his head and grin.

Returning from the garage with two suitcases, Parker stepped carefully through the sea of clothing draped over furniture and piled in tidy stacks covering almost every inch of floor space. He placed both suitcases in the only free spot left in the room before relaxing on the floor beside them.

"I don't think these suitcases will hold half of this stuff," he observed.

"I know." She put her hands on her hips and looked around the room. "Maybe I'll have to ship some of this."

Parker laughed. "Kate, why do you need so many clothes?"

"I don't know," she moaned.

"Annabella does have a washer and dryer, doesn't she? If you're willing to wear something twice, perhaps you could make use of her appliances so you don't have to take so much stuff."

Kate continued to pull more clothes out of her closets while listening to Parker.

"Katie, I'll probably get out there to visit you a couple of times, and maybe you'll even make a trip home. You can use those trips to exchange your wardrobe. Also, the last time I checked, California had department stores specializing in women's clothing, so if you forget something, you can always buy it."

"I know."

"I think you should go to California and relax. Your work's primarily done. It's now in the hands of David and his director and the crew."

"I know, that's what I'm afraid of." She couldn't tell him that guilt was also driving her anxiety. She would be sneaking behind Parker's back to help Martin. Being up-front about the situation made sense, except Kate wasn't sure her desire to help Martin was that innocent.

"Let it go, darling. David will safeguard your baby. Don't try to rationalize your being in California for the whole shoot because they need you. You're going for moral support and to enjoy the camaraderie that goes with the making of a movie."

Kate straightened her back upon hearing his comment. "How did you make the transition from the amount of clothes I'm taking to the fact I'm not needed?"

"I didn't mean it that way. I'm sorry. I just want you to stop worrying about everything."

She struggled to soften her anxiety with a smile. "So my nervousness is driving you crazy. You're probably anxious to get rid of me, after all." She sat on the floor alongside Parker.

"How did you guess?" He tipped up her chin and kissed her on the lips. "Once you're gone, I can golf all day and play poker with the guys every night, belching and farting at will."

"You hate poker," she reminded him. "And besides, don't forget about Rusty." She pouted her lips in a Shirley Temple impersonation. "He needs you to take him on hikes and feed him snacks from your barbecued leftovers."

"I won't forget our dog. I'm not the one who's deserting him. Do you realize this is the longest time we will be separated since we got married? I'm going to miss you."

Seeing the tender sadness on Parker's face awakened her desire. "Ah, come on, now. I'm not deserting Rusty, or you either." She rubbed her fingertips over his leg and softened her voice. "We promised each other conjugal visits, remember?"

"Two or three times in one month isn't worth an entry in my diary!"

"Oh, poor baby." She hugged him. "It'll be all right. I promise I'll make your trips very memorable." She eased her caressing hands slowly around to unbutton and slip off his shirt, all the while nibbling him seductively on his ear. Kate moved her lips down the naked curve of his neck to his shoulder and taunted him by trickling her finger tips along the inside of his leg.

Reclining his body into the stacks of surrounding clothes, Parker let his wife completely undress him, while he drifted into an euphoric trance. Kate raised above Parker and slowly pulled her tee shirt over her head and stepped out of her shorts. Parker smiled as he watched, then pulled her back beside him. They smothered each other with penetrating kisses, their bodies rolling and tumbling among the cotton and silk of Kate's stacks of clothing.

Early the next morning, Kate methodically loaded her Jeep Cherokee, while Parker tucked himself away in his den—a pointed reminder to Kate that he still had reservations about her long stay in California. She overrode his coolness with a demonstrative, loving goodbye. He warmed to her embrace, but with a certain restraint that disappointed her. She wondered what had become of the passionate lover from the evening before.

The two-day drive to California was smooth and long. Kate let her mind wander over the Rocky Mountain passes, through the scenic red canyon lands and piñon pine-covered passes of Utah, and into the seemingly unreachable horizons of the Nevada desert.

She listened to her cache of CD's. Chopin, Mozart and Beethoven accompanied her throughout the initial miles of worrying about Parker. She felt badly about leaving him for so many weeks and even wondered if their marriage was solid enough to withstand this separation. Of course it was, she voiced to herself. Two hundred miles later, she thought about turning around. Then, she grew angry over Parker's cool send-off, which fueled her determination to continue. Why was Parker making this so difficult for her? She needed to fulfill her aspirations beyond Parker's embrace. If this movie production became a test of their marriage, then perhaps their relationship wasn't what it should be.

Four hundred miles farther, crossing the state line into Utah, the freedom created by distance triggered a metamorphosis from the caring mountain wife into the determined career woman she had once been. Thoughts of daily household chores and responsibilities faded away. For the first time since marrying Parker, her solitary purpose was to follow her passion to work in the business where she once had thrived. Parker would have to accept her choice to work again. Her aimless hikes spent plotting story lines and developing characters, months of secluded writing, and years of patiently waiting had finally allowed Kate a chance to reinvent herself.

Crossing the glaring white salt flats, Kate played Barbra Streisand singing "I'm Gonna Live and Live Now" over and over again until she felt a fearless energy building up inside of her. The inspiring song from *Funny Girl* had always lifted her spirits and focused her determination when she was younger. By Wendover, Nevada, she was sailing through dreams of Hollywood premieres and an Emmy Award for her screenplay. When night fell, nostalgic memories of her past career and the glamorous world she had once inhabited lulled her into a fitful sleep at a roadside motel in Elko. Anticipation woke her at five in the morning and rushed her back onto the interstate.

Throughout the second day, her brain dashed through an outline of the schedule that lay ahead of her in California. At the crest of Donner Pass, she flipped on a Bruce Springsteen CD and soared into the state where she had been born and raised; where she had created, coddled and achieved the dreams of her future; where winters were short and summers long; where she had loved and lost and won again. Over the summit and down the foothills, through the Sacramento Valley and into the San Francisco Bay Area, she reminisced. To her chagrin, blurry images of Martin entered her thoughts and clouded her first glimpse of the San Francisco skyline. She admonished herself for allowing him to intrude on her view. She tuned in a Bay Area radio station playing oldies but goodies from her parents' era. She reverently listened to Judy Garland singing, "Somewhere Over the Rainbow."

Kate pulled into her parents' driveway late in the afternoon for her promised visit. A hand-painted "Welcome Home" banner hanging over the garage door celebrated her arrival. Her father's artwork raised her spirits and offered hope for an angst-free visit. She ran a comb through her hair and dabbed on lipstick before sliding out of her Jeep onto legs stiff after two days of driving. Though standing on solid ground, she felt like she was still moving. Running a finger over her dirt-caked car, she made a mental note to wash off the road grit before heading to Annabella's.

Expecting her parents to be in the backyard on this warm day, she entered through a side gate. She spotted her mother first, nipping newly sprouted weeds from her well-manicured garden. The older woman wore a long-sleeved blouse, trousers, shoes and socks, a wide-brimmed straw hat, gloves, dark glasses and heavy makeup. Unlike Kate, who worked outdoors in sleeveless tops and shorts, her mother protected her alabaster skin like a badge of honor.

Kate smiled at the incongruity of their lives. Her mother pampered rose bushes. Kate scattered wildflower seeds.

Kate's father, colored a deep bronze from his afternoons spent baking in the sun, lounged by their swimming pool reading a book. Kate wished she had time to go fishing with him, but knew her schedule wouldn't allow that luxury.

Upon seeing Kate, her parents put aside their tools of relaxation and welcomed her with warm hugs. After ushering her into the shade of the patio eaves, the trio settled into deep wicker chairs and sipped on sun tea while catching up on the niceties of their lives.

The afternoon flowed smoothly with no sign of her mother's emotional land mines that often peppered their visits. Kate could detect no edge or neediness in her mother's voice. In fact, the woman was uncharacteristically calm. Kate knew to be cautious, yet began to relax with the safeguard of her father nearby.

"What do you hear from Les Madison?" her father asked.

"Funny you should ask. I haven't heard from him since last year's Christmas letter. But Becky showed up at my front door a few weeks ago."

"No!" Her mother chimed in with disbelief in her voice. "Why on earth?"

Kate shook her head. "I'm bewildered myself. Basically, I think she wants to be friends again."

"And you're up for that, after she dumped you?" asked her mother.

Kate shrugged. "Perhaps, I'm an easy touch. Her friendship meant a lot to me once. And she must feel something similar, or why would she have contacted me? If nothing else, her appearance has tapped my curiosity."

"I, for one, am glad," said her father. "You two were inseparable as kids. Friends like that are hard to come by."

"Thanks, Dad. I knew you'd understand."

Finding comfort in her father's good spirits, Kate leaned toward him and asked, "Speaking of old friends, what do you hear from Doc Swanson?" The polite query flagged a turn in their conversation. They all knew what Kate was really asking. And Kate assumed her father would respond with the same code phrase he always used to put her at ease until the next time she asked the same question.

Doc Swanson had delivered Kate and half of the neighborhood's children, including Les and Becky. He was one of those rare doctors who made house calls and kept in touch with the patients he had known since birth. More to the point, he had helped Kate through her closeted pregnancy during an era when unwed mothers were looked upon in shame. Because of the steps he had taken to protect Kate's reputation, Doc was the only source who could lead the child of that pregnancy back to Kate.

Worried looks passed between Kate's parents. Her father put his hand on his wife's knee as a signal to let him speak. She responded by leaving the two of them alone. The scar of Kate's unwanted pregnancy was an unfortunate sidebar in their family history, something her mother never discussed.

"There was a fire, Kate."

"Oh, no. When did this happen? Is Doc okay?"

"A week ago. He was hospitalized, but doing fine now. That tough son-of-a-gun wouldn't let a little thing like a fire keep him from his weekly poker game. Miraculously, he didn't suffer from any burns. Just smoke inhalation."

Kate sighed with relief. "Thank goodness he's okay. How bad was the fire?"

He looked into Kate's eyes as he spoke. "All of his records were destroyed. His entire building—gone."

"I see." Kate's heart fell into a cavernous pit and she struggled for breath. "If I understand you correctly, the paper trail linking me to an adopted child has literally gone up in smoke." She looked down to gather her thoughts. She had always imagined the child she had given away might want to find her someday. She and Doc thought they had a foolproof plan in place to accommodate a child's search for a biological mother.

"Kate, those papers were never a guarantee your child would come looking for you. You know that."

"I do. But the sad truth is, Dad, my need has grown more acute over the years, not less. Especially, since I can never have another child."

"I understand how your miscarriage has made this more difficult for you."

"Doc might have died in that fire. All those years ago, I never imagined anything happening to him.

"Doc isn't gone. He can still be of help if that day should come."

"But he won't be around forever." She put her hand on her forehead. "How stupid could I be? Don't you see? Without him, the paperwork means nothing anyway."

Her father reached over and took her hand. "You need to put it behind you, Katie. Doc found a wonderful family for your child. He promised you that."

"I know. I know." Kate offered the sliver of a smile, but her insides churned. The losses incurred by her two pregnancies enveloped her like the final curtain of a stage play one would never forget. She had often referred to her screenplay as her baby. Now, it truly was the only creation she would be allowed to nurture. There was little solace in this inanimate replacement for a living, breathing child.

The next morning, Kate and her mother lingered after breakfast in the sun-drenched kitchen, the scene of many conversations between them over the years. Though they had their differences, there were few secrets between them.

"I envy you, dear," said Kate's mother. "You're living a life of opportunities I never had."

"You've had a good life."

"I had you. Something I've been mostly proud of."

Kate smiled. It was all too clear to what her mother was referring. "Had I known then what I know now, I might have kept that baby."

"But you wouldn't be the success you are today."

"Did I tie you down, Mother?"

"Not at all. I worked on many charities, which your father and I still support today. I have my garden, my bridge group, and of course, all my dear friends."

Yes, thought Kate. Those were the friends her mother shielded from the shameful knowledge of her pregnancy years ago.

"Women of my generation were expected to have children, not a career. You were a groundbreaker, Kate. You rose through the ranks into jobs women never had before. You opened doors for all those who are following behind. Unfortunately, many women today believe they can have high-powered careers and children, and do them both justice." Her mother rested her elbow on the back of her chair, seemingly confident about what she was about to say. "I think the children of these 'super-moms' are being slighted. The civility of our culture will eventually suffer because of it. At least you didn't make that mistake."

"You're probably right about that." Kate ran her fingers casually through her silky hair. Her mother's conciliatory mood prompted Kate to believe she could safely broach the subject of Lily and Martin. Her need to talk about them had been gnawing at her for weeks.

Leaving as many details intact as she thought appropriate and neutralizing her emotions for Martin, Kate told her mother about meeting Lily and how Martin had asked for her help in uniting him with a daughter she never knew he had.

Her mother sipped her Earl Grey tea from her favorite porcelain tea cup. Listening. Expressionless.

Ignoring the absence of any visible signs of compassion from her mother, Kate continued her lengthy saga, all the while hoping for support from her mother. She talked about her first meeting with Lily and how she had ultimately invited Lily to stay with her and Parker. It wasn't until she told her mother of Lily's connection to Martin that Kate realized she had made a mistake.

Her mother's blank expression had shriveled into a prune-like scowl. Her mouth was pursed and her eyes squinted with disgust…not the sign of quiet sympathy or understanding for which Kate had hoped.

"So, now you're looking for someone else's daughter to fill the shoes of the one you gave away? Why do you think you can suddenly be a mother to this…this… What was her name? Lily. A perfect stranger."

"She's not a stranger. She's Martin's daughter, and I'm not trying to be her mother."

"But you welcomed her into your home and got her a job on your movie project. That is something a parent does. Katherine, I don't understand how you can invest so much energy in Martin's daughter.

You know better than to put yourself into the middle of other people's problems."

Kate winced from the criticism that always carried a painful sting when it came from her mother.

Her mother continued. "I always liked Martin. We got along very well. Maybe you should have married him in the first place, then you wouldn't live so far away from me."

"Mother, that's not a good reason to marry someone."

"Katherine, why are you so wrapped up in Martin and his daughter? Is there something going on between you and Martin?"

Caught naked, thought Kate. She should have known her mother would sense the resurgence of her primordial preoccupation with Martin.

"No. I'm not involved with Martin. I'm just helping him the way I would want to be helped. That's all."

"It doesn't seem like a smart idea to me. You could get hurt."

Kate threw back her head, then looked at her mother and sighed. "I'll be fine."

Her mother gave her a look of uncertainty, which made Kate feel more compelled than ever to help Martin.

By the time Kate arrived at Annabella's flat later that afternoon, she found a stack of messages waiting for her from David, which she expected, and one unexpected message from Martin.

Kate called David immediately. He had arrived in San Francisco over the weekend. One of his requests for Kate was to call Martin and confirm the arrangements for shooting at the Napa winery.

The mere suggestion of talking to Martin set her heart pounding with anticipation. She thought she would have moved beyond these nervous emotions by now, but apparently not. Kate gritted her teeth. She hadn't anticipated the need to deal with Martin so soon. She wanted time to plan a contingency of comebacks for every possible scenario he might throw at her. She decided to unpack and join

Annabella for a glass of wine first.

"So, you told your mother about your involvement with Lily and Martin. Awfully brave of you," observed Annabella.

"Stupid is a better word." Kate peered into her wine glass to hide from her thoughts. She suddenly looked up, as if prompted by a ripple in her wine. "As much as I'm enjoying this wine, it is only a diversion from the inevitable. I might as well call Martin and get it over with. I'm acting like a timid teenager. I'm an adult, so I might as well behave with the self-confidence and control I wish I possessed."

"Atta girl," Annabella encouraged. "Keep talking like that and you might start to believe it."

"Oh, shut up!" Kate snapped back with a laugh.

Kate retreated to her bedroom to make the call, her stomach knotted with nerves. She dialed the only phone number she had for Martin—his office number. It annoyed her that he hadn't given his home number to her. How typical of him to withhold that, she thought. She knew it was his way of maintaining control over when and if she could reach him, yet he thought nothing of having access to her at any time. Which brought another thought to mind. How did he know when she was arriving at Annabella's? Did he still have that private investigator tailing her?

Martin's phone rang several times before someone answered. "Mr. Kelly's office."

Kate recognized the officious female voice from her last conversation with Martin's secretary. "Mr. Kelly, please?" asked Kate, just as business-like.

"Mr. Kelly is not available at this time, may I take a message?"

"Please let him know Ms. Cochran returned his call."

"Ms. Cochran, Mr. Kelly asked me to see if the production schedule for your movie was available yet."

Kate relaxed. There would be no interaction with Martin today. "Actually, I'm not sure. Tomorrow is the company's first day in our San Francisco offices. I'll have someone messenger one over, if it's ready."

"He would appreciate that. Thank you for your help."

"You're welcome." Kate hung up the phone and rejoined Annabella in the living room. "Whew. That was easy." She sank into an overstuffed chair and reached for her wine.

"Let me guess. He wasn't there."

"Right." Kate laughed.

"Did you find out what he wanted?"

"The shooting schedule. I wonder why."

Annabella shrugged. "He probably wants to keep track of your whereabouts."

"Don't kid around, Annabella. This situation with Martin isn't an easy thing for me."

"I know, darling. I'm sorry. But seeing you all worked up like this brings back memories of the turmoil and trauma that used to surround your relationship with him before you married Parker. His having a daughter, well…"

"I'm not worked up. And there is no new interest on my part."

"Are you sure?"

Kate shielded her eyes from the sun that had begun to shine through the louver blinds. "No, I'm not sure. You're beginning to sound like my mother!"

Annabella walked across the room to shut the blinds for Kate, then turned and put her hands on her hips when she spoke. "Now that was a low blow."

"It was meant to be. You know something else that bothers me? How did Martin know I would be here?"

"I told him." Annabella poured them more wine, then stretched out on the sofa.

"You told him! Annabella! When did you talk to him?"

"He called last week and asked me when you were due back here."

"What else did he want to know?"

"That was it. I didn't see any problem in telling him since he does have some involvement in the film."

"I never should have let David talk me into asking Martin to help secure the winery."

"Kate, why are you so uncomfortable about all of this? Is there something going on between you and Martin you haven't told me about? Are you still in love with him? Is that it? Do you feel guilty about spending time with him?"

"I don't want to spend time with Martin."

"Kate, it's okay to spend time with an old friend. It doesn't mean you're going to sleep with him." She gave Kate a sideways glance. "Does it?"

"Of course not," Kate shot back, as if trying to convince herself as well.

"Maybe you do need to spend some time with him so you'll remember how he took you for granted and was downright neglectful of any relationship he pretended to have with you. At least, that's how it appeared from where I stood."

"Are you trying to rationalize the need for me to spend time with Martin?"

"My lips are sealed, Kate." Annabella put her thumb and forefinger to her pursed lips and twisted them before flicking the invisible key back over her shoulder. "You know you can trust me, no matter what you decide to do. I'm only suggesting that perhaps there is still some unfinished business between the two of you."

"You might be right, but seeing Martin makes me feel like I'm betraying Parker."

"If anything, it might be the best thing you can do for Parker. If a part of you still loves Martin, no matter how minute it may be, it'll get in your way. It's a portion of your heart you are withholding from Parker. Your wonderful husband deserves all you have to give. So, why not see Martin so you can do whatever is necessary to discard the old baggage?"

"So, Martin's just old trash, eh?"

"Like yesterday's news!"

"I don't know, Annabella."

Annabella dramatized her words with a thick European accent of indiscernible origin and held the back of her hand to her forehead for emphasis. "I've said all I'm going to say. Madam Herznegovia the Horrific Soothsayer is growing weary." Returning to her normal voice, she continued, "It is something you have to live with, not me. I just don't want to spend the next month screening all of your phone calls in case Martin calls here again."

"You're right. If I deal with this in a very straightforward manner, there should be nothing wrong with my associating with Martin, just like I'll be working with everyone else involved in the production," insisted Kate, searching for stable ground. She got up to leave the room. "I think I'd better call Parker and let him know I arrived safely at your place."

CHAPTER FIFTEEN

Monday morning, Kate drove down the eastern slope of Telegraph Hill to the flats, where railroad tracks once connected a grimy warehouse district to awaiting ships docked on the nearby wharfs edging San Francisco's bay. Today, a colorful community of refurbished buildings welcomed Kate with flowering window boxes and glass entry doors with polished brass fixtures and elegantly lettered signs. Somewhere in the middle of this neighborhood was a maze of cramped, windowless offices bursting with resourceful people ready to embark on the fanciful trip of movie making.

Black numbers two feet high identified the red brick warehouse Kate was seeking. All of the parking places were filled, so Kate drove around the building until she found a spot next to the loading dock where the indentation of railroad tracks could still be detected under the new pavement. Upon entering the building, Kate found herself in the middle of what might appear to be chaos, but to her trained eye, was actually a platoon of soldiers organizing for an invasion. This gathering of demanding, focused individuals was enthusiastically coordinating efforts to build sets, gather props, design costumes, order equipment…all discussing their needs and ideas at the same time to anyone who would listen.

Kate smiled at the bustling activity happening because she had written a screenplay. Not recognizing anyone, Kate headed for the only person who was stationary—a twenty-something girl handing out paperwork to newly arrived crewmembers while continuing to answer the phones and hook up her newly delivered computer equipment.

"Can you tell me where I can find David Backus?" Kate raised her voice over the din.

The girl answered Kate without looking up from the confusion of tangled computer cords. "He's down the hall, third office on the left. At least, that's where he was five minutes ago."

Kate continued, "By the way, are you the person who would messenger a production schedule to Martin Kelly?"

"I'll take care of it." The girl looked up at Kate with a reassuring smile.

Kate thanked her and began moving down the hall, hearing David before she saw him.

"Damn it! We've got to have that set built by next week if it's going to be our cover set. How many more carpenters do you need?"

Kate peeked her head around the edge of the doorway and directed a quizzical expression toward David to ask if she should come back another time. David was sitting at the far side of a large round table that filled the cramped room. Seeing Kate, he motioned for her to come in. Seven other people filled all of the chairs around the table except one. She recognized Ken Ferrer, the incorrigible location manager, and Mat Bloomberg, the veteran cinematographer. She assumed the youngest person in the room must be Jonas Waring. She quietly eased onto the empty chair next to David and listened while the set designer, Mark Harrington, assured David the set construction in question would be completed on time.

"Everyone, meet Kate Cochran, screenwriter extraordinaire and our co-producer," David announced to the group.

She spilled an easy smile across her face, hoping to hide her delight upon learning that David had taken up her offer to act as "co-producer." She thought he had invited her to this production meeting as an observer, but instead, she heard him tell the group about her responsibilities in working with the set designer and Ken Ferrer. She was to be an integral member of the design team to coordinate the overall look of the sets and locations. Kate listened with some embarrassment as David espoused her qualifications and how lucky they were to have the use of a writer who also had a successful career in production. She was more fascinated than anyone to hear about her duties as co-producer, but didn't want to let on that she, too, was hearing about her new job for the first time.

When the meeting was over, Kate patiently waited for the hangers-on to finish their conversations with David and leave the room. Then, like a schoolteacher reprimanding a student, Kate took hold of David's earlobe between her thumb and forefinger and pinned him to a corner of the room where she moved him against the wall so he couldn't evade her. "David, what was that all about?"

"What? You mean your co-producer job?"

She knew he was needling her and persisted with her own question. "Why didn't you discuss the details with me first?"

"I did."

She shook her head. "You did not!"

"Just weeks ago, you asked if you could help with any of the production details. I believe I told you then that I thought it was an interesting idea. Now, if you don't want the job..." he teased.

"You know I do."

"I figured you'd get bored just standing around every day with nothing better to do than pick on me. Our meetings and discussions over the past few weeks confirmed my decision. You brought up too many suggestions I hadn't thought about yet. So, we might as well channel your thoughts in a direction that will make constructive use of your talents. And by the way, I've already talked to your agent and he's drawing up a contract that includes compensation for both of your jobs. You know, Kate, you really should keep in better contact with him, even if you're not motivated by money."

"Yes, you're right. Especially since my agent is your agent. I hope there won't be a conflict of interest." She knew the smile on her face was sarcastic.

David replied using his best Bogart imitation. "You can count on it, sweetheart. And Kate, try to keep your ideas within our budget."

Kate let David move away from the wall as she gathered her notes from the table. "Don't worry. And besides, I know why you're doing this for me. I promise I'll stay out of your way."

"Kate, don't misunderstand me. I really want you to be closely involved with the look of this movie. So please, do work your magic."

A very grateful Kate kissed David smack on the lips. "Thank you."

"You're welcome. But watch the kissing stuff, it could be misconstrued as sexual harassment." He winked at her before he walked from the room, leaving Kate alone to absorb the thought of her new responsibilities. Her moment of introspection lasted only a few seconds.

"Kate, can I have a word?" Jonas had entered the room when Kate's back was to the door. Startled by the voice breaking through her thoughts, she jumped slightly.

"Jonas. What is it?" She immediately regretted the edge to her voice.

"I didn't mean to startle you. Are you still upset with me?" He sounded cautious.

"Oh, Jonas. If you only knew what a rage your phone call sent me into. Your timing couldn't have been worse. No. I'm not upset anymore." She smiled. "I hear the rehearsals went very well."

"Yes, I think they'll bring better performances from our actors and more depth to your characters."

"I'm glad."

"And I'm glad you're not mad at me anymore. I've got a couple of things I would like to go over with you to make sure we're all in sync. Would this be a good time?"

"Sure."

Jonas led Kate down the hall to a closet-sized work space he had commandeered for the day. Before Kate turned to follow Jonas into his office, she and Lily spotted each other at opposite ends of the hallway. Kate waved to her and was about to call out her name when Lily put her index finger to her lips to signal Kate's silence. Kate gave Lily a quizzical look, but said nothing and squeezed into Jonas's office. She would have plenty of time to talk to Lily later.

Kate looked for Lily after her meeting with Jonas, but couldn't find her. Finally, she approached the efficient young production secretary, who now had her computer up and running, and asked if the girl had seen Lily.

"She left to deliver a production schedule to Martin Kelly's office," explained the secretary.

"She what?" shouted Kate. Just then, David came down the hall from his office. Kate turned to him and tried to sound more controlled as she asked, "Why was Lily sent to deliver Martin Kelly's production schedule? I thought it would be messengered over to him."

"What's the problem? Lily is our production assistant. That's what she does—pick up and deliver things, run errands, make coffee."

Kate apologized to the production secretary for yelling at her and walked away from David with no explanation for her outburst. How stupid of me, thought Kate. Of course Lily would be the one to deliver a script to Martin.

She was wild with concern and a complete feeling of helplessness. Martin wanted a choreographed meeting with Lily. Not an unexpected appearance. There was nothing Kate could do but let fate take its course. Still, she worried that none of this was fair to Lily. She blamed herself for the booby-trap she had unwittingly set for the unsuspecting girl. Kate felt she had betrayed their friendship by not telling Lily about Martin beforehand, and worried that Lily would never forgive her.

Kate's mind whirled. She was oblivious to the bustle of activity around her.

Suddenly, she was furious with Martin for drawing her into his conspiracy by telling her about Lily in the first place. It was an untenable, awkward situation that wasn't of Kate's making. She looked for a phone to call Martin, to warn him. Of what? To behave? To pretend he didn't know whom Lily was? To pull Lily into his arms and confess that he's her long-lost father? To lie about Kate knowing Martin is her father? Oh, hell! What difference did it make? Lily wasn't her daughter. She'd only known the young woman for a few weeks.

Kate was becoming the guardian of Lily's happiness. She knew it was presumptuous, but she was drawn to the girl. Perhaps her mother was right...Kate had claimed Lily for the daughter she would never have.

Maybe it was a good thing that father and daughter were thrown together like this. After all, it was inevitable the two would meet. Kate just hadn't thought it would happen on Lily's first day in San Francisco.

Kate hadn't prepared herself for this scenario. In fact, she realized the only thing she had been worried about was her own relationship with Martin, not Lily's at all. Martin did have her mesmerized, but this incident was helping to put a new perspective on the real reason Martin was back in her life. It was because of Lily, not to rekindle his love for Kate.

She was such a fool. Suckered in again by his charm and charisma. Annabella was right, she did have to clear her mind of Martin Kelly's cobwebs.

An emptiness settled in her stomach.

Unable to find a parking space near Martin Kelly's office building, Lily pulled the production company's staff car into a yellow loading zone and placed the Zuni Productions delivery placard on the dashboard. The transportation captain had insisted the placard would save her from any tickets or towing, so she decided to trust his theory.

She dashed across the sprawling white marble plaza, squinting against the blinding bounce of reflecting sunlight, barely dodging a small group of office workers hidden in the brilliant glare. After reaching the building, she burst through one of the tall glass doors into a three-story terrarium of jungle-dense growth that dominated the lobby's periphery.

Lily slowed her pace to mark time with other pedestrians heading to the elevators in the center of the building. Her blue jeans, green Nike cross-trainers and bright red blazer quarreled with the subdued, tailored business attire surrounding her. She smiled when she said, "Penthouse, please," to a gentleman pushing floor buttons for other passengers.

She was the only person left on the elevator when the doors opened onto a dimly lit, long and narrow foyer. Two mammoth, flower-filled urns perched on matching pedestals flanked a splashy modern painting hanging on the wall facing her. Stepping off the elevator, Lily took a deep breath to gather herself and along with it, she inhaled a deep whiff of the aromatic flowers.

An embarrassing fit of allergic sneezing shook her. She pulled out a Kleenex to blow her tickled nose and walked toward the bright sunlight at the end of the foyer. After passing another elevator marked "Private," she rounded the corner into a spacious marble-floored room with a broad expanse of wraparound windows, much like an observation deck on a ship. "Oh my gosh," she uttered quietly to herself, overtaken by the seamless birds-eye view of the sparkling white city and the sweeping blue of San Francisco Bay.

"Beautiful view, isn't it?"

Lily turned to find the source of the deep, melodious, voice. A finely dressed, heavy-set black woman, whom Lily hadn't noticed upon entering the area, rose from a nearby desk.

"Yes, it is," said Lily.

"That's why I like working here." The woman continued talking as she walked over to Lily. "There's no better view in the city." She was at once warm and motherly, comforting Lily with an easy nature that made the girl feel like she belonged in these elegant surroundings instead of on a playground, as her clothes suggested. After pointing out some of her favorite sights, the woman asked Lily if she could help her find someone.

Lily explained her mission and that she was looking for Mr. Kelly's office. The woman ushered Lily into a private elevator and inserted a key into a slot in the foyer's mahogany paneling that closed the elevator doors on Lily. Not feeling any movement, she wasn't sure she had gone anywhere when the doors reopened. She was looking at the same view, but through a bank of French doors. They opened onto a landscaped terrace with gravel walkways lined with miniature English-style hedges meandering through a garden splashed with zinnias, pansies, marigolds, flowering bushes and an ivy topiary of the Golden Gate Bridge. A tall hedge blocked Lily's full view of a bronze sculpture of three graceful dolphins frolicking through a burst of fountain spray. She made a mental note to avoid the terrace for fear of setting off another allergy attack.

This time, Lily found the secretary before the secretary found her. "I'm looking for Mr. Kelly's office."

"This is his office." The woman enunciated with a raised eyebrow and a watchful eye, as if questioning the appropriateness of Lily's presence in her elite corporate realm.

Lily ignored the woman's arrogance. "I'm from Zuni Productions. I have a production schedule for Mr. Kelly."

The woman toned down her uppity attitude. "Thank you very much. I'll see he gets it."

"I wonder if I might say hello to Mr. Kelly?"

"Is that necessary?"

Lily shrugged. "Our production secretary told me he will be helping us with the movie. I thought it would be nice to meet him now, since I'm here."

"I'm afraid Mr. Kelly isn't expected back in the office for another hour."

Lily thought about lingering in the serenity of this idyllic office with its understated elegance, art-lined walls and unlimited view, but remembered her car and knew she couldn't leave it too long in the yellow zone. She handed the envelope to the woman and left.

"Kate. Kate?"

The voice broke through the mist of Kate's foggy consciousness, snapping her back into the present. Kate was surprised to find herself standing alone in a corner of the production office and wondered how long she had been staring into space.

"What?" asked Kate, coming out of her trance-like state. She turned to see a beaming Lily standing beside her. "Lily!" Kate froze in place, waiting for a reaction from the girl to give her some clue as to what had transpired at Martin's office.

Lily hugged Kate, so Kate hugged her back, feeling some sense of relief.

"Boy, were you deep in thought."

"Yes, I guess I was. How are you?" Kate heard the concern in her own voice and tried to gather her composure.

"I'm having so much fun. You will not guess where I have been."

Kate swallowed hard and braced for what she was about to hear. "Where?" she asked, trying to maintain her equilibrium.

Lily dove into the details of delivering a production schedule to the most gorgeous office she had ever seen. She gushed to Kate about the rapturous view and the English sculpture garden, and how she never imagined such an office was possible. Throughout Lily's animated description, Kate tried to picture Martin in this setting.

"I wonder what kind of person has an office like that," finished Lily, dreamily.

"Then you didn't meet Mr. Kelly?"

"No."

Kate rolled her eyes toward the ceiling in relief.

"Kate, before you drift off again, I have a favor to ask". Don't tell Jonas that you got me my job. Okay?"

"Okay. But why?"

The light in Lily's eyes was still glowing. "It's a silly game we're playing. He wants to know how I got my job, and I won't tell him."

Kate laughed, thankful for Lily's good spirits. But her relief was temporary. She knew she would be hearing from Martin sooner than she'd originally expected.

CHAPTER SIXTEEN

Martin Kelly, weary from a long negotiating session with a ruthless adversary, pulled his martini-beige Jaguar into his private basement parking space in the Kitty Murphy Building on Montgomery Street. He had dreaded the confrontation with Maxwell Bedford for weeks. The man could get nasty when he was being outgunned in a lucrative business deal. At stake was prime development property on the outskirts of Santa Rosa. Though Martin might have felt exuberant for handily winning round one, he knew Bedford's lawyers would be hard at work preparing new stumbling blocks to unnerve him in the next round.

When Martin pressed the elevator button for the penthouse, he was undecided about whether he was headed for his office or the apartment he kept for himself adjacent to the sculpture garden. When he stepped off the private elevator, habit carried him to his office. He raised his hand to his secretary, Donna, signaling silence as much as a greeting as he walked by her desk and into the sanctuary of his corner suite. He dropped his coat and briefcase on the leather couch and sank into his desk chair, swiveling his back to the desk to find a moment of peace in the empty sky beyond his office windows. He didn't see the buildings climbing the San Francisco hills, or the lurking fog entwining its tentacles around the base of the Sutro Tower. Nor did he hear the mounting noise of five o'clock traffic clogging the narrow streets far below.

After allowing himself only a few lost moments, Martin picked up his phone to call Bethel, his partner. No answer. He tried two other numbers and still couldn't locate her.

A haphazard pairing aligning two strangers in a scavenger hunt at a long-forgotten party had unwittingly led Martin and Bethel, an unlikely pair, into a twenty-year business partnership. Awed by each other's ingenuity for finding and securing impossible items on their scavenger list, Martin and Bethel decided they should put their skills together in business.

What started out as a joke, proved to be a most satisfying, profitable, long-term working relationship and mutual admiration society. They could read each other's thoughts and rarely had to finish a sentence when they were together, which saved them a lot of time in meetings, yet baffled those around them, who often had to have things explained later. Together, their passion for developing prospective business deals was so electric, a friend once misconstrued their relationship as a romance. They laughed at the improbable concept. Why would anyone want to ruin a successful business relationship with sex?

In their personal lives, Martin and Bethel were light years apart. Unlike Martin's freewheeling single life with no commitments, Bethel's earth mother sensibilities had graced her with the love of one man, three children and one grandchild. Her husband, a retired high school teacher with a PhD, who now wrote textbooks, completely understood his wife's appetite for business. He loved her dearly and tolerated Martin's late night business calls.

Martin turned to see his secretary standing in the doorway. "Donna, would you please find Bethel for me? She's disappeared again."

She gave Martin a knowing smile. "I think she's filling in for Vicki this time."

"Well, please find someone else to replace Vicki for awhile." Martin was exasperated, but appreciative of his partner's kindheartedness. He also knew filling in for Vicki on the lower level of their penthouse offices was Bethel's favorite respite and a great excuse for her to spend the day staring out the window. Bethel called it her creative time.

When the gentle woman with the melodious voice finally walked into his office, Martin just shook his head. "Goldbricking again,

Bethel?"

"Just escaping for a few hours. I didn't notice when you came in, or I would have been up here sooner." She relaxed in the leather chair across the room from Martin's desk. "Before we get bogged down about your meeting with Maxwell Bedford, I think you should know that you had a visitor today."

"Donna didn't tell me anyone was here."

"Donna didn't know the significance of a certain delivery person."

"Donna knows better than to bother me with unnecessary details. Get to the point, Bethel." Martin was irritable and too tired for a guessing game.

"This was a delivery girl"—she paused—"from Zuni Productions."

Martin pulled himself up from his slouched position as if the delivery girl had just walked into the room. His eyes darted around his office for any signs she might have left behind. "Lily? Was it Lily? Did you see her?"

"Yes. And yes."

"How did you know it was her?"

Bethel remained very calm in contrast to Martin's sudden anxiousness. "I knew it was Lily the minute I saw her. She has your coloring, your blue eyes and your mouth. Fortunately, she doesn't have your ears."

"Don't kid with me, Bethel. I can't believe I wasn't here. Did Donna know who she was?"

"Of course not. Miss Perfect hasn't a clue about anything around here except the details of your business needs."

"Bethel, lay off Donna. Without her, I couldn't function."

"No, she just makes you think that's the case."

Martin ignored Bethel's jab. "So what was she like?"

"Martin, I'm only going to say this one more time. If you really want to know what your daughter is all about, then it's time for you to arrange a meeting with her. You have spent her entire life learning about her from other people. I refuse to be one of those people. She deserves more."

"You're right, as usual. I have a plan. In a few weeks, or even days, I will meet my daughter face to face. Which is one of the things I need to talk about with you. I'm going to hang around the set while they're shooting at White Oaks. So I'll be away from the office a number of days in the next few weeks or so."

She folded her arms across her chest. "So, what's your plan?"

Martin got out of his chair and began to pace behind his desk, his mind racing to formulate a plot that would pass muster with Bethel. He looked out the window as he spoke so he wouldn't have to see the disappointed expression on her face. "All right, here's the deal. I need to bring you up to speed about my meeting with Maxwell Bedford. You were right, it was best you weren't there today. Your presence at the next meeting will be much more effective. We won today's round, hands down, but I think Bedford's got something up his sleeve he's saving for another day. I'll have Donna type up my summary of the points we discussed today."

"Martin," she interrupted. "I'm not talking about your plans for Bedford. I know that deal will eventually go our way. Stop changing the subject."

Martin turned back toward Bethel and mindlessly fiddled with some pencils on his desk. "I'm getting to that part." He sighed and fell into his chair. "The timing really couldn't be better. I've done all I can until you ply your talents with Bedford's goony lawyers. And based on the nasty mood I left him in, Bedford's going to drag this on for several weeks, at least. So that gives me time to spend on the set."

"I think I'm getting the picture. My turn to work while you hang out with the Hollywood crowd."

"Right."

"Maybe the leading man will get sick, and they'll notice you standing in the wings and call upon you to take over and save the movie!"

"Very funny."

"So that's your plan?"

"That's it."

"What do you mean, that's it? Are you just going to hang around and watch Lily as she does whatever it is she does on the set?"

"For awhile, yeah. Besides, they might need my help around White Oaks."

"Oh, Martin, you're so dense sometimes."

"I've got help. Kate is going to help me."

"Kate Cochran? Martin, you didn't drag her into this." Bethel was well aware of the history between Kate and Martin. Over the years, she and Kate had become close friends. After Kate and Parker married, Bethel let it be known to Martin that he had let the best woman he'd ever met get away from him.

"Please don't start with me. I have my reasons."

Bethel threw her arms up in resignation. "You're right. There's no need for me to get in the middle of this." She marched across the room and leaned over Martin's desk to make her point. "I know this situation with Lily has been an unsettling part of your life. The fact that it may finally be coming together for you is exciting. But you need to be careful. This reunion could change people's lives. There's bound to be some pain and disappointment lurking in the wings, and it could be your pain as much as anyone else's. It could all collapse around you."

"I know. And I appreciate your concern. I'm more anxious and nervous about this than any business deal I've ever worked on. Maybe by eliminating some of my business distractions, I will think more clearly about what to do about Lily...so I don't make a mess of things."

Bethel answered with an ambivalent smile.

Martin knew that look all too well. She had always been more than generous in praising his business acumen, but often reminded him that he deceived only himself with his well-intended innuendos about marrying the appealing woman who currently accompanied his tuxedo on high-profile occasions and shared his rare weekend retreats to Palm Springs. Bethel claimed he was afraid of intimacy and being rejected.

After years of being single, even Martin did not know what he was waiting for anymore, and conveniently blamed Bethel for his marital status. He claimed she had spoiled him from loving anyone else because she was the only woman he could talk with for hours about land development deals, building costs, environmental impact studies or even sports, without having to discuss his feelings or personal needs. And Bethel usually obliged him by never pressuring him about anything but business.

Until recently, Martin's business had been a convenient escape from the reality of his aloneness. On those rare occasions when he thought of anything else, he had confined himself to memories…happy ones. He tried to focus on the sweet-smelling wisteria outside his parents' bedroom window, but not his parent's constant bickering that ended only when his father left for work each morning. He remembered the drops of sweat spotting his driveway during a game of one-on-one hoops with his dad, but not the times his dad called him a loser for getting bad grades or for failing to take out the garbage. He remembered the freshly cut grass on a newly sodded football field, the resounding crack of crunching helmets and plastic-padded bodies scrambling to snatch a fumbled football, but not the searing pain of ruptured ligaments that ultimately shattered his lifelong dream to play pro football. He remembered the freckles on Kate's nose that popped out after spending a day at the beach, but not the times he canceled their dates at the last minute. And not the day he learned she was marrying another man.

And now, he was allowing wishful thinking to diminish the terrifying possibility Lily could reject him. He was her father. She was his flesh and blood. He believed their reunion could only have a rewarding ending.

Kate walked into Annabella's flat just as the answering machine picked up the phone. When she heard Martin's voice, she darted to pick up the receiver. "Martin, hold on while I turn off the recorder."

Their conversation was filled with cordial niceties about Kate's drive from Colorado and the health of her parents. But underneath was a sense of immediacy on both of their parts. They agreed to meet at the Marina in half an hour, dressed for running.

Kate arrived before Martin. She found an empty station on the par three exercise course and began to stretch.

The park was filling with after-work business people eager to unwind with their individual exercise regimens. A few sailboats dotted the bay, holding their own against the incoming tide, while a slippery fog prowled outside the Golden Gate Bridge, waiting to consume what remained of the warm summer day. Kate spotted Martin walking toward her dressed in a tattered gray sweatshirt, maroon shorts and a fairly new pair of running shoes. He's really come for a workout, she thought. It was good to see him like this. She smiled as he approached.

"Want to run for awhile?" he asked.

Their best times together had often involved vigorous sporting activities. That's when they were the most relaxed and the happiest.

"Come on," he urged her, and they were off.

She easily matched his pace and in so doing, felt the mental stress of her day begin to dissipate. They ran along a narrow dirt path where lush grass had once flourished before the daily stream of joggers usurped the strip to save their legs from pounding the unforgiving sidewalk. Sometimes Kate ran behind Martin to let oncoming runners pass by them.

After a short time, the freedom of running allowed them to relax into the steady rhythm of their breathing. Martin picked up his pace, and Kate stayed with him. She could see the sculptured dome of the Palace of Fine Arts in the distance. Accustomed to running at seven thousand feet in Colorado, she felt she could run forever at sea level. Martin waited for a break in traffic before leading them across the street, where they continued to run on the sidewalk. Kate felt her muscles loosen and her strides become easier and longer.

They reached the grounds of the Palace of Fine Arts, and Kate thought Martin would stop, but he kept running through the colonnades toward the center of the artful dome and around to the open lagoon. She was getting out of breath and walked for a short time until she saw him heading back toward her. Kate started running again to get a head start on their return.

When he caught up with her, they ran shoulder-to-shoulder, energy pulsing between them. About two hundred yards from where their cars were parked, Kate took off in a full sprint, expecting Martin to do the same.

Near her car, Kate was bent over with hands resting on her knees when Martin finally jogged up along side of her. "Nice job. That was an impressive sprint."

She stood and laughed, trying not to breathe too hard. "Thanks."

Martin brushed a wisp of Kate's hair away from her face.

Their eyes met. Kate reached up to touch the hair he had swept aside.

"Thanks for meeting me here," he said. "I've got to go back to the office to finish up some work. But after tonight, I will have some breathing space in my schedule. I want this situation with Lily to be my first priority. After what happened today, I understand the need for some planning. Did you know she came by my office?"

"Yes. It totally unnerved me." Kate rested her hands on her hips while stretching side to side.

"Me, too. It made me realize I'm not ready for a chance meeting. I'd like to work out some sort of strategy. At least, that's what Bethel preached to me today."

"Dear Bethel. She always knows what's best, even if we never did. How is she?"

"Just as wise as always. She misses you."

"I miss her, too. Please send her my love. So, what's your strategy with Lily?"

"I don't know, Kate. I need your help. That much I do know. Could we get together tomorrow sometime to talk about it?"

Kate was puzzled. "What's wrong with talking now? You sounded so anxious on the phone."

He grimaced. "I know. But the run helped calm me down. I'll be able to focus on Lily better after I tie up some loose ends at the office."

Kate shook her head, annoyed. "Always business."

"Tomorrow will be different, I promise."

Kate rolled her eyes. "I have no idea if I'll have time tomorrow." She explained to Martin that her job as writer had been expanded to co-producer, adding new responsibilities to what used to be a light workload.

"That's a good thing, isn't it?"

"Yes." She smiled. "But it means I'll have to call you in the morning when I know my schedule."

"You won't forget?"

"I won't."

"You promise?"

How ironic. He was prodding her not to forget a commitment, when it was he who had reneged on promises in the past. "Martin, I promise." She was growing impatient with his childishness. The dialogue was the same as fifteen years ago, except now, she didn't adore him for it. She was irritated.

CHAPTER SEVENTEEN

The next morning, set designer Mark Harrington pressed Kate to spend the day scouting White Oaks with him. Knowing they would need Martin to gain access to the property, Kate called him and arranged for him to meet them there. As representative of the property's ownership, he had the authority to oversee the owners' interests, answer questions and set parameters for use of the existing buildings and vineyards the production company requested for filming.

Martin was a legitimate participant in the production, necessitating his presence on the set where Lily worked. There was no need for trumped up pretenses. How dense could she and Martin be, thought Kate. Why hadn't they realized this earlier?

Kate drove up to White Oaks with Mark, Mark's set decorator and the construction coordinator. The three men had worked together for almost fifteen years on countless films. When it became clear that Kate understood the working rhythm of the men's tight nucleus, they readily fell into conversation with her over the work that lay ahead.

Martin was waiting when they arrived at the decaying, yet grandiose, vineyard gate. The group spent the next two hours walking the property, taking pictures and measurements, and reformulating their initial plans to better incorporate the ambiance of the natural setting. Having read the script the night before, Martin better understood their needs. He suggested they use the interior of the house and barn to save on construction costs. The other men jumped at this opportunity.

Kate was grateful for Martin's generosity, even though she believed he had no idea how many nicks and scrapes would result from the filming. On the other hand, the house was in such a state of disrepair, some modifications might be necessary to improve the house for filming. She made a note to be sure the location agreement covered any possible damages that might occur from the project.

Once they had scoured every gully and dusty knothole on the property, it became apparent Kate and Martin were extraneous baggage. After awhile, Mark suggested that he and Kate drive back into the city while the crew finished up on their own.

After leaving Mark with a key to the front gate, Martin led Kate to his car. "How about lunch?" he asked her.

"Sounds great. I'm starved."

Kate assumed they would eat somewhere nearby. Instead, Martin headed north to Santa Rosa and asked if she felt like seafood. Without much thought as to what he had in mind, she agreed to seafood.

After they had bypassed Santa Rosa and reached the outskirts of Sebastopol, she looked at him suspiciously. "Are you lost?"

"Nope," he answered, winding his way through a hilly residential area into a dark valley of towering redwood trees and rustic summer cottages. He continued driving through the tiny village of Occidental and onto a one-lane road that crept through the damp forest until it reached the sunny ridge above the valley.

"Isn't this a little out of our way for lunch? Where are we?"

"You'll see."

Leaving the redwoods behind, they drove onto a sweeping ridge of rolling pastures with closely cropped grass. Kate discovered the reason for the short grass when they crested a knoll and watched as a man and two Australian shepherd dogs herded sheep across the road into another pasture.

"Where are we?" she asked again.

"God's country."

"This is beautiful. I had no idea anything like this existed around here."

A few more miles of the single lane road took them to the edge of a bluff, hundreds of feet above the coast highway and the Pacific Ocean rolling into the horizon. Kate lost herself in the majesty of the view until Martin turned into a driveway leading to a quaint, two-story Victorian. Though the house had been given a gingerbread facelift of brightly colored blues and corals, and the dirt parking area was now paved and lined with wine barrels of fresh blooming daisies, there was no mistaking the roadhouse where he had taken her for dinner more than twenty years earlier. Back then, they had driven up the coast highway to find the restaurant.

Martin parked the car and rested his arms on the steering wheel. "Recognize this place?" he asked her with pleasure in his voice. "New owners and a gourmet menu instead of the greasy spoon we first went to, but the same magnificent view!"

Kate tried to overcome a sudden wave of anxiety rising inside her like an onrushing tsunami as her thoughts propelled her into the past. She certainly did remember this place. It had been the summer before her first year in grad school. Martin had been visiting his fraternity brother and Kate's next-door neighbor, Les Madison. Les had introduced them at a neighbor's swimming party. During the rest of his two-week stay with Les, Martin had spent at least half of his time with Kate. He had taken her to the roadhouse his last night in town for a brave plunge into a devilish fish stew—fish tails included—and two bottles of wine.

Afterward, Martin had driven Kate down from their high perch on the bluff for a stroll on the deserted beach and a closer look at the moon's silvery trail glistening across the ocean's surface. The intoxicating pleasure of consuming their exotic dinner, the relaxing influence of the local wine and his strong masculine presence enveloped her with an euphoric sense of security she had not felt before. When he took her in his arms, she let opportunity prevail. They made love on the sandy beach as the calming surge of breaking waves carried her sensibilities out to sea. He left the next day, and a few weeks later, she was packing for grad school.

Kate wanted to abandon her memories before they tugged her deeper into the abyss where secrets still lingered from that intoxicating night of pleasure. She turned to Martin and hoped for strength to calm her senses as she responded to his question. "Yes, I remember this place. I didn't realize you were so sentimental."

"When it comes to you, there is very little of which I'm not sentimental. I'm only sorry we didn't meet again until three years after that summer."

"But you let me get away a second time."

"What is it with you women?" He laughed. "Just yesterday, Bethel reminded me you were the best thing that ever happened to me, besides having her as a partner, of course. Then, she reprimanded me for letting you get away."

"She's right, you know."

They left it at that and went in to have lunch.

Over crab salads and iced tea, they talked about Lily and how he might meet her. They agreed that while it would be easy to explain his presence at White Oaks, he wasn't scheduled to be there until the second week of production. Martin didn't want to wait that long.

Kate suggested a dinner party at Annabella's.

"Too stiff."

They threw out more ideas until Martin finally hit on one. "Golf. We all like golf. Bring her out to the Olympic Club. I'm a member. If she's as much of a golfer as I understand, she may jump at the chance to play the course. We've hosted a few U.S. Opens, you know."

"You don't have to convince me about the privilege of playing at Olympic. It's on Parker's top-ten list of dream courses he hopes to play someday."

"Okay. It's decided."

Kate sighed, relieved to settle on anything at this point.

Martin began to embellish on his plan. "It should be your idea to include Lily. Make it look like someone else dropped out, and she's a substitute."

Kate held up her hand to stop him. "Let's not make this more complicated than it is already. I'll simply ask her if she wants to play golf with us, period."

He agreed and suggested they all meet for brunch before their tee time, to which Kate agreed.

Martin folded his arms over his chest. "After this initial meeting with Lily, things will develop naturally without you as the go-between."

So it was all worked out. A shiver ran down Kate's spine.

That night, during a phone call with Parker, Kate let it slip she might be playing golf at the Olympic Club on Sunday. Without hesitation, he leaped at the opportunity to fly out and join her.

Kate scrambled for an out. "I think we already have a foursome. Besides, who will take care of Rusty?" With a shameful wince, she took a long, ragged breath to steady herself. "I'll try to set something up for you on another weekend."

"Is golf at the Olympic Club one of the perks of being a writer?"

"No. It's because I'm the co-producer of *Love Among the Vineyards*." She was pleased to surprise Parker with her news and eager to avoid further details about her scheduled day of golf.

"Co-producer! That's wonderful! David is a more astute businessman than I thought."

Kate delighted in Parker's compliment. "So, you see, I'm not just another extraneous person they have to feed at lunch!"

"You never were."

Before they hung up, Parker told Kate that Becky Madison had called, wanting Kate's phone number in San Francisco. He warned Kate about a sense of urgency he heard in Becky's request.

Kate assured Parker there was nothing to it and told him she had, in fact, suggested Becky come to San Francisco to be an extra in her movie. "I made the offer never expecting her to take me up on it. Maybe she's decided it would be fun after all. Did you give her Bella's number?"

"Yes. I hope that was okay."

"It's fine. I already sent it to her in one of my earlier letters. I guess she must have lost it or something."

"Or something." He paused. "It's like she has a split personality, Kate. One minute she was very solemn and the next she was a gossipy, chatty Cathy, asking about Rusty and our wildflowers, the rock garden and my golf game. And she asked about Lily, though not by name."

Kate couldn't remember whether she had told Becky about Lily in one of her letters or not, but assumed she must have. "She can be odd," was the best explanation Kate could offer. "Thanks for letting me know, darling. I love you."

He responded in kind, and they hung up.

"Golf at the Olympic Club," proclaimed Lily with enough enthusiasm to practically knock herself over backwards in her chair. "Totally fabulous."

"I assume that's a yes," said Kate in a moderate voice, trying to downplay the invitation. She looked around the production office to see if anyone heard Lily's outburst, then pulled her chair closer to Lily's desk so they could speak more quietly.

"Definitely. Yes. My grandfather told me a feast of golfing lore when I was little. But his favorite story was his eyewitness account of the 1955 U.S. Open at the Olympic Club. Jack Fleck beat Ben Hogan in an eighteen hole playoff."

"I didn't know that."

"Not many people do. My grandfather loved that course and always dreamed of teeing it up there. Now I will get to play it for him. I practically know the layout of every hole without ever having seen it."

Lily politely asked Kate about the other players in their foursome, but it was clear to Kate that Lily wouldn't have cared if they were playing with the King of Siam or a beggar from India.

"Martin Kelly is our host," said Kate.

Lily looked at her with a blank expression.

"You delivered a production schedule to his office earlier this week."

"Oh yeah, the one with the gorgeous office." Her eyes lit up. "Is that why I'm invited to play golf?"

Kate offered a vague response to avoid lying. "Just be thankful you're getting to play."

Lily shrugged and seemed to take the invitation at face value.

Kate rose and patted Lily on her back. "It will be fun to spend the day together."

"I'm very glad of that," agreed Lily. "We've both been pretty busy lately."

On her way out of the office, Kate literally bumped into Jonas. "Umph."

Jonas instinctively reached out to steady Kate. "Are you okay?"

Kate laughed. "Yes, thanks." She started to continue on her way, but hesitated. "Jonas, how would you like to join Lily McGuire and me for golf on Sunday?"

The spontaneous invitation flew out of Kate's mouth. She didn't even know if he played golf. She'd been searching her mind for a possible foil to offset a potentially awkward day and to take the pressure away from her role in the forthcoming match up. Why not Jonas?

"I'm flattered by your invitation. Unfortunately, I've got meetings with David and the actors who are arriving on Sunday." He shrugged. "Besides, I don't play golf."

"Oh."

Jonas tipped his head sideways and leaned slightly toward Kate. "Did Lily put you up to this?"

"Afraid not. It was my idea."

CHAPTER EIGHTEEN

Kate picked up Lily at the Embassy Suites in plenty of time to meet Martin for brunch before golf. Lily's nervous excitement about playing the famous course was contagious. While the younger woman wiggled restlessly in her seat, Kate whistled nonsensical tunes that jived with Lily's movements. They teased each other about topping their first tee shots into the trees while everyone in the clubhouse was watching and wondering who had let them on the course.

Lily rolled her excitement into a rapid monologue based on what her grandfather had told her about how to play the course. "And then there's the dog leg right, but watch out for the water on the left and the sand trap in front of the narrow green. Fleck flew that green, but chipped within ten inches to save par. On the next hole, the cypress tree midway down the left rough will catch a hook every time, so aim right like Hogan did, unless you have a tendency to fade your drive, then you might strengthen your grip and…"

"Lily, stop." Kate tried to control her laughter. "You'll have me so confused I won't know how to hold a golf club on the first tee, let alone hit the ball more than two feet."

They both laughed.

"Sorry. I'm just…"

"Nervous? I noticed." Kate was nervous too, but more for Martin than herself. She knew he must be on edge about meeting his daughter for the first time. She was glad she had not dragged Jonas along.

Late in the week, Kate had tried to back out of Martin's golf outing. His scheme was misguided—a mere trick on Lily, she had insisted.

"What kind of friend am I to either one of you for going along with this? A Benedict Arnold, that's who."

"You're overdramatizing," was Martin's comment.

Thinking he might be right, and seeing Martin's utter dismay at the possibility of losing her support, Kate caved. Martin tried to boost Kate's courage with the assurance he would not allow Lily to blame her for the role she was playing in connecting father and daughter.

Martin had a fitful sleep on the eve of his meeting with Lily and finally got out of bed at four o'clock in the morning. He went running at first light, then tried to distract himself by reading the Sunday *Chronicle*. When that failed, he tried watching the Sunday morning parade of talk show pundits. Eventually, he showered and drove over to the course, still two hours before Lily and Kate were scheduled to meet him.

Killing time on the driving range, he mindlessly hit practice balls that seemed to stare back at him in defiance of his attempts to perform the normal, rhythmic swing that had rewarded him with a respectable, single-digit handicap. Instead, he sliced the irons and hooked his driver.

On the putting green, he chatted and laughed aimlessly with fellow members. Finally, he worked his way to the front steps of the clubhouse and paced back and forth, searching for Kate and Lily in every car that drove through the entry gate.

Upon turning her car into the club's driveway, Kate spotted the distant figure of a man pacing in front of the stately clubhouse and knew at once it was Martin. "Here we go." She took a deep breath and looked over at Lily, then patted the girl's knee. "Don't worry, you'll make your grandfather proud."

Lily smiled at Kate. "I want to make you proud, too."

Kate drove through the parking lot and pulled up in front of the building. Martin waved and walked down the clubhouse steps to the open window on Lily's side of the car, where he looked into the smiling face of his daughter for the first time.

Kate thought she saw tears forming in his eyes and wondered if he might be regretting the public meeting he had set up. It was too late to stop the charade now.

He managed to direct Kate to the golf bag drop area and walked the short distance behind the car to help the women with their clubs. He had the bags out of Kate's car the minute she'd braked to a stop, then showed her where to park the car and how to return to the clubhouse.

When the two women finally joined Martin at the entrance, Kate noticed something different about him—a vulnerability she had never seen in him. Striding ahead of Lily, she kissed him on the cheek and whispered into his ear. "Are you all right?"

He nodded that he was okay and squeezed her hand.

Kate knew it would be easy to mistake the tenderness Lily saw in Martin's face as being directed toward Kate. Lily had witnessed a similar exchange between Martin and Kate at Dottie Emerson's cocktail party in Denver. Like then, there appeared to be more to this occasion than the meeting of old friends. But in time, Kate trusted, the truth of the day would eventually dispel any misconceptions Lily might have.

Lily came alongside Kate with the meekness of a child privy to something she shouldn't have witnessed.

Seeing Martin's gaze focus on the full form of his daughter, Kate put an arm around Lily's shoulders. "This is Martin Kelly."

Lily reached out to shake his hand. "How do you do."

"And you are Lily McGuire," said Martin, putting both of his hands around hers. The sparkle in his eyes outshone his smile. "I hear you're quite a golfer." His manner radiated warmth and charm.

Lily reacted with an uncharacteristic giggle that caused her to blush.

Kate took a few steps back from father and daughter, as if to make way for the energy emanating from the force of their meeting. Even if Lily had no idea of the magnitude of this moment, Kate certainly did.

Martin let go of Lily's hand but his gaze remained fixed on her. "How about brunch?"

"I'm famished." Lily looked at Kate as if silently asking the older woman to break the fervor of Martin's intensity.

"Me, too," said Kate.

Martin ushered them through the columned portico to the entrance of the clubhouse and down the trophy-lined hallway to the dining room. He had reserved a window table affording them a spectacular view overlooking the natural amphitheater surrounding the eighteenth green where some of golf's legendary players had walked.

Feeling like she was balancing plates on the end of her nose, Kate broke the strain among the three with polite conversation about the weather and her busy days of pre-production. Lily showed her ease by recounting her impression of Martin's office and how spectacular it was, which finally rousted Martin out of his silence with an open invitation for Lily to visit anytime.

Once the conversation began to flow more easily, Kate retreated into the role of observer. She leaned back in the booth and anxiously tapped her foot on the floor...waiting, waiting. Now that the anticipation was over, she wasn't sure she had the fortitude to help Martin through the rest of the day.

Fortunately, father and daughter found they had a lot in common. They matched each other with golf witticisms and tales of athletic endeavors from biking to baseball. Both had suffered knee injuries—his from football, hers from ballet. They even touched on politics, an area where each bowed to the other in polite disagreement.

"Who else is playing golf with us?" asked Lily.

Kate and Martin looked at each other. Martin answered. "It's just the three of us. I hope that's okay."

"Sure," said Lily. She looked to Kate.

Kate shrugged and turned her hands upward to show she was fine with the group.

Just then, the maitre d' interrupted them to remind Martin of their tee time in ten minutes.

Lily excused herself from the table.

"She's beautiful," Martin said to Kate.

"She's got your blue eyes."

He smiled at Kate's observation, then added, "She's quite charming, too. Isn't she?"

"Like her father." Kate's heart pounded with jealousy. He had a daughter, and she did not. The remembered whisper of newborn life she had given away isolated Kate from Martin's joy. She saw sunny skies radiating newfound love over this man who had always protected his emotions with the reserve of a cloudy day. She tried not to show her sorrow and doubted he would have noticed anyway. Inhaling deeply to soothe her nerves, she rose from the table before Martin could see the blur of moisture gathering over her eyes. "I think I'll catch up with Lily," she said without looking back at him.

"See you on the tee box," he said.

Kate forced aside her anxieties about Martin and Lily when she stepped onto the first tee and concentrated on the business of golf. Driver in hand, she picked an aiming point near the right edge of the cypress-lined fairway that would set her up for an easy second shot toward the green. Her muscles weren't loose, and she pulled the ball into the trees on the left. She declared a mulligan and hit a second ball that made her happy.

After all three teed off, they strode down the fairway in jaunty style with their caddies in close pursuit. Kate moved over to Lily and asked, "So, why didn't you make a bet on the round with Martin like you did with Parker?"

Lily chuckled. "Do you think he's the betting kind?"

"You might be surprised about the chances he's willing to take."

Lily continued to walk alongside Kate on the first couple of holes, asking questions about Kate's friendship with Martin. Had she ever worked with him? Did she think he was handsome? Did he know Parker?

Kate admitted she and Martin had dated for awhile before she married Parker. Lily followed with more inquiries about Martin, and whether or not he had a girlfriend. Finally, Kate got a little annoyed and asked Lily what was on her mind.

"Just curious." Lily shrugged. "I'm sorry. I didn't mean to pry.

Martin's a very interesting man. I think I understand why you used to be attracted to him."

My God, thought Kate. Does Lily think Martin and I are having an affair? Or worse. Is she attracted to him? The second option stopped Kate in her tracks. She glared at Lily.

Stopping alongside Kate, Lily must have read the older woman's thoughts. "Don't misunderstand. He's not my type," said Lily. "Too old and not artsy-craftsy enough."

Kate felt instant relief. "How about Jonas?"

"Don't distract me from my golf game," said Lily as she took the seven iron her caddie was holding for her.

"That goes for you, too," whispered Kate in Martin's direction as she watched him hit a low shot out from under a tree.

"Nice out," observed Lily.

"Thanks," he replied.

After Lily hit her shot, Kate suggested it might be polite if the two of them spent a little more time socializing with their host. "I could use a little course knowledge on how the hell to play some of these holes so I don't keep landing in the hidden bunkers."

"I could use help in reading the greens," added Lily.

Later, Martin took his turn at pumping Kate for information. "Were you and Lily talking about me earlier?"

Kate sighed, disappointed by his prodding. "She was asking about us, to be specific."

"What do you mean, 'us'?"

"She knows we used to date, and I think she believes there still might be something between us."

"Is there, Kate?"

"Don't go there." She spoke softly while waiting for Lily to hit her next shot from the far side of the fairway. "And let me make something else clear to you. I don't intend to tell you about every conversation Lily and I have. I'm not here for that. I'm doing you a favor, which has put me in an uncomfortable position." She gritted her teeth and forced a smile. "My payoff is getting to play this glorious golf course. I'm ashamed for allowing myself to be so easily coerced and bribed by you. Now, go talk to Lily." She gave him a light pat on the back and walked away to find her golf ball.

How had she fooled herself into believing this day could be about golf? Clearly, her mind had been clouded by the shadow of her unsettled relationship with Martin.

Martin chunked his next shot into a bunker and almost fell down when he stepped on the rake at the edge of the sand. Kate saw him close his eyes with embarrassment, but he laughed and shook his head to acknowledge his blunder. He missed several more easy shots over the next few holes until finally settling down and regaining his composure.

Walking up behind Lily as she crouched to line up her putt on one of the greens, Martin cleared his throat. "Want some help? It's a bigger break than it looks."

"Please." Lily smiled at him.

Martin placed a hand on her shoulder while pointing out the line of the putt, then stepped away to watch her execution. Her ball barely missed the hole. "Bravo. You really know how to follow instructions."

Lily smiled again. "I had good advice."

Standing on the next tee box, Lily walloped her drive to the exact spot Martin had suggested she aim. He clapped his hands in admiration. Lily saluted putting the tip of her fingers to the brim of her hat, like a golf pro does to the fans.

A mixture of pleasure and jealousy flitted through Kate as she watched the two of them saunter down the fairway, shoulder to shoulder, laughter ringing out, arms moving through the air to trace the line of Martin's missed shot into the trees.

It wasn't until after she had dropped Lily at her hotel that Kate lowered her guard and noticed the tightened muscles cinching her body into a giant knot of stress. A short time later, comfortably ensconced in Annabella's flat, sipping on the wine Annabella had poured for her,

Kate began to feel her cares fade.

"I'm not of sound mind," said Kate. "Why else would I have helped Martin with this charade today? He's got to tell her soon, or I will."

"What happened when he saw her?" asked Annabella.

Kate was happy to unburden her load with a rehash of the day's drama. "It was like a movie. I choked up at the look on Martin's face when he saw Lily for the first time. I thought he was going to burst into tears."

"No kidding! What was he wearing?"

Kate rolled her eyes. "He looked gorgeous, of course. Expensive gabardine trousers, a yellow cashmere sweater, those broad shoulders…he's in such fabulous shape. Totally flat stomach."

"I love the ripples in a man's muscled stomach."

"Maybe I ought to get the two of you together."

Annabella laughed. "What about Lily? Did she have any idea she was spending the day with her father?"

"Not a clue, as far as I know. She seemed preoccupied with me…like she was watching out for me. I think she concluded that all those feelings emanating from Martin were directed at me. She kept bringing up Parker, hoping to remind me that I'm married and should ignore Martin, or something. It was so ironic. In all the years with Martin, I never saw him as sweet and attentive as he was with Lily today. He was gaga over her, and a little uncertain how to act. If only he'd let down his guard like that with me years ago. Things might have been different."

"Still second guessing? You've got to resolve these old feelings."

"Don't I know it. I almost lost it at lunch today. She is the daughter I might have given Martin. And today I got a glimpse of what I always knew was inside of him, but was never able to bring out. He was funny. He was silly, loving and thoughtful in spite of the apprehension he must have been experiencing…all to make Lily comfortable. And she used all of those same attributes to make me comfortable. They are a lot alike. Lily and I didn't talk about it, but I know she felt my discomfort today."

"Oh, Kate. It's all so melodramatic. But you have Parker."

"You don't have to remind me about Parker, too, Bella. I love that man, and he loves me in a way Martin never could. I know how lucky I am."

"But?"

"But, I guess I'll always feel something for Martin. Although I wish those feelings would simply fade away and stop haunting me."

"When does he plan to tell Lily the truth?"

"I have no idea. And you know what? I've done as he requested. I introduced them. Now, I can get back to my film, which starts production tomorrow morning. Martin's on his own from here on."

"We shall see," said Annabella.

CHAPTER NINETEEN

Lily dragged her golf clubs into her hotel room and flopped on her bed before noticing the flashing red light on the telephone. She pressed the button and listened to the message.

"Denise and Simon arrived this morning. Come join us for dinner at the Union Street Brew Pub at seven."

Hearing Jonas's voice on the message restored energy to her weary body. She'd had a lovely time with Kate and Martin, but welcomed the opportunity to shake off the strange feeling she had carried home from her day. The sensation wasn't due to the straight-laced atmosphere of the Olympic Club. It had emanated from Kate and Martin. There was something about their vibes that had kept her from relaxing.

Jonas, Denise and Simon were half way through their first beers when Lily arrived at the pub and spied them. She wiggled her way through the overflow of Sunday revelers until she reached a point inside the front door where she caught Jonas's eye. Instead of waving her over, he walked through the bustling sea of tables to greet her with a gentle kiss on her lips as he took hold of her hand.

Lily stepped back from the unexpected kiss and looked at him with a wry smile of pleasure. Still holding her hand, Jonas led Lily back to their table where she hugged the two actors, Denise and Simon, before sitting in the chair Jonas had pulled out for her.

"So, how was golf today?" asked Jonas with a knowing smile.

"What?" Lily was caught off guard by his query. His question signaled the end of the secret she had enjoyed keeping from him since the first day they met. She knew he had put two and two together.

"You know, that game with long sticks and a dimpled white ball," added Simon.

"Oh, that silly game. All right, I guess." Simon and Denise may not have known the significance of Jonas's question, but Jonas did. Suddenly, his knowing who her mentor was didn't seem to matter anymore.

"What do you mean, just all right? Didn't you play at the Olympic Club?" asked Jonas. "A classy place from all I've heard."

"The course was fabulous. Have you ever played it?"

"I almost did today—with you."

"You did!" Now he had raised her curiosity.

"Kate Cochran asked if I wanted to join your group, said it would be good public relations or something."

"Oh, really." She wasn't sure what to make of Kate's invitation to Jonas. "Too bad you didn't join us. We had a lovely day."

"Well, so did we," offered Denise. "I bribed Simon with lunch at Fisherman's Wharf so he would keep me company while I explored the shops on Pier 39. He ended up buying more junk than I did. Then we dragged ourselves back to the hotel because Jonas insisted on going over our scenes for tomorrow."

"We are here to make a movie, after all." Jonas signaled a waiter. "Let's order."

After their early dinner, taskmaster Jonas sent Denise and Simon back to the hotel to study lines and get a solid beauty rest before their six a.m. calls the next morning.

"Now"—Jonas moved his chair closer to Lily—"what was that golf game really about today? Why was Kate so desperate to have me join you?"

"I didn't know she was."

"You make it sound like you didn't know she asked me."

"I didn't."

"Oh." His voice dropped. "I thought maybe you had wanted me there."

"Is your ego in need of a boost or something?" she teased. "I didn't even know you played golf."

"Actually, I don't. I've been a little busy making movies."

"How fortunate for you."

"Damn right. So are you some kind of wonderful golfer or something?"

"I play."

"Your modesty means you're probably quite good. Is Kate how you got your job on the movie?"

The question was inevitable. There was no point in playing dodge ball anymore. She leaned across the table to speak right to his face. "Yes. Are you happy now?"

"Yes. But I still like you, maybe even more."

"What do you mean?"

"Kate's a class act. A little uncertain about her writing skills, but she's got a good production background. Once we got past her insecurities and she found out I wasn't the egotistical prima donna she'd anticipated... Let's just say I like her, okay? Is she a friend of your family?"

"Kate is my friend."

"However you two are linked, I'm especially glad you're part of this production company, Lily."

"Me, too."

"I mean, on a personal basis."

Lily gulped. Flashes of fleeting Hollywood romances and the oversexed directors and producers portrayed in so many movies filled her imagination. She didn't want to get suckered in, but if she didn't risk a leap of faith, how could this relationship move one way or the other? She found the courage to say what was on her mind. "Since that night at your beach house, I have felt something special with you, Jonas, like we are connected in some way. Maybe on a spiritual level, or something." She rolled her eyes. "Please don't laugh."

"I'm not laughing. There is something special between us."

"But the thing is this, I'm not very experienced with older guys," she continued. "So, basically, I'm suspicious about everything you say."

"Good for you. You should be. I would be cautious, too. So, let's take it slowly. I love being around you. You're sensitive and straightforward…a very refreshing commodity in my world. I've been burned, too."

"I've not actually been burned, yet. I'm just afraid of being burned." Lily longed to tell him more about herself and the real reason she decided to work on Kate's movie, but she couldn't risk it, yet.

"So what is your ideal scenario?" he asked.

"Friends. How about if we just ease our way into being friends?"

"And what if we decide we want something more than that?"

"You mean sex?"

"Well, yes."

"No sex. Not during production. If we are still drawn to each other when this is all over, then we can discuss it."

"How did you become so wise at your young age, Lily?"

"It's not wisdom. Just sheer fear."

Jonas laughed. "I think I'm falling in love with you right this minute. I already know I love your honesty. Is it okay to admit that much?"

"You can say anything you like. It's your actions I'll be assessing."

"I'll take that as fair warning." Jonas took Lily's hand and turned his attention to the band whose thunderous music began to fill the room.

CHAPTER TWENTY

Kate and David met at seven in the morning for the first day of shooting. Equipment vans, the catering truck, and portable dressing rooms lined one block of the neighborhood park across the street from the Pacific Heights flat of Denise's character. Busy crewmembers had already littered the sidewalk with cables and lighting equipment. Bundled against the brisk chill of morning fog, David and Kate toasted the start of production with their Styrofoam cups of bitter coffee from the catering truck.

Soon, Kate ventured into the flat for a closer look at the morning's progress. The space overflowed with crew members, klieg lights, cables, camera equipment, and Mark Harrington's set decorations. Overall, Kate was pleased with the look Mark had achieved. It wasn't the pink femininity of flowery pastels she had described in her screenplay, but it was cozy. Made more so by all the equipment crowding every spot of open floor that wasn't occupied by furniture.

Kate overheard some crewmembers groaning about having to work in such tight quarters. She hoped she and David had not miscalculated their needs when they chose this location. The young woman who lived in the apartment had taken the day off work to watch the shooting. She sipped a cup of coffee and peered into the living room from the safe haven of her kitchen, occasionally venturing out to cautiously move a piece of her own furniture from being bumped by a piece of incoming equipment.

Suddenly, the authoritative voice of the assistant director roared above the clatter. "Everyone not involved in setting up equipment, please vacate now!"

"It's my apartment," said the shy woman clutching her coffee mug. "I hope you don't mean me, too."

Kate stepped backward over some cables into the hallway, where she bumped into Mark. She had been the only expendable person in the flat.

"Sorry," he said.

"My fault. I need to get out of here. I'll catch up with you later. I've got some things I'd like to go over with you."

Mark gave her a thumbs-up signal and moved into the overcrowded apartment to help move furniture.

Back outside, Kate rejoined David, who was now talking with Jonas.

"How's it going in there?" asked Jonas.

"A trifle hectic, but there's synchronicity in their movements," offered Kate.

"Music to my ears. I'd better get to work myself. I'll see you both later." Jonas left them to join the pulsing activity in the flat.

"How much longer are you going to hang around here?" asked David.

"I'd like to watch them shoot the first couple of scenes."

"Me, too. Did you give casting the names and addresses of the extras you want to include?"

"Not yet, but I will."

Just then, Annabella drove up and honked her horn.

"Who else? It's Bella," said Kate. She raced over to the curb to prevent Annabella from leaning on her horn again. "Bella, what are you doing here so early? The sun's barely up."

"On my way to the gym. Got to get myself in shape if I'm going to star in your movie, darling! I missed you this morning and wanted to wish you luck. How's it going so far?"

"Until you drove up, everything was fine. Since you announced your arrival to our sleeping neighbors, I'm not so sure."

A sheepish expression washed over Annabella's face. "I'm sorry, I wasn't thinking. I got excited when I saw all the activity and those handsome crew members dashing around in their butt-hugging jeans."

"You're certainly observant for this hour of the morning."

"Just enjoying the scenery. I may still be half asleep, but that doesn't blind me from noticing a sexy man or two. When's lunch?"

"Probably around twelve-thirty."

"Good, I'll be back then."

"Annabella, would you do me a favor? Bring my address book when you come for lunch. I've got to give casting Becky Madison's address and phone number."

"Who's Becky Madison?"

"Geez, I thought I told you about her. She's an old childhood friend of mine. We recently reconnected after many years. I invited her to be an extra in the movie. I'll tell you more later."

"You got it, girl. Ciao." She waved and drove off. Kate walked back toward the flat where Lily was standing.

"Was that the infamous Annabella?" asked Lily. "When do I get to meet her?"

"Morning, Lily." Kate gave her a motherly kiss on the cheek. "She'll be here for lunch."

"Good. I have a lot to talk about with her."

Kate couldn't imagine what Lily might want to discuss with Annabella. She was about to ask when she spotted Mark Harrington emerging from the building and left to speak with him. Lily moved on to respond to a call on her walkie-talkie.

The immediacy of first-day problems preempted lunch with Annabella for Kate and Lily. By the third day of shooting, things had settled into a routine. David and Kate continued to rendezvous for breakfast from the catering truck every morning. Filming started by eight or eight-thirty, lunch was at twelve-thirty, and they wrapped by seven each evening. Much of Kate's day involved paperwork, production meetings, or going over dialogue with the actors. Dailies were scheduled each night at eight-thirty at a screening facility near the production office. Kate usually fell into Annabella's apartment by ten.

When time allowed, Kate sunk into the shadows where she could observe with quiet fascination as everyone worked and moved mysteriously as one entity, stealthily maneuvering their skills to perform one harmonious operation, interspersed with laughter and resolve. To Kate, it was a carefully choreographed ballet—a syncopation of organized pieces coming together at the right moment because everyone knew what was needed to inject life into her screenplay. Misunderstandings, lighting problems, ill-fitting wardrobe, equipment breakdowns, missing props...all were easily remedied by the ingenuity of men and women who knew how to make magic within the demanding time frame of a movie schedule, where everything was needed and supplied upon demand.

"Bella, I'm exhausted, but I can't sleep. Let's go out for a drink." Kate had just plopped onto Annabella's sofa after the third day of shooting.

"Do you feel like dancing?"

"I'm not that energized. And I still need to be up early."

"Okay. We can go to Jedediah Smith's."

"That sounds like a joint in Colorado. Isn't there some place closer?"

Annabella laughed. "It's just up the hill. It used to be a corner grocery store, now it's our neighborhood watering hole. You'll like it."

Kate found Jedediah's pub comfortable and friendly. Several people knew Annabella and gave the two women a warm greeting. Two older men played darts in the back corner. A young couple whispered intimately over the tiny wooden table separating them. Small groups chatted around the other tables.

Annabella and Kate perched on the two empty stools at the bar. "A glass of your finest Chablis," said Kate to the bartender.

"Same for me, Walter. I'd like you to meet one of my all-time best friends, Kate Cochran."

"Kate." He nodded while pouring her wine. He looked barely old enough to drink, himself.

"Nice to meet you, Walter."

"Walter's the best bartender in all of San Francisco."

He shot Annabella a look of warning.

"Uh oh. Looks like there's a bit of history here," said Kate. "If it has to do with Annabella's former drinking habits, I can only imagine."

"I'll drink to that." Annabella raised her glass.

Walter smiled at the two women and moved down the bar to serve another customer, leaving Annabella to listen as Kate recounted her first few days of production with the enthusiasm of someone who had just discovered the ecstasy of a chocolate fudge sundae.

"And how's Lily doing?"

Kate shrugged. She knew Annabella's innocent question would certainly lead to talk of Martin, a bog she had hoped to avoid. Kate sighed and pictured herself in hip boots sloshing into a muddy marsh. "Great, I guess. We've all been so busy, I've hardly seen her."

"Any word from Martin?"

There it was. "Not a thing, thank God. But now that you mention it, I'm surprised he hasn't made at least one appearance. You haven't talked to him, have you?"

"Nope."

"It's odd. Sunday was such an intense day. I thought he would want to talk about it, or at least thank me for bringing his daughter to him."

"Maybe he decided to leave you alone for awhile."

"No. That would have been the selfless thing to do."

"Aren't you being a little hard on him?"

"I don't think so. Not after the emotional day he put me through on Sunday. You saw what a wreck I was. He hasn't thought about anyone else except himself in this whole situation with Lily. And what about Lily? We haven't been truthful with her at all."

"Yeah, I'll go along with that."

"Whose side are you on?"

"I was agreeing with you. I'm on your side and Lily's. So, when am I going to meet Martin's long lost daughter?"

"She was asking the same thing about you."

"Really? I was going to stay away from the set the rest of this week, but maybe I could stop by to meet Lily."

"Whatever. It's fine with me. Let me know when you want to come, and I'll make sure she'll be there."

"How about tomorrow for lunch?"

"Okay. Come to the set at twelve-thirty."

Annabella arrived the next day in time to watch some filming before lunch. The crew was set up to shoot a scene on the front sidewalk of the flat. A small group of curious neighbors had gathered to watch from a safe distance. Lily stood among them like a sentry, making sure they were quiet during the takes.

Annabella sidled up alongside Kate, who was positioned next to the soundman. She wore a set of earphones so she could hear the quiet dialogue from their position about twenty yards away from the actors. The two women whispered "hello" to one another, then turned to watch the actors, who were beginning their first take.

"Rolling," said the cameraman.

"Speed," yelled the soundman.

The assistant cameraman clacked the slate. "Act one. Scene fifteen. Take one."

"Action," called Jonas.

It was a dramatic scene in which Denise's character was upset with Simon's character. The two actors began moving along the sidewalk as crewmembers pushed the camera down tracks strategically laid to follow alongside the actors through this relatively long sequence. As rehearsed, the actors walked slowly to a position on the sidewalk where they stopped to recite their dialogue. They hit their marks exactly. Denise delivered her first line. Simon said his line, then slapped her across the face. Denise instinctively slapped him back, leaving both of them paralyzed and the crew waiting in a frozen silence.

"What the hell was that?" bellowed Jonas, rushing up to the actors.

"Cut!" yelled the first assistant director.

"Wasn't that part of the scene?" Annabella whispered to Kate.

"Not even close."

"What are they saying? Can you hear?" Annabella poked Kate on her arm.

Kate put a finger to her lips to signal Annabella to be quiet and pointed to her earphones. Kate had learned years ago that the soundman was the best source of information on a set. He was able to swing the long boom over people and eavesdrop on whispered conversations no one else was meant to hear.

By the time Jonas reached them, Denise and Simon were bent over in laughter.

Kate listened with her headset as the actors explained to Jonas about Simon's attempt to get a spontaneous reaction out of Denise by inserting his own ad lib. Kate smiled and removed her earphones to update Annabella.

"Remember the look on Shirley MacLaine's face in *The Turning Point* when Anne Bancroft threw a glass of whiskey at her?"

"Of course. That was a great scene."

"During filming, MacLaine was expecting them to use colored water. Instead, Bancroft substituted real whiskey for the water. Being the pro she is, MacLaine stayed in character when the real whiskey surprised her, and that take is in the film. Simon tried to do something like that with Denise. But Denise doesn't have the savvy of Shirley MacLaine."

Jonas clapped his hands to get everyone's attention. "Let's get back to work, people."

It took several minutes for Simon and Denise to settle so they could try the scene again. Then they started to giggle at the beginning of two more takes. By now it was after twelve-thirty, so Jonas called the lunch break.

"*The Turning Point*! I loved that movie," said Annabella, following Kate toward the catering truck.

"Shhhhh. Not so loud. Everyone will know how old we are."

Just then, Jonas walked by them. "Can you believe those two? They think they're MacLaine and Bancroft."

"You know about the whiskey scene from a 1977 film?" asked

Annabella.

"Doesn't everyone?"

Kate took a moment to introduce Annabella to Jonas, then proceeded to share information she had recently learned about him. "Jonas saw almost every movie ever made before he was old enough to drive. His father was the film editor at a television station in Bakersfield, so he screened each film that was bicycled through the station."

"A slight exaggeration, but I've seen most of the best and more than I want of the worst." Jonas turned to Annabella. "It's nice to meet you. By the way, I understand you're responsible for finding us local actors to fill out the casting. Thanks for your help."

"My pleasure. In return, I want you to be sure to have the camera focused on my best side when I make my debut as one of the grape pickers."

"You got it!"

Kate and Annabella strolled across the street to the catering truck to take up positions at the end of the lunch line. Moments later, Lily joined them.

"Kate, hi. I've been looking all over for you. Mark Harrington needs you at the brokerage firm location. He said there's a problem. They may need a rewrite."

Kate grimaced. "There goes my lunch. But all is not lost." She put her arm around Lily and Annabella. "You two have wanted to meet each other. Now, you can have lunch all by yourselves." After perfunctory introductions, Kate rushed off to meet with Mark.

Annabella and Lily loaded their trays with salads, veggies, a baked potato and dessert, then found an empty spot at one of the long tables set up in the adjacent park overlooking the Mission District sprawling below.

"You certainly have a healthy appetite," observed Annabella.

"You, too," said Lily, indicating the food on Annabella's tray.

Annabella looked down at the heaping amount of food in front of her and laughed. "So I do."

They ate their lunch while sharing polite conversation about the weather, the production and college until Annabella turned their attention to the person who brought them together in the first place. "So, what do you think of Kate?"

Lily finished a bite of food before answering. "She's great. If it wasn't for her, I'd be lost."

"Really?"

Lily looked at the people sitting at the far end of their table before responding in a quieter voice. "I guess you could say I went to Colorado in search of myself. I wasn't sure how long I was going to stay, but after I met Kate at Dottie Emerson's campaign headquarters, things got better. Kate made me feel like I belonged somewhere."

Annabella raised an eyebrow. "How's that?"

"It's complicated. My mother and I have some unresolved issues I'm dealing with right now. When Kate and Parker let me stay with them, I felt safe."

"What do you mean safe? Are you in any kind of danger?"

"Oh no. It's nothing like that. After dorm life, it's nice to be in a family situation."

"How nice that Kate and Parker have been there for you. It seems like you and Kate have become very close."

"You think so?" Lily tipped her head as if to ponder Annabella's remark. "That must mean Kate has said some nice things about me. I like her very much." She shifted around in her chair. "Now I get to ask you some questions."

"Okay, shoot."

"How long have you and Kate been friends?"

"Forever."

"Did you know her in college?"

"No, we met in L.A. a few years after college."

"So you know almost everything there is to know about her."

Annabella looked at Lily, wondering if her concern showed on her face. "What is it you want to know, Lily?"

"Am I that obvious?"

"Like a sledgehammer."

Lily cringed. "It's just that I feel so close to Kate, like she's a"—she looked down at her half-eaten plate of food as if asking for help—"like a sister or something."

"Or maybe a mother figure?" Annabella peered over the top of her sunglasses to look directly into Lily's eyes. "She is old enough to be your mother."

Lily shrugged her shoulders.

"Kate told me you haven't seen your mother in awhile. Maybe you see something in Kate you miss about your own mother."

Lily stopped her fork in mid-motion and put the uneaten bite of food back on her plate.

The older woman continued. "I may be out of line here, but I'm a little worried you and Kate might be reading more into your friendship than really exists. I would hate to see either of you get hurt."

"I'm not sure what you mean. Kate and I are just friends."

"That may be true. But I get the impression you want something more from Kate. For reasons I won't get into, Kate doesn't need another emotional upheaval in her life right now."

"Annabella, I assure you, there is no need for you to worry about your friend."

Annabella leaned back in her chair. "I'm sorry. I can see I have overstepped my bounds. I didn't mean to make you feel uncomfortable."

Lily rolled her shoulders to shrug off the awkward moment. "It's okay. I appreciate your concern."

Both women took a few bites of their dessert before Lily continued in a lighter vein. "A group of us are going dancing tomorrow night. Why don't you and Kate come with us?"

"Hey, I'd like that. Leave goody-two-shoes Kate to me. I'll make sure she comes."

"Perfect." As the people around them started migrating back to the set, Lily excused herself and headed after them.

Left alone, Annabella drummed her fingers on the table and stared curiously after Lily.

Later that afternoon, the first assistant director asked Lily to check the identity of the well dressed businessman standing near some equipment. Turning to see who he meant, she realized it was Martin. After reassuring the assistant director the "suit" was okay, Lily walked over to Martin.

"Mr. Kelly," she said.

"Martin," he corrected her. "You said I should come and watch, so here I am."

"I actually thought you'd be too busy. It's nice to see you again." She felt stiffness in his manner and tried to soften the moment with some levity. "You know, you really stand out in that business suit. It's chez chic, but well, as you can see"—she gestured toward the crew with a sweep of an arm—"things are a little less formal around here."

"I see that," he chuckled, scanning the workers in jeans, sweatshirts and cutoffs. "I'll remember to dress accordingly the next time I come by. How's everything going?"

"Fine. I think. Want to move in for a closer look?"

"I'd like that."

For the next hour, Martin and his daughter stood shoulder to shoulder, observing Jonas direct the actors and the crew through the filming of an exterior scene. Occasionally, Martin would glance discreetly at Lily

"In all the years I've known Kate, I've never been on a movie set," Martin whispered into Lily's ear. "This is fascinating."

Lily put a hand over her mouth to muffle her voice. "It's fun, isn't it? This is actually the first chance I've had to watch any of the shooting myself."

"I'm glad to be initiated with you, Lily."

"Same here," she said, agreeing without giving it much thought.

When there was a break in the shooting, they walked over to the catering truck for a cup of coffee.

"I enjoyed playing golf with you Sunday," Martin said. "You're a joy to watch."

"Thank you. I had a lovely day. It was nice of you to include me."

"Perhaps we could play again while you're in San Francisco."

Before she could answer, Lily spotted Kate who must have just returned from her meeting with Mark Harrington. She appeared to have been watching Lily and Martin from a distance. "Kate, over here," she called out with a wave. "Come join us for coffee."

Kate waved back and walked over to them.

"Hi, Martin," she said in a flat voice.

He answered with a smile.

"Did you get things straightened out with Mark?" asked Lily.

"I think so. I need to find David, though. Have you seen him?"

"Yeah, he was around earlier. I'll go find him." Before Kate had a chance to stop her, Lily walked off, leaving her with Martin.

"Problems?" asked Martin.

"Just a small one. We can handle it with a minor rewrite. Have you been here long?"

"Not very. An hour or so." He stepped back and gave her one of his long looks. "You're radiant, Kate. You really thrive on all this, don't you?"

"I didn't know it was so obvious. It's fun to be working again, especially on my own project. And a little scary." Regardless of her earlier fears, Kate knew she was coming into her stride as each day of shooting progressed. Like an athlete in training, the harder she worked, the more she could handle–meetings, rehearsals, set checks, dinners, dailies, minor crises.

"I'm proud of you. I know how hard you've worked and how much crap you've put up with over the years."

"Yeah, I guess I have." She kicked the dirt in a comic "awe shucks" gesture.

"I remember those late nights we used to sit up talking about the trials and tribulations of your job. You were balancing a lot of super egos and heavy hitters in those days."

"I was in way over my head."

"No you weren't. They were lucky to have you around. You're a talented woman."

"I didn't think you paid that close attention to my career."

"I was there during most of it. Remember?"

Martin's admiring gaze made her feel uncomfortable. She didn't know what to say.

Martin filled her silence. "I'd like to take you and Lily to dinner tonight. Are you available?"

She sighed. "I can't. We have dailies until about nine. Perhaps Lily can meet you."

"I don't think she'll go with me unless you join us."

Kate resigned herself to the inevitability of his invitation. "You're probably right. How about meeting at nine, but no place fancy. This is how I'll be dressed." She stretched out her arms to model her sneakers, powder blue jeans and sweater.

"You're on. Will you ask Lily?"

"I'm not going to play this game much longer." She drilled him with her glare.

"I know, and you're right."

Kate showed up at the restaurant without Lily. "I'm sorry Martin. She already had plans and didn't feel comfortable breaking them at the last minute."

"I understand." Kate could hear the disappointment in his voice. He went on, "Will you still have dinner with me?"

"Yes." She smiled and consoled him with a pat on his shoulder before sitting opposite him. "I'm famished."

This time, their meeting was relaxed. Absent was Kate's edginess and bitterness toward their past. She was in a good mood. They quickly ordered, and she joined Martin in a glass of wine from the bottle he had already ordered.

"The dailies are really looking good," said Kate. "I love what the actors are doing with my characters. The production's right on schedule. I think I owe Jonas, our director, a big hug."

Kate rambled on about her days on the set like she had done years ago with him. He chuckled over her embellished version of Simon slapping Denise and shocking the entire crew into silence and Jonas's love of old movies.

"How many times have you seen *An Affair to Remember*?" he asked her.

Kate laughed. "Too many times to count. And what's your favorite movie?"

"I assume you want me to name a romantic movie, not *The Guns of Navarone*."

She quickly moved the bottle of wine over to her side of the table. "Give me the right answer, or you'll get no more wine."

"Okay, okay. How about *Casablanca*?"

"Good answer!" She poured more wine into his glass.

Martin told Kate about his current hassles over the property in Santa Rosa and the ingenious plan he had hatched with Bethel to solve their problems. "The lawyers won't know what hit them when Bethel is through." His eyes lit up. "It's going to be beautiful. She'll enter like the wonderful earth mother she is, then stalk them into submission like a coyote."

Kate joined in his laughter. "I wish I could see Bethel in action."

"Me, too. But if I'm there, it'll spoil everything."

It was better than old times. Their guards were down, allowing an evening of mutual enjoyment to flow between them. As much as they might have wanted to sustain this newfound ease in their friendship, Kate's weary body had run its course for the day. The clock struck midnight. They went their separate ways.

CHAPTER TWENTY-ONE

Kate felt remarkably happy and relaxed when she tiptoed into Annabella's flat. Preparing for bed, she saw a note resting on her pillow.

We're going dancing Friday night with Lily and her gang. You're already committed so forget any excuses. You deserve a night of retro abandon. Bella.

Why not, thought Kate. She slipped under the comforter and fell asleep the instant her head touched the pillow.

It was dark when she heard the phone ring. A minute later, Annabella nudged her on the shoulder.

"What's wrong?" Kate asked, groggy, but jarred with middle-of-the-night fear. "What time is it?"

"It's okay. It's almost six. Parker's on the phone." On her way out of Kate's bedroom, Annabella raised the blind to allow the rising sun to lighten the room.

Kate picked up the receiver by her bed.

"Good morning!" came his chipper voice. "I know it's early, but I wanted to catch my darling wife before she put on her producer clothes."

"How nice." She melted back into the bed. "Good morning, my love. I'm sorry I haven't called but we've been going like crazy, and I haven't been getting home until late."

"I figured as much."

"How are you?"

"I'm fine. How's it going?"

"Great. I'm having a ball. I forgot how much fun this can be. Although by the end of next week, I may be bored silly."

"I doubt it. But I don't want you to get so caught up you won't want to come home again."

"Don't be a silly fool. This is fun, but I miss you and Rusty, too. How's my boy?"

"Rusty is just as stubborn as ever. He hangs out by the garage door waiting for you to come home every night."

"Ahhhh. Are you still planning to come out next weekend?"

"That's partially why I'm calling. They've called a divisional meeting in Houston for that weekend. There's no way I can get out of it."

"Oh, no. I was so hoping to see you."

"I know. Me, too."

"What about Rusty?"

"Nancy said she'd take care of him. It's only for three days."

Just then, Kate's alarm clock went off. She fumbled around and finally put a stop to the buzzing. "Sorry about that."

"I'll let you go, darling. Call me this weekend."

"I will. Love you."

"Love you, too."

That night, Kate went dancing with Lily and her gang as promised, but fatigue led her home early. She promised everyone a better exhibition the following weekend.

During the next week of production, the company shot scenes at various locations around the city. Martin came by the set, sometimes twice a day. Annabella popped in and out, too, usually around lunchtime. Occasionally, Martin, Annabella, Kate and Lily were all there at the same time to watch the filming. Kate was often the brunt of their jokes when the actors screwed up her dialogue. Mostly, they whispered their comments to one another as if they were playing telephone. Sometimes Kate would pull Annabella away to leave Lily and Martin on their own. It was during these times the two women felt the most discomfort in knowing the secret of Lily's real relationship to Martin.

One day, Martin and David appeared on the set at the same

moment. It was the first time they had actually met face to face, though they had known about each other for years through Kate.

Kate watched them from a distance, noticing that David seemed to relish the opportunity to goad Martin. "So, you're the infamous Martin Kelly," she heard David say. "I always thought you were a mythical character in Kate's imagination. Phaethon comes to mind."

"I'm not quite sure how to take that," replied Martin. "My classical training is severely lacking, as I am but a mere mortal."

"Phaethon was mortal, also." A devious grin sliced across David's face.

Kate decided it was time to join the pair. She walked over to them and put an arm around David's waist. "I apologize for David's haughty manners." Kate spoke in a lighthearted fashion, hoping to deflect the edge in David's comment. "He's overly protective of me sometimes."

"I can see that. I assume Phaethon is not such a nice character." Martin turned to David and asked, "What have I done to warrant the use of your sword?"

"Phaethon meant no harm, either."

Martin turned to Kate with a questioning look.

Kate threw her hands up in self-defense. "I don't know who Phaethon is either."

"I'm sorry," said David, in an apparent attempt to make amends for his rudeness. "I owe you a debt of gratitude, not insults. Without your assistance, we might be shooting a chunk of this film in an Escondido avocado orchard instead of the Napa Valley wine country."

Martin engaged David in small talk for a few minutes, adding little to the conversation, which eventually allowed David to withdraw to something more needful of his attention. Before he left, David invited Martin to watch dailies anytime he wished. Martin politely accepted David's peace offering.

"What was that all about?" Martin asked Kate when David was out of view.

She grimaced. "I may have cried on his shoulder about you in years past. But I was a bit surprised at his reaction toward you, myself. His lack of diplomacy was out of line, especially since you're involved with the film."

"Perhaps I should charge you combat pay for use of the property if I'm going to be attacked with hostility by the executive producer."

"David has been a good friend to me for years. He's always been a good listener, and I took advantage of his friendship to uh, well, share some of my heartaches."

"And I was one of your heartaches?"

"No. You *were* the heartache."

"Yes, I've been getting that picture from you over the past couple of months."

"Hey! I hate to interrupt," said Annabella walking over to join them. "It's Friday, Kate. We're invited to go dancing again after dailies tonight. I said we'd go."

"I guess so."

"How about you, Martin? Want to join us?" asked Annabella. "We're going to this new swing club."

Martin looked at Kate with an expression that seemed to ask for her guidance. She elected not to give him any and remained silent. He turned back to Annabella. "Let me think about it."

Not wanting to appear rude, Kate relented and offered words of persuasion, until he agreed to join them. Afterward, she kicked herself for encouraging him. She thought he might prove to be a drag and inhibit their spirits with his button-down tendencies. She wanted to let her hair down and go wild with the crew, not worry about whether or not Martin was having a good time

The Will Rockit Dance Club pulsed with jumping, gyrating dancers of all ages. Jonas, Lily, Denise, Simon, and some crewmembers were already working up a sweat to Bette Midler's rendition of "Boogie Woogie Bugle Boy" when Kate and Annabella arrived. Exhausted from an intense week and feeling every day of her forty-plus years, Kate led Annabella to the bar. Throwing caution aside, she ordered a gin and tonic instead of her normal glass of wine.

Both women were looking at the bottom of their cocktail glasses by the time Martin arrived. They readily accepted his offer to buy them another drink while the trio sat at the bar and watched the others dance.

When the music slowed to the Johnny Mathis classic, "Chances Are," Martin smiled at Kate and offered his hand to lead her to the dance floor. Taking her in his arms, he gazed at her, then pressed his cheek against hers and guided her easily around the dance floor. The familiar comfort of his hand on the small of her back and the smell of his after-shave released a flutter of butterflies into her stomach and aroused her tactile memories. The hunger she once felt for him overcame her like an alcoholic taking a drink after years of sobriety.

After two more dances, Martin returned Kate to the bar and ordered fresh drinks for her and Annabella. Then, he led Annabella onto the dance floor as Kate sipped her cocktail and surrendered to the flow of the evening.

When the Village People's "YMCA" blasted over the room, Jonas and Lily pulled Kate into the circle of their gang of actors and crewmembers. The liquor had done its work. Kate was feeling no pain.

The beat went on into the night. The room got hotter as the intensity of the dancing increased. More participants crowded onto the floor until no one could tell who was dancing with whom. Everyone shimmied, did the pony, boogied, screamed and tossed their heads with laughter. Around midnight, Martin pulled Kate aside and offered her a ride home. She started to follow him until a passing hand towed her back into the crowd of dancers. She laughed and threw up her hands as if surrendering to the music and waved goodbye to Martin. A few minutes later, Martin returned and slipped something into one of Kate's pockets. Not giving it any thought, Kate smiled and wished him a good night as Simon twirled her around to the big band rumblings of Harry James.

Just before two a.m., Annabella and Kate stumbled out of the club into a blast of cool San Francisco air. The intoxicated friends giggled with youthful frivolity. Kate slipped her hands into her pockets to keep them warm and discovered the note and a key Martin had placed there. The note included an address and three words:

Please join me.

The doorman waved down a passing taxi and the two women jumped in. Kate relaxed into the seat. She held Martin's key in one hand and touched her face with the other, remembering Johnny Mathis and the warmth of Martin's cheek against her own. Other memories of their happier times together rose to the surface. On an impulse and without a word to Annabella, Kate gave the cab driver the address on Martin's note.

Annabella's mouth dropped open. "That's the financial district. Martin's…"

Kate interrupted Annabella before she could finish her sentence. "I want you to drop me off on your way home."

"Are you sure?"

Kate answered by repeating Martin's address for the cab driver. She didn't look at Annabella, but she could feel her friend's piercing look of disapproval, which in Kate's inebriated state held little sway. Dancing with Martin had already transported her back in time.

They drove in silence until they reached Kate's destination. Stepping out of the cab, Kate pressed a twenty-dollar bill into Annabella's hand to pay the fare. "If you follow all the rules you never have any fun."

"I don't think you're thinking straight."

"I'm fine." She tapped the roof of the taxi to send the cab on its way. Turning Martin's key in the palm of her hand, Kate looked up at the Kitty Murphy Building towering over the deserted plaza and sauntered toward the skyscraper. After walking around the base of the building, she found a side door where a security guard seemed to be expecting her. He escorted her onto an elevator that took them to the penthouse level, then onto the small elevator Lily had taken a few weeks earlier.

"Ma'am, when you get off the elevator, walk to the far right side of the sculpture garden to the private apartment hidden behind the only unmarked door at the end of the hall."

Kate patted the guard on his shoulder and assured him she could find her way. She hoped she was right. Everything seemed to be moving, including the doors. Scouring all possibilities, her blurry eyes finally happened on a door that didn't have a sign. She searched around in her pocket for the key before realizing it was already in her hand.

Inside the apartment, dim lights allowed her to avoid bumping into anything. It was completely quiet. Martin must have gone to bed, she thought. She steadied herself with one hand on the wall to stop the whirling sensation in her head before following the lights that spilled from overhead and pooled like stepping stones down a hallway that lead her to an open door.

Enough light entered the room so she could see the mold of Martin's body under the rumpled blankets on the bed, but she couldn't tell if he was awake and watching her, or not. She hoped he would say something if he was, but the room was still.

"Martin?" she whispered. There was no answer. She couldn't even hear shallow breathing, but remembered he had always been a quiet sleeper. She stepped out of her shoes in the hallway and walked into the room, draping her jacket over the back of a chair as she passed by. She thought she would feel better if she could just lie down. At the edge of Martin's bed, on the opposite side from where he lay, she took off her outer garments, letting them fall to the floor. Still no response from Martin. She eased under the covers alongside him and felt relief in resting her intoxicated body into a horizontal position.

Kate lay there for several moments, a little perturbed he might really be asleep. She began to lightly caress his back.

"Oh, yes," he whispered. "Whatever you do, please don't stop."

Kate took a deep breath and closed her eyes while she continued to move her hands up and down his back, pressing harder when she felt the tight muscles around his shoulders. "How does that feel?"

"Much better."

Her hands roamed lower and found he was naked. After awhile she stopped rubbing. "Martin?"

He rolled over to face her. "Am I dreaming? Are you an apparition of my desire?"

Kate smiled.

He ran the back of his fingers over one side of Kate's face, then tilted her head toward him, kissing her lightly on one cheek, then the other. "You feel real enough."

"Perhaps you should make sure." Her breathing increased when he ran his fingers lightly down her arm and took hold of her hand. He entwined her fingers through his and gently squeezed.

"You feel so good," he murmured.

Lost in the darkness, Kate could only imagine Martin's smiling eyes. They held each other, content for the moment. Kate slowed her breathing to match Martin's deeper rhythm.

Finally, he kissed her softly on the lips, then a second time, then again, longer and more passionately. Kate answered his hunger with a seductive moan and flirtatiously rolled over on her side, facing away from him. She reached back to pull him close to her. Martin kissed her shoulders and curled his body around hers.

A laser streak of morning sun shot through a narrow crack in the wooden shutters, silently piercing Kate's motionless sleep and arousing her body. She was alone under the covers.

In her first flash of consciousness, she didn't know where she was. She looked around to see the details of the room for the first time. She roamed her disquieted mind and throbbing head to fix on the details of the night before, but nothing appeared before her except the mortifying realization she was in Martin's bedroom. After rolling out of bed, Kate grabbed the wrinkled heap of clothes she had left on the floor and stumbled into the bathroom. She put herself back together as best she could and wandered out of the bedroom to find Martin.

She called out for him.

"Straight down the hall," he responded.

She followed his voice into a kitchen that opened onto a plant-filled solarium a few steps lower than the tiled kitchen floor. Martin was seated in the sun-drenched room in front of a sweeping view of the city.

"I smell coffee," said Kate.

Martin put aside his newspaper and spoke in a soothing voice. "Can I get you some?"

"Don't move. I can get it." She poured a mug of the black stuff, hoping it possessed enough strength to bring her back to life, then walked down the steps to sit on the plump sofa opposite Martin. She looked round at the cheerful garden room filled with the kind of wicker furniture that was actually comfortable. "Very nice."

"Thank you."

Kate sipped her coffee and glanced at Martin, who seemed to be waiting for her to start their conversation. She cleared her throat. "I hope, that is, I think, I owe you a thank you for not letting me do something I would regret for the rest of my life." She was convinced she would have remembered if they had made love, even though she didn't remember how she had gotten to his apartment in the first place. Kate thought she would suffocate while waiting for the response that would relieve her fears.

"You're welcome. You should have no regrets. Almost nothing happened, Kate."

She tipped her head sideways. "What do you mean, almost nothing? I was a little confused about some of the details when I woke up this morning."

"We kissed a little and held hands. Then you fell asleep."

"That wasn't my intention."

"It certainly wasn't. You had me going for awhile."

Kate dropped her head into her hands. "Oh, shit." She felt incredibly uncomfortable and wished she could vanish.

"It wasn't easy for me, but I did stop." He gave her a reassuring smile. "Nothing happened below the waist."

Kate laughed nervously. "Just like bashful high school sweethearts, eh?"

"That's right. However, I owe you an apology for luring you into harm's way in the first place. I hope my actions—rather, lack of action—will finally prove to you how much I really do love you. Perhaps, for the first time in my life, I put your interests before my own selfish desires."

Martin leaned toward Kate with his elbows resting on his legs and his hands clasped together. "You had too much to drink, otherwise you never would have followed me home. Don't forget, I've known you for over twenty years. You are much too loyal a person to succumb to adultery. I wanted you last night, Kate, but not under those circumstances, not when I knew the emotional price you would pay afterward. If we were ever to make love together again, beyond what happened last night, I would want you with all of your faculties intact, and with a clear conscience. I let myself be intoxicated by the festivities of the evening, but after I got home I realized I wasn't being fair. I didn't expect you would actually come."

"Then how come you left the lights on?"

He laughed. "Because I hoped things would be different. When you did come, there was no other explanation except you had had too much to drink. Remember, I know what a cheap drunk you are. Did you have another gin and tonic after I left?"

She hung her head in mock shame and held up two fingers.

"There. I rest my case. I'm sorry, Kate. I was out of line asking you to come here."

"But I'm the wench who slipped into your bed."

Martin smiled, but said nothing. He watched Kate drink more of her coffee.

She sighed. "Well, perhaps it's time for me to get out of here before I cause you any more trouble."

"Don't go yet." Martin moved to the edge of his chair and reached toward Kate. "You've never been anything but a sheer joy in my life. I made a big mistake in ever letting you go, but I know my time has passed. Bella has told me what a wonderful marriage you have."

"I told you that, too."

"Yes, but after our lunch in Denver, when I witnessed all the anger you still held for me, I didn't expect you to tell me anything to the contrary, even if you had the worst marriage on record. Bella, on the other hand, has no agenda with me. She always keeps me in my place with her brutal frankness. Did she tell you she called me a selfish interloper?"

"She was only looking out for me."

"You do a good job of that yourself. When you told me about your life with Parker that day in Denver, you radiated happiness and contentment. I just didn't want to believe it. I'm truly happy for you and envious of Parker. I apologize for my arrogance in assuming I could simply walk back into the center of your world."

"Thank you, Martin. It means a lot to hear you admit that. Not to diminish my love for Parker, but I have a confession to make as well." She shrugged her shoulders. "I still miss you sometimes." Noticing a quizzical look on Martin's face, she laughed. "Don't be confused. I'm not saying I want to restart anything."

He smiled and looked deep into her eyes.

Kate returned his smile and held his gaze. "It's all so confusing sometimes. I find myself thinking of you at the oddest times—usually when I'm peeling an orange for breakfast. But before I'm finished, thoughts of you vanish. Don't you think that's odd? Especially, after all these years."

He looked down for a moment. "I'm flattered. I assumed I was long forgotten."

"It's only a flicker."

He put both hands over his heart. "I'll take an occasional flicker."

"Martin, you know what else disturbs me?"

"What?"

"The fact that you haven't told Lily the truth, yet."

The glimmer drained from his eyes. He fell back into his chair, engulfed by its soft cushions. "I'm afraid to."

"You've got to tell her."

"I just haven't been able to get her alone."

"Make it happen soon, Martin. This situation isn't fair to Lily. She's gotten used to having you around the set. She's more relaxed with you now. She likes you."

"You make that sound difficult to believe."

"You know what I mean. Martin, you're a big boy, a successful businessman who has always been able to handle the most complicated and difficult challenges."

"This is different."

"No, this is personal. You're not afraid to lose in business, but you're afraid to lose in your private life, so you don't take any risks. You're stymied by fear. Well, get over it. If you don't come forward with the truth, then you'll lose her like you lost me."

They stared at each other. Kate had made her point and let the silence underscore its validity. She knew she had penetrated his emotional armor.

Almost a full minute passed before Martin spoke. "My tentative plan was to talk to her when the company moves up to Sonoma. I'm hoping there will be fewer distractions up there. Perhaps I can get her alone, then."

"Whatever. I don't mean to be a nag, but you were the one who asked for my help. So now, I'm advising you to take the initiative, before you lose her for good."

"I never would have had the courage to approach her in the first place if it hadn't been for you. I owe you."

"You already repaid me by being a gentleman last night, saving me from my own reckless behavior. Now, I've got to go. I know Bella must be thoroughly disgusted with me after last night. I've got to polish my tarnished tiara and let her know I'm not an adulteress after all."

As Martin walked her to the elevator, Kate surveyed her surroundings and the impressive sculpture garden she hadn't been able to see the night before. "Lily was right. You do have an extraordinary compound up here."

From their vantage point, the sculpture of three dolphins frolicking in a fountain dominated the garden. The dolphins reminded Kate of Lily's ring. She stopped and turned to Martin. "Was it you who gave

Lily the dolphin ring she wears on her necklace?"

"Yes."

"I still have the dolphin ring you gave me, too."

"And I have my icon," he said, gesturing toward the sculpture. "You will always be a force in my life. Both you and Lily."

Kate's mouth dropped open. She put a hand over her chest to still her pounding heart as she realized the profound significance the three dolphins held for Martin. Then, melancholy stilled the emotional upheaval in Kate. She turned to him, saying, "Don't let your fear of rejection get in the way, Martin. You're running out of time. Please, tell Lily the truth. Soon."

Martin smiled and kissed her on the cheek. "Goodbye, my dear Kate."

She stepped onto the waiting elevator and held Martin's gaze until the doors closed.

CHAPTER TWENTY-TWO

"Kate, you don't need to explain anything to me," said Annabella as she scrubbed the stains out of her kitchen sink. "I don't want to know."

Kate hovered near Annabella, trying to get her full attention. "Bella, if you'll just listen for one moment. I've been trying to tell you, we didn't have sex. Oddly enough, the humiliation I felt when facing Martin this morning seems to have freed me of his hold over my emotions. I think the fear of what might have happened scared me straight."

"Really, Kate. I'm not a fool. You don't deny you spent the night with Martin. You were probably too drunk to remember if something did happen. I blame myself for not trying to stop you."

"Annabella, please! You know I wouldn't lie to you about this. I'm not confused about where Martin belongs in my life anymore. What can I say to convince you? It's important you believe me."

Annabella finally dropped her sponge into the sink and turned to face Kate. "I believe you. Okay? I'm sorry for my outburst. It's none of my business anyway."

"You aren't just patronizing me?"

"No. I believe you. It's just that I was so angry with you. I couldn't believe you would do that to Parker. Remember when you and Parker became engaged and I told you that I was worried you might be prone to having an affair?"

"Not a flattering comment about my character, I might add."

"I apologized. But I thought you had lived up to my expectations last night. I've been sick with worry about what it would do to your marriage."

"Oh, Bella. An affair would destroy the trust in my marriage, something I never want to lose." The women settled at the kitchen table while Kate continued. "I admit it looks bad. I drank too much and behaved like a slut last night. Worse yet, over the past weeks, I allowed myself to regress into old patterns with Martin. I'm embarrassed and ashamed of myself." Kate shivered. "It's complicated. This whole thing with Martin and Lily has brought back painful memories. Something happened many years ago that I've never told anyone, except Parker, and even he doesn't know all the details."

Annabella's eyes widened.

"I can't tell you everything. But it might help if I could talk to you about it. You mustn't tell anyone, though. Especially Martin."

"Why not Martin?"

"Because he's changed. He's softened. I'm afraid of how he might react." The phone interrupted Kate before she had a chance to continue.

Annabella reluctantly answered the phone and handed it to Kate. "It sounds like Jonas."

"Okay... Sure... Not a problem." Kate hung up the phone and turned to Annabella. "I'm sorry, I've got to go."

"Right away?"

Kate nodded. "Jonas and David want to make script changes before filming begins at White Oaks."

"What crummy timing."

"We can talk later." She hugged Annabella before retreating to the guest room.

After downing a couple of aspirins to relieve her throbbing headache, Kate was about to step into the shower when the phone rang again. It was Becky Madison. In all that had been going on, she had forgotten about Becky.

"Would you be able to pick me up at the airport on Monday?" Becky asked.

"Yes, of course."

Kate took down the flight information and told Becky to look for her red Jeep outside the baggage claim area. She hung up the phone and immediately wondered how her schedule would allow her to meet Becky when the company was moving to their Sonoma location on Monday.

Kate spied Becky waiting in the passenger pickup area when she arrived at the airport in her red Jeep. Because of the work she had completed over the weekend, Kate had managed to schedule time to meet her old friend. Becky threw her carry-on into the back, climbed into the passenger seat and leaned over to hug Kate.

"I can't believe you really came!" said Kate. "It's good to see you."

"Same here. Two meetings in less than four months after not seeing each other since college … I hope we're not overdoing it."

"I don't think so." Kate laughed, but thoughts about the folly of inviting Becky had already cluttered her mind. What could she have been thinking? She already had her hands full with the production, and the situation with Martin and Lily. Now, she must find time to feed an old friendship she wasn't sure she even wanted. Fortunately, Annabella had volunteered to usher Becky through the long days of filming.

Kate drove into the city, where they met Annabella for lunch at the wharf. Settled at a window table, Annabella and Becky, who were both going to be extras in the movie, fell into a light repartee between mentor and student. Mainly, Annabella extolled the virtues of being a good extra, while Kate listened, occasionally offering her own advice to Becky on how to be a modest part of the scenery.

"Don't do as Annabella does. Do as she says," warned Kate. "Annabella's a bit more of a ham than most extras, but she gets away with it."

"Oh Kate, how much exuberance can we emote as grape pickers?" asked Annabella. "No one will even be able to see our faces as we stoop over grapevines, let alone recognize us. The wardrobe lady told me we'll be wearing baggy shirts, overalls and big straw hats. Jonas will probably shoot us with our sweaty backs to the camera anyway."

"True."

"This may be normal stuff to y'all, but it's my first time on a movie set, and I'm excited," proclaimed Becky.

"Then let's hit the road." Kate motioned to the waiter for the check. "We can drop our stuff off at the Sonoma Valley Lodge on our way to our main location at a vineyard called White Oaks. I'd like to see how the staging is progressing this afternoon. How about you, Bella?"

"I can't get there until later tonight." Annabella turned to Becky. "I'll meet up with you at the hotel in the morning."

When Kate steered her car through the gates of White Oaks, Becky clasped her hands together so tightly her knuckles turned white. After parking the Jeep in a shady area near the stone barn, Kate jumped out, but Becky remained seated for a moment pondering her next move. She hadn't anticipated a set visit that might put her face to face with Lily so soon. Her mind reeled with anxiety, pushing aside all reason. Staring blindly through the windshield, her eyes flickered back and forth, not focusing on anything in her view. She hadn't been thinking clearly since Lily's furtive flight from college and subsequent refusal to see her in Denver weeks earlier. Desperation had driven Becky to Sonoma to find the reason for Lily's distant behavior. She ached for reassurance that their mother-daughter bond was still tight.

Adrenalin pumping, Becky stepped out of the Jeep to catch up with Kate. As they drew closer to a group of trailers, Becky slowed her steps and warily scanned the area for any sign of Lily. From the middle of the vineyards that stretched up the hills that formed the intimate valley of White Oaks, she could hear the distant drone of directions being bantered about as men moved equipment, cables and giant reflectors around two stoic stand-ins positioned between rows of overgrown vines. Long canes and shoots from struggling grapevines, desperately in need of pruning, obscured the original symmetry of vines that had once flourished on the property. No one seemed bothered by the tendrils of dried mustard plants and scratchy weeds that must be brushing against their legs.

Becky stopped in the shadow between two of the trailers. It seemed a good place to hide. "I don't want to be in the way. Perhaps I'd better wait here for you."

"Don't be silly." Kate linked her arm with one of Becky's and continued to walk. "Come with me."

Kate poked her head in the door of a trailer marked "Makeup," then stepped inside. "Hi, everyone. What's up?" She motioned for Becky to join her. "I'd like you all to meet my oldest friend, Becky Madison."

Becky cautiously joined Kate in the trailer where she was introduced to Jonas, Simon and Denise who sat side-by-side in barbershop-like chairs. She smiled with relief at not seeing Lily. "And don't any of you ask us how long we've known each other."

Jonas, Simon and Denise laughed and exchanged pleasantries.

"Hey, Kate," said Jonas. "We were going over some of our script changes. Things are really moving along in our set-up. We're going to have time to film a couple of scenes this afternoon."

"That's great. David will be happy to get a jump on his schedule."

"Kate, have you seen Lily around?" asked Jonas. "I've got an errand for her."

"Sorry. Haven't seen her. But I'll send her your way if I do." Becky followed Kate out of the trailer. "Lily's our production assistant," said Kate. "A really neat girl. If we don't run into her here, I'll bet she's helping out at the production office back at the hotel. You'll meet her tomorrow, for sure."

Becky nodded somewhat uncomfortably. She moved away from the trailer and cautiously glanced back down the driveway. There was no sign of Lily, only some men laying down a truckload of sod between the barn and the house.

"Let's take a closer look," said Kate pointing at the group of men. "Mark Harrington's our set designer. He and his crew are preparing the area for our wine festival—a glamorous party scene you'll be in, along with your starring role as a grape picker."

"From migrant worker to ritzy party-goer. Quite a transformation. Do you think my acting abilities can handle the range?" joked Becky in an attempt to cloak herself in a veneer of calm.

As the afternoon wore on, it became apparent that Lily was not on the property, which allowed Becky to stop looking nervously over her shoulder. Upon returning to the hotel, Becky made excuses to Kate about needing sleep after her long travel day and retreated to the safety of her room, where she lit a cigarette and immediately called her brother, Les.

"I'm about to make my daughter hate me forever and alienate Kate for the second time in our lives."

"What are you talking about?" asked Les.

"I'm here in Sonoma where Lily is working on Kate's film."

"What? I thought you were going to that seminar in Europe."

"Change of plans. I want to see my daughter, even if she doesn't want to see me. We haven't spoken in weeks. That's not like her. We've always been able to work out our differences. Something's going on with her."

"So you're sneaking around Kate's movie set to ambush Lily?"

"I'm out of control, Les. I haven't been able to sleep in weeks." Her voice quivered as tears began to fall. "I've cancelled appointments with my clients for no reason. My house is a mess, and I'm smoking too much again."

"Calm down. This is so unlike you." Les continued in a slower, softer voice. "You're a dedicated therapist and incredibly conscientious. You're not acting rationally. Maybe you need some professional help."

"It's too late for that. I've got to find Lily and talk to her."

"You sound possessed."

"You're not far from wrong. A demon from my past has turned me into a conniving mother obsessed with the fear of losing her daughter. And, I'm using an unsuspecting Kate to wangle my way into Lily's new world. Can you help me? How can I turn this around in my favor?"

"Go home. Tonight. Let Lily come to terms with whatever it is she's looking for."

"I wish I could do that. But I'm a mother. I want to fix whatever is keeping her from me—even if it means spying on her. Tell me how to proceed, or at least temper my paranoia."

"You're the therapist. The only things I see are flashing red lights warning you to abort your scheme. When Lily catches you, which she will, she'll resent you for sure. Leave now. Things will work themselves out. You've always had a tight relationship with Lily. You're not going to lose her."

"I wish it were that simple."

Early the next morning, Annabella and Becky were among the first to arrive at White Oaks where organized pandemonium had already descended upon the peaceful valley. The entire force of the film's cast and crew was assembling to shoot the biggest scenes in the production. Annabella spotted Lily at work near a group of trailers. She seemed to be in charge of directing the actors to their appropriate trailers and getting them to and from wardrobe and makeup. But, there was no sign of Kate.

Eventually, thirty extras arrived who had been bussed in from a central meeting place in downtown Sonoma. Upon the suggestion of an assistant director, who seemed intent on having everyone in their proper staging areas, Annabella and Becky soon joined the other extras. All were costumed in their grungy, migrant worker attire and waited in various forms of repose under a shady grove of oak trees hidden behind the farmhouse. Some of the extras were Hispanic laborers who couldn't speak English. Try as she might, Annabella couldn't make her Italian sound like Spanish. Her attempt at friendly banter left everyone laughing in appreciation of her arm-waving pantomime. As the morning wore on, she abandoned the rigors of speaking another language and rejoined Becky.

Annabella settled under a tree near where Becky was pacing and puffing on a cigarette. "Why don't you relax? It could be awhile." She patted the ground next to her. "Join me."

"How long will it be until they need us?" Becky dropped to the ground and stubbed out her cigarette.

"Hard to tell. But believe me, once they move us into those vineyards under the hot sun, you're going to wish we were back under these trees. Want to take a walk, find something to drink?"

"I'd love to do both. I'm thirsty, and I'd like to see what's going on." Annabella encouraged Becky with a light jab of her elbow. "I think our being old friends of Kate's might afford us special privileges."

"Where is Kate, anyhow?" asked Becky.

"When I saw her in the production office this morning, she said something about a meeting in San Francisco with an exec from the TV network. She'll probably show up later this afternoon."

Both women stood and brushed grass and bits of debris from the back of their clothes.

"We've been here for almost two hours and haven't done anything. How come they had us get here so early?" asked Becky.

"Welcome to the movie business. Hurry up and wait. We're the lowest sub-species on this movie and the most expendable. We're being paid to be on the ready. We're like those gangly vines out there— scenery, or atmosphere, as some might call us."

They rounded the farmhouse and ambled toward the barn, which was about a hundred yards from where the catering truck was parked. Along the way, they passed men draping party lights on poles around the newly sodded area. Almost everyone else was working with Jonas in the vineyards.

Annabella waved at Martin and Lily, who were standing by the catering truck. As she and Becky drew closer to the pair, Annabella was aware of Becky freezing in her tracks. She turned to see why the woman had stopped in time to see Becky pull her straw hat down to shade her face. She walked back to her. "What's the matter? You look as though you've seen a ghost."

Just then, someone called for Annabella and Becky to join the rest of the extras proceeding up the slope into the vineyards. Apparently, Jonas was ready to shoot his first master shot with the extras.

"We'd better get going," Becky urged Annabella.

"Don't you want some water?"

"No, no. I'll be fine." Becky turned and quickly walked off to merge with the group on the slope.

Annabella shrugged her shoulders and continued to the catering truck, intent upon getting some water before she joined the activity.

"You look awful," said Martin.

"So awful I hope you barely recognized me," replied Annabella. "I don't want my friends to watch this movie and be able to pick me out in this get-up. I'm saving my glamour shots for the party scene where I get to play a wealthy landowner!"

"Who was that walking with you?" asked Lily, her eyes continuing to follow Becky's figure as the woman walked into the vineyards.

"Oh, that's a friend of Kate's. Someone she's known since they were kids. Becky Madison. You can meet her later."

Annabella watched a look of, what seemed to be, startled disbelief drain the color from Lily's face. Odd, she thought. That was the same expression she had just seen on Becky's face. Then she noticed that Martin seemed to stiffen at the sound of the name, as well.

"Are you sure that's her name?" Lily asked, clenching her fists by her side.

"Yes. Why?"

"No reason. It just sounds oddly familiar." Lily's voice was clipped and strained. "I'm sure it's only a coincidence. You'd better get going, Annabella. Didn't they call for all of the extras?"

"Yeah. I'll see you later." Annabella poured a cup of water and scooted up the hill.

Somehow the idea of seeing Martin and Lily together hadn't crossed Becky's mind. His unexpected presence had knocked her off balance. Partially hidden by the spindly growth of vines, and stuck in the middle of all the extras, she struggled to follow Jonas's directions while surreptitiously keeping an eye on Lily and Martin. In time, she saw them part and watched until her daughter moved out of sight. When she spotted Martin again, he was plodding his way up the hill toward her before positioning himself behind the soundman, presumably to watch the filming.

After several takes, Jonas let the cast and extras take a break while his crew set up for the next shot. Martin and Becky eyed each other and gravitated to a shady spot away from everyone else.

"It's been a long time, Skipper." Martin spoke in a gentle tone.

"I haven't been called that since college." She stood on guard with her arms folded across her chest. "How did you recognize me in this get-up? I thought I was incognito, especially hidden under this droopy straw hat." To prove her point she lifted the wide brim to reveal splotches of dirt the makeup lady had wiped across her face to further obscure her identity.

"The hat doesn't conceal your distinctive walk. And, Annabella confirmed my suspicion when she mentioned your name."

The hint of a smile curled into a frown. "What are you doing here?"

"I'm representing the cartel that owns this property."

"Really. How nice. But that's not the only reason y'all are here, is it?" she said in icy tones.

"It isn't the real reason at all, and you, of all people, should know that better than anyone."

"I don't know if I know anything anymore."

"What does that mean?

Becky ignored his question. "I saw you talking to Lily. Does she know who you are?"

"No."

Becky bit her lip and looked suspiciously at him. "How did you find her?"

"It doesn't matter how I found her. The important thing is, I've been able to spend time with her over the past couple of weeks. But she didn't mention you were going to be here."

"She doesn't know. I wanted to surprise her."

"That explains her behavior at the catering truck. Based on her reaction when Annabella mentioned your name, your being here isn't a surprise anymore."

"Shit," said Becky under her breath.

"I guess Lily's in for a lot of surprises."

"What other surprises, Martin?"

"I'm going to tell her who I am."

"You can't do that. You promised you'd stay out of her life."

"That's when she was younger. She's an adult, Becky. And, I think she wants to know who her father is."

"But you have no right!"

"I have every right. She's my daughter."

Martin and Becky were oblivious to the second assistant director's call for all of the extras to return to their positions. Annabella's two-fingered whistle finally got their attention.

"I think you're wanted back on the set," said Martin.

"I know." Becky clasped her hands together as if to plead with him. "Please don't do anything until we talk some more." Then she reluctantly hustled off, holding onto her hat to keep it from flying off as she hastened her return to the waiting crew.

Back on the set, Becky's gaze anxiously scoured the grounds in search of Lily, but she was nowhere in sight. Ironically, Becky's disguise had trapped her on a hillside vineyard. She found it hard to concentrate on Jonas's directions, but some deep sense of decorum kept her from making a ruckus to find Lily while she was on Kate's movie set. It seemed like agonizing eons before Jonas called for the next break in shooting.

After looking everywhere, Becky eventually found an assistant director who informed her that Lily had returned to the production office at the hotel.

"Can someone take me there?" she asked him.

"Afraid not. There aren't any drivers available until we wrap at the end of the day."

Becky bit her lip and looked around. She had to do something. She spotted Annabella and approached her, asking, "Do you think I could borrow your car?"

"We're still needed in the next scene," said Annabella. "We can't leave now. Besides, I loaned Lily, our production assistant, my car. Is there anything wrong?"

"I, ah, I forgot something at the hotel and hoped I could make a quick trip there before they need us again."

"I'm afraid we're stuck here until the bus can take us back to town with the other extras. We could call the production office and see if Lily has time to pick up what you need and bring it to you."

Becky dropped her head. "No. That won't be necessary."

When Kate finally arrived at White Oaks late in the afternoon, Annabella wasted no time in cornering her. "First, tell me about your meeting in the city this morning. By the big grin on your face, I'm guessing it went well."

"They like the daily footage they've seen so far and want to schedule *Love Among the Vineyards* during the February sweeps."

"February sweeps. That is prime airtime. They must love your film. Probably means lots of publicity, too."

"They're sending up a publicist and photographer to gather photos and interviews with the cast members."

Annabella looked around. "Kate that's fantastic, but I need to talk to you about something else." She put a hand on her friend's arm and led her behind the barn, where she practically pinned Kate against the stone wall. Kate had no choice but to listen as Annabella related the story of Becky's odd behavior earlier that day.

"We were going for some water. Next thing I know, she turned and practically ran in the opposite direction. You should have seen the expression on her face! Lily had almost the same expression when I mentioned Becky's name. Even Martin looked weird. Don't you think that's odd?"

Kate looked at the stack of files she held in her arms and then at Annabella. "Forgive my lack of concern, but I'm a bit preoccupied with production issues right now."

Annabella placed her hands on Kate's shoulders. "I saw Becky and Martin talking during one of the breaks, so I invited Martin to join us during lunch. They acted as if they had just met today. But I know they've met before. It was so obvious. They were uncomfortable with each other. Don't you see? That only happens when people already know each other."

"Bella, it's your overactive imagination. You've been standing around too long today with nothing to do. Look, I've got some things to check on, and I think they need you back in the vineyards." Kate pointed toward the extras moving back up the hill.

Annabella sighed with exasperation and rushed off to join the extras.

Back at the Sonoma Valley Lodge, the production manager directed Martin to a conference room the film company was using as an additional office. Here, Lily was answering telephones for the missing production secretary.

"Hi, Lily."

Lily looked up, seemingly startled by the sound of his voice. She leaned back in her chair and folded her arms over her chest. "What are you doing here?" she challenged.

Martin spoke with caution. "I've come to invite you to dinner."

"Are you all in on it?"

Martin spoke softly. "In on what, Lily?"

"Sneaking my mother onto the set to spy on me?"

"Lily, it's important we talk. That's why I want you to come to dinner."

"Will my mother be there to surprise me? I saw the two of you talking today."

"No. I can promise you that. I had no idea she was going to be here either. I'm just as shocked as you are. My God, I haven't seen her in years."

"I'm a little confused. How do you know her?" The ringing phone interrupted them. She jerked the receiver to her ear, but spoke calmly to the caller. After writing a note, she slammed down the receiver and glared back at Martin.

Martin fought Lily's icy stare with gentle words and the reassuring warmth of a father. "Lily, please. It's very important that we talk. Please say you'll come to dinner tonight. I'll tell you everything then."

CHAPTER TWENTY-THREE

At seven sharp, Martin watched Lily drive up the long gravel driveway to the sprawling, red tile-roofed hacienda he had borrowed from a friend for the two weeks of filming at White Oaks. He stood in the open doorway and greeted her as she stepped onto the front porch. He was dressed casually in khaki pants, a light golf shirt and sandals. Lily was in white slacks and a hot pink designer tee shirt topped off with garish, dangling earrings that nearly brushed the top of her shoulders. As if to announce her arrival, Lily flicked her fingers through the earrings, setting off a jangling noise.

Martin laughed at her youthful gusto. "I hope you didn't wear those earrings on my account."

"Pretty obnoxious, aren't they?" She offered Martin an uncertain smile. "I'm meeting Jonas later, so thought I'd have a little fun with these."

"I'm glad you decided to come, with or without those earrings." He stepped aside to let her into the house and guided her through the Spanish-style living room. The space was filled with overstuffed leather couches, a hanging tapestry and opulent antique tables blooming with giant vases of hydrangeas, foxgloves and delphiniums. A wall of glass doors opened onto the gracious outdoor courtyard where a towering azure-tiled fountain splashed water from its monolithic center. Beyond the terrace, acres of vineyards surrounded the home.

It was a very warm summer evening in the Sonoma Valley. Lily readily accepted Martin's offer to join him for a glass of wine on the patio.

They sat opposite each other in a grouping of cushioned, wrought-iron chairs nestled under an olive tree in a corner of the courtyard. For several minutes, they shared small talk about the house and the ornamental garden of blooming flowers surrounding them. Except for the fuchsias, impatiens and bougainvillea, they both pleaded ignorance to the names of the other plants. All the while, Martin's foot twitched in time to his finger nervously tapping the back of his watchband.

"Gardening isn't what you wanted to talk about with me, is it?" prompted Lily.

Martin was uncharacteristically nervous, even more so than during his first meeting with Lily at the Olympic Club. He got up and started pacing, fully aware that Lily was watching his every move. "I'm not sure how to begin."

"How about telling me how you know my mother."

"Skipper. That's what I used to call her."

"Skipper? I'm a little confused."

"Your mother is Skipper. I invited her to go sailing on our first date, but she was afraid of sailing, so my fraternity brothers gave her the nickname of Skipper, and it stuck throughout college."

"So you met at the University of Washington?"

"That's right."

Lily pulled herself up a little straighter in her chair and set her wine glass back on the table next to Martin's untouched glass.

Martin could see he had Lily's full attention as he began to recount his college romance with her mother. "I'm not sure she liked her nickname, even though it was meant as a term of endearment. I understand she dropped any reference to 'Skipper' and 'Becky' after college and preferred to be called Rebecca. I guess Rebecca sounds more professional than Becky, but why did she change her last name from Madison to McGuire instead of Thompson, her husband's name?"

"I don't think she ever took his name, especially since he died so soon after they were married. As long as I can remember, we have always used McGuire."

"Sounds like a woman with an identity crisis," observed Martin.

"It must run in the family. I've been a little confused about my own identity lately."

Her comment boosted Martin's courage to reveal his relationship to her, but before he could continue in that vein, Lily interrupted him.

"What was she like in college? Please tell me more."

"Didn't she ever tell you about her college days?"

"Not a word. She resides strictly in the present. Only thinks about what's important today. Rather ironic, since she spends all day delving into her patients' pasts. She says it's necessary to help them move into the present."

"The 'Skipper' I knew was fun, almost flighty sometimes. She never missed a party and instigated most of the practical jokes our group of friends enjoyed. She had a great sense of humor. Occasionally, she would withdraw and get very moody, but those periods never lasted more than a couple of days. But in her senior year, she changed."

"How so?"

"She stopped going to parties and spent her time studying at the library. She had raised her sights to graduate school. Becky and I went together for almost two years before breaking up during our senior year. She dumped me for her first love, Donald Thompson. He had returned to Washington to finish his senior year. He was very studious, more of an egghead academic. I guess he represented the intellectual she so desperately wanted to become herself."

"And he had money," added Lily.

"No. I don't think he did. As I recall, he was from a middle class suburb of Chicago. Why would you think he had money?" As soon as he asked the question, he understood that Lily might be fishing for a clue to her benefactor, the identity of which he would soon reveal.

"No reason," she responded, disavowing her question with a flip of her wrist. "I was just wondering."

Martin walked over to the table and took a sip of his wine to calm his nerves. "Before I go on, I did promise you dinner. Are you hungry?"

"A little."

"If you like salmon, I'll fire up the grill.

"That would be just right."

Martin hardly touched his dinner while he filled Lily's appetite with more stories about his days with Becky in college. When he saw that Lily had finished eating, he knew he couldn't put off the inevitable any longer.

"There is something else about your mother and me that it's time you know. Your mother tried to convince me otherwise today. And for years, I let her have her way. But after getting to know you these past few weeks, I think you can handle the truth."

"This sounds ominous." Lily shifted in her chair.

Martin cleared his throat and leaned toward Lily a bit. "Even though your mother broke off our relationship, we still remained friends. During our last year in college, when she and Donald had a falling out, Becky and I went out together a few times. That's when it happened."

"What happened? Don't stop now."

"That was the summer of 1967. Becky was a very desirable young woman."

Lily nodded her head matter-of-factly. "So, you had sex with her."

Martin leaned back in his chair and looked out on the golden glow cascading across the lush green vineyards as the sun melted behind the rolling Sonoma hills. He glanced at the fountain's crystal waters hoping to catch a muse, but his words stuck in his throat. He turned back to face Lily, who gently folded her hands on the table. His fists were clenched so tightly that his nails dug into his wet palms.

"Lily, that was the summer you were conceived." Seeing no reaction from her, he continued. "I'm trying to tell you that I'm your father."

Lily's mouth fell open. Martin saw the color drain from her face. All went still around him. He could no longer hear the water splashing from the fountain. A flood of discomfort stiffened his bones. His throat tightened in anticipation of her response. But Lily seemed trapped in her chair. No words came from her. Her head bobbled like a cupie doll in a '57 Chevy.

Finally, Lily broke the deadly silence. "Martin, I don't know what to say. That's impossible."

"Please, just listen to all I have to say."

"Martin…" She tried to interrupt him, but he ignored her and continued talking.

"I'm so sorry I wasn't there for you while you were growing up. I didn't know about you at first. Your Uncle Les and I were fraternity brothers. He's the one who eventually told me about Becky's pregnancy. My immediate reaction was to ask Becky to marry me, but she had already married Donald. She told me to leave her alone. Selfishly, I was relieved. We never loved each other that way, and I wasn't ready to get married. But I felt responsible for our child. When Donald was killed in the automobile accident right after you were born, that's when I started a trust fund for you. I didn't have much to deposit in those first few years, but after awhile, when I started to make some real money, I added more and more. If I couldn't be a part of your day-to-day life, then I wanted to provide you with the security and choices money could buy."

"You're the one who set up my trust fund?" Martin could hear astonishment in her voice.

"Yes. I wish your mother would have at least told you that much about me."

"She only alluded to some mysterious friend. I used to think she meant Donald, or maybe his parents." Lily looked down in her lap, than back at Martin. "I don't know what to say."

"This must be a lot for you to take in. I know you'll need time to absorb it all."

"Who else knows this?" she asked.

"Your Uncle Les has known for years, but your mother convinced him not to tell you. And, Kate knows. I told her about you this spring and asked for her help when I learned the two of you were already working together on that campaign. She was uncomfortable in keeping this a secret from you, but reluctantly agreed to keep quiet at my insistence."

Lily shifted uncomfortably in her chair. "Kate knows?"

"Please don't be upset with Kate. She wanted me to tell you from the very beginning. But I was afraid. After seeing your mother today, I knew I couldn't wait any longer."

"How did you know I was in Denver?"

"Your Uncle Les told me, but I hired a private eye to find out where. Les disagreed with Becky's decision to keep me away from you. But even though he kept me informed about you, he remained loyal to Becky by never revealing where the two of you lived. Looking back on it, I think Becky changed her name to McGuire to make it more difficult for me to find you.

"Les told me about your golf, your love of ballet, and what you were studying in college. I took up golf when I heard your grandfather was teaching you how to play. I hoped some day we might play together, and we have, haven't we?"

"But why now? After all these years?"

"Les told me you left college this spring before finals and without telling anyone, and had essentially run away from Becky as well. That's when I got worried and hired a private detective to find you."

It was Lily's turn to pace around the fountain. She nervously poured more wine, but left the glass sitting on the table. "I don't know how else to say this. I don't believe you can be my father."

Martin turned his chair to keep her in his sight. "For reasons I will let your mother explain, it could not be Donald. It was not just your uncle who told me I was your father. Becky admitted this to me just months before you were born, although she tried to deny it later."

"But you didn't believe her." Lily circled the fountain again. "Oh, my God. You have believed a lie for so many years. This is so incredibly difficult." She grabbed her dangling earrings with both hands that stopped the tinkling sound echoing in the courtyard. The gesture seemed to unlock an emotional floodgate as tears streaked down her cheeks and words tumbled uncontrollably out of her mouth. "My mother, 'Becky,' 'Rebecca,' 'Skipper,' whatever anyone wants to call her, had a miscarriage when she was seven months pregnant." Lily covered her mouth with two clinched fists and spoke up at the sky with words that reeked of frustration and anger. "Why am I the only one who seems to know this?"

Martin saw pain and confusion in Lily's demeanor. He wanted to hold her in his arms to calm her. He struggled with words. "What are you saying? She gave birth to you, a beautiful baby girl."

"No, Martin. That's what she let you and me and everyone else think."

"Lily, I can see you're in denial, perhaps shock. But what I have told you is the truth. If I'd known it was going to be this traumatic for you, I would have insisted your mother be here so we could have told you together. I have made a mess of this, and you're the one who is suffering, the last person I ever wanted to hurt. I am so sorry, Lily." He rose and walked over to console her.

Lily threw her hands up and moved away from him. "I'm sorry, Martin. Maybe you're right. I need time to think. I'm sorry to rush off but I've got to go." With that, Lily raced through the hacienda to the front door, leaving Martin standing alone in the courtyard. He could hear her fumbling with the massive door handle before freeing herself from the house.

Once in her car, Lily drove off into the darkness, tears blurring her vision. At first, she was unsure of what to do next. She knew she couldn't go back to the hotel. She feared her mother would be waiting for her. Thankfully, she calmed down enough to remember that Jonas was expecting her at the Winery Café.

After pulling into the café's parking lot, Lily ran a comb through her hair and dabbed at her teary eyes before summoning the calm to walk into a public place. Once inside the Winery Café, she spotted Jonas waiting at a corner table and walked over to him.

"Lily, you look terrible. What's wrong?" Jonas got up to pull out a chair for her.

She pushed away swelling tears with both hands. "I was hoping I wouldn't look as washed out as I feel." Jonas put his arm around Lily, who began to weep. "I'm so embarrassed. Can we go outside?"

"Of course." Jonas threw money on the table to cover the cost of his beer. With his arm still around her shoulders, he led Lily outside and helped her into his car. He walked around to the driver's side and slid in next to her. The only light illuminating them shimmered across the parking lot from the restaurant.

"I don't know how much longer I can keep this all to myself," she murmured through her fading tears.

"Keep what to yourself? What's happened, Lily?" Jonas looked intently at Lily.

"I wish I could tell you."

"Did Martin say or do something to upset you tonight?"

Lily answered with silence.

"What did he do?" demanded Jonas in urgent tones.

"Nothing. Nothing. He was a perfect gentleman." Lily exhaled a deep sigh while fumbling through her purse for a tissue. "I guess you could say, my predicament has something to do with, oh, I don't know...self-discovery. And, I don't mean in the New Age sense. I recently learned something about myself that has turned my life upside down, and tonight, it got more complicated. It's not a life and death thing," she added when she saw his worried look. "I thought I had everything figured out until tonight. Then, Martin surprised me with a missing chunk of the puzzle I wasn't expecting. I'm afraid I reacted very badly and ran out on him."

"I'm confused. I thought you barely knew Martin."

"That's true. But it turns out, he knows my mother. Oh, yes. Did I tell you that my mother is one of your extras in the movie?"

"What?"

"Yep. I didn't know about it, either, until I saw her on the set today." Lily shook her head to display her own disbelief at her mother's sudden appearance. "Jonas, the last thing you need right now is to hear about all my problems. You've got your hands full with the film."

"Lily, I can focus on more than one subject at a time."

"I don't want to be another one of your projects."

"You know what I mean. We're friends. I care if you're in trouble, and I want to help you."

"I'm sorry about all the drama. I don't mean to be so mysterious, either. God, I must seem like a silly schoolgirl to you."

"You don't strike me as someone who cries over nothing. I'm sure there is something major going on here. Talk to me, Lily. Perhaps, it will help you get a better perspective on things."

"It would help. I desperately want to confide in you and almost have a couple of times. I thought I was going to tell you tonight, but, just being with you has given me the strength not to tell you. Goofy, eh? It's just that…there are people involved whom I care about, and I can't risk alienating them. It's important they don't find out about me from someone else. Not that I don't trust you." She brushed his cheek with her hand. "I think you'll understand once I do tell you everything, and I promise I will. Now that my mother is here, I have a feeling my secret will be out in the open sooner than I had planned." She wiped at her remaining tears and blew her nose. "There. I'm better now." She moved closer to him and smiled. "Maybe, if you kissed me, I'd feel even better."

Jonas took her hand. "I thought I couldn't touch you until after we finished making this movie."

Lily responded by leaning over and kissing him. He wrapped his arms around her and eagerly responded to her overture.

"You're a wonderful kisser," she said, drawing slightly away from him so she could rest her head on his chest.

"I'm sorry about whatever is upsetting you. But, I'm glad it led you into my arms. It's been hard being just friends with you these past weeks."

"I know. For me, too. But…

"But?"

"Oh Jonas, my life has become a bubbling pot of confusion. The excitement of a new relationship right now might cause it to boil over. I don't want to risk our relationship by over-spicing the stew just yet."

"I think I understand. But, maybe we could share a few hors d'oeuvres?"

Lily laughed. "Yes, I'd like that."

Lily and Jonas tentatively pressed their lips together like two innocent teens experiencing their first kiss. Wrapped in their desire, they managed to sustain a modest level of growing passion for longer than they thought possible. Finally, it swelled beyond the appetizer stage, and instinctively, they pulled away from each other. There would be a next time and a better time.

On first glance, Kate spotted a subdued and preoccupied Becky across the hotel lobby, but by the time they converged, a smile had camouflaged her despondency.

"Everything okay?" asked Kate.

"Fine. I'm just a wee bit tired I guess. It was a long day out there. I stopped by the production office, but the secretary said that everyone had gone to dinner. I'm glad I found you."

"Are you up for some Mexican food with me and Bella?"

"Sure, why not?"

During dinner, Becky was congenial but quiet. Annabella was the queen of restraint per Kate's insistence that she avoid any talk of Becky's strange behavior at White Oaks earlier that day. But after the last sip of her second Margarita, Annabella broke the truce. "I didn't know you knew Martin Kelly."

Kate shot Annabella a look of warning, but was interested to hear the answer herself.

"Why do you think that?" asked Becky taking a sip of her Coke.

"Oh, after seeing the two of you together today…you seemed pretty chummy."

"I wouldn't call it chummy. It was quite a surprise to see him. We went to college together." She looked down at her plate and pushed bits of food around with her fork.

Kate noticed Becky's discomfort, but wanted to satisfy her own aroused curiosity. "I forgot Martin had gone to the University of Washington. Didn't he belong to the same fraternity as your brother?"

"Yes. That's how we met. But how would you know that?"

Kate brushed off her question. "Just one of those things you pick up along the way. It never occurred to me that you and Martin might have known each other in college, but of course you would have. What a lucky coincidence to run into him here." Kate smiled and nodded with resignation, hoping Annabella would take that as a signal to drop her inquisition.

But Annabella continued to bait Becky. "I bet you've got some fun college stories. What kind of a wild man was Martin in college?"

"Y'all will have to ask my brother for those details."

Later, when the three women returned to the hotel, Annabella headed up to her room while Kate and Becky drifted out to the deserted swimming pool to enjoy a few more moments of the warm summer night. They removed their shoes at the edge of the pool so they could dangle their feet in the refreshing water and lay back on the deck to view the star-packed sky. The moment was reminiscent of the many summers they had shared together as children.

"This is nice." Kate spoke softly as if to keep her words from rustling the still air.

"Brings back a few memories," said Becky. "Hide-and-seek with the neighbor kids, camp-outs in your backyard, snipe hunting with anyone who didn't know better."

"Skinny dipping in my parents' pool at midnight, stealing apples from the Peterson's tree," added Kate.

"We never stole any apples."

"I know. But it sounds adventurous."

They laughed, then drifted into their own thoughts.

Eventually, Becky sat up and pulled her legs out of the pool into a cross-legged position. "I hate to interrupt this magical moment, but I've got to talk to you about something rather important."

"Okay, shoot." Kate was still lost in the stars and didn't notice the tightness in Becky's voice.

"Kate, I haven't told you much about my daughter and why she was in Denver."

"Uh huh," acknowledged Kate, half-listening. "Did you finally get in touch with her?"

"In a manner of speaking, yes."

"Good, I'm glad to hear that." She swished the top of the water with her feet.

"Aren't you curious about what happened between us?"

Kate sat up but left her feet in the water. "I'm sorry for appearing indifferent. I rarely ask about anyone's children. Since I don't have children, I usually focus on other things."

"Oh, I didn't know that subject was taboo with you."

Realizing her admission sounded heartless, Kate attempted to explain. "The truth is, the topic of children stirs up a lot of emotions in me lately. You see, I recently had a miscarriage, and the upshot of it is, the doctor told me I can never have children. The emotional pain is still pretty raw for me."

"I'm so sorry," said Becky. "I didn't realize."

"I'm learning to deal with it. Unfortunately, the desire to be a mother seems to be one of those primal whispers that reside for all eternity in a woman's subconscious…at least, mine. Something to do with defining our womanhood, I think."

"Have you thought about adopting?"

"We talked about it, but decided against it." Kate pulled her feet out of the water and turned to face Becky. "Years ago, I chose a career over love and children. Now that I have love, it's too late for children. If I had tried to have a career and children, I would have been mediocre at both. I don't think children deserve compromises when it comes to having a parent available when they need one. Too many children of working parents fall near the bottom of a long list of priorities."

Becky grimaced but didn't interrupt as Kate continued.

"What some may view as selfishness on my part is just the opposite. By not having children while working full time, I saved an innocent soul from the heartache of being a neglected, latchkey kid. That may sound harsh, but I'm a firm believer that children need a strong family unit to survive today. I think raising children is probably the hardest and most important thing anyone can do in their lives."

"Whoa, pretty strong opinions on a subject you have never experienced."

"Don't get me started on the problems with kids and working parents. As you can see, it arouses the zealot in me. If people are lucky enough to have children, then they need to make the full-time commitment that goes with it. Some friends accuse me of treating my dog like a child. I think that's better than some parents who think of their children as pets whom they leave alone while they pursue the brass ring. I chose to pursue what, luckily, turned into a gratifying career for me. One I'm revisiting with this movie."

"You're really wound up." Becky leaned back on her elbows, as if to create distance from Kate. "You always did overpower me when you had a point to make."

Kate saw Becky's annoyed expression and put her hand across her mouth. "Oh, God. I know sometimes parents don't have a choice about working."

"It's okay. You're not a parent. You can't possibly understand about raising kids today."

Kate resented Becky's dismissive comment, but felt perhaps she deserved it. She tried to recover her gaffe. "So please, tell me about your daughter. I would like to hear about her, in spite of what I said earlier."

"I was...am...ambitious like you, Kate. Often the demands of my career have come before my daughter. But as a single, working mom I did everything I could to give her what I thought she needed. Not to brag, but she is a very smart and beautiful young woman. She is a far better daughter than I deserve. Unfortunately, Lily and I had a major falling out that I'm not sure I can repair."

"Lily?" It was too much of a coincidence not to be the same Lily, thought Kate.

"Lily McGuire is my daughter."

A thick silence fell between them.

"I don't believe it." Kate's comment was barely audible. This was reminiscent of her conversation with Martin months earlier when he told her Lily was his daughter. "Then you and Martin Kelly were more than just friends in college?"

"What do you know about Martin? What has he told you?"

"Martin and I have known each other for years. I know that he's Lily's father and her benefactor."

"Martin isn't Lily's father."

"What do you mean he isn't her father? Hasn't he provided Lily with a rather generous trust fund?" Kate was aggravated and suspicious of Becky's conflicting information.

"I don't know what Martin has told you, but obviously a lot. My brother, and certain circumstances, led Martin to believe he was her father. I tried to tell Martin otherwise years ago, but he didn't believe me. When my husband, Donald, died in a car crash a few weeks after Lily was born, I didn't know how I was going to support her. Martin offered to help, but I begged him to stay out of our lives. It may not make sense, but I was afraid he might try to take Lily away from me.

"I changed my name to McGuire and moved away so he couldn't find us. It was my brother who kept Martin informed about Lily over the years. How could I know Martin would feel such a paternal connection with Lily after seeing her once when she was barely two years old? And I didn't know he had kept up with the trust fund until much later."

Kate shook her head in disbelief. "I don't get it. If, as you claim, Martin isn't Lily's father, then why would Les tell Martin that he is? And if Martin isn't Lily's father, then what rightful claim would he have on her? The Martin I know would never take a child away from her mother."

Becky reached for a towel on a nearby chair and wrapped it around her body. "Let me explain. Before we decided to get married, Donald and I had a fight. To retaliate, I took up with Martin again." She shrugged her shoulders. "Martin and I had, shall we say, a passionate relapse during our brief reconciliation. When I got married later that summer, I was pregnant. That's why Martin thinks the baby is his."

"What about the trust fund? Why haven't you told Lily where it came from?"

"I didn't realize it had grown so large until Lily turned sixteen, when one of Martin's lawyers wrote me a letter saying the money was available for Lily's college education. I think Lily assumed it came from Donald or his family."

"And you just let her think that?" asked Kate.

Becky answered with a dismissive shrug of her shoulders.

"Why so many secrets, Becky? What are you afraid of?"

Becky shook her head in silence.

The night air was cooling down. Kate walked over to get a towel and sat in a nearby chair.

"Becky, did you know Martin and I..." Kate hesitated to search for the most apt way to posture her on-again-off-again love affair with Martin. She took a deep breath and started again. "Martin and I have known each other for years and are very close friends. Not long after you came to my house in April, I ran into Martin at a fund-raising event. He had come to Colorado to find Lily, too. He located her, but was reluctant to approach her, so he asked for my help. Coincidently, I had just met Lily for the first time several days earlier. But I didn't know she was your daughter." Kate knocked the palm of her hand against her head. "Oh, I think I'm beginning to see. My meeting Lily in Denver wasn't a coincidence, was it? You told me the day you came to my house that she might come looking for me, which totally baffled me at the time. Why would she want to see me? Does she think I'm her benefactor?"

"I honestly don't know."

"Yet, you thought she might come looking for me. What aren't you telling me? I'll give you a pass for not telling me much about Lily in April, but why didn't you tell me about her before you came to San Francisco?" Kate's building anger didn't wait for an answer. "I think my dense little gray cells are beginning to light up." She pointed a finger at Becky. "You found out Lily was working on my movie and used me to get to her." Kate shook her head. "Lily is another pawn in your game, of that I'm sure."

"Kate, I didn't use y'all. Y'all invited me, remember?"

"Don't split hairs with me. And stop with that *y'all* business. You're not from the South. You knew exactly what you were doing. We were once very close friends. Why couldn't you have been honest with me? You know, Bella suspected something odd was going on. As usual, she was right." Kate jumped to her feet and stood with hands on her hips, looking down at Becky, who remained sitting by the pool. "I'm losing my patience. I assume you're not going to tell me anything more."

"I'm sorry."

"Sorry doesn't cut it. If you have family problems to work out, please do so, but not on my movie set. I will not tolerate any disruption caused by you. I can't prevent you from staying at this hotel." Kate thought for a moment. She was on a roll. "Or maybe I can. Your room is reserved for this production, with which you are no longer associated. Lily has been a fantastic asset to this production, and I don't want her job to be jeopardized by an intruding mother who has to sneak around and con people in order to be close to her daughter. You and Lily will have to confront your problems away from her work."

Becky stood to face Kate. "I think you're overreacting."

"Becky, I'm tired. I've been working long hours and weekends on this movie. I don't have time for this. I don't like being deceived and taken advantage of. You have done both. I am in the middle of the biggest project of my life, and I won't let anyone, not even you, ruin one moment of the sheer joy I am experiencing with this production. Martin has pushed the envelope a bit far, himself, but at least he's been honest with me." Kate grabbed her shoes and stormed back into the hotel.

In a seething fury, Kate knew she would not be able to sleep, so she went to Annabella's room in the hope of being able to vent. She listened at the door for the sound of a television before she tapped lightly and called out Annabella's name. Kate heard the rattle of the chain as Annabella removed it from the door and took that as her cue to explode into the room, almost knocking Annabella backward. Annabella sat on the bed to be out of the way while Kate paced madly about the room, relating the jumbled details of Becky's incredible revelation.

As she neared the end of her story, Kate began to feel some sense of relief. "What a mess. What a mess." Shaking her head, she finally sat on the bed next to Annabella.

"Poor Lily," added Annabella. "Do you think her mother is lying about Martin not being Lily's father?"

"I don't know what to believe. But I owe you an apology. You said something was strange about Becky's behavior. Who could have imagined this mess? Have you seen Lily tonight?"

"Not since this morning. She's probably with Jonas. I think they have something going."

Kate smiled. "That would be nice. Right now I'm more concerned about Lily being ambushed by Becky. Did you tell me Lily saw Becky today?"

"She saw her all right, from a distance. Lily borrowed my car and left White Oaks right after that. Now I know why."

"I feel somehow responsible for this," said Kate. "Lily must think I set up this whole thing. She must think I'm a monster."

"I think you need a drink." Annabella raided the honor bar for a mini bottle of Jameson's whiskey to help calm Kate's nerves. She grabbed a brandy for herself. They talked for awhile longer before Kate finally retreated to her room.

The message light was blinking. Kate reluctantly called for her messages in case David or Jonas needed her about the production. The only message was from Martin:

I told her. Please call me. Lily needs time to sort this out, so I won't be around for awhile.

Kate was concerned for him, but preferred to console him with a return call the next morning. The whiskey and her exhausted emotions induced her into fitful sleep.

The next morning, the alarm woke Kate at six, hurling thoughts of
Martin and Becky to the forefront of her mind.

Daylight sneaked through a slit in the curtains, allowing enough light
to show Kate's exhausted body where to find the bathroom. Soon a
pelting shower of water began to bring her back to life. Kate heard the
muffled sound of her phone ringing, but chose not to answer it in fear
it might be Becky or Martin. Once dressed, she called for her messages
and learned it was Lily asking for a ride to the set. Kate sighed in
resignation and called the girl.

Twenty minutes later, Kate pulled her car up to the front entrance
of the hotel where Lily was waiting for her. Kate was apprehensive. She
knew Lily must be flush with emotions after her meeting with Martin
and the unexpected appearance of her mother.

"Morning, Lily."

Lily offered a half-hearted smile and slid into the front seat.
"Thanks for giving me a ride."

Kate eased the car away from the hotel grounds and onto the
highway. A quick side glance told Kate that Lily was keeping her gaze
fixated out the passenger side window.

"Are you okay?" asked Kate.

"Uh huh."

"I'm sorry, Lily. I didn't know Becky was your mother."

"I know."

"I fired her last night."

Lily laughed. "You did?"

"I didn't have a choice."

"You're being awfully nice about all this, Kate. I thought I might
have to resign today. I'm the one who owes you an apology."

"I figured one of you had to go, and Jonas would kill me if you quit.
Maybe you can repay me by telling me what's going on."

"I will. Soon."

"This weekend?"

"That would be best," Lily agreed.

They drove the rest of the way in silence until Kate pulled inside the gate at White Oaks and parked the car.

Lily turned to Kate. "I had dinner with Martin last night. I'd like to talk to you about that, too."

Kate looked over at Lily and put a reassuring hand on her shoulder. "I thought you might. Speaking of Martin, I got a message from him last night. He said he wouldn't be on the set for a few days.

"That's a relief. Thanks for letting me know."

Lily slid out of the car and headed off to start her day. Kate lingered behind and watched Lily until the girl disappeared behind the barn.

CHAPTER TWENTY-FOUR

By the end of the week, all seemed back to normal to Kate. She had become immersed in a fifteen-hours-a-day schedule like a workhorse plowing the fields. She fell into bed each night with a mind relaxed by work. As far as Kate knew, Becky was no longer around, Martin was keeping his distance, and Lily seemed amazingly calm after the emotional upheaval she had endured earlier in the week.

"I have a surprise for you." Lily stood opposite Kate at the long dining table near the catering truck where Kate was having lunch with Jonas and some of the actors.

"You're going to come away with me for the weekend!" said Jonas enthusiastically.

Lily shook her head at him. "Jonas! This is a surprise for Kate."

"For me?" Kate loved surprises, but after Becky's disturbing ambush earlier in the week, she was leery. She saw a sparkle of delight on Lily's face, so decided it was safe to take the bait. "What could it possibly be?"

"Turn around, and you'll see."

Before Kate had a chance to turn around, hands rested lightly on her shoulders and lips nuzzled her neck. Kate whirled around in her chair to see Parker grinning down on her. "Parker!" she cried, jumping up and knocking her flimsy, plastic chair over. She threw her arms around him and held him close, fighting back her tears. "I'm so glad you're here!" And she was. She had had no idea how much pressure had been building inside of her until she felt it wash away in the protection of his arms.

After several moments, Kate realized the group was watching them. She released Parker and turned to them, smiling proudly. "Everyone, this is my husband, Parker." She wiped away a tear escaping down her cheek.

"Hi," they all chimed. Parker returned their welcome, then politely excused himself and Kate. He winked at Lily before walking off, arm-in-arm with Kate.

"How did you get here?" Kate asked.

"Lily picked me up. Company business. A special delivery package for one of the producers." Parker grinned at her. "Now, where can we go so I can kiss you properly? I've missed you terribly."

She led him inside the farmhouse, to a room taken over by the wardrobe department. Racks of clothes packed the tiny space.

"This will do." Parker shouldered his way around the racks to a back corner. Kate stepped into his arms. Their embrace grew from tender and caring, to passionate and wanting. Both instinctively started to tug at the other's clothes until Kate pulled away.

"Whoa, I guess you did miss me. We can't do this here."

Parker laughed. "Why not?"

Kate laughed with him. "I'd like to disappear with you for a few hours, but then everyone will know what we're doing."

"So?"

"So, let me take care of a few things first and then we can leave."

Parker reluctantly agreed. A few minutes later, they sauntered over to the set, and joined Annabella as she watched the actors rehearse their next scene.

"Kate's doing a fabulous job," Annabella told him. "The filming is going along great!"

"That's good to hear." Parker stretched his arm around Annabella's shoulders. "I'm so glad you've been here for Kate during the shooting."

"I think Kate has a new future as a screenwriter," Annabella added.

Parker smiled and raised an eyebrow.

Jonas's call for "quiet on the set" forced an end to their conversation.

Two hours later, Parker and Kate relaxed in her hotel room, after their afternoon lovemaking. Their naked bodies were closely entwined on the bed as the late-day sun poured through the window, draping them in its warmth

"Why didn't you let me know you were coming?" asked Kate.

"Because I know you like surprises."

"How did you know how much I needed you?"

"I wasn't sure. You've been a little preoccupied in our past few phone conversations. I was getting concerned. I tried to lure you home for the weekend, but you didn't seem interested."

"I don't remember even discussing it."

"Exactly. So I decided to come to you."

"I guess I have been operating on 'overwhelm.' I'm sorry."

"My lovely wife." He warmed his words with a smile. "Your compulsive, single-minded work ethic is not new to me."

"And that's why I love you so. You love me, in spite of myself."

"Yes, I do."

They laughed and rolled into each other's arms.

They went out for an early dinner so Kate could be back in time to view dailies. But she never made it to dailies.

Sipping their favorite wine with dinner, their conversation overflowed with talk of his work, their friends in Colorado and the progress of her film.

At one point, Parker checked his watch. "You'd better get going."

Kate thought for a moment. "I think I can miss the dailies tonight."

"You should go. We'll have the entire weekend together."

Kate looked down and bit her lip. "Actually, there are a couple of things I'd like to…ummmm…talk to you about."

Parker wrinkled his brow. "Okay. If that's what you want." He settled back in his chair.

Kate leaned forward in hers and folded her hands on the table. She felt her stomach flip from calm to knotted dread. What she wanted to tell him would certainly change the mood of their harmonious reunion. "I don't think I told you that Becky was here."

He sipped on his wine. "Somehow, I'm not surprised. You showed signs of wanting to see her again that day she came to the house. Did she ever connect with her daughter?"

Kate looked up at the ceiling then back at Parker. "I'll get to that." She swallowed hard to dislodge the weeks of deception she feared would singe the bond of their marriage. She reached across the table and took his hand. What had possessed her to think she could shield Parker from her involvement with Martin, to say nothing of Martin's relationship to Lily? Her seemingly harmless secrets now weighed her down with regret. "I should have told you about all this weeks ago."

Parker squeezed her hand and looked at her affectionately, which gave Kate added courage to continue. She began with the first accidental meeting with Martin at the political fundraiser. Kate didn't notice any marked difference in Parker's demeanor at the mention of Martin, so she proceeded to tell him about their subsequent lunch in Denver when Martin asked for her help in uniting him with his daughter.

A look of bewilderment crossed Parker's face. "Martin has a daughter?"

"Brace yourself. This might be a little hard to take." Kate paused. "He thinks Lily is his daughter."

Parker's mouth dropped open. He pulled his hand away from Kate's. An uncomfortable silence swelled between them until Parker spoke with forced restraint. "What do you mean he thinks? And why the hell did he ask for your help?"

She felt the bitterness in his words and raised a hand to calm him. "It's complicated."

"I can only imagine."

Kate ran her fingers through her hair and gulped a breath of air to fortify her nerve to continue. "I had no intention of helping him. But then, I needed his assistance in convincing the owners of White Oaks to let us film on their land. And...there is Lily. She seemed in need of a family. And Martin appeared to be the father her mother never allowed her to meet."

"And just what did helping Martin entail on your part?"

Kate dropped her head, then looked back at Parker. She had his attention. But his facial muscles were taut, a sure sign of his building displeasure. Knowing it was best to get it all out at once, she continued. "I helped him work out a plan to meet Lily without her knowing who he really was. We played golf together one day, then he started hanging around the set to get to know her better."

"That's when you played at the Olympic Club?"

Kate nodded her head.

Parker rolled his eyes. "And all this time, Lily still didn't know that he was her father?"

"Right." Kate grimaced. "But here's where it gets complicated." She poured more wine into each of their glasses. "I'm glad you're sitting down. This is another shocker." Her next words were slow and deliberate. "Becky is Lily's mother."

Parker froze for a moment in stunned disbelief. "That can't be." His expression changed to one of uncertainty.

"There's more."

Parker fell back into his chair and crossed his arms over his chest. His jaw was clenched, and his eyes locked onto Kate as if he were braced for an attack. Tension filled the air. The burden of her disclosure weighed heavier on her than it had moments earlier.

"Becky told me that Martin isn't Lily's father. And I think that Lily told him that as well."

"And Martin didn't believe her," added Parker.

"You're getting good at this." Kate smiled.

He did not return her smile. "You think? Do you have any idea how it feels to be left in the dark about all this, especially your secret meetings with Martin?"

She shook her head.

"Why Kate? Why keep this from me?" He tapped his fingers on the table. "You know what, though? As betrayed as I feel right now, I'm sad for Martin. I don't like him wending his way back into your life, but I feel sorry for the bastard. This business about Lily must be painful for him. He and I have been played for fools. He's chased across the country for a child who might not be his after all, and I invited this same young woman into our home and treated her like my own daughter. Ironic, don't you think?" Parker's body had twisted into rigid formality.

"It isn't Lily's fault. She's a victim of Becky's lies, too. Maybe not lies in the truest sense, but certainly lies of omission. Lily didn't know about Martin until a few days ago."

"I guess that makes me feel better about Lily. As for you and Martin, I only wish you would have told me about seeing him from the beginning."

"I wish I had, too. I wanted to, and I would have, if it had been anyone else but Martin. Somehow, I felt guilty about seeing him. Because he and I... Well, you know. In the beginning, it felt like I was doing something wrong by seeing him. As time went on, I was afraid to tell you. I think if it had been any other male friend, I wouldn't have thought anything about it. Can you understand that?"

"Not really. Maybe you aren't being honest with yourself. Perhaps you do still love Martin. Is that why you feel guilty?"

She realized she might have overstepped the limits of Parker's tolerance and understanding, and in doing so, she may have magnified the ambiguity of her connection to Martin. Her heart pounded. "Oh my God, Parker. Is that what you really believe? I once loved Martin, a long time ago, like you must have loved some other woman before me. But not anymore. Seeing Martin again has actually clarified my feelings toward him." She turned up her empty hands. "Nil, nothing. There is no spark."

"So you admit you've been confused about your feelings for Martin all these years?"

She dropped her head into her hands to gather her thoughts before replying. She owed her husband an honest answer. She looked back at him. "If you put it like that, I guess I would have to say, yes. He was my first love. Over the years I spent with him, he became a habit. He was convenient. And then, he became one of the memories squeezed into the gray recess of my brain." She paused and took a deep breath. "But you...you are the blood that flows through my heart every moment. Your life is my life. Your pain is mine." Kate threw her hands up into the air. "Oh God, I'm making a mess of this. You are the most important reason for my wanting to be alive. I don't want to lose you over this."

They sat in silence while the waiter cleared the table.

"Coffee?" asked the waiter.

Parker looked at Kate who nodded. He held up two fingers for the waiter. "Two, regular coffee, please."

Parker didn't speak again until after the waiter returned with their coffee. A painful silence for Kate, who waited and worried about what Parker was thinking.

"This is a lot to take in," he finally said.

Kate bit her lip and waited.

Parker rose from his chair and pulled it around the table so he was sitting next to Kate. She turned toward him when he took one of her hands into both of his.

"I know you love me," he said. "I'm trying to be adult about this, but I just don't like the irrational picture that forms in my head when I think of you with him...under any circumstances. You and I married later in our lives. Of course we had other relationships before we met. But it's you I married, and you I love."

The curve of her mouth crept upward as Parker continued.

"For better or worse, we will stick together. You have found yourself in the middle of another family's problems. They aren't our problems. So let's not make them ours."

"You're right." She squeezed his hand for reassurance.

Parker signaled the waiter to heat up their untouched coffee. "I suspect there is more to this story."

Kate looked at him with alarm. "What do you mean? I've told you everything."

"There is something about Lily that's pestered my curiosity since I first met her."

Kate sat stone-faced, not daring to think about the implications of Parker's words.

Back at the hotel, Parker led Kate through the lobby and out into the private hotel grounds to stroll in the embracing warmth of the sultry summer evening. It was so different from the brisk nights in Colorado that would send them back indoors for jackets and blankets whenever they wanted to observe the summer stars. Walking near the swimming pool, Kate thought she heard someone's whimpering cries skimming across the still surface of the water, but she couldn't see anyone.

"Did you hear anything?" she asked Parker.

"It's probably a cat or something."

She crinkled her nose in disagreement. "Let's find out."

She guided Parker to the far side of the pool where a path led into a lush garden. They stepped onto the path, and the crunch of gravel beneath their feet resounded in the night. It must have alerted someone of their presence because the crying stopped. They continued to follow the winding path until they came upon a small opening where the sound of someone sniffling alerted them to a lone figure huddled on a stone bench.

"Lily?" asked Kate, walking over to the bench. Parker held back.

There was a tiny gasp for air as Lily tried to stifle her flow of tears. "Oh, hi." She looked up at them with a sheepish smile. She wiped her nose with her wrist. "Have you guys been enjoying your reunion?"

"We *were*," said Parker. "What's wrong, Lily?" He left the shadows and stepped closer.

Lily sniffled and released a brooding sigh. "Everything's just ducky."

Kate joined Lily on the bench and rummaged in her purse to find a tissue. "Can we do anything?" She handed Lily the tissue.

Lily wiped her eyes and blew her nose. "This seems to be my week for tears. I'll calm down in a bit."

"What happened?" asked Kate.

"My mother and I really got into it tonight—accusations, raised voices, tears, that sort of thing. We both said some things we shouldn't have."

"I thought she had left," said Parker, supported by a nod from Kate.

"I guess we're all mistaken in that belief," said Lily. "She couldn't make a quiet exit without having her say first."

"Lily, I don't want to add to your troubles tonight. You have clearly been through enough with your mother already. But the time has come for you to tell me why you're here," said Kate. "It's apparent that you and I have connections to Becky and Martin. So it doesn't seem possible that your meeting me this spring was a coincidence."

Lily nodded.

"I thought not." Kate sighed and looked at Parker, then back at Lily. "We need to talk about it this weekend."

"I promise."

"It's a beautiful night for a walk," said Parker. "How about it? Lily, will you join us?"

"I don't want to intrude."

"Come on," said Kate. "A walk will do us all some good."

Kate placed Lily between herself and Parker, and they each put a comforting arm around the girl as they strolled through the garden. Finally, Parker interjected a little humor when he launched into his mush-mouthed impersonation of Bill Murray from the golf movie *Caddy Shack*. "It's a Cinderella Story. Lily McGuire, out of nowhere, about to become the Master's Champion."

It worked. Lily laughed and added her own line, "Be the ball, Parker. Be the ball."

The trio explored every corner of the garden before Kate and Parker walked Lily back to her room.

"Thanks for getting me home safely," said Lily.

"Our pleasure," said Parker. He looked at Kate, then back at Lily. "I have an idea. Why don't you join Kate and me in Carmel for the weekend?"

Lily put a hand to her chest with a look of surprise. "I couldn't possibly."

Kate glanced at Parker with uncertainty, then picked up on his idea. "We won't take no for an answer. Have you ever been to Carmel and Pebble Beach?"

"No."

"Then that settles it," said Parker. "It will be the perfect setting for you and Kate to have that talk you promised her."

Lily tipped her head and shrugged. "Okay. I'd like that. Are you sure it's okay?"

"Meet us at nine o'clock tomorrow morning in the lobby," said Parker.

Upon reaching the door to their own room, Parker and Kate paused and looked at each other. Parker shrugged his shoulders. "What else could we do?"

"I know. Even with her mother in town, I feel responsible for her." Kate stopped directly in front of Parker to command his full attention. "Did you ever wonder why she came to stay with us in the first place?"

He nodded and spoke softly. "I'd like to know what's really going on."

"I'm suddenly nervous."

Parker put a comforting arm around Kate and led her into their room. "We'll find out this weekend."

CHAPTER TWENTY-FIVE

Rugged Cyprus trees shaped by years of ocean breezes enhanced the storybook appearance of shops that lined the streets where Kate, Parker and Lily strolled in Carmel-By-The-Sea. They visited specialty boutiques, art galleries and courtyards, and though tempted by an array of merchandise, the trio's only indulgence was to fill their picnic basket with a deli lunch of cheese, prosciutto, French bread and wine.

When the noontime sun finally broke through the morning shroud of fog, Kate felt a sudden sense of urgency to their day. She knew they might have sun on the beach for only a few hours before rising temperatures in the Carmel Valley would suck the fog back into its belly. This might be her best opportunity to talk with Lily.

"The fog seems to have lifted," said Kate. "I'm ready for the beach."

"Me, too," said Lily.

Parker drove them down to the beach through narrow streets slipping around giant evergreen trees that dedicated city planners had prevented from being cut down. Pre-World War II cottages, designed by the writers and artists who first lived in them, crowded every street. Some nestled behind groomed hedges, others were surrounded by bright red geraniums, dancing fuchsias and glowing impatiens that flourished in the manicured gardens. A few newer, glass-walled homes stretched above the treetops for a glimpse of the Pacific.

Once at the bottom of the hill, where the ocean came into full view, Parker eased the car into a spot on the edge of ice-plant-covered bluffs that dropped onto the beach. By now, the morning fog had retreated far enough from shore so the trio could see the slow rolling swells cresting out of the fog to form sun-splashed walls of sparkling water that crashed onto the white sand.

Kate led the way down a stone stairway cut into the bluff, and flipped off her sandals when she reached the beach. Parker followed suit and immediately started walking after Kate, jamming the balls of his feet into the fine sand. The deliberate maneuver emitted a high squeaky noise, sounding to Kate's sensitive ears like fingernails on a chalkboard. It was a tradition she knew he wouldn't stop no matter how much she pleaded, so she ran ahead to a large piece of driftwood they could use as a backrest. She laid out the blanket and put her shoes on two of the corners to keep it from fluttering in the light wind. By the time Parker and Lily reached her, Lily had learned Parker's technique of noisy sand walking and joined him in running squeaky circles around Kate to announce their arrival.

"That's enough." She feigned disgust at their gleeful taunting. Parker and Lily both fell to their knees on the blanket, throwing sand everywhere. "Now look at all that sand!" Kate made them get up while she shook the sand out of the blanket and spread it back down again.

"How can you expect to keep sand off of everything when you're at the beach?" teased Parker. Turning to Lily he said with a wink, "We go through this every time we come here."

"Yeah, first he drives me nuts with his squeaky sand walking, then he gets sand on everything."

Lily laughed. "So, what's the next ritual?"

"Next, we go down to the water and let the white foam curl over our toes and screech about how cold the water is," explained Parker.

"It's always cold. The water only gets to about fifty-six degrees," added Kate.

Lily followed Kate and Parker to the water's edge, where they took off in a jog, dashing in and out of foam and salty water that turned the white sand to a wet gray. Kate managed to execute her customary set of acrobatics, flipping cartwheels to the cheers and applause of Parker and Lily.

With their lungs sufficiently filled with fresh sea air, they returned to their blanket, energized and ready for lunch. Parker served the food, and sea gulls swooped down to pester the picnickers, boldly waddling closer and closer to the edge of their blanket. Kate warned Lily not to give the flock any crumbs or they would be eating out of her hand next. By the end of their lunch, one bold interloper managed to sneak behind them and peck at the empty basket.

"Hey," yelled Lily, jumping up to scare him away. She ran through the cluster of birds with her arms spread out like an airplane, twirling in circles like a whirling dervish until she was so dizzy she sat in a giggling heap on the beach. She picked up a handful of warm, dry sand and let it slip through her fingers. "Thank you both so much for bringing me here." She swept her arms through the air with balletic grace and picked up more sand. "This ocean, these hungry sea gulls and these teensy-weensy bits of squeaky sand have transported me into another world. Ahhhhhhhh." And with that, she fell backward onto the sand to bask in the baking sun.

"I think the wine has gone to Lily's head. How about a walk?" Kate asked.

Parker replied, "Not for me. I'd rather take a nap. You girls can sober up with a walk."

"I'm not drunk," stated Lily. "Not from the wine. I'm intoxicated by all of this beauty." She swept an arm far above her head while remaining in her prone position.

Parker and Kate gave each other a knowing glance. Rising to her feet, Kate started down the beach. "Come on," she urged Lily. "Keep me company."

"Happy to." Lily jumped up, brushed off her clothes and shook her head to rid herself of sand, then ran a few paces to catch up with Kate.

"I'm glad you like my beach," said Kate when Lily was at her side.

"I love your beach. Do you get here often?"

"I've been coming here since forever, or so my mother tells me. Apparently, I was only a few weeks old on my first visit."

"Are you close to your parents?" Lily asked.

"Mostly. I get along fine with my father, but my mother and I have kind of a love-hate relationship. Like most mothers and daughters, I guess." Not wanting the conversation to be about her mother, Kate downplayed their turbulent relationship and shifted the focus onto Lily. "How about you? Did you resolve anything with your mother yesterday, Lily?"

"She ripped into me pretty good."

"Do you want to talk about it?"

Lily sighed and dropped her head back to gather her thoughts. "She's a complicated woman. I think she's good at her career, but somewhat distracted as a parent. Luckily for me, until I reached high school, she let me stay at her father's home every summer. My grandfather adored me, and I idolized him. I used to wish I could live with him most of the time. I went everywhere with him. My mother usually took me places when it was convenient for her. Anyway, come Labor Day, she'd return from her travels to get me home in time for the new school year."

"She couldn't have been that bad."

"I guess not. It's just that I loved to be outdoors doing things, but she preferred museums and cultural events that were boring to me. It was my grandfather who taught me how to play golf and got me started with my ballet lessons. I think my mother was jealous of our relationship because he seemed closer to me than he was to her." Lily picked up a piece of driftwood and threw it into the breaking surf. "She didn't tell you she changed her name from Madison to McGuire, did she, Kate?"

"No, she didn't."

Lily shook her head. "If it makes you feel any better, her entire life with me has been a lie."

Kate hesitated, not sure what to say to Lily after that pronouncement. She looked around and noted that the beach was beginning to fill with people: young mothers dipping their infants' toes into the ocean for the first time, self-conscious teenage girls clad in shorts and halter tops flirting with surfers preparing to tackle the fast-breaking waves, an older couple strolling by hand-in-hand. Kate and Lily jumped aside when an Irish setter scampered by, pulling its owner along by its taut leash.

Finally, Kate said, "You know, your mother and I were best friends growing up. We used to share all of our secrets. I don't understand why she didn't tell me about you. It's very odd. Even strangers tell me about their kids. Were you and your mother ever close?"

"I'm just getting to know her."

"She's certainly a different person from the one I knew as a kid, I'll grant you."

Just then, a trio of junior high school boys came splashing after a soccer ball caught in the ankle-deep surf that rolled up the beach toward Lily and Kate. Lily intercepted the ball, showing off some fancy footwork of her own before kicking it back to one of the boys as she and Kate continued on down the beach.

"She's not the mother I thought she was at all," continued Lily.

"How do you mean?"

"She's not my mother," stated Lily, matter-of-factly.

Kate was startled. "Lily, you shouldn't disown your mother, no matter how you might feel about her abilities as a parent. Being a parent, especially a single mother, is the toughest job in the world. In time, you'll be able to forgive her for whatever she may have done."

"No. That's not what I mean. She isn't my real mother. I was adopted."

Kate hadn't expected this bombshell. She stopped walking to focus her full attention on Lily, who held Kate's gaze. The roar of the ocean filled the silence while Kate tried to digest what she had just heard. Her heart began to race. A capricious notion flooded her consciousness, a dream too painful to let surface if she was wrong. She shoved it down as best she could. "Does Martin know this?"

Lily looked puzzled. "Martin?"

"I mean. Oh, boy. This is awkward. I thought you already knew about my part in bringing you and Martin together."

"Kate, why is Martin the first thing that pops into your mind?"

Kate shrugged and turned up her hands. "Martin and I plotted for weeks about how he could meet you. Besides working on my movie, helping Martin meet his daughter and all the complications that came with that, which I won't get into, has been on the forefront of my mind for weeks." Kate wrinkled her brow. "And now I guess he really can't be your father. I don't know whether to laugh or cry."

"Don't worry. Martin told me how he twisted your arm to keep you from telling me about him."

"It never occurred to me you might not be his daughter." Kate was rattled, shaking inside. She forced herself to talk. "Martin is a good man. His intentions were honorable, otherwise I never would have tried to help him. I feel terrible that I put you through all this with him."

"It's okay. I understand." She put a comforting hand on Kate's shoulder. "There was no way Martin or you could have known the truth. I didn't discover that I was adopted until a few months ago. I did try to tell him that he wasn't my father the night I had dinner with him, but he wouldn't listen to me. I didn't know what else to do but run away. Very childish, but I panicked. He didn't deserve that. He's always been very nice to me."

"Becky tried to tell me Martin wasn't your father, but I thought she was just trying to keep you from Martin," said Kate. "To me, her explanation left room for the possibility that he still could be your father."

They resumed their walk down the beach, away from the crowds. Kate was grateful to be moving again, hoping the activity might calm her nerves. She didn't want Lily to detect her rising anxiety. She stretched her arms above her head and inhaled a deep Yoga breath.

Lily broke the silence. "I plan to pay back the money I used from the trust fund he set up for me."

"I don't think that will soothe the pain he's going to feel at losing you a second time. Did you know he's kept track of you throughout most of your life?"

"That's what he told me. It's a little creepy since it turns out he's not my father."

"When did Becky tell you that you were adopted?"

"She didn't."

"Then how—"

"The man I thought was my father, Donald Thompson…"

"Your mother told me he died in a car accident a few weeks after you were born."

"He did. His parents verified that part of Becky's story. She never talked much about Donald, and I always thought it was strange that his parents, who would have been my grandparents, never wanted to see me. After all, I would have been their first grandchild. So, this past spring, I went to see them. What they told me turned my life upside down."

Kate led Lily over to a ghostly hulk of bleached driftwood resting at the base of a steep bluff that bordered the Pebble Beach Golf Course above. The two women sat side-by-side on a smooth section of the log, gazing across the undulating kelp beds on Carmel Bay as Lily recounted her story.

"Mrs. Thompson answered the phone when I called. She seemed very confused about who I was and called her husband to the phone. At first, I thought I had the wrong Thompsons. But when I asked if their son had been killed in an auto accident twenty years earlier, he finally realized who I was and agreed to meet with me.

"When I arrived at their house, they seemed very uncomfortable. They asked a few questions about my mother and about where I was going to college and what I was majoring in. You know, things you would ask your friends' children. Finally, they asked me why I wanted to see them. I was surprised by their question. I told them I came to meet my grandparents. That's when the world as I know it disintegrated. I'll never forget their startled looks.

"Mrs. Thompson started to talk until her husband shook his head to stop her from saying anything more. But Mrs. Thompson persisted. She asked me how old I was. When I told her, she turned to her husband and said if I didn't know the truth, then it was time I learned. They argued for a few minutes, almost as if I wasn't there. Then, Mr. Thompson got up and left the room. I assumed he wanted no part of what she was going to tell me."

Lily squirreled her feet under the warm sand as she continued. "I think Mrs. Thompson started to have second thoughts when she was alone with me, but I encouraged her to tell me whatever it was she thought I should know. That's when she moved over and sat in the chair next to mine, gently held my hand in hers and said, 'My dear, our son wasn't your father.'"

"Oh, Lily." Kate turned toward the young woman. "I can't imagine how that must have felt."

Lily tipped her head. "It was unexpected, to say the least. I remember my body whirling and my insides flipping upside down. I knew in my mind that she must be mistaken. I reassured myself that her son was the same University of Washington student who married my mother. I thought the shocked expression on my face would give Mrs. Thompson a sign to let me catch my breath before she continued, but she kept on."

Kate closed her eyes. She couldn't imagine how hurtful it must have been for Lily to learn of her adoption from a stranger instead of her mother. She thought of the betrayal Becky had unnecessarily inflicted on Lily and bit the inside of her cheek to hold back her sorrow. No wonder Lily was estranged from her mother.

Lily continued in a subdued monotone as if to avoid reliving the heartbreak she had already suffered from the words of Mrs. Thompson. "She told me her son was not able to have children. That's why he decided to marry Becky, even though she was pregnant with another man's child. She tried to soften the blow by telling me how much Donald and my mother loved each other, and that my mother didn't love the guy who fathered me."

Kate put a hand to her forehead, a little confused. "I thought you said you were adopted."

"Let me finish," said Lily adjusting her position on the log. "Mrs. Thompson proceeded to tell me that Becky lost her baby. The child was stillborn in her seventh month of pregnancy. Kate, I'm not sure of this, but based on what Martin told me about my mother, I think he could have been the father of the baby my mother lost."

Kate looked up at the sky and shook her head. Her mind was reeling as Lily talked.

"Donald and Becky were pretty shook up over it. I guess it was a difficult time. Becky's mother had just died of cancer, so they kept the baby's death a secret from her family. They didn't want to burden them with another loss. When Becky's family doctor presented them with an option to adopt, they agreed. I guess they never told anyone where I really came from."

Lily looked out at the ocean and spoke softly as she finished her story. "The doctor had another patient, an unmarried, pregnant graduate student who was planning to put her baby up for adoption. That baby was due the same time Becky's baby should have been born. Apparently, the doctor acted as the intermediary. Mrs. Thompson told me it was all very legal."

Tears were streaming down Kate's face. When Lily looked over and saw Kate's tears, she also began to cry. "Did she remember the doctor's name?" asked Kate, looking back at the ocean, anxious for what might come next.

"She found his name in some of her son's old papers."

"Was it Dr. Swanson?" asked Kate, already knowing the answer. She turned to face Lily, who seemed transfixed by the breaking waves thundering on the beach. "Did you go to see Dr. Swanson, Lily? Did he tell you who your real mother is?"

Lily nodded. "Yes to all your questions."

Kate put her arms around Lily and pulled her close as they both wept. Kate could hardly breathe. This day was a gift, a miracle she hardly felt she deserved, yet it had actually, finally, come.

"Oh Lily, Lily, Lily," she cried, rocking her daughter in her arms like an injured toddler. The words almost stuck in her throat, swollen with emotions. "Why didn't I guess who you were? You reminded me of someone, from the first day we met. But then, Martin said you were his daughter, so I assumed that's why you seemed so familiar to me."

"Kate, I wanted to tell you right away, but you were so involved in your movie, I couldn't get your attention. Then I thought it would be best if we got to know each other better. Especially since I didn't know how you might react. I didn't want you to reject me before I had a chance to get to know my real mother."

"You must have had some idea I wouldn't reject you. I was very explicit with Dr. Swanson. I gave him written permission to give you my name and whereabouts if you ever did come looking for me."

"I wasn't sure. So much time had passed."

"And what do you think of the woman who gave away her own daughter?"

"I'm sure you had your reasons."

"They were selfish reasons. I wanted to finish college and have a career. A child might have prevented me from achieving my dreams. Everyone assured me I was doing the best thing for my baby and for me. It was Becky, the woman who fed and cared for you, who was the unselfish one. She took you in and loved you. I know she loves you, Lily."

"I know she does. But right now, I'm angry with her for not telling me the truth."

"She did the best she knew how. She had already lost one baby and her husband. Perhaps she feared losing you to the discovery of a birth mother."

"Don't defend her. That's not why I'm here. I want to know who I really am. I want to know where I came from, and why I'm athletic and love ballet. Learning of my adoption has actually helped me understand why I always felt like a misfit with my mother, and why she and I are so different. I thought I must be more like my father, but she never would talk about him. That's why I went to see Donald's parents. I was looking for myself. I never expected to have another life thrown at me. Please, tell me who I am."

Kate took hold of Lily's hand. The two women sat side by side for a time without talking, allowing themselves to absorb the impact of their true relationship. Eventually, Kate stood and pulled Lily up alongside her. She found a tissue in her pocket and wiped her daughter's tears, then her own. She smiled and looked at Lily with loving eyes. She was thankful for the bond they had already formed since their first meeting at the Denver campaign headquarters weeks earlier. That seemed like so long ago.

"Lily, in answer to your question, I'm still trying to figure out who I am. If you're at all like me, it may take your entire life to learn who you are, but I'll try to help you." Kate looked at her watch. "This is an important day for you and me, but I'm worried that Parker might be getting anxious about us. We've been gone almost two hours."

Lily nodded. "Maybe we'd better head back."

Walking arm in arm, Lily and Kate made the long trek back to where they had left Parker.

"I was beginning to worry, but I can see you're both okay," he said with arms relaxed by his sides.

"We're better than okay," chirped Lily.

Parker turned to Kate, as if looking for a hint at what had transpired, but he only got a Cheshire grin. Kate squeezed Lily's hand before letting her daughter go. "We had a great talk. Now, I'm ready for a shower. Want to head back to the Lodge?" she asked Parker.

Kate looked at Lily, sensing in her daughter an excitement that emanated beneath a tranquil veil of serenity. She wondered if she, herself, projected the same mood, and glanced over at Parker in time to catch his quizzical expression. She realized that wanting to leave the beach before the afternoon fog rolled in was unlike her. But he didn't question her. He joined the women in gathering their gear and returning to their car, during which time Kate and Lily kept a quiet watch over one another with knowing smiles. Very little was said on their fifteen-minute ride to The Lodge at Pebble Beach, where Parker had made reservations for them to spend the night.

Once in their suite, Kate's emotions erupted into a volcano of sobs and tears that shook her entire body. It was an outburst held at bay since Lily's birth. Parker guided her to the bed where she sprawled on her stomach with her head buried in a pillow to smother the noise of her crying. He sat beside her with his hand softly rubbing her back. Moments later, Kate sat up and allowed Parker to hold her, almost afraid that if he didn't, she would vanish like the mist into the sea.

"Kate? What is it?"

Kate couldn't speak through her sobs. Her stiff body continued to shake until the sobs turned into whimpers, and she began to calm down.

"Has this got to do with your talk with Lily?"

She barely slipped out the word *yes* between the gasping breaths that come after uncontrollable crying. Parker continued to hold her as she slowly struggled to regain her composure.

Kate's thoughts suddenly tumbled beyond her talk with Lily. She sat up cross-legged on the bed next to Parker and pushed the hair back from her face. Parker handed her a tissue from the nightstand.

"Parker, why did you ask Lily to come to Carmel with us? This was supposed to be a special weekend for you and me. I could have talked to her some other time." If he already knew that Lily was her daughter, she worried about what else he might know. When he didn't answer right away, she prodded him further. "Parker? Why did you invite Lily along?"

"Because she's your daughter." There was silence and then he added, "Isn't she?"

"Yes. Yes, she is." She put her hands over her mouth. It was still hard for her to believe. "She told me on the beach this afternoon."

"I hoped that might be why you took so long on your walk. And how do you feel about that?"

She smiled at his careful question. "Happier than I've ever been in my life. And scared, confused, guilty, ashamed, elated. But how did you know she was my daughter?"

"I've always known that someday, your daughter would walk into your life. Before we were married, you told me you had left an easy trail if your child ever wanted to find her mother. And Lily is so much like you. She has your guts and determination, and the need to know the why of everything. A daughter of yours would eventually want to know the who of her real parents. The first time she ever came to our house I saw you walking through the door. She has your broad smile, your cheekbones, your elegant grace and tomboyish zest for enjoying life. She even has some of your mannerisms."

"Like what?"

"Like, she pulls her ear when she's thinking, and she can't talk unless she's gesturing wildly with her hands. And she has your feet."

"My feet? Hmm. I never saw any of that."

"That's because you've been trying to ignore her since she came to stay with us."

"I have not."

"Kate, you have. You were so preoccupied with finalizing your script and the movie deal, you hardly even noticed *me* on some days. But with Lily, it was like you didn't want her at our home. Oh, you were always nice to her, but you were somehow removed. I thought perhaps the idea of her being your daughter had crossed your mind and you didn't want to become attached to a false hope, so you remained somewhat reserved."

So he had noticed something different about her behavior back then. "It was a confusing time…for many reasons. But why didn't you say anything to me?"

"What if she hadn't been your daughter? I knew you secretly looked for your daughter in every young girl you passed on the street. I didn't want to open that wound needlessly and risk the hurt it would cause you."

"Parker, she wants to know who her father is."

"That seems logical. Did you ever tell her father you were pregnant with his child?"

"No." Kate's heart pounded. Revealing that part of the equation would be a painful price to pay for having Lily in their life.

"Then perhaps, you should ask his permission first, before you tell Lily who her father is."

"I already know his answer. He wants her to know."

Parker wrinkled his brow with a quizzical look. He didn't pursue the question that caused his puzzlement. Instead, he asked, "When are you going to tell her?"

"I wanted to tell you first." She slipped off of the bed in search of a Kleenex. "I need to blow my nose." Gesturing toward the honor bar she said, "Maybe you could get us a Perrier or some seltzer to drink."

Kate disappeared into the bathroom to splash her face with water and clean the smudged mascara from around her eyes. Finding relief behind the closed door, she decided to jump into the shower to give herself a few more moments to gather her emotions. She let the water wash over her body until she lost track of time. When she came out wrapped in one of the hotel's lush terry cloth robes, she found Parker sitting on their balcony overlooking the golf course along the ocean's edge. She followed his gaze to a group of golfers who were finishing their round on the eighteenth green. She wished she were part of the foursome instead of facing the confession that might ruin her marriage.

Standing behind Parker, she put her arms around his neck and embraced him for a moment before moving aside to sit in the chair next to him. "This is not easy for me."

"I gathered that by the length of your shower. I thought you might need something stronger than a Perrier, so I poured you a glass of wine." He nodded toward the small table in front of him that also held a half-eaten bowl of mixed nuts.

"Thanks." She robotically picked up her glass and took a sip. She was too concerned about what Parker's reaction would be when she told him about Lily's father to care what she had to drink. "I would have told you everything before, but I thought it wasn't relevant. It was a detail from my past that was just that—part of my past. And I didn't want to tell you because I lacked the courage. Now, I have no choice."

"You still don't have to tell me."

"Oh yes, I do. When you hear who her father is, you'll understand why I never told you. Please know that it's the only secret I've ever kept from you. And now, I'm glad that you will finally know everything." She stared across the churning ocean for some sign of how to proceed, but nothing spoke to her. She put a hand on Parker's thigh, an intimacy she instinctively needed to draw closer to him. "Before I begin, please tell me that you love me, because I love you so much. More right now than ever."

He reached over and squeezed her hand.

Kate closed her eyes and exhaled to release some of the pressure from her pounding heart. Parker said nothing but kept his focus on Kate. She wasn't sure he was looking at her with concern for the apprehension she was feeling, or just stoic resolve to hear her out. The latter worried and annoyed her at the same time. More importantly, she knew he was listening, no matter what the outcome.

"We only dated for a week or so while he was visiting his fraternity brother, who happened to be an old friend of mine, Les Madison." She saw his head tilt slightly in recognition of a familiar name. "Yes, Becky's brother. It was the summer before my first year in grad school. Becky didn't come home that summer, so she never knew I had dated this guy, and I had no knowledge he was Becky's old boyfriend. And then I let it happen. It was only one time, his last night in town. I was young, infatuated and obviously stupid. The two bottles of wine at dinner didn't help either. I didn't see or talk to him until several years later."

Parker started to interrupt her, but Kate stopped him with a squeeze of her hand that still rested on his leg. "Please, let me just get through this while I have the courage." She withdrew her hand to take a sip of her wine. "When I found out I was pregnant, I knew two things. The future I wanted for myself did not include a baby at that point in my life, and I didn't want to abort the baby. That left adoption as the only alternative. I never told the baby's father about the pregnancy because I didn't want someone I hardly knew making decisions for me. Back then, the father wasn't much of a factor in those decisions like he might be today."

Kate rubbed her fingers along the stem of her wine glass. "As expected, my mother's reception to the news was entirely self-centered. She shipped me off to Doc Swanson for an abortion. My sensitive mother." Kate couldn't help the drooling sarcasm she heard behind her words. "To her, being an unwed mother was something that happened to other girls, not an intelligent graduate student like her daughter. She was more concerned about what her friends would think than she was about my well-being. The motherly love and support I needed, never materialized."

Parker shook his head, disbelief dulling his eyes.

"So, Doc and I worked out a plan. Ultimately, he found a newly married couple to adopt my baby. It was not at all unusual in the sixties for a doctor to circumvent the system and write in the adoptive parents' names on the original birth certificate. That would obfuscate any shame on my family or me. I lived with my aunt during the final months of my pregnancy, so none of my parents' friends or neighbors even knew I was pregnant. I didn't speak to my mother again until several months after I had given birth. That way, she could pretend her daughter was away at school instead of in the next town giving birth to her illegitimate grandchild. To this day, we have never spoken of my pregnancy."

Parker's face reflected the pain Kate felt from her mother's ostracism. He squeezed her hand and started to say something, but hesitated as Kate continued in a lifeless tone that was the only way she could communicate the painful events of her past...as if she were telling someone else's story with the detachment of a newspaper reporter.

"Today, Lily helped to fill in the blanks regarding the part Becky played. I didn't know it then, but at the same time I was pregnant, Becky was also expecting a baby. It appears that it was Martin Kelly's." Kate looked for a reaction from Parker when she mentioned Martin's name, but seeing his stone-faced expression, she plowed forward. "This was while she was engaged to Donald Thompson. Donald loved Becky, so he married her, knowing she was pregnant with another man's child. Apparently, Donald was not able to have children. Anyway, they lived in Berkeley while he worked on his doctorate. About two months before I was due, she lost her baby."

Kate took a shaky breath and plunged on with her story. "Doc was

Becky's family's doctor, too. When he learned of Becky's loss, I guess he thought my baby would be the child Becky and Donald could never have together. Doc and I had agreed to keep everything confidential like a regular adoption, so I never learned who the parents were, and vice versa. As you already know, I asked for a clause in the adoption agreement permitting the doctor to reveal my identity if the child ever requested the information. He and his lawyer set up the whole thing. Very neat and tidy."

"So who is Lily's father?" Parker asked.

She took a deep breath and bit the inside of her cheek. "Martin Kelly."

"I'm confused. I thought you said Becky lost his child."

"She did." Kate dropped her head, then looked back at him. "Martin was Becky's college boyfriend and her brother's friend I dated that summer. He is Lily's father." She paused to let him grasp the ironic circumstances of Lily's birth and adoption. When he didn't say anything, she nervously continued with her explanation. "At the time I became pregnant, I never dreamed I would ever see Martin again, let alone become involved with him. Our paths didn't cross until almost three years later when we met at a party in L.A."

"And you never told him?"

She shook her head. Parker pressed his lips together and fell back in his chair with his hands limp by his side. Kate fiddled with the front of her robe, watching him.

If Martin hadn't been her ex-lover, Kate imagined that Parker and Martin might have been friends. They were both successful businessmen who appreciated the achievements of others. On the few occasions when circumstances had brought them together before he and Kate were married, Parker had enjoyed Martin's dry sense of humor and quick wit. But as his wife's ex-lover, Martin was someone Parker would have preferred to keep at a distance. Now, his intrusion in Parker's life with Kate was unavoidable. Martin was the father of her child.

Finally, Parker said, "I'm shocked, but what can I do about it?" It was a rhetorical question, but Kate had an answer anyway.

"I hope you can accept it as part of my past. That you will be understanding and never stop loving me."

"Kate, that part of your past is very much in the present." The sharpness in Parker's voice punctuated his dismay. "You never kept your pregnancy a secret from me, but it was an abstract part of your past. Now, your daughter has a lovely face. She also has a father who, coincidentally, was a significant part of your life for many years. He's always been like an ex-husband in my mind. Kate, your old baggage is sitting on our doorstep. It's like being married to a divorced mother. It complicates things. I'll need some time to sort this out."

Fear plunged into Kate's gut, chilling the sun's lingering rays that grazed their terrace as she said, "We both need to digest all of this, but can we do it together?"

He fixed his stare on the ocean, blind to the seagulls soaring over the shoreline, deaf to the roar of the waves as the tide sent them crashing against the sea wall only to dissolve into a misty spray settling gently into a fairway bunker. Kate reached over and took both of his hands in hers and tried to get him to look at her.

"I need time, Kate," is all he would say.

"Parker, I love you. Martin is nothing to me but an old friend now."

"And the father of your only child. Something we will never share together. It hurts, especially since the father is Martin. He is salt in my wound. "

"But Lily thinks you're great. She enjoys being with you more than she does Martin"

He glared at her. "Don't patronize me."

This was not the reaction Kate had anticipated. Instead of Parker's normal demeanor of common sense understanding, he appeared to be engulfed by jealousy and resentment.

"Parker, I love you. You are the man I married, not Martin."

"I know that, Kate, but he has a connection to you I never will." Parker's voice was tight and forced. "He was my rival when you and I first met. I thought he was out of your life, but now he never will be.

Adjusting to Lily as your daughter is one thing. But Martin..."

"Please don't be angry."

"Damn it, Kate. I am angry. How could you not have told me he was the father of your child?"

"I hoped it would never matter. I just never imagined I would ever have to tell anyone."

"How naive!"

She knew he was right. Regret overtook her like a fever. She collapsed into the back of her chair, defeated, not knowing what she could do to ease his pain and anger. She had never seen him like this before. Her head fell forward into her hands, but tears wouldn't come.

Parker left her alone on the terrace and walked out of their room.

CHAPTER TWENTY-SIX

"Thanks for meeting me, Becky," said Martin. His demeanor was guarded.

The two were sitting on a stone bench in the rooftop garden outside of Martin's office in San Francisco. An unusually hot summer day in the city had kept the late afternoon fog at bay, but it didn't warm the chill that lay between them.

"I'm not sure I can help you, Martin. Lily is a very headstrong young woman with a fairytale vision of what life should be."

"She strikes me as a very serious young woman who knows what she wants."

"And what might that be? You'd know better than I would since I understand you've spent more time with her lately than I have. She apparently doesn't want to be around me anymore."

"You sound bitter."

"No. I'm a realist as well as a mother who is having a hard time letting go."

"I understand that many parents suffer through a difficult transition when their children leave home for college."

"There's no need to explain that to me. In case my brother left out a few details of my life, I did manage to get my PhD in psychology." She folded her hands on her lap. "Yes, I know that Les was the one who kept you informed about Lily's life all these years. But that's history. This is a great deal more complicated than separation anxiety. I've made a grave mistake with Lily, Martin...one she may never forgive me for."

Martin looked at Becky with concern, surprised that she would admit a mistake to him. "I'm listening."

She nervously ran her fingers over her lips. "Basically, I misled Lily into believing something that isn't true. I prefer to call it a lie by omission. It's the same lie that allowed you to be misled all these years."

"What do you mean?"

Becky stood up and walked across the gravel path. She turned back toward Martin with her arms crossed over her chest. "Actually, I did tell you the truth. Lily isn't your daughter. But, you never believed me. What I couldn't tell you was why you can't possibly be her father. That would have jeopardized everything."

Martin stretched his arms above his head, clenched his fists, then brought them back down and grabbed hold of the bench with both hands. "You and I may have had our differences, but I know you always tried to do your best with Lily, even if it included keeping me away from her. And really, that was as much my doing. Your desire to raise her on your own made it easy for me to get on with my life without the worries or responsibilities of raising a child."

"Martin, she isn't your child."

"Look Becky, let's not play this game anymore. Remember, I was the guy in college who inflicted the accidental blow to Donald's testicles in a lacrosse game. We both know he couldn't have children. Of course she's mine."

"Do you think you're the only guy I ever slept with in college? I see your ego is still intact."

"I used to know you pretty well. A casual affair or a one-night stand wasn't in your DNA. And we both know that."

"Don't be so smug. I'm not the same person anymore."

"Perhaps not, but that doesn't change what happened between us."

"Ahhh, the past. That's what this is all about. The problem is, you think you know the past, but you don't. I understand Lily already told you that you aren't her father.

"She did," he acknowledged.

"But you didn't believe her either."

"No, I didn't. She was understandably confused and shocked when I told her I was her benefactor and her father. Apparently you let her believe Donald was her father. Why? I might understand your motivation if she had actually known him, but he died when she was only weeks old. Why couldn't you have told her that her real father was alive? Why did you keep your whereabouts a secret from me? What were you afraid of? Shit, Becky, you even changed your last name, presumably to make it harder for me or anyone else to find you."

"You are a very stubborn man, Martin. I told you from the beginning Lily wasn't your child."

"But I know she is!"

"No, she isn't." Becky dropped her voice to a whisper as she continued. "It's true I was pregnant with your child. But I lost her, Martin. I lost our baby."

As she spoke, the indelible anguish of a mother's loss rose through Becky's words and washed over Martin. He leaned toward Becky, instinctively knowing that what he was hearing was finally the truth.

"She was stillborn when I was seven months pregnant." Tears welled up in her eyes. "Please believe me. That is the truth." She turned her back to him and looked across the city, as if trying to gather her emotions.

"But Lily?"

Becky turned back to face Martin. "Lily is adopted."

The air stilled and the city fell silent. Martin felt the color drain from his face. Sudden emptiness numbed his body. The years of waiting and wondering what it would be like to finally meet his daughter faded into a lifeless wasteland.

Becky sat beside Martin and continued. "The baby was stillborn just a few weeks after my mother passed away from cancer. I didn't dare put my father through another heartbreak right then. We were all devastated by my mother's death, so I begged Donald not tell anyone about the baby. I went into a deep depression after that. Poor Donald was terrified I might do something to harm myself.

"What about Les? Didn't he know what was going on?"

She turned up the palms of her hands. "I completely withdrew from everyone for weeks after losing the baby. We were living across the bay at the time. Donald was working on his doctorate at Berkeley, and I was supposed to be very pregnant, so it wasn't hard to find excuses to be left alone. We all needed time to grieve for my mother, so I guess it didn't seem odd that Donald and I kept to ourselves."

She paused apparently gathering her thoughts. "One day, I went for a checkup with our family doctor in Palo Alto and told him how devastated Donald and I were about not being able to have children of our own. That's when he told me about a patient of his who wanted to give up her baby for adoption. We jumped at the opportunity, but still didn't tell my family about having lost my own baby. About the time I was originally due, we were given our new baby, Lily."

Martin buried his head in his hands, his elbows pressed on his legs. He felt Becky's hand on his shoulder.

"I'm so sorry, Martin. I didn't mean to hurt you."

"Go on," he said in a strangled voice. "Tell me the rest of it."

"When we walked into my father's house with the new baby, everyone assumed she was ours. My father's spirits soared when he learned we had named the baby after my mother. He was certain Lily was the reincarnated spirit of my mother. I think Lily saved his life. She gave him something to live for again. Three weeks later, Donald died in an automobile accident. There was too much heartache in our lives to tell my father the truth."

Martin listened with disbelief as she continued.

"Somehow, my family's belief that Lily was my birth child made her connection to me even stronger. You were the only complication, but I thought you would lose interest and be relieved, even thankful, you didn't have a child to support."

"But I did feel responsible!"

"And my dear brother, Les, was no help. I had no idea he continued to keep you informed about Lily's upbringing until only recently. Otherwise, I might have told you about the adoption before this. I'm sorry, Martin. I never expected you would care so much."

"What about Lily? Does she know she's adopted?"

Becky sighed. "Yes, but she didn't find out from me. She found out quite by accident in the process of looking for you, her benefactor.

Martin pressed his fingers into his forehead, devoid of all feeling.

Kate waited over two hours for Parker to return to their hotel room. She spent the first hour withdrawn, huddled in a corner of the terrace, wrapped beneath her bathrobe...inadequate protection from the bitterness of Parker's departure. Her mind had been too numb to carry herself inside to a warm room. When she finally did retreat indoors, she remembered Lily was waiting for her call. She had no idea what she would tell Lily about Parker's absence.

With or without Parker, Kate was determined to celebrate her reunion with Lily. She made a dinner reservation at The Lodge's elegant Club XIX restaurant and then called Lily with the arrangements. With the help of makeup and a colorful Laisse Adzer ensemble, Kate felt outwardly presentable again. She grabbed her room key and left to meet Lily.

"Kate, wait up." Parker called out to her from the far end of the walkway. "Where are you going?"

She turned and waited as he rushed toward her.

"Are you meeting Lily?"

"Yes."

"I want to come with you. I think it's important we present a united front to her."

She slumped her shoulders. "Parker, I don't want to put up a false front for Lily's sake. She will see right through us. If you're not sure where you stand, I certainly understand. Please take however much time you need to decide. Now, if you'll excuse me, I don't want to keep Lily waiting any longer than I already have."

Parker moved closer to her. "Having me for a husband or Lily for a daughter are not options. You must take us both." He gently placed his hands on her shoulders. "Don't you know how much I love you? Even Martin Kelly can't ruin what we have together. I think we both agree on that point."

Kate looked up at him.

"But you can't blame me for the jealousy and rage I felt when you told me he was the bastard who got you pregnant."

"He's not a bastard," she whispered. "I was just as much to blame for what happened."

He squeezed her shoulders. His voice softened. "I understand. More important, Kate, Lily is your daughter. I'm already very fond of her. Why wouldn't I be? She's part of you. It took a lot of courage for her to walk into your life and win you over the way she has. You could have rejected her."

"I tried to."

He smiled. "But you succumbed."

"I adore her," admitted Kate. "From the moment we first met, she felt like a soul mate. But later, I thought it was because she was Martin's daughter, and that scared me."

"But it's okay, now."

"Yes." Kate felt a burden of fear lifted from her. Parker wasn't going to leave her. She felt anxiety slip away and began to feel the exhilaration of being united with her daughter.

"So, what are we waiting for?" asked Parker.

"Are you sure?"

Parker took Kate into his arms. "I've always wanted a daughter who can play golf. Lily will be a ringer in our father-daughter golf tournament in September."

She held him tight and whispered into his ear. "Thank you."

Parker returned to their room to clean up, and Kate continued on to meet Lily.

While waiting for Parker to join them for dinner, Kate and Lily had a few moments alone at their table.

"I imagine you have a lot of questions, Lily, including who your father is."

Lily nodded. She looked beautiful in a simple silk dress. The scoop-neck design allowed the perfect showcase for Lily's dolphin ring that rested against her skin on the end of the gold chain. The auburn hair that Lily normally pulled back with a clip hung in gentle curls around her face. She listened attentively as Kate spoke.

Kate reached across the table to hold Lily's hand. "I promise, we'll have a lot of time for me to explain everything to you, but for tonight, I'm hoping we can simply enjoy each other's company." Kate threw up her hands, then clasped them together and leaned into the table toward Lily. "I'm so overwhelmed to be sitting across the table from my daughter. I don't know if I'm of a mind to be able to tell you much of anything right now."

Lily's eyes sparkled. Her posture was straight, but her manner was relaxed. "That's okay. I was really scared to tell you who I am. But I know that everything will be okay from here on, Kate. Mother. Can I call you that, now?"

Kate smiled. "Yes, if you want. Although, it's going to take me a little time to get used to answering to 'Mother.'"

"This is pretty new for both of us."

"That's for sure. But how are you doing, Lily? Are you adjusting okay since learning about me?"

"I think it will all get better now that everything is out in the open. Keeping my adoption a secret these past few months has been really hard. Sometimes, I thought I would burst from the need to talk to someone about it. Poor Jonas. He came to my rescue one night when I broke down in tears, but never pressed me for details. He has been incredibly wonderful to me."

"Do I detect something going on between you two?"

Lily tipped her head with a coy smile. "Maybe. We're still in the exploratory stage. Mostly, I've been too mixed up to know what I'm feeling. But today"—she straightened in her chair—"I feel like a child on Christmas morning. I'm excited and happy, yet a little anxious about what mysteries are still hidden in the unopened packages under the tree."

Kate laughed. "I can certainly understand that. And I hope you won't be disappointed."

"I'm also a little concerned about my mother...er...Becky."

"Mother. Becky is your mother, too, Lily."

"Yes, she is. And I do love her. In many ways, I can love her better now because I understand why we're so different. My creative bent has always clashed with her analytical, scientific mind. I never felt the flow I feel with you, Kate. Everything has finally fallen into place. You seem to understand me."

"You might be a little premature in that assumption. But I hope we'll spend enough time together so we really do get to know one another. But don't abandon Becky because of me. That would crush her. And it wouldn't make me happy, either."

"She's going to be shocked when I tell her that you're my birth mother."

"What may shock her more is to learn that I was pregnant the same time she was." Kate sighed. "It's too bad that both of us were too ashamed to confide in each other at the time. Sad, really." Kate clasped her hands together and rested them on the table in front of her. "Right now, I'm still annoyed with Becky's recent behavior, but she and I were like sisters growing up, and I've missed her. Maybe sharing a daughter will bring us together gain. I think she and I can find a way to make that happen."

Lily nodded. "I hope so."

Kate took hold of Lily's hand and shook her head in amazement. "Having a daughter is going to take some getting used to. Something I'm very much looking forward to."

Once Parker joined them, Kate, Lily and Parker celebrated their new family over scrumptious dinners of handmade Orecchiette pasta, venison loin, cassoulet of lobster and duck confit. After a final toast, the trio escaped to the deserted golf course where heavy fog swallowed them into its quiet hold and allowed them to stroll along the ocean's edge in their own cocoon.

Later that night, Kate and Parker talked about what lay ahead regarding Lily and how all the pieces would fit into their life. The one point Kate was anxious to resolve was Martin's role. After all she and Martin had gone through with Lily, Kate didn't want to keep this a secret from him any longer than necessary. It was Parker who surprised Kate by suggesting they call and invite him down for the day. And so it was decided. Parker would arrange an early tee time for him and Lily to play golf the next morning while Kate met with Martin.

Kate was waiting on The Lodge's grand terrace overlooking the eighteenth green when she heard Annabella's voice boom through the lobby. "There she is, Martin!"

Kate wasn't sure what to make of Annabella's unexpected presence. Why had Martin brought her with him? Hadn't he sensed Kate's desire to talk to him alone? She left the balcony to join them inside.

"Hello, Kate," said Martin. They gave each other a tentative hug, and she let him kiss her on the cheek. He looked drawn and tired.

"Well, don't I get a welcome too?" demanded Annabella.

"Of course," said Kate, giving her friend a hug. "I just didn't expect you."

"When Martin told me he was coming down here to see you, I offered to keep him company on the drive. You know how I love it here."

"Bella, we don't need a chaperone." Kate wasn't fooled by Annabella's motive for coming with Martin. She knew Annabella was going to do whatever it took to protect her from Martin's advances this time.

"Of course not," Annabella said raising a suspicious eyebrow.

Kate rolled her eyes at Annabella and said, "Martin, will you excuse us a minute?" She took Annabella's hand and led her back across the lobby and onto the terrace. After glancing over at Martin to make sure he was not within hearing distance, Kate drew closer to Annabella and whispered, "What are you doing here?"

Annabella leaned away slightly, as if trying to escape Kate's disapproval. "Martin came to my house last night looking for you. He was absolutely devastated. Becky told him Lily isn't his daughter." She stopped and waited for a reaction from Kate, but when nothing dramatic happened, she asked, "Did you hear what I said?"

"Yes. As you may recall, Becky tried to tell me that several days ago, but I didn't believe her. But that doesn't explain why you're here."

Annabella looked puzzled about Kate's nonchalant attitude. As if stating the obvious, she explained. "Martin got the call from you after he left my house last night. He called and told me about your invitation to meet you here. Kate, I couldn't stand aside and let you make the mistake of a lifetime."

"What are you talking about?"

"What happened to Parker? Why did you ask Martin down here? Are you crazy? Do you want to ruin the best marriage I've ever known?"

Kate sighed and shook her head at her overly protective friend. "Annabella, I love you. You are too precious. But things are wonderful with Parker and me. Oh, there were a few frightening moments yesterday, but things couldn't be better."

"Thank God. I've been so worried about you."

"I know, and I'm sorry my normally uneventful life erupted while I've been staying with you. You've been very understanding, and I appreciate the breathing room you've given me. If our roles had been reversed, I'm not sure I could have kept my mouth shut if you had been as misguided as I have been." Kate was still ashamed and embarrassed about the night she spent at Martin's. "Bella, something very exciting has happened."

Annabella picked up on Kate's excitement. "What? What?"

"If I tell you, you must promise not to react or respond in any way. Martin is watching us, and I don't want him to see you go nuts on me."

"I promise."

"You are so emotional. I'm not sure I can tell you right now. Martin deserves to hear this first."

"Martin? Why does he get to know first? You're pregnant, aren't you?"

"Bella! No, and please keep your voice down."

"Then what?"

Kate put her hands on Annabella's shoulders, partially to steady her own nervous exuberance, but mostly to contain Annabella. Then she whispered, "Lily is my daughter."

Annabella's mouth dropped open and her eyes widened. Kate issued an emergency warning when she saw the shocked expression staring back at her. "Please don't say anything, and for gosh sakes, close your mouth." She shook Annabella's shoulders to defrost the frozen expression on her face before letting go of her.

"I'm speechless. Then Becky was telling him the truth. Poor Martin."

Kate would tell Annabella about Martin's role in the drama soon enough. For now, she wanted to be alone with the father of her child. She smiled to herself, knowing that her revelation would be fodder for Annabella's story mill for years to come.

"Are you happy about finding your daughter?" It was an obvious question, but it was the best she could do. Annabella was the closest to being speechless Kate had ever seen her.

"I'm ecstatic. And Parker is very happy for me," she added in anticipation of Annabella's next question.

Annabella rolled her shoulders back to assume a perfect posture, as if trying to gather herself. "Okay. So, I'm out of here. I'll get a taxi into Carmel and leave you alone." She looked across the room at Martin. "How much time do you need with him?"

Kate's irritated grimace told her all she needed to know.

"Okay," said Annabella. "Leave a note with the concierge when it's okay for me to return. I'll keep checking in with him." She looked to Kate for approval.

"That would be fine," agreed Kate, thankfully.

The two women walked back into the lobby chattering about golf. "A truly dumb game," insisted Annabella. "I'd much rather spend my time chasing after a six-foot man with dimples than a white, good-for-nothing golf ball with dimples."

When they rejoined Martin, Kate looked at him and shook her head. "She's right, you know. What is the fascination with such a frustrating game?"

Annabella whisked out the front door with a promise to return after a spending spree at all of her favorite shops in Carmel. Kate and Martin laughed in appreciation of Annabella's *joie de vivre*. Kate was relieved they were now alone.

"I thought you'd be happy to see her," Martin offered as an explanation for Annabella's presence. "Actually, she threw herself on me, sort of a mercy mission to bring her shopping. But I knew she was worried about the two of us being together. She thinks we need a chaperone. Do we?"

Kate barely noticed the curl of Martin's smile. Nor did she hear much of what he was saying. She was looking for Lily's features in his face. "Do we what?"

"Do we need a chaperone? It would make me very happy if what Annabella feared is true."

"We're going to need a lot more than that," she teased provocatively, easily falling into the pattern of innuendo and fun that used to dominate their conversations.

"You've got my attention."

Her mood turned from fun-loving to serious. "Can we take a drive?"

"My car's just outside." He instinctively reached out and took her hand like he always used to. She felt the reassuring grip of his strong hand and did not pull away. When he looked down on her, she gazed into light blue eyes that mirrored Lily's.

They skirted the tourist traffic clogging the coastal route of the popular Seventeen-Mile Drive by taking a local shortcut through the forest. The narrow road eventually returned them to the ocean on a section of wind-swept beach close to the Pacific Grove Gate.

Kate directed him to turn into the parking area near Fan Shell Beach. Tourists rarely stopped there anymore because the fan shells no longer washed up on the beach.

"A deserted beach. Very romantic," Martin said.

Kate stepped out of the car into the windy vista, savoring the salty air blowing through her hair and filling her senses with the fishy smell of kelp.

"We used to spend a lot of time at the beach together."

"A few weekends," she corrected him.

"But they were special times."

Martin followed Kate on a worn path down a slight embankment covered with ice plants, to a rocky outcropping. At high tide, this area would be surrounded by ocean waves.

"This okay?" she asked, gesturing to the flattest rock she could find.

"Perfect."

They sat together, savoring the dramatic view. After a few minutes, Martin broke the silence. "This feels good, being here with you like this. But I know better than to hope you have something romantic in mind."

"There was a time when I wanted nothing more than to have this quiet time with you."

"I was a fool to let you get away."

"Yes, you were." She smiled. "But I think we've recently covered that territory."

"Then why am I here, alone with you? Is it about Lily?"

"Yes."

"You'd better let me go first." He brushed his windblown hair back from his forehead. "I owe you an apology. I dragged you into something that is a lie, and I'm very sorry. I know you've gotten emotionally involved with Lily in your efforts to help me."

Kate tried to interrupt him but he wouldn't let her.

"Becky finally told me the truth about Lily." The tired, worn look Kate noticed when Martin first arrived, returned to his face as he continued. "She isn't my daughter, Kate. Becky was pregnant with my child, but it was stillborn. My daughter died." His voice trailed off.

Kate waited.

"All these years, I thought I had a daughter I would someday be able to meet and spend time with. I lost you, Kate, and now I've lost a daughter I never even had."

Kate saw the moisture in his eyes and a single tear escape down his cheek. She took his hand in hers. Any confusion she might have had about her emotional attachment to Martin had been stilled by compassion. At last, she had quenched her primal thirst for their romantic past. Yet, in a moment, she would give him a gift that would connect them for life—not as lovers, but as two people who share a child.

Breinigsville, PA USA
21 October 2010
247803BV00001B/136/P